WANTING SHEILA DEAD

This Large Print Book carries the
Seal of Approval of N.A.V.H.

A GREGOR DEMARKIAN NOVEL

WANTING SHEILA DEAD

JANE HADDAM

THORNDIKE PRESS
A part of Gale, Cengage Learning

GALE
CENGAGE Learning™

Detroit • New York • San Francisco • New Haven, Conn • Waterville, Maine • London

GALE
CENGAGE Learning™

Copyright© 2010 by Orania Papazoglou.
Thorndike Press, a part of Gale, Cengage Learning.

Thorndike Press® Large Print Mystery.
The text of this Large Print edition is unabridged.
Other aspects of the book may vary from the original edition.
Set in 16 pt. Plantin.

LIBRARY OF CONGRESS CATALOGING-IN-PUBLICATION DATA

Haddam, Jane, 1951-
    Wanting Sheila dead : a Gregor Demarkian novel / by Jane Haddam.
        p. cm. — (Thorndike Press large print mystery)
    ISBN-13: 978-1-4104-3206-3
    ISBN-10: 1-4104-3206-8
    1. Demarkian, Gregor (Fictitious character)—Fiction. 2. Murder—Investigation—Fiction. 3. Television personalities—Fiction. 4. Connecticut—Fiction. 5. Large type books. I. Title.
PS3566.A613W36 2011
813'.54—dc22   2010037283

Published in 2011 by arrangement with St. Martin's Press, LLC.

Printed in the United States of America
1 2 3 4 5 6 7 15 14 13 12 11

PROLOGUE

No day is so long as the day of a murder.
— Rudyard Kipling,
"Love-o'-Women"

1

The line began to form in front of the great double doors of the Milky Way Ballroom at just after six in the morning. By ten, when the rain started to fall, it went to the end of the block and around the corner and to the end of the block again and around the corner again. It was at least four women across. Nobody could pass through any of those stretches of sidewalk except by walking half in the gutter.

Olivia Dahl was standing at the window of the third-floor office when the lightning first lit up the sky. She had been in the office since six herself, but not always in the window.

CLIPBOARDS, she had written across her steno pad, and BALLPOINT PENS, as if she were about to forget, either. This was the first day of the new season, the day without which the season could not happen, and

Olivia, as always, had had a perfect memory for details.

The phone buzzed on the desk behind her. Sheila Dunham's voice came into the room like battery acid over a bullhorn. That was a metaphor that made no sense. Olivia didn't care. It fit exactly.

"I don't know where the hell my blue dress is," Sheila said. "What the hell did you do to my blue dress? And I don't care if Oprah *is* God, she's a fat pig and I don't want her near the auditions. Why the woman thinks she has to make a statement about everything on the planet is beyond me. Find my blue dress, for God's sake, or I'm going to fire you."

Sheila wouldn't fire a stock boy on audition day. She would not fire Olivia ever. Olivia knew it. She stayed where she was at the window, watching the rain come down in sheets and the women hold newspapers over their heads for protection. There would be at least another forty-five minutes before the doors opened. Even then, only a few of the women would be let inside at a time. You'd think some of them would have watched a weather forecast before they'd come out this morning.

"Olivia," Sheila's voice said.

Olivia turned her back to the window and

leaned against the sill. It was impossible to see faces that far down, anyway. She straightened her skirt and put her hands in her hair. She was fifty years old, but she was as rail thin as she had been in the second grade.

"Stupid cow," she said. She said it, looking straight at the intercom on the desk. "Somebody really ought to slit your throat."

2

Back home, Janice Ledbedder had promised herself that she would not let herself get caught in The Midwestern Thing. "The Midwestern Thing" was what she called the need to be *nice* all the time, even if being nice meant losing out on something for herself. She had been nice about her boyfriend going out with her very best friend. Now she didn't have a boyfriend or a best friend, and she spent a lot of her time thinking about ways to kill people. She had started to worry herself. Maybe she was exhibiting red flags. "Red flags" was what they called it when somebody started behaving very weirdly, right before they got a 30.06, and shot up everybody they'd ever known in school.

The rain was very thick, but Janice had an umbrella. Very few other people did. Janice was nervous about being in Philadelphia. She didn't think it as bad as New York, but it was a city. Black people lived here, and people who didn't speak English. It was nothing at all like her little town in South Dakota. That was another part of The Midwestern Thing. She couldn't help feeling out of place.

Next to her there was a girl in a green raincoat with no umbrella, and with nothing else, either, not even the newspapers so many of the girls were holding over their heads. The girl in the green raincoat was a blonde and very thin, and she looked oddly familiar. The rain had plastered her hair to the sides of her head. There were rivers of water coursing down her cheekbones into her neck.

"Here," Janice said, shoving the umbrella sideways so that it covered the other girl's head. "You can't stand out here like that. You're going to die."

"Thank you," the blond girl said.

Janice looked around to the front of the line. The doors were still closed, but they weren't too far back, only three or four rows from the front. Janice looked at her watch. It was a Timex watch. Everybody in Marshall, South Dakota, got a Timex watch when they graduated from junior high school.

"It's quarter to eleven," Janice said. "That's not too much longer to wait. Aren't you glad you came out early? The girls at the back are going to be a mess by the time they get inside. You should be all right, though. I mean, you know, you need to dry off a little, but you've got the raincoat, and it's like I said, it won't be much longer. Of course, I've been here all night. It took everything I had just to get the bus ticket down here. I had a little money left over, but when I saw what the hotels cost I nearly died. Who's got that kind of money to stay in a hotel room? I'm Janice, by the way. Janice Ledbedder. I'm from Marshall, South Dakota. You've probably never heard of it."

Janice took a deep breath. This was yet another part of The Midwestern Thing. You started talking and you couldn't stop.

The blond girl seemed to have shrunk into her raincoat. She didn't look at all familiar anymore.

Janice started to feel a little worried. "Are you all right? You look sort of sick. Do you need to sit down? I could save your place in line if you needed to go somewhere and sit down."

The blond girl shook her head and stood

11

up a little straighter. "No," she said. "No, I'm all right. Sorry. I'm a little tired. I'm Emily."

"Oh, I like the name Emily," Janice said. "It's so old-fashioned. It reminds me of *Little Women*. Not that there was anybody in *Little Women* named Emily, because there wasn't, but it's that kind of name. Old-fashioned. And New England. You don't happen to be from New England, do you?"

"I'm from Merion," the blond girl said.

"Merion?"

"Merion, Pennsylvania," the blond girl said. "You're in Merion. We are. This is Merion, not Philadelphia proper."

"Oh," Janice said.

"It's — the townships all sort of bleed together."

The blond girl was making an effort. Janice understood that. She herself was making an effort, too. She was so nervous, she was ready to burst.

"Isn't it awesome, the way people come from all over the country to take part in these things?" Janice said. "They've had girls from every state in the Union be on *America's Next Superstar*. And there have been girls from other countries. Well, you know, not right from other countries. I mean people from other countries who live here now. Look at all the girls here. I mean, just look at them. I didn't know there would be so many trying out."

Janice paused. People should talk, she thought. People should say things and not make other people uncomfortable.

"There are only thirty places," Janice said. She had begun to feel desperate. Emily was standing right up against her shoulder. Janice could feel Emily's breath in her hair. "And thirty is just the first round. If you get picked for the thirty there's another round where they take it down to twenty, and then another where they take it down to fourteen, and it's only fourteen that actually get to be on the show. Well, you know what I mean. They always show some of the losers for the thirty and the twenty to — I guess — make it dramatic, but it's only the fourteen who get to live in the house. I'll just die if I don't make it into the house. I really mean it. I came all the way down here from South Dakota, and everybody I know back home knows I did it, too, and if I just get dumped back out with nothing they'll all laugh at me. I won't be able to show my face. And I can't hardly show my face now, considering. It's terrible."

"Excuse me," Emily said. She stepped out from under the umbrella and turned a little away. The rain came down on her hair again.

I'm talking too much, Janice thought. Easterners didn't like it when you talked too much.

Emily turned her back to her and put her hands in her pockets.

That was when the crowd surged for the first time. The wave coming from behind pushed Janice almost off her feet and into the back of a girl in a pink vinyl motorcycle jacket.

3

Andra Gayle was not a fool, and she was not a hick from the sticks, either. She was from New York. She knew, as the girls around her didn't — she could tell, because she was listening — that being on a reality show was not going to turn her into a superstar. Nothing was going to turn her into a superstar. She was not pretty, and she had none of the usual talents. Her great blooming Afro of red hair shot out from her skull like an animated cloud. Sometimes she looked in the mirror and imagined the cloud could talk.

The rain was coming down very steadily. The drops were so thick, they were less like drops than like the stream that comes from a faucet whose drip has been neglected for years. Some of the girls had taken off their coats and put them around their heads. Others were using those huge pocketbooks that everybody had thought were hot about two and a half years ago. Andra had neither. She had bought a copy of *The Philadelphia Inquirer* from a little mechanized kiosk instead. She had a picture of the latest mayor of Philadelphia on her head, along with a thick tall headline that made it sound as if the entire state of Pennsylvania was mad at him.

Andra hated the state of Pennsylvania. She hadn't seen that much of it. She'd come in on Amtrak just the day before, and stayed at a Holiday Inn for an amount of money that made her stomach hurt. Still, she couldn't imagine that the rest of the state would be any better, even if it was different. There was no point in a city that wasn't New York. Even Los Angeles only existed because of the movies.

"And the government," Andra said.

The girl next to her turned and stared, but there wasn't any time to do anything about it. A wave of energy seemed to ripple through the crowd around them and everybody was shoved suddenly forward. Andra wobbled on her ankles. Then she stumbled first forward and then to the side. Somebody far in the back started screaming. It didn't sound frightening, or pitiful. It just sounded stupid.

"For God's sake," the girl who had looked at Andra said. "What are they doing back there?"

"Screwing around," Andra said.

"I don't think they should be screwing around," the girl said. She was wearing a light windbreaker jacket and a very odd hat. It had a brim like a baseball cap, and a band that went around the head, but nothing that went over the top. What the hell use was that going to be? It was raining. The girl's hair was getting wet.

"They ought to open the doors," the girl said. "It's ridiculous out here. Somebody's going to get sick and end up suing."

"I think it's only a couple of minutes," Andra said.

"I think they should let everybody into the building as soon as they open the doors. They won't, of course, because they enjoy the ritual of it. It's part of what sells the television program. It's still a damned stupid thing to do. I'm Grace Alsop, by the way. I'm from Connecticut."

"I'm Andra Gayle."

This was not true. Andra was no more "Andra Gayle" than she was a natural

16

redhead. She took the hand that was not holding the newspaper on her head, and turned it over and over in the rain. The girl beside her made her very nervous. It was the way she talked, and the way she held her body, and the clothes she wore. It was an atmosphere. Andra looked down at the ground. Grace Alsop was wearing plain little ballet flat shoes that looked more expensive than Andra's mother's last phone bill.

Of course, Andra's mother hadn't paid the last phone bill. Andra's mother never paid bills, and never had paid bills, in all the time Andra had known her. Andra had started to pay the bills when she was old enough to quit school and go to work. This month, she hadn't paid them because she'd needed the money to come here. Her mother was back there in Morris Heights, living without electricity and shooting up heroin in the dark.

"You've got to wonder, don't you?" Grace said.

"Wonder what?" Andra said. She knew, now, what bothered her about Grace. Grace Alsop smelled like money.

"Why people come to audition for something like this," Grace said. "Look at how many there are. I hadn't expected there to be this many. There has to be a couple of hundred girls just on this part of the block alone."

"There were more than that," Andra said. "There were tens of thousands of audition tapes. Didn't you send an audition tape?"

"Well, yes, of course I did," Grace said. "But I thought that was just —"

"Just what?"

"Well, you know, just to weed out the people with mental health problems, or things like that," Grace said. "They must get a lot of crazies, don't you think? I mean, on *American Idol* you have to be able to sing, or something. And on *America's Next Top Model* you at least have to look like a model. But with this. Well. You don't have to be anything, do you?"

"You have to be female," Andra said.

"Yes, you do. Did you ever wonder why that was? My friends back at school say that they're just trying to pick the next Paris Hilton, or something like that, the next person who's just famous for being famous. Which is pretty funny, if you think about it."

"Is it?"

"I think it is," Grace said. "I mean, the Hilton sisters are famous because they have lots of money. I'll bet nobody here has lots of money. Do they really think they're going to make a career out of having people pay them to go to parties?"

"I don't know," Andra said.

"Don't you?"

Grace stepped away a little. Andra was suddenly aware that this other girl was looking her up and down, really looking at her, and for the first time. There was a light in those pale blue eyes that was not very pleasant.

"I'm just here on a dare," Grace said. "I'm going to law school next year. Lawyers actually do make lots of money, if that's the kind of thing you're into."

Grace turned her back to Andra and eased off a little into the crowd, and Andra wrapped her one free arm around her waist.

Grace was right, she thought. There were hundreds of girls here. There were too many girls. Andra had thought that the audition tapes would be the thing that weeded out most of the competition, so that when she showed up at the Milky Way Ballroom there might be fifty or sixty other girls, and then a fast whittling down to the thirty and the twenty and the fourteen. Instead, there were girls everywhere, and some of them were pretty, and some of them could probably do something other than just stand there and look cute.

She took the newspaper off her head and

looked at it. The mayor of Philadelphia was black. The president of the United States was black. All around her there were black people doing things, but none of them were the black people she knew. Back in Morris Heights, there was a limited number of options. You could sell drugs. You could take drugs. You could run numbers. You could go on welfare if you had a baby or got very old. You could have the kind of job where you took the bus into Manhattan, and cleaned offices or worked in dry-cleaning places or did something else nobody could see you doing. You couldn't even go to Manhattan to be a waitress, because in Manhattan all the waitresses were white college girls who wanted to go into acting.

Andra put the paper up over her head again. She was soaked through and shivering. She wished she could afford a cell phone. But then, there was no point in calling her mother. Her mother would have found a way to get high. She'd be lying on the living room floor because she'd just sold all the furniture again. Or she'd be five blocks away at somebody's house. Or she'd be staggering along the street as if she were one of the living dead. She'd be somewhere.

Even so, Andra thought, it would be good to have a phone, so that she could check in, or ask somebody else to check. Assuming she knew anybody with a working phone.

Up at the head of the line, the doors began to open.

4

Mary-Louise Verdt had been the first person to stand in line this morning, at just after six o'clock, and she would have been earlier if she had been easy in her mind about staying out on the street here after dark. She'd heard the girls behind her talking. She'd even talked to some of them. By now, she knew she wasn't even in the city of Philadelphia proper. It felt wrong to her for the producers of the show to be doing what they were doing. If the show was going to be called *America's Next Superstar — Philadelphia,* then it ought to be in Philadelphia, and not someplace else, no matter how close.

When the doors opened, Mary-Louise was still first in line, in spite of the doubling up and the pushing and shoving and rain. There had been a lot of rain. Mary-Louise was glad to be out of it, stepping through the doors into a wide lobby with what looked like velour on the floor and the walls. It reminded her of the lobby in that movie

21

theater in the Jim Carrey movie, *The Majestic*. She hadn't much liked that movie. She liked movies where people went through a lot of funny troubles and then got married.

There was a long table right in the middle of everything. There were four women at the table, each holding a clipboard, with little signs in front of them that said A TO D, E TO H. Mary-Louise found the one at the very end, U TO Z, and went there. The woman at the clipboard looked a little hassled. The lobby was dark and damp and humid. Mary-Louise put on her brightest smile, but the woman with the clipboard didn't notice it.

"Your name is . . . ," the woman said.

"Verdt," Mary-Louise said. "Mary-Louise Verdt."

"And you're from?"

"Holcomb, Kansas."

The woman with the clipboard didn't react. It made Mary-Louise a little annoyed. Almost everybody reacted to that "Holcomb, Kansas," or at least everyone at home did. One of the most famous murders in the history of America had happened there. People still talked about it.

"Do you have your letter?" the woman with the clipboard said.

Mary-Louise reached into her oversized

purse and got the letter, still in its envelope, from the little side compartment where she always kept her phone. She handed it over, and then she couldn't help herself.

"This is the biggest thing, back home where I'm from," she said. "I mean, it was even in the paper. Just my getting the chance to come in and interview. But I just knew I'd get the chance to come in and interview. I know I'm going to get to be on the show, too. You've got to really want things, do you know what I mean? You've got to really want them. That's the only way anybody ever gets anywhere. And I really want this."

She might as well have been talking to a statue. The woman with the clipboard was not paying attention. She read through the letter for, what felt like to Mary-Louise, the third time. Then she handed the letter back and pointed to the right.

"Through those doors," she said, "you'll find a corridor and a series of rooms. You go to the blue one. It's painted blue. It won't be hard to find."

"Yes, of course," Mary-Louise said. "I'm sure I won't have any trouble."

"Someone will come in and call you when it's time for your interview. If you're off in the bathroom or somewhere when they call you, they'll come back in five minutes and call a second time. If you don't answer then, either, then too bad. You go home."

"Yes, of course," Mary-Louise said. "I'm sure I won't have any trouble."

"That way." The woman with the clipboard pointed right again.

Mary-Louise stepped away from the table. Girls were crowding in, pushing each other, but they were stopping well back from the tables. There was something intimidating about the tables. Mary-Louise had to admit it: There was something intimidating about a lot of the girls, too. She was sure she was dressed all wrong, but she couldn't quite put a finger on why.

She went to the doors on the right. She looked across the lobby and saw that there were also doors on the left. This place was called a ballroom. Maybe they held dances here. Maybe there were dressing rooms. She had no idea.

She went through into a narrow corridor and looked around again. It was a shabby place. The carpet here was worn. The paint on the walls was faded.

The first room she came to was painted a sickly color of pink. There were already two girls in there, looking at magazines. The second room she came to was beigy-brown.

It was empty, and it smelled a little bad, as if somebody had left a sandwich in the wastebasket overnight. She went farther along the hall and found it, the blue room.

Mary-Louise went in, and looked around, and put down her purse. There were windows. She went to them and tried to look out, but the only view she got was of a blank wall. She got her purse again and sat down in a big chair in the middle of everything. Then she took out her phone.

She was in the middle of calling her mother when she heard a voice from the hall that said, "Oh, for God's sake."

She looked up and saw a woman standing in the door, very thin and businesslike, running a hand through her hair.

"For God's sake," the woman said again. "You can't have that here. Didn't they tell you you couldn't have that here? I don't know what I'm going to do if they haven't bothered to confiscate any of them."

"Excuse me?" Mary-Louise said.

The thin woman came into the room and snatched the phone from Mary-Louise's hand. "The phone," she said. "You're not allowed to have a phone. Well, a camera phone, actually, it's the pictures she cares about, but this is a camera phone, isn't it? Everything's a camera phone these days."

"Excuse me," Mary-Louise said again. "It's a very expensive phone. My boyfriend gave it to me for my birthday."

"I don't care if the pope gave it to you," the thin woman said. "You're not allowed to have camera phones in here, and you're not allowed to have them at all during the competition." She reached into the pocket of her jacket and came up with a small pad of Post-it Notes. "What's your name?"

"Mary-Louise Verdt," Mary-Louise said. "But —"

"You'll get it back when you leave," the thin woman said. "Honestly, I can't believe they didn't remember this. I hope all of them haven't forgotten it. You said your name was Word?"

"Verdt," Mary-Louise said. "V. E. R. D. T."

"Right," the thin woman scribbled something on the Post-it Note and stuck it to Mary-Louise's phone. The woman's hair seemed to have wired out and gone crazy in just the minute or so she'd been in the blue room.

Mary-Louise was wondering if she should make one more protest about the phone when another girl came up to the door, smiled faintly at the thin woman, and tried to squeeze in. She was a very unusual-

26

looking girl. She was wearing almost nothing but leather, and she had seven piercings in the left side of her nose alone.

"What about you?" the thin woman asked. "Do you have a phone?"

The new girl looked confused. "Yes, of course I have a phone. Do you need to use it for something? I mean, I'm sure —"

"Show it to me."

The new girl reached into an oversized purse that was very much like the one Mary-Louise had, and came up with a Samsung Propel.

The thin woman rolled her eyes. "For God's sake," she said. "You're not allowed to have a phone."

Then she took the phone, brought out the pad of Post-it Notes, and demanded that the new girl deliver her name. Mary-Louise didn't really hear it. Everything was happening so fast, and the thin woman seemed to be angry.

"I've got to go out and stop them before they do more of this," the thin woman said. "Then I've got to get people to confiscate all the phones. This is a complete load of crap. It's going to hold us up for half an hour."

Mary-Louise tried to think of something to say, but nothing came to her. Then the thin woman was gone. She'd left the door open, so that Mary-Louise and the new girl could look out into the corridor where girls were arriving from the lobby, all of them looking insecure.

"Well," Mary-Louise said.

"Do you know who that was?" the new girl asked. "That was Olivia Dahl."

"Who's Olivia Dahl? Is she famous?"

"She is if you follow the show," the new girl said, "or if you read the supermarket newspapers. You know the ones. She's Sheila Dunham's personal assistant. She runs everything around here."

"Runs how?"

"Oh, you know — does the scut work, and organizes everything, and makes sure things get done. Everybody says she should have been promoted to executive producer years ago, but Sheila Dunham won't have it. She likes to pretend she does everything herself."

"Oh," Mary-Louise said.

The new girl sat down in one of the other chairs. Nobody else had come into their room. Mary-Louise wished they would.

"They're shoving each other like maniacs out there," the new girl said, "and it's still raining. There's going to be a riot. Wouldn't that be something else?"

Mary-Louise didn't know what it would

be, but she did know that this girl was not going to make it through the interviews.

This girl didn't care, and Mary-Louise did, and caring was the only thing that really mattered.

5

Coraline Mays had never intended to enter this competition. She had never even seen the television program, although she'd heard it talked about often enough. Practically everybody back in Southport talked about it, and then complained about the way Sheila Dunham behaved, and who got picked to stay and who was made to go. Even the people at Coraline's church did that. To Coraline, it seemed somehow very wrong to be watching something that you knew was full of sin, just so that you could complain about the sin later.

This was the very back of the line. It had only been in the last minute and a half that they had moved far enough forward, and turned enough corners, so that Coraline could see the entrance doors to the building. The entire idea of a ballroom made her nervous. It wouldn't be the kind of ballroom Cinderella had danced in. It would be the kind that Jane Fonda had danced in, in that movie Coraline had seen at her friend

29

Miranda's house one afternoon when Miranda had broken up with Keith again. Miranda broke up with Keith a lot. Coraline had been with her own boyfriend since their freshman year in high school, and she expected to get engaged to him as soon as they got off to college. Or, rather, as soon as Miranda got off to college, to Liberty University, to get her teaching degree. Michael was talking about joining up with the Marines.

Coraline had an umbrella. It wasn't a very good one, and it had cost nearly twenty dollars, but she had needed to buy it off one of those street stands with the newspapers. She hadn't expected the rain. She hadn't expected the crowd of girls. She had almost been late, and she wondered if that was because she didn't really want to be here at all.

"Oh, thank *God,*" the girl next to her said. The girl was very short and she had a lot of rings on. She also had tattoos. There was a big green and black snake down the side of her neck. Where Coraline came from, girls only got tattoos when they were . . . when they were . . . well — not right with the Lord. That might be the best way to put it.

The girl with the tattoos had an umbrella, too. If she hadn't had one, Coraline would have offered to share her own. People she didn't understand made Coraline very nervous, but she knew there was only one way to bring souls to Heaven, and that was to be as good a Christian as possible in your everyday life. Coraline didn't think she was an especially good Christian — she could think the most awful things about people; she had to work like the dickens to make sure she didn't say them out loud — but she could try, and trying was something she was good at.

"We are actually moving," the girl with the tattoos said.

Coraline realized that the girl was actually talking to another girl, who was standing beside her. This other girl was also very short, and did not seem to have brought her own umbrella.

The girl with the tattoos turned to Coraline. "Hey," she said. "I'm Linda Kowalski."

"Hello," Coraline said, and suddenly she could just hear her own accent, like a joke on a television show. "I'm Coraline Mays from Southport, Alabama."

"Well, you sound like you're from Alabama," the other girl said, the one without the tattoo. "I'm Shari Bernstein. I'm from Scarsdale."

"It's a town in New York," Linda Kowalski

said. "You can't just do that. You can't just assume that everybody is going to know where Scarsdale it."

"Everybody *does* know where Scarsdale is," Shari said.

"I'm about ready to pop," Linda said. "I can't believe they left us standing out here in the rain. And I've got a million rosaries on me, and I'll bet all of them are wet."

"You didn't look to me like the kind of person who would be carrying around rosaries," Shari said.

"My mother gave them to me," Linda said. "She wants me to win. But it's no big deal. I mean, it's not like you can't have a tattoo here and there, and still be a good Catholic. I don't have tattoos of the devil or anything. It's just a snake."

"It's a snake the size of a swimming pool," Shari said. "And I'll bet you got it some night when you were out drinking. I make it a point only to drink when I'm safe in my own home. When I go out, I stick to one rum and Coke, or a glass of wine. You never know what's going to happen to you when you go out."

"That's just because you don't have advantages," Linda said. "You blow a gasket some weekend and what happens? You go to temple and feel guilty. I go to confession and get it all taken care of, and then I'm on my way."

"It won't help you much if you end up with a warthog tattooed on your ass next time."

Coraline looked up toward the head of the line. She really could see it now, and she could see that they were letting girls in one by one, or more like five by five. They were letting them in, in little clumps, at any rate. There was somebody with a clipboard.

Coraline was very cold, and she was wet in spite of the umbrella. There was a lot of wind. Rain kept slashing against her legs, and she had nothing on her legs but stockings. She wrapped her arms around herself and tried to think. It was all very well for Pastor Thomas to talk about what an influence she could be, and how much the world needed the example of a good Christian girl. How did he know what she would be like when she got away from home and around people who weren't even Christians at all, or didn't like them? She had heard that Sheila Dunham didn't like Christians, and Sheila Dunham was running this whole show.

Besides, even people in the media who were in parts of the country who did like Christians went wrong. Think about Nashville. Country-music singers were always talking about how much they loved Jesus, and yet they ran around drinking themselves to death, and taking drugs, and sleeping with people they weren't even married to or . . . well, or anything. There was something that went wrong when people got famous. Coraline was sure of that.

"Hey," Linda Kowalski said. "You know, I think you've probably got a good chance to get on the show."

"Excuse me?" Coraline said.

"I think you've got a good chance to get on the show," Linda said again. "I mean, you must be practically the only person here from Alabama —"

"People get on this show from the South," Coraline said quickly. "There was a girl just the season before last who was from Mississippi."

Coraline didn't know this from her own experience. Her mother had told her about it. Her mother watched the show every single week it was on, and she watched the extras and specials where they interviewed winners and contestants and talked about what they were doing now. Coraline's mother thought it was absolutely the most wonderful thing in the world that Coraline was going to try out for this show.

"Pastor Thomas is right," Mama said. "The world could use the example of a good Christian girl. Besides, honey, you're the prettiest girl in this town and a hundred more like it. You're prettier than Miranda ever could be. That has to count for something."

Coraline didn't know what counted for what, and she didn't care. She had figured it out. Rosaries meant Catholic — Linda Kowalski was Catholic. And temple meant Jews. Shari Bernstein was a Jew. There was a Catholic church back in Southport, a really tiny one, but Coraline had never met any of the people who went there. She had never met a Jewish person at all. Her throat felt very tight. She thought she was going to cry.

"For God's sake," Shari said. "She's just about ready to collapse. You're scaring the hell out of her."

"Oh, no," Coraline said. "No, really. I'm just nervous. I'll be all right in a minute —"

The surge could not have come from directly behind them. There wasn't much of anything directly behind them. There was still a surge. Coraline felt herself pitching sideways, against Linda Kowalski's back. Shari Bernstein caught her so that she didn't fall.

"What is going *on* around here?" Shari
said.

Then the surge hit again, and Coraline
found herself thinking that it was like an
invisible wave. It came up out of nowhere
and crashed over her head, and then —

— she was lying flat on the ground, in the
rain, with mud streaming up the back of
her right hand.

6

Grace Alsop had no patience, really, for the
sort of person she was running into. First
there had been that girl on line, she couldn't
remember her name — Andra, she'd called
herself, as if anybody had a name like that,
and hair nobody had ever had — and now
there were these people in here, one after
another of them. There were so many frilly
little dresses and tops, Grace wanted to run
around pulling the flounces off. There were
so many tattoos and piercings and hair
frizzed out and dyed improbable colors. . . .
Well, she supposed she should have expected it. She'd watched the show half a
dozen times before doing her audition tape,
and then she'd watched it three or four
times more before coming for this interview.
She did have a *vague* idea of what was going on in this place. She'd made sure,

though, not to have *more* than a vague idea. That was part of the point.

The room she was sitting in was pink. The girls she was sharing it with were all nervous. Grace wasn't nervous at all. She did feel a little sorry for one blond girl sitting in a corner chair, hunched down as if she were about to die. As for the rest of them, Grace didn't know what to say. There was one standing there in the middle of the room looking like Andy Warhol with gangrene, a big neon lime green streak in her white blond hair — where did they come up with these things, really? Did they expect to get jobs someday, jobs that weren't just clerking in a convenience store or tending bar in the kind of place where people had fights with bottles? Maybe they didn't. Most of them weren't in school. Grace had already figured that out.

The blond girl with the green streak was talking to the company at large, as if she'd been hired to deliver a lecture.

"They say they don't like bitchiness, but it isn't true," she said. "They're always looking for at least one bitch. They want a good season. They want people to watch. You need a good bitch for that."

"They'll take that awful girl who stepped on my ankle," somebody in one of the seats said. "I wish they'd make this all faster. I'm so nervous, I'm going to pee myself."

"They won't take you if you spend all your time cussing," another girl in another seat said. "They don't want to have to bleep out every word you say. There was that girl from California and it was like all she could say was, um —"

"The 'f' word," yet somebody else said.

"They can't hurry too much," the blond girl with the green streak said. "They want you to meet all the judges. And, you know, I don't think it's a good sign if you're in and out of the interview in a minute and a half."

"Oh, God," the first of the girls in the chairs said.

The door to their room opened and a young woman with a clipboard stepped in. She wasn't the important woman who'd come by at first to make sure none of them had been allowed to keep their cell phones. Grace had been sort of impressed with that woman. This was somebody unimportant. She looked frazzled.

She looked down at her clipboard and frowned. "Grace," she said. "Grace Al . . ."

"Alsop," Grace said.

"That's it," the young woman with the clipboard said. "Would you come with me?"

Grace couldn't have been more relieved.

She wasn't sure what happened to girls when somebody with a clipboard came to fetch them, but she knew they didn't come back to the room, at least not right away. Two of them had already disappeared from the pink room.

The young woman was holding the door to the hallway open. Grace went through it and looked around. The hallways and the lobby here reminded her of an old movie theater back in Connecticut. Years and years ago, it had been a vaudeville theater, and now it was barely hanging on with competition from the multiplexes at the Danbury Fair Mall.

"It's just along here," the young woman said. "You'll have to wait for a minute at the door. They don't like dead air, if you know what I mean, so we have to get it all set up in advance."

They passed through a set of doors that led into the ballroom proper, but from the side, so that they didn't have to pass through the lobby. Grace was curious. Was there a reason they weren't supposed to see each other? There were canvas curtains hung all across the ballroom. She could hear the murmur of voices coming from one end. The young woman with the clipboard made her sit in a row of chairs all the way on the other side of the room.

"It'll just be a minute," the young woman with the clipboard said.

Grace looked around. The ballroom was empty. It was all very odd. A moment later, another young woman with a clipboard entered, leading a perky-looking sort of girl with her hair plastered almost entirely to her head.

"I had an umbrella," she said, "but it didn't seem to work after a while."

"Too bad," Grace said.

"I'm Mary-Louise," the other girl said. "Mary-Louise Verdt."

"It's better if you don't talk out here," the new young woman with the clipboard said, in a whisper. "They don't like the noise. And she gets, you know."

The new young woman with the clipboard left, and Mary-Louise giggled.

"You hear all these stories," Mary-Louise said, not so much whispering as speaking very loudly in a hiss. "About Sheila Dunham, I mean. That she's crazy. That she screams at people and throws things. Do you think she's going to do anything like that today? I'd give a lot to see it. I mean, if I didn't get on the show, it would be something I could talk about when I got back home."

Grace already had enough to talk about when she got back home, or back to school, which was more to the point. She looked down at her hands.

"I met a girl in line," Mary-Louise said, "who said she'd murder somebody to get on this show. Wouldn't that be amazing? If something like that happened? It would be on all the television stations and you'd be hearing about it forever."

"You'd be living through it first," Grace said.

Mary-Louise looked startled, but she didn't have time to say anything else. The older woman with the clipboard — the one Grace thought of as important — had come out from behind the screen on the other end of the room and was advancing toward them. She had a name tag on that said MISS DAHL.

"It's Miss Alsop I'm looking for," she announced as she came up to them.

Way up at the other end of the room, a girl stumbled out from behind the canvas curtains. It was obvious she'd been crying.

"Never mind about that," Miss Dahl said, because Mary-Louise was staring. "If you can't handle the interview, you can't handle the show. And if you can't handle the show, you can't handle being a celebrity. Believe

41

me. I've seen it. Will you come with me, Miss Alsop? It's right up front here."

Grace could see where it was. She didn't need to be told. And she wasn't nervous, either. This was not the kind of thing she did. This was not the kind of thing anybody with any sense did. It was stupid people who went on shows like this. They had to go on shows like this. They couldn't get the grades to get into a decent college, never mind graduate from one. They didn't have a hope in hell of having a real career.

The space between the chairs on one end of the ballroom to the curtains on the other end was endless. It went on and on, and the longer Grace tried to make herself walk across it, the drier her mouth felt. Her head hurt. Her feet hurt worse. The shoes she was wearing seemed to have shrunk on her feet.

Miss Dahl stopped at the curtains and pulled them back. Grace could see a line of people sitting at a table with a tablecloth on it. She tried to remember who had been the judges on the shows she had watched, but her mind was blank.

"Don't make a fuss," Miss Dahl said. "They don't give a damn. And she really doesn't."

Grace stepped through the curtains, took

a deep breath, and looked around.

Sheila Dunham was the only face she recognized, and Sheila Dunham looked so triumphantly furious, Grace almost turned around and ran.

7

If there was one thing about this entire day that had made Ivy Demari really happy, it was definitely the part where that woman had come around and taken all their cell phones. Normally, Ivy liked her cell phone, as much as she liked her NDS, her PSP, and that little handheld arcade game thing her sister had given her for Christmas last year. She liked her computer and her subscription to World of Warcraft, too. Every tattoo on her body except for the butterfly on her neck had to do with World of Warcraft or *Lord of the Rings,* and she was here to tell the world that geek girls were not necessarily fat misfits in Starfleet uniforms.

Of course, Ivy had no problem with Starfleet uniforms, either, but she did think it was a little excessive when people wore them to jury duty.

What Ivy didn't like about her cell phone, today, was that Dennis wouldn't stop calling her on it. He had called at least forty times while she'd been standing in line.

She'd had the phone out of her pocket so often she'd begun to be afraid it would be ruined by the rain. There was a lot of rain, too. There was also wind. Ivy had never been in a hurricane, but she had begun to wonder if that was about to end. And then there was all that shoving.

"It's the wrong thing for you," Dennis had said, over and over again. "You don't belong with those people. It's like you want to change into one of the pod people. You're going to start going on about world peace —"

"Of course I'm not going to start to go on about world peace," Ivy had said.

"— And about helping other people," Dennis had continued. "You know how those people talk. How all they really want, besides world peace, is to help other people. We talked about it. We agreed. It's stupid."

"Of course it's stupid," Ivy had said, but then her mind had wandered, and she had known that Dennis had noticed it. It wasn't that she had changed her mind about the pod people. It was just that she didn't necessarily want to spend her life holed up in an emotional bunker, keeping the world at bay by looking as weird as possible and talking in a code nobody but other geeks could understand.

By the time the woman had come to take her cell phone, Ivy had been ready to hang up on Dennis and turn the damned thing off. The only thing stopping her was the knowledge that she would surely have to go back home someday. She didn't want the scene she knew would come if Dennis got her voice mail every time he tried to reach her.

The woman who had come to take their phones was holding back the canvas flap. Ivy stepped into the little interview area and looked down the table at the judges. She knew all the judges. At home, they watched the show and threw popcorn at the screen when something really stupid came on.

The judge in the middle was Sheila Dunham herself. Ivy thought she was trying to look fierce. What she actually looked like was . . . desperate.

Somebody cleared his throat. It was one of the men. Ivy wasn't sure which one. If she'd had to guess, she would have said Pete Waldheim. The other two of the men were gay.

Sheila ruffled the papers in front of her and ran a hand through her thick black hair. Her face had the hard angles of someone who'd had too many lifts after taking too many drugs. Her mouth was the mouth of a

45

world-class bitch.

"So," she said, "tell us something about yourself."

Ivy put her hands behind her back. "My name is Ivy Demari. It used to be Demaris, but my father changed it —"

"Your father changed it?" one of the men said. That was Johnny Rell. He was the gay guy who practically screamed gay. The other one, Mark Borodine, you only knew was gay because he said so.

"My father changed it," Ivy said.

"Why?" Mark asked.

"I don't know," Ivy said. "I was a baby at the time."

"Do you think he was trying to hide something?" Sheila said. "Had he been in jail? Was he covering up for something he did?"

"It wasn't much of a change," Ivy pointed out. "If he was covering something up, he'd have changed it to Smith or Petrelli or something, I think."

The only other woman was Deedee Plant. Ivy was not old enough to remember when any of Deedee's television series had been on the air in real time, but she'd seen all of them anyway. *The Family Tree,* that was one of them, about a family whose last name was Tree and there were seven children.

Everybody had terribly serious teenaged problems, like whether people liked them or what they were going to do if they didn't get a date for the prom.

Deedee Plant was leaning in and staring. "Is that a real tattoo on your neck," she said, "or one of those temporary ones?"

"It's a real one," Ivy said.

"Do you have a lot of those," Deedee asked, "you know, all over your body?"

"I have a few," Ivy said.

"Where?" Sheila asked.

"Well," Ivy said, "I've got one in the small of my back that's a picture of the one ring that binds them . . ."

"*Star Wars*," Sheila said.

"*Lord of the Rings*," Ivy said. "It's J. R. R. Tolkien. He's —"

"Where are you from?" Sheila asked.

They weren't really like questions anymore. They were more like demands. It was very stuffy in here, and very hot. Ivy thought she was sweating. She knew she was having trouble trying to breathe.

"I'm from Dallas," she said.

Suddenly, Sheila Dunham was leaning so far forward, she was nearly climbing over the table.

"Dallas," she said. "That's where they tried to kill Kennedy. They did kill Kennedy. He died. I've seen the pictures. Are you a racist?"

"Excuse me?"

"That's what they've got down there in Dallas," Sheila said. "Racists. That's why they killed Kennedy. They didn't like it that he gave all those rights to black people. Are you a racist? Do you think racists should be superstars?"

"Well," Ivy said, and suddenly it was no trouble at all to breathe. Everything was perfectly fine. "I do have an irrational revulsion against all Romulans. But I don't think it's likely to come up on *America's Next Superstar.*"

"What the hell is a Romulan?" Sheila demanded.

Pete Waldheim was smirking. "It's an alien race. From the *Star Trek* series. It's —"

"Illegal aliens?" Sheila demanded.

"Aliens from space," Pete said again.

"Christ," Sheila said. "What do you think you're doing? Are you wasting our time? Because, let me tell you, we've got a lot of people out there who'd like to be where you are now. They didn't get invited to these interviews."

Ivy wanted to point out that lots of people had been invited to these interviews, hundreds of them. She'd just spent several

48

hours standing in line with them.

"I'm not going to put up with racists on my show, no matter what kind of racists they are," Sheila said. "I'm not going to put up with fag haters, either. Are you a fag hater?"

Johnny Rell was wincing. Mark Borodine was staring at the ceiling.

Ivy said, "I'm not a fag hater, but I understand why it is everybody keeps expecting you to turn up dead."

8

Alida Akido had been feeling confident all morning, even when she was standing out there in the rain at the back of that God-awful line. It was easy to see, just by looking around a little, that there were almost no other Asian girls trying out for this cycle. They dotted the crowd like separate little miracles. They were also completely impossible. One of them was Korean, so Korean that her face was as flat and ugly as a pancake with acne. One of the others was that Asian-indeterminate that spelled mixed ancestry with a white person, or maybe even worse. Alida had never understood the mania Americans had with pretending that race didn't matter. Of course race mattered. Race said everything you needed to know about a person, at least as it applied to people in any of the other races. You saw that very clearly in Japan.

The panel at the front of the room was all trying to look encouraging, except for Sheila Dunham, who always looked sour. Alida stood very straight and waited, patiently. There was something about the girls she'd been seeing all day. None of them could be patient. None of them could be calm. They were all jumping and hopping all over the place.

"So," the one called Deedee Plant said, "your grandparents were in a Japanese internment camp in World War II —"

"My great-grandparents," Alida said.

"What?" Deedee said.

"My great-grandparents," Alida said again. "I'm only nineteen. It was a long time ago."

"Your great-grandparents," Deedee said.

Pete Waldheim leaned in and tried to look aggressive. Alida nearly giggled.

"I think the point here," he said, "is that we'd like to know if you knew these people. These great-grandparents. The ones who were in the internment camp."

"I knew my great-grandmother a little," Alida said. "She died when I was six. My great-grandfather died before I was born."

"Your mother died, too, didn't she?"

50

Sheila Dunham said.

Alida would never in her life have done anything as stupid as take a deep breath, or shift on her feet. The important thing was not to let go of your emotions, only to look as if you had. There was something else the Americans had a mania about: showing your feelings. Only idiots and savages showed their feelings on their faces, as if it didn't matter who could see what.

Alida was counting to thirty in her head. Finally, she said, "Yes. My mother is dead. She died when I was twelve."

"And how did that feel?" Deedee said. "Could you tell us how that affected your life? You were just at the age when girls most need their mothers."

"I want to know how she died," Sheila said. "Did you kill her?"

"For Christ's sake," Pete said.

"It's a perfectly legitimate question," Sheila said. "Remember that girl they let into Harvard a few years ago? Then they found out that she'd been convicted of killing her mother, and they had to take it back. Have you been convicted of killing your mother?"

"I haven't been convicted of anything," Alida said. "And my mother died of breast cancer."

"Is that an issue you feel strongly about?" Deedee said. She sounded as if she were rushing. "A lot of our contestants have causes they want to advance if they win the competition. Maybe breast cancer can be yours."

"I've thought about that," Alida said.

And it was true. She had thought about it. Everybody had a cause in America. Everybody wanted to help the world. Everybody wanted the world to like her. That was the problem. The world never liked really successful people; it envied them. Alida wanted to be envied.

Sheila was staring at her. Alida did not smile. She was not surprised at the questions: They were the kind of questions Sheila was famous for asking. Sheila Dunham made a career out of being an uncivilized jerk.

"Well," Sheila said.

The panel leaned in toward each other, whispering. Alida was not worried. Sheila took a clipboard and wrote something on it. She passed it around. The others also wrote something on it. Then they gave it back to Sheila. If you had perfect calm, perfect poise, perfect self-control, you could stand in a crowd of people and have them all believing you weren't a savage.

Sheila looked at the clipboard and then handed it across the table to that Miss Dahl who had brought Alida in to the panel. Miss Dahl looked at the clipboard and nodded.

"Come with me," Miss Dahl said.

Alida nodded to the panel — she'd seen the show a million times; she'd seen the clips from this part of it; she was supposed to look sincere and strained and to thank them for considering her and tell them how desperately she needed to do this with her life.

"Good luck," Deedee said.

Alida smiled this time, and then followed Olivia Dahl out of the canvas-enclosed area. She was just passing through the flap to what appeared to be yet another corridor at the back when she heard Sheila Dunham say to the other judges:

"You're going to regret that one. She's got all the emotion of a dead fish."

The corridor went through a long stretch of what looked like high school lockers, to a back staircase.

"This way," Olivia Dahl said, climbing.

Alida followed her.

"I need you to stay in this room until you're called again," Olivia said. "That may take another hour or so. There are still a lot of girls who have to be interviewed, and of course there are always borderline cases that have to be reinterviewed and rediscussed. You're in neither of those categories. You'll be in the initial thirty, which means you'll appear in at least the first episode of the new cycle."

"Thank you."

"There's no point in thanking me. I had nothing to do with it. The other girls in the room up here will also be part of the first episode of the new cycle. But you've got to remember that none of you is on the show or in the house yet. Once we've made the determination of just which thirty of you there will be, we'll film an episode where first ten of you will be eliminated, then another six, and the fourteen left standing will be cast for the show proper. Do you understand all that?"

"Yes," Alida said.

"You've watched the show?"

"I watch it all the time."

"Good," Olivia said. "You wouldn't believe how many people try out for this thing without ever bothering to watch the show. What's the point, really? It's not even good strategy. Well, never mind. Up here."

They were in a dark upstairs corridor, carpeted and wallpapered just like the corridors downstairs, all dark and fuzzy-velour.

Olivia opened a door and held it back. Alida looked in on a small crowd of girls, some of whom she recognized from the line and the waiting room, some of whom she didn't. There was that girl with the thick green streak in her white-blond hair. There was that Southern girl who looked like she was dressed to go to a very formal PTA meeting.

"This is Alida Akido," Olivia said in a very loud voice.

Alida stepped into the room proper, and behind her, Olivia pulled the door closed and disappeared behind it. Alida looked from girl to girl. Some girls were sitting. Some girls were standing. Some girls were all the way down on the floor.

She'd gone about halfway around the room when she finally noticed the black girl, and then it was all she could do not to make a face. It wasn't just a black girl. It was a black girl with a bright red Afro that looked like a Brillo pad in the electric chair. It was a black girl with "ghetto" screaming out all over her.

And it didn't help that Alida knew that both she and the black girl were in this room for the very same reason — because *America's Next Superstar* didn't want to look like it was prejudiced.

55

Alida shrugged slightly, and then turned away, looking for somebody to talk to who wouldn't be an annoyance or a threat.

9

Olivia Dahl thought she had a headache, but she wasn't sure. She would have a headache, when all this was over, because she always did. Right now it only mattered that she kept going without hurting anyone, and especially without hurting Sheila. Executive assistants were supposed to worship the ground their celebrity employers walked on, but Sheila wasn't that much of a celebrity, and Olivia was from Brooklyn.

She looked into the big room where she had put the final thirty. She counted them off. She had already made sure that there was plenty of video from the interviews. They could go through all that later and pick what they wanted to use. That was always a difficult choice to make. You wanted some losers as well as some winners. The viewers liked to second-guess the panel, and they really liked to watch the tearful exit interview with some poor girl who'd washed out completely before the game even got started. It was also important not to make everything too obvious. You didn't want the audience to know who was going to end up in the house before the elimination that got them there.

Olivia counted a third time — there should be thirty, there were thirty, she had to stop obsessing like this — and then retreated to the hallway outside to check on the recording equipment. There were a dozen men and women out there, carrying heavy things and tripping up everything with wires.

"Don't forget," Olivia told one of them, "it's like a news show, not a movie. You have to get them when they talk and it has to be clear. We don't get to come back in and put the sound on later."

"Yes," said the man she was talking to. He looked faintly contemptuous. She blushed. Some of these people had been working with them forever. She could never remember them from one season to the next.

"Fine," she said.

She turned around to find Sheila walking in among the wires. She looked smug as hell.

"Did you get that thing about whether she'd murdered her mother?" Sheila said. "That's got to go in the final cut. Don't you think? God, I'm beginning to like this. I thought I'd hate it when it started, but I'm beginning to like it."

"You thought it was the end of your

career," Olivia said.

"That's when I didn't realize the potential," Sheila said. "It's gotten huge, this reality thing. Oh, not the crap, you know, twelve people screwing one another's spouses and voting each other off some island in the Pacific. I don't understand why anybody watches that kind of thing. But this stuff. The competitions. They're the biggest thing since television started."

"If you say so," Olivia said.

"*America's Next Top Model* is in a hundred and thirty-two countries, did you know that? I want this to be just as big. Give us a few more seasons and we will be. It's just a matter of striking the right balance."

"Right now it's a matter of you remembering what you're supposed to say in there. Please tell me you've been paying attention to the notes. We had to film you four times last season, and after a while the responses get a little stale."

"You can cut and paste the responses. You can always use — who the hell is that?"

Olivia looked up. A girl was picking her way through the wires toward the door to the room where the thirty semifinalists were waiting. Maybe they didn't call them semifinalists. Olivia couldn't remember. She did remember this girl, who looked very familiar.

"Who are you?" she demanded.

The girl flushed. "I'm sorry," she said. "I didn't mean to cause any trouble. I just wanted to use the ladies' room, and I —"

"Who *are* you?" Olivia said again.

The girl flushed again. "I'm Janice Ledbedder?" the girl said. "I'm from South Dakota? I'm really sorry. I hope I haven't missed anything, or made a problem or something, I just really needed to use the ladies' room and . . . and —"

Olivia checked back through the pages on her clipboard to the one with the thirty girls listed on it. She went through the names one by one. Janice Ledbedder was about a third of the way down.

"Ah," Olivia said. "All right. Here you are."

"I haven't caused any problems?" Janice said. "Because I really didn't mean to. I mean, I really didn't, I just wanted —"

"You haven't caused any problems," Olivia said. "Just go in and sit down. Really. Go in and sit down. We're about to start."

"Do you always go around dressed like that?" Sheila Dunham said. "I mean, honey, you look like you should be greeting people at the door to a Walmart."

Janice flushed yet again. Olivia pushed her toward the door. Janice went through it and disappeared.

"Save that for when the cameras are rolling," Olivia said, "and don't tell me it's all part of the image. I manage your image. I know better than you do that you have no need to act like a complete and utter bitch twenty-four seven."

"It's one of the perks of the job," Sheila said. "I don't think I ever realized, before I started doing this, just how much I wanted to say that I wasn't saying. I mean it. You worry about your career and whatever and you keep it all bottled up inside. I don't keep it bottled up inside anymore. I let it all right out there. And it's wonderful. Besides, half these people deserve what they get. Can you really believe there are hicks this stupid in this day and age?"

Olivia wanted to say that Sheila had always let it all right out there, if she'd had enough to drink. That was how she'd ended up on a reality show to begin with. Olivia, however, never let anything out, and wouldn't, even if they were paying her. She checked her clipboard again, pawed through a few pages, found the one she wanted and said:

"All right. You go in through that door

over there. You'll find yourself behind a curtain. Wait for the music to cue up and then come through. We've got it set up so that there's a little platform there. After that, it's up to you to remember what you're supposed to say."

"I remember what I'm supposed to say," Sheila said.

Olivia watched her go through the other door. Then she herself went through the one she'd sent Janice Ledbedder through. She looked around at the girls. She nodded to one of the men behind her and the spotlight went on to the place where the curtains would part. Olivia looked at the crowd one more time and then —

"Thirty-one," she said.

"Quiet," the man closest to her said. "We're rolling."

Olivia was still staring at the crowd. She counted. She counted again. There were thirty-one. She thought of Janice Ledbedder out in the hall. She looked across the heads of the girls and at as many faces as she could catch, but she couldn't find what was wrong. She went to the front and stood just behind Sheila at the podium.

Then the music started, and the curtains parted just slightly, and Sheila was out there in front of everybody. Her long red dress glittered in the light. Her long black hair looked as fake as it always did. Olivia told herself that it wouldn't matter. There were thirty Gucci bags on tables in the next room, twenty with a picture of a girl in them. If one of the losers had snuck into this room she'd be weeded out before any more filming got done before that, because she wouldn't have her picture in any of the bags. This was not a crisis. There was no need to turn it into a crisis.

"The thirty of you standing before me today," Sheila Dunham said, "represent the end of one very long process, and the beginning of another. Whether you realized it or not, we have been watching you in this room for the last hour. We've been watching what you say and what you do, and we've come to the second decision of the three decisions we'll have to make today. There can be only one *America's Next Superstar.* There can be only fourteen girls in the house in Bryn Mawr. That means that sixteen of you will have to leave before this day is over. This time, we will eliminate only ten of you, and then there will be another test. In the next room —"

Olivia saw the girl move forward, a little blond girl, pretty enough, but mousy and small.

"— there are tables, and on those tables are Gucci bags, one for each of you. In twenty of those bags, there are pictures. If there's a bag with your picture in it, you will go on to the next test. If there is not, then you will have to go home, immediately. When I step back —"

The blond girl had gotten closer. Nobody was paying attention to her. Some of the girls were straining toward the faint line that told them how far back they had to stay. The girl was not moving past that line. Olivia moved forward herself. She had to stay outside the range of the cameras.

"— you will be allowed to go through these curtains, through the door behind them, and search for your picture. On the count of three. One —"

This time, the little blond girl did move forward over the mark.

Then she raised her arm, pointed it directly at Sheila Dunham, and it was only when the shot was fired that Olivia realized she had a gun.

■ ■ ■ ■

Part I

■ ■ ■ ■

Everyone is interested in murder, in
theory if not in practice . . .
— Theodore Dalrymple

ONE

1

For most of his life, Gregor Demarkian had cared very little for, or about, murder mysteries. He had tried a few, over the years. In the army, he'd read the books he'd found in the base libraries close at hand. Those had been mostly "hard-boiled," and he'd found them completely ridiculous. It was odd, these days, to think that he'd ever been as young as that, but he hadn't been so young that he hadn't been able to figure out that real private detectives did not go chasing around the landscape solving murders that police forces couldn't, or wouldn't, solve themselves. Besides, he never much liked the way the police were portrayed in the works of people like Raymond Chandler. He did not think the police were habitually corrupt. He did not think the local business community was habitually corrupt, either. He did not think America could be explained by some grand collusion of the police and the capitalists, for the sole purpose of . . . well, he had never been able to figure out what the villains in hard-boiled novels really wanted. There was money, but it had never seemed to him to be a big enough reason for all the nonsense that was going on, nonstop, in an apparent attempt to destroy the soul of the country.

There was light streaming in the window now, good light for six o'clock in the morning. That was how he knew spring was coming. He looked down the long line of his body. He was lying flat on his back in bed, which was how he slept. It annoyed the hell out of his new wife that he slept that way, instead of tossing and turning the way she did.

"It isn't natural," she'd told him, on several occasions. "It's not like you're sleeping at all. It's like you turn into a statue when you close your eyes, and then Pygmalion's kiss has to wake you up."

"The kiss is the princess and the frog," he'd reminded her. "I don't think Pygmalion kissed anybody."

"Galatea. And you don't know. I can tell."

Bennis was not laying next to him in bed now. She was in the shower. Gregor could hear the water running. He looked back down that long line of his body and reached for the book he'd left lying in bed when he fell asleep last night. He usually had the sense to put a bookmark in it and put it on the nightstand. He picked it up. It was *At Bertram's Hotel* by Agatha Christie. He'd been given it by his closest friend in Philadelphia — by his closest friend in the world, maybe — and he was shocked to find that he enjoyed it very much. It was not realistic, but it was not trying to be. The police were not played for fools. But it wasn't that. It wasn't that at all.

"It's a metaphor," he said.

"What?" Bennis had just come out of the shower. She was wearing his bathrobe. She was always wearing his bathrobe rather than her own. If he let her have it and got himself a new one, she would abandon the old one and go for the new one. Gregor had no idea why this should be. He *did* know that her skin held a tan very well. She was still almost as brown as she had been in Jamaica. That was where they had just been on their honeymoon.

"It's a metaphor," Gregor said. He did not say that he found her remarkably and oddly beautiful, because he's said that before. Marriage was supposed to change the conversation at least a little bit. "The

Agatha Christie book Tibor gave me. It's a metaphor."

"A metaphor for what?"

"You were the English major," Gregor said. "A metaphor for the reality of crime and evil. No, that isn't it. A metaphor for the good of social order."

"The good of social order? Are you sure Tibor hasn't been lending you the nonfiction?"

"Social order is a good," Gregor said. "It's what makes everything else possible. If you're running around all day worrying about getting murdered, or if you can't open your store in the morning without worrying about getting robbed, then you don't get very much done. You expend all your energy on self-protection. If you want art and music and railroads, even, then you have to have social order. And it can't just come from the police."

Bennis had let the robe slip to the floor, which was . . . interesting. She had her back to him, but still. He hadn't moved off his back. Now he did, rolling over to his side as she started to get dressed. He wanted a better look. Maybe he was wrong. Maybe marriage didn't change the conversation, not the little unspoken one that ran through people's heads.

"Real murders," he said finally, "aren't like the murders in this book — except, actually, sometimes they are. I'll get to that later."

"You've been thinking of this in your sleep?" Bennis asked.

"Partially," Gregor admitted. "I think of lots of things in my sleep. I sometimes have really rude dreams about you in my sleep."

"You weren't sleeping."

"Murders," Gregor said. "Your ordinary run of murder in the real world is not like the murder in this book. Your ordinary run of murder in the real world is monumentally stupid. It's the product of a combination of drugs, alcohol, and IQs that would look good as golf scores. Or it's the casual brutality of organized crime, which, Mario Puzo and Marlon Brando notwithstanding, doesn't do much better on the IQ scale."

"You'd have to say James Gandolfini now," Bennis said. "Or Tony Soprano. Tibor says his students don't know who Marlon Brando was."

"It doesn't matter," Gregor said. "The thing is, we've already made provision for that kind of crime. It's built into the structure of society. I don't care what kind of policing you have, there's going to be that kind of crime. I don't care how perfect you make your society, either. You can raise and lower the incidence of that kind of thing, the street mugging, the home invasion, usually by arresting people and putting them away for a long time. Did I tell you that I hold to the retribution and punishment side of what we should do about criminals debate?"

"Several times," Bennis said. "Almost every night when we watch the news."

"It's not that I think it's impossible to rehabilitate a criminal. Every once in a while you get one who should be rehabilitated —"

"Tibor's students."

"Some of them. However. Lots of them can't be rehabilitated because they don't particularly want to be. So there's that. I don't understand why it is that reformers can't see that. And they really can't. They think you're a monster when you suggest that some people will only leave the rest of us alone when they're locked up."

"Well," Bennis said, coming to sit down on his side of the bed. She was nearly dressed, now. She had on jeans and a long sleeved T-shirt under a short-sleeved one. She was not wearing socks or shoes. "It's depressing, if you think about it," she said. "It's depressing to think that there will always be evil and violence in the world.

People would like to think, even I would like to think, that there are ways to get rid of it forever."

"There are no ways to get rid of it forever," Gregor said. "That's Tibor's department. God gets rid of it on the last day, if I remember the Sunday school lessons of my childhood."

"You don't believe in God," Bennis said.

"I don't think I do," Gregor said, "but that's beside the point. Reality is what it is. We will never get rid of all the evil and violence in the world. There will always be murder. There will always be cruelty. There will always be robbery. We can make those things happen less often by catching the people who do them and putting them in jail and keeping them in jail. And making sure there isn't an upside — that jail isn't something . . . Did I tell you that when I was first in the FBI, I had a job in this one small town in Wisconsin — kidnapping detail, something. And I met this guy who *deliberately* committed a rape — deliberately, mind you — every spring he was out of jail. And do you know why? Because he wanted to be in jail. For the winter. It was the only way he could be sure of being out of the cold for the winter. It was the craziest thing I ever saw. With the three-strikes laws these days, they'd put him away for good now."

"Maybe that was what he wanted," Bennis said. "Maybe he was one of those people who only feel entirely comfortable when they're locked up. Didn't you tell me about that once?"

"Yes, I did. Where was I?"

"You were depressing me." Bennis got up and started walking around the bedroom. "You were telling me that there would always be evil and violence in the world."

"Ah. I know. Yes. There will always be evil and violence in the world, but we're not really all that worried about that. We know what that is. We expect it. But we also expect everybody else, the people who aren't these sorts of low-life thugs, we expect those people to behave themselves. We don't police them the way we police the others. Hell, we can't. There are too many people in any society to police them all effectively, unless you're North Korea, and that's no society any of us want to live in. So we let the rest of the population go about its business, sort of on the honor system."

"You really think of all this in your sleep, do you?" Bennis said. "Didn't I buy new socks? From L.L.Bean? I keep thinking I remember putting them away, but I'm not sure."

"They're in the top center drawer of the highboy," Gregor said. "They're in little plastic wrappings. It's when the ordinary people, the people we expect to be on their good behavior, it's when they start doing things they shouldn't that we have to worry. Because if we can't count on the ordinary people, the good people, to do good even if they're not being watched . . . well, that way lies chaos. That way lies a society that can't be governed at all. Can you see that?"

Bennis had found her socks and sat down on his side of the bed again to put them on. Bennis was forty-eight, but she still dressed like a college girl, and she oddly still looked like one. The enormous cloud of black hair was as thick as it had been when Gregor first met her. He expected it was dyed, but he didn't ask. Her body was as slim as it had been, too, though, and that he couldn't help wondering about. The woman ate like a horse, and she ate all the things his Armenian mother and aunts had eaten and gotten fat on. The really odd thing was the sides of her eyes. Bennis had no crow's feet. Gregor knew she had never had plastic surgery. It would have been a kind of miracle, except that he wouldn't have cared about crow's feet.

"Weren't you making some kind of point?" she asked.

"Yes," Gregor said. "Yes, I was. I was making a point about Agatha Christie. Her books are not unrealistic. They're just metaphors."

"Metaphors for social order," Bennis said. She was being half solemn.

Gregor sat up. He hated sitting up. It hurt his back.

"Metaphors for the need for social order," he said. "Because the kinds of murders she deals with are rare in the real world —"

"They weren't rare in her fictional world," Bennis said.

"— but they do happen." Gregor was going on as if Bennis wasn't talking. This was sometimes necessary. "They do sometimes happen. And they have to be dealt with immediately when they do, because they're the most dangerous kind of crime. Much more dangerous than some thug idiot who starts staging home invasions and beating and killing the crap out of everybody. We *know* how to deal with *him.* We *need* to know how to deal with *them,* and we don't."

"Them?"

"The middle-class criminals. The 'nice' ones who do plotted murders, and other things. What we do now is look at the thug idiot and shove him in jail pretty much indefinitely. We look at the polite criminal and we make all kinds of excuses. We offer services. We offer reduced sentences and mitigated sentences — house arrest, probation, parole, whatever. And we're dead wrong. We should lock these people up for as long or longer than we lock up the thugs. Because these people are more dangerous than the thugs."

"Is that what you want to do with the Bernie Madoffs of the world?" Bennis asked. "Lock them up?"

"Well, we did lock Madoff up," Gregor said, "but in that kind of case, the only thing that would really do would be for us to take all their money. And I mean all of it. They should become acquainted with soup kitchens and homeless shelters."

"Get up and get dressed," Bennis said. "Tibor is probably already waiting for us at the Ararat."

"You don't want to get me started on Bernie Madoff," Gregor said.

Bennis got out of the way so that he could move, and Gregor went into the bathroom to take a shower. She was right. Tibor would be waiting for them.

And maybe, just maybe, Tibor would have

more of these books for him to read.

2

In the beginning — well, Gregor thought, no. The beginning was his childhood, when this small neighborhood in Philadelphia had been long blocks of tenements filled with people who barely spoke English.

In the *second* beginning then, in the time since Gregor had come back to Cavanaugh Street from the District of Columbia, from the time when he had retired from the FBI and come back home to do what ever it was he thought he could do here — from then, he and Father Tibor Kasparian had had a nearly invariable routine. Every morning at six, Gregor would get up, shower, shave, and get into clean clothes. Then he would go down to the street and walk toward the Ararat Restaurant. Halfway there, he would find Fr. Tibor Kasparian coming out from behind the church, where his apartment was. Then they would go on to breakfast.

This had been their routine even after it had become apparent to anybody who was watching that in spite of the fact that Gregor and Bennis had separate apartments in the same brownstone, the apartments were separate in fact but not in spirit. Bennis usually took more time, or less, than Gregor to dress. She usually had things on her mind, even if it was only something she was doing with Donna Moradanyan Donahue. Donna didn't eat breakfast in the Ararat these days: she had one small boy and an infant at home. Still, Donna did manage to be there at some point every morning, and Donna and Bennis always seemed to have something they needed to do.

This morning, Tibor was not waiting in front of the church. Gregor knew that he would be in the Ararat in the window booth, where they always sat. It was not a rejection. It seemed, instead, to be a kind of acknowledgment of Gregor's marriage. Now that Gregor was married to Bennis, Tibor did not wait for him to come by for breakfast. This made absolutely no sense.

"Are you all right?" Bennis asked him.

They were walking past the church, which was on the other side of the street. The Ararat was on this side of the street. Gregor sighed.

"I was thinking about Tibor," he said.

"Is there something wrong with Tibor? Look, he's in the window. He looks all right to me. Is there something I should know?"

"Why doesn't he wait for me in the mornings anymore? Because we're married? Does that change breakfast? And why do we come down to the Ararat together? We never did before. You never even wanted to."

"That's what this is about? You're having a delayed reaction to our getting married?"

Gregor sighed again.

They were at the Ararat now. Tibor really was sitting in the window booth. The Ararat still looked the way it always did, in spite of the fact that it had picked up a good deal of dinner traffic over the years. It was still a fairly basic diner, just one that served a lot of Armenian food.

Gregor pushed open the big plate glass door and held it for Bennis to go in. Then he came in himself and nodded to Linda Melajian. The Melajians owned the Ararat, and Gregor knew that old Mikhail Melajian had been sick on and off now for a year. He couldn't imagine that the Ararat would close. Maybe Linda would take it over, or her brothers.

Gregor went to the booth and slid in next to Bennis. The booth was half a joke between the lot of them. It was low to the floor, the way booths were in the Old Country. The older they all got, the harder they found it to get in and out of the thing.

"What do you figure people do back in Armenia?" Gregor said. "I mean, the old women, and people like that? Do they get down on the floor and just get stuck there?"

"They are more used to it than we are, Krekor," Tibor said.

Linda came to the table with the coffeepot and started pouring. "Good morning," she said. "I thought I'd better warn you. The Very Old Ladies were here when I first opened up this morning, and I mean first. They were here when I unlocked for myself, never mind opening up the restaurant itself. And they've been waiting ever since. And now they're staring at you."

"They're staring at Gregor," Bennis said confidently. "They don't mind me anymore because I'm married to him."

"They're always going to mind you," Gregor said. "You were practically living with me first. Never mind, you know, the thing with not belonging to the church."

"They really are staring at you," Tibor said.

The three of them managed to look at the Very Old Ladies all at once, and to look away again all at once. The problem with the Very Old Ladies was that they always looked ready to pronounce doom on the world around them. The head-to-toe black they wore was not a help. Bennis and Tibor and Gregor all looked down at their hands and then up at each other.

"Well," Bennis said. "I still don't think they're going to come over here and lecture me about living in sin. If they were going to do that, they'd have done it years ago."

Linda came back with a rack of toast. Gregor found himself enormously grateful to have that to concentrate on.

"So," he said, taking toast and a couple of little packets of honey to put on it, "I was telling Bennis this morning. Agatha Christie wrote metaphors."

"Oh, very good, Krekor," Tibor said. "That's it exactly. She writes very important metaphors, too. She writes —"

Bennis tapped on the table. "You two are not going to do this this morning," she said. "My point is perfectly valid. If it isn't valid, then you should say so. And if you can't say so, then I say it's time for Gregor here to get off his ass and do something."

Gregor had put enough honey on his bread to reconstitute a beehive. He put it all down on the little round side plate that was part of the standard Ararat table setting.

"I have been doing something," he said. "First, I got married. Then, I spent nearly a month in Jamaica —"

"You went on your honeymoon and complained the whole time," Bennis said.

"That's not doing something. You need to go back to work."

"Why?" Gregor asked. "I don't need the money. Even without you I don't need the money. I've been working a lot the last couple of years. I'm tired of it."

"You're not tired of it," Bennis said. "You're just annoyed with it, it's not the same thing. And you need to do it because you're driving me crazy going on the way you are now. You are not a person who does nothing comfortably."

"I'm perfectly comfortable," Gregor said.

"I'm not," Bennis said.

"And besides . . ." Gregor said, watching Linda come across the room with their breakfasts. Linda Melajian was infallible. She knew what all the regulars ate, and even knew when they were going to vary the usual. In Gregor's case, she knew what he ate when he was alone with Tibor, and what he ate when Bennis was at the table. When Bennis was at the table, there was a lot of fruit.

Gregor looked down at the fruit and cheese and thought about breakfast sausages. Then he said, "I can't just jump out of bed in the morning and go to work. Somebody has to hire me. Nobody is interested in hiring me at the moment."

"That's not true," Bennis said. "And you know it."

"Nobody suitable is interested in hiring me at the moment," Gregor said. "I consult for police departments. There's a reason I consult for police departments."

"You don't always insist on police departments," Bennis said. "And I think this would be good for you. Good for you in every way. And it would get you out of your shell."

"I'm not in a shell, and you just want a chance to go snooping around that television show."

"What television show?" Tibor asked.

"I never snoop around," Bennis said, "and if that's all I wanted, I could get my brother Christopher to do my snooping for me. It would be good for you. And they asked."

Tibor had a three-egg double-cheese omelet, two sausage patties, hash browns, and bacon. Gregor would have killed for any of it.

Linda Melajian came back one more time and leaned over to whisper. "They just asked me to warn them when it looked like you were about to leave. So you're warned, if you get my drift."

"At least it isn't a reality show," Gregor said.

"What reality show?" Tibor asked.

Bennis leaned across the table. "*America's Next Superstar* has rented Engine House from my brother Bobby —"

"But I thought he'd lost the house," Tibor said. "There was some settlement about securities law —"

"Well, yes, there was," Bennis said. "But you know about Bobby. He's —"

"A world-class con man," Gregor put in.

"That, too," Bennis said, "but he's especially good at conning the government. Anyway, he's had Engine House back for at least a year and a half now but he doesn't live in it because, really, who could? It's thirty thousand square feet and it was built before anybody knew anything about insulation."

"Robber barons didn't need to know about insulation," Gregor said.

"Yes, I know," Bennis said. "My great-grandfather was a robber baron. Whoopee. This is not news. Anyway, it's sitting out there in Bryn Mawr, empty, and it's huge and just the kind of thing for reality shows — you know, a 'palatial estate' as they put it — and so *America's Next Superstar* rented the house. You know, to be the house where the girls all live and there are eliminations. I don't know. I've only watched the thing once or twice —"

"Me, too," Tibor said. "I prefer *America's Next Top Model*. I don't like the woman on *America's Next Superstar* so much. She's, she's —"

"A dyed in-the-wool bitch," Bennis said. "Yes, I know. I actually met her once, before she was reduced to doing reality shows. She used to interview for the *Today* show. Then she asked Katie Couric — on the air, I'm not making this up — she asked Katie Couric if the stress of being married to her was the reason her husband died of cancer. And that was that."

"I think I heard about that," Tibor said.

"Everybody heard about it," Bennis said.

"So there has been another murder in your house in Bryn Mawr?" Tibor said.

"It's not my house," Bennis said. "It's the family house, and Bobby got it in my father's will. No, there hasn't been a murder, or anything else in the house. It was before that, when they were doing the final auditions. They held them in this place in Merion, and somebody shot at Sheila Dunham."

"Just shot at her?" Tibor asked.

"Well, in front of a crowd of people," Bennis said. "Just stood up and shot at her. One of the girls who hadn't been eliminated, I think. Oh, I don't know. I really don't. They arrested the girl, and she's sitting in jail somewhere. She's just been sitting there. She doesn't ever talk, apparently. And she didn't have any ID on her, so they don't know who she is, and she isn't saying. And that's where it stands, I think. So the show asked Bobby to ask me to ask Gregor —"

"To do God only knows what," Gregor said, "since there's no murder here, and I'm not the kind of detective who tracks down missing identities. The police will figure out who this young woman is, eventually. They're good at that kind of thing. And they have resources I don't. There's absolutely no point in my going around doing nothing particularly sensible —"

It was the tip of old Mrs. Vardanian's walking stick that Gregor noticed first. All the Very Old Ladies used walking sticks, although most of them didn't seem to need them to walk.

Gregor sat back and away from his food, feeling a little breathless.

"Mrs. Vardanian," he said. "Good morning. Ladies."

The Very Old Ladies nodded in unison. They were like a Greek chorus, those women, a Greek chorus made up of Furies, or Harpies, or something else equally intimidating.

Mrs. Vardanian picked up her walking stick and pounded it on the floor.

"There's something going on down at Sophie Mgrdchian's place," she said. "And I think you ought to go down there and look into it."

Two

1

It had been late fall when Gregor Demarkian first moved back to Cavanaugh
Street. He had a tendency, when he was
indoors, to imagine it always that way: dark
and cold, and with that wet sting in the air
that promises snow.

It was now late spring, though, and the air
was thick and warm, and the landscape was
bright. The fronts of the town houses that
lined both sides of the street looked washed.
The windows of the stores looked as if
they'd been polished. Back down the street
a bit, back toward his and Bennis's own
apartment, the new Holy Trinity Armenian
Christian Church glittered in the way that
could only happen if women had come out
to wash the sidewalk in front of it.

"Probably hired someone," Gregor said to
himself.

"What?" Bennis said.

The Very Old Ladies had led them out onto the sidewalk, and were now marching them down the block in the other direction from the church. The air smelled like something in the country. Gregor wasn't sure he liked it.

"They probably hired someone," he told Bennis. "The sidewalk in front of the church has been washed down, and I know the city didn't do it. When I was growing up, the women did it, the married women, but I can't imagine them doing it now. Can you see Lida Arkmanian out here with a tin pail on her hands and knees, scrubbing the sidewalk?"

"Maybe if the pail were Gucci," Bennis said.

The Very Old Ladies were marching relentlessly forward. They moved faster than you'd think they would, but not really fast. Gregor was just reluctant to catch up with them. By now, there was a little parade of people moving along: the Very Old Ladies themselves, Gregor and Bennis and Tibor, one of the Melajian boys (who'd probably been ordered to report back), Sheila Kashinian and Hannah Krekorian and Lida.

They passed Ohanian's Middle Eastern Food Store and Lucy Ohanian came out, the youngest of the girls, the only one left on the street now that the rest of her siblings had gone off to college and jobs. Gregor always found it incredible how many children people in this neighborhood still wanted to have.

They got to the Donahue town house and Donna came out, looking a little disheveled. Her husband Russ was just behind her, holding the baby, and keeping Tommy from running out into the street.

"What's going on?" Donna asked Bennis as she caught up to them. "You look like some kind of procession. I thought there was going to be a casket."

"We don't know where we're going," Bennis said. "Mrs. Vardanian and company came and grabbed us, and here we are."

"There's going to have to be a casket for somebody if she keeps up this pace," Gregor said.

They had crossed another intersection. Now they were in that part of the neighborhood that was exclusively residential. The first block of it had good-looking town houses on both sides, well kept up and repaired. The Kashinians had their place in this block, and there were three houses divided up — like the house Gregor lived in in the other direction — into floor-through apartments. Hannah Krekorian had one of those.

The block after that one was not so pretty. It was not a slum. No part of Cavanaugh Street was a slum anymore. Gregor supposed it had been one when he was growing up here, and instead of floor-throughs the apartments had been more like rabbit warrens. Still, it had always been clean, what with women washing sidewalks, and other women washing clothes so often that lines of the things had seemed normal to him, a part of the architecture.

He snapped himself back to the present. The present was not bad. He liked his life these days. The Very Old Ladies had stopped, and the whole crowd of people who had followed them was now standing in front of a tall brick town house that looked like it hadn't been cleaned in forty years. There was mail in the mailbox out front. It must have been left from the afternoon before.

Mrs. Vardanian mounted two of the steps up to the door and looked the house over. "There," she said, sounding satisfied about something. "That's what we want you to do something about."

Gregor looked the house over one more time. "What's what you want me to do something about? I can't fix up the house, if that's —"

"No, no," Mrs. Vardanian said. "It's not the house. It's Sophie Mgrdchian."

"She's the woman who owns the house," one of the other Very Old Ladies said.

Sometimes Gregor could not keep the Very Old Ladies apart in his head, except for Mrs. Vardanian who was easy to remember because she had a lot in common with the bogeyman of his childhood.

Gregor tried to think of what he was supposed to say here. "Is she a friend of yours?" he asked.

"What difference does it make if she's a friend of ours," Mrs. Vardanian said. "Of course she is, or she used to be. She doesn't go out very much, not even to go to church these days. Her husband Viktor died —"

"In 1984," yet another of the Very Old Ladies put in. "I remember the funeral. It wasn't a very big funeral. There's a niece, I think, in New York somewhere."

"It's California," the first of the Very Old Ladies said.

Gregor was beginning to feel a little dizzy trying to remember who was saying what.

"Here is what we want you to do," Mrs. Vardanian said. "We want you to find out what has happened to her."

"Has something happened to her?" Gregor asked.

"Yesterday," Mrs. Vardanian said, "I saw a woman come out of this house and leave the neighborhood. She came back in a taxi half an hour later with grocery bags. It was not Sophie Mgrdchian."

"Maybe it was the niece," Gregor said, "or, I don't know, the sister? Brother? Whoever had the niece?"

"It's a niece," one of the Very Old Ladies said. "Sophie's two sisters are dead. It was a terrible thing, really, there were practically no children. One of Viktor's brothers had a daughter. But the niece can't be more than, I don't know —"

"Forty," Mrs. Vardanian said. "She's probably younger. This woman looked as old as Sophie. And she was —"

"She was messy," the third Very Old Ladies said.

"She was dressed in layers," Mrs. Vardanian said positively. "The way homeless people dress. And she wasn't Armenian, not even close. And she was too tall."

"Tall," Gregor repeated.

"Sophie was barely five feet," one of the Very Old Ladies said. "This woman had to be about five seven or eight."

"So," Mrs. Vardanian said, "what we want

94

you to do is find out what happened to Sophie Mgrdchian. I know we haven't seen much of her in the last fifteen years or so, but that doesn't mean we're going to stand by and let some strange woman kill her off and steal her house."

"You think somebody has killed Mrs. Mgrdchian and stolen her house because you saw somebody you don't know bringing groceries there yesterday?" Gregor said. "Maybe it's a friend. Maybe she's got a visitor. Maybe —"

"She doesn't have a visitor," Mrs. Vardanian said. "I know every single person Sophie could have as a visitor, and it wasn't any of them."

"We weren't just watching yesterday," one of the other Very Old Ladies said. She sounded a little sheepish. "We've been, well, we've been —"

"We've been watching for a week and a half," Mrs. Vardanian said flatly. "We've been staking the place out, the way they do on the television. And this woman has come in and out, and there's been no sign of Sophie. Not a sign."

"Why didn't you just knock on the door and ask what was happening?" Gregor said.

"We did," one of the other Very Old Ladies said. "Nobody answered."

"And she was in there at the time, that woman," Mrs. Vardanian said. "I could hear her moving around."

Gregor didn't say that he'd thought for years that Mrs. Vardanian was deaf as a post, because it was only half true. He didn't understand why these women thought that whoever was in that house would be more likely to answer his knock than theirs.

He sighed a little and went up the steps past Mrs. Vardanian. He stopped at the door. It needed to be painted. He rang the bell. He could hear the bell sound in the hollow spaces beyond the door. Nothing happened.

"You can't just leave it at that," Mrs. Vardanian said. "You're a policeman. You can go into the house."

"I'm not a policeman," Gregor said, "and even a policeman can't go barging into people's houses for no reason. He has to have probable cause to believe a crime has been committed, or he has to have a warrant, and I've got neither."

"You do have cause to believe a crime has been committed," Mrs. Vardanian said. "We told you."

Gregor pressed the bell again. He listened to the distant bell sound again. Nothing happened.

"Maybe Mrs. Mgrdchian is sick and has a nurse's aide staying with her to do for her," Gregor said.

"If Sophie Mgrdchian was sick and wanted to get somebody in, we'd have heard about it," Mrs. Vardanian said. "She'd have called for the priest. You don't take chances with that kind of thing."

Gregor looked back at the door. Maybe Mrs. Mgrdchian was deaf, and the woman who was with her — if there was a woman with her; if this wasn't just Mrs. Mgrdchian herself and the Very Old Ladies having vapors — maybe the woman who was with her was deaf, too.

Gregor raised his fist and pounded against the door, hard and flat, making a big booming noise that he thought almost anybody could have heard. When nothing happened yet again, he raised his fist one more time, gave one more hard pound . . . and the door popped open.

"The door's open," Mrs. Vardanian said. "Very good. We can go in there now and look around and nobody can blame us. The door's open on a city street and that means —"

"I don't really think we ought to go in there," Gregor said.

"Oh, don't be such a coward," Mrs. Vardanian said, pushing her way up the stairs and next to the place where Gregor was standing. "I don't know what's wrong with young people today. They've got no initiative. They've got no —"

But by then Mrs. Vardanian was looking at what Gregor himself was looking at: the small, thin body of a woman lying across the foyer carpet, flat on its face. Just beyond her there was another woman, taller and thicker and wild-eyed, standing very still.

"My God," Mrs. Vardanian said.

Gregor got out his phone and punched in 911.

2

The paramedics and the police arrived first, but only by a hair. The man from the Mayor's Office arrived right behind them, and he didn't care half so much about blocking the flow of traffic on the street. Of course, by that point, there was no flow of traffic on the street. The taxis had seen the logjam and had taken alternative routes, radioing in to any other drivers who might need the information. The ordinary motorists were just stopped in their tracks. Some of them had gotten out of their cars. If anybody had to go anywhere in a fast car with lights and sirens flashing, there was going to be a problem.

The man from the Mayor's Office was somebody Gregor recognized, but not well enough. He was very young, and very white, and had that look about him that so many of John Jackman's aides had. John liked to hire graduates of all the Ivy League schools that had once turned him down.

The young man threaded his way through the crowd and up to where Gregor and Bennis were standing, just off the now open front door. The denizens of Cavanaugh Street were out in force. Even the ones you'd expect to stay in their stores and restaurants just to keep them running were there. Gregor spotted three of the Ohanians and two of the Melajians. The Very Old Ladies were as close to the door as the uniformed personnel would let them, and closer. As soon as all the uniformed backs were turned, they crept in again.

"Murder," Mrs. Vardanian was saying. Viola Vardanian said nothing under her breath. It had been decades since she could hear a voice pitched that low — unless it was a voice delivering really good dirt on somebody she knew, and then she could hear it coming all the way from Trenton.

The young man made it the rest of the

way up the steps and held out his hand. "Mr. Demarkian? I'm David Mortimer. Mayor Jackman sent me."

Bennis snorted a little in the background. Gregor ignored her. "How do you do, Mr. Mortimer. Except I think I've at least met you once, I just couldn't place you. I hope John is well."

"The mayor's fine, as far as I know," David Mortimer said. "He thought you might need some help with whatever's going on in there."

"I don't know what's going on in there," Gregor said.

"It was murder," Mrs. Vardanian said. She made her way across the front stairs as if nothing and nobody was in her way. She took David Mortimer by the lapels of his very expensive suit jacket. "It was murder," she said again. "We've been saying it for days now, and nobody would listen to us. I knew that wasn't Sophie Mgrdchian going in and out. I've known Sophie Mgrdchian all my life. Damned fool woman in a lot of ways, but she wasn't that tall American thing coming in and out —"

"You're American," Gregor said blandly.

"I was born in Yerevan," Mrs. Vardanian said, "and so was Sophie. And I told you this morning that something was wrong. I

100

told you."

"She did tell me," Gregor admitted. He pointed across to the other two of the Very Old Ladies. "The three of them did. Apparently, they've been watching this other woman, the one we found in there with the body, go in and out, and —"

"For God's sake," somebody said from inside the house, very loudly.

Gregor and the crowd all turned to look in unison. All of a sudden, there was a fury of activity. People were running in and out of the house. Somebody climbed into the ambulance and started up first the motor, and then the lights and sirens. Two uniformed police officers raced out of the house into the crowd and started clearing the street.

"Let's get a pathway, let's get a pathway," one of them said. His voice sounded loud enough to be coming out of a bullhorn, although it wasn't.

"I wonder what's happening," Bennis said.

"My guess," Gregor said, "is that we don't have a murder quite yet."

There was another flurry of activity, and four paramedics came down the stairs carrying a gurney with a woman strapped to it. She had an oxygen mask over her face.

"She's alive?" Mrs. Vardanian asked,

sounding stunned. "She was dead. Dead on the floor. We all saw her."

They had done more than see her. Gregor had actually tried to take a pulse while they were waiting for the paramedics to arrive. He hadn't gotten one, or at least he hadn't detected one. He felt like an idiot.

"I'm not trained for this," he told David Mortimer. "I tried to see if she were alive, but I couldn't get anything in the way of a pulse, so I just assumed —"

They all watched as the screaming ambulance edged through the crowd. Police were now running up and down the block and onto the next one, pushing people back onto the sidewalk. Three other police cars had arrived and blocked off the side streets so that the ambulance would have a clear path. The crowd was doing what crowds do. It got back on the sidewalk. It fell off again.

The ambulance let out a long series of screaming wails at a volume Gregor thought must be something new, and then it was free, careening off into the street with all its lights going and an equally lit and screaming police car following it.

Gregor looked at David Mortimer. "There's another woman in there," he said. "She was just standing there."

David Mortimer jerked his head in the

direction of the door and began to move. Gregor followed him. Everybody in the city knew John Jackman's aides. Nobody bothered them. David Mortimer led Gregor through the little clusters of police officers as easily as if the scene had been entirely unpopulated.

When they got in through the front door, Gregor saw that the woman he had first seen standing over the body was still there, and still standing. There were half a dozen police officers standing in front of her, but she did not looked worried, or frightened, or — anything. She looked blank.

David Mortimer went up to one of the police officers and whispered in his ear. The police officer turned around and held out his hand.

"Mr. Demarkian," he said. "I'm Officer Kelsowicz. I'm glad to meet you."

"What's going on with the woman?"

"We don't know." It was another officer, a woman. She didn't offer her name. "We've been trying to talk to her," she said. "She seems to be drugged, or maybe mentally ill. It's hard to tell."

"Do you think anyone would mind?" Gregor asked.

"Oh, no," Officer Kelsowicz said. He put his hand out and tapped the officer nearest the old woman on the shoulder. When the officer turned, Kelsowicz said, "It's Gregor Demarkian. He wants to try to talk to her."

"Gregor Demarkian," the third officer said.

A fourth officer looked around. "That's Mortimer from the Mayor's Office," he said.

"But it's Gregor Demarkian," Officer Kelsowicz said.

Gregor stepped forward and put an end to the confusion. Now that he was up close and paying attention, he could see that the woman was not only old and shabby, but very clean, shiny clean, as if everything about her — her clothes, her body, her hair — had been newly washed and sort of polished. She was wearing some kind of perfume, or cologne, too. It smelled like flowers, but not any particular one.

Gregor held out his hand. "Hello," he said. "I'm Gregor Demarkian. It's very nice to meet you."

The old woman looked delighted. "It's very nice to meet you!" she said. "It's very nice to meet you!"

"You can call me Gregor, if you like," Gregor said. "I'm not sure what you want me to call you."

"Oh, you call me Lily, just like everybody," the old woman said. "Lily. Lily flower.

That's what my mother used to say. She used to say that I looked just like a lily flower. That was before the helicopters came, you know, back in the days when there was grass. I used to like the grass. I liked the smell of it."

"I like the smell of it, too," Gregor said. "There isn't much of it, in the city. Except in the parks."

The old woman leaned very close to Gregor's ear. Her breath was sour with age and, he thought, lack of dental work, but her teeth had been brushed. He could smell the mint of the toothpaste.

"I don't go into the parks anymore," Lily said. "I used to. I used to go there for the grass. There are children in the parks. Did you know that?"

"Yes," Gregor said. "I knew that."

"Some of them are real children, but some of them are not," Lily said. "People like to disguise themselves as children sometimes. You have to be careful. It's like that old story. The sheep in wolf's clothing. My mother used to tell me stories. Before the helicopters came."

Gregor nodded. "My mother used to tell me stories, too. That was right down the street. I grew up on this street. I lived in an apartment a couple of blocks from here, but that building is gone now. Did you grow up here?"

"Here?"

"In this house. I don't remember seeing you around, but this is a couple of blocks away. I might not have noticed you."

"I notice you," Lily said. "You're right there. I can see you."

"I am right here. I was wondering if you grew up in this house, that's all."

Lily backed away a little. She looked around. She looked back at Gregor.

"The helicopters came," she said. "They came and they ran all around the yard, and then there was water. It was like being on an ocean, but it wasn't. There are whales in the oceans. There's the Loch Ness monster. I read about that in the newspaper. I don't think that was this house. Do you?"

"No," Gregor said. "I don't."

"Am I someplace I'm not supposed to be? I'm always someplace I'm not supposed to be these days. I don't know how it happens. I thought I was all right in this house, though. There was a lady, but she fell down. She gave me soap for my hair. And then the helicopters came. But not here. It wasn't here. And there was water."

"I think it would be a good thing if you let these people take you to a hospital,"

Gregor said. "I don't think you're feeling very well."

"She wasn't feeling very well," Lily said. "She fell down. My mother didn't fall down. She fell into a hole. It was a big black hole. I read about those in the newspaper, too. Do you read the newspapers? I don't know if I can believe them. They disguise themselves as children sometimes. It's very wrong of them."

"I'm sure it is," Gregor said.

He stepped away and motioned to the policewoman who had been closest when he first came up. She moved forward and took Lily by the hand, not by the arm.

"Come on," she said. "We'll just take you to the hospital and see what the doctors have to say."

"I don't like the hospital," Lily said. "They yell at you there."

For a split second, Gregor thought he would have to step in again, but Lily was going without a struggle, walking along hand in hand with the policewoman as if they were two best friends from second grade.

THREE

1

It had been raining when Olivia Dahl first
woke up in the morning. It had rained all
through her sweep of the morning news
shows, local and national and cable. It was
raining now, as she took her clipboard down
the long back hall to where Sheila Dunham's voice was emanating, that grating
Connecticut caw that always sounded halfway between trailer park and drunk.

"Of course I'm going to do *Good Morning
America,*" Sheila was saying. "Do you think
I give a flying fuck whether that little bitch
from the *Today* show still has friends? It
wasn't my fault she drove her husband off
the edge of a cliff and he got cancer just to
get away from her. And that's what happened, don't believe anything else. Stupid
bitch."

It was halfway possible that Sheila *was*
drunk. It wasn't likely. In spite of all the

rumors, Sheila didn't usually drink first thing in the day. People just needed an excuse for her behavior.

"God, what do you have on?" Sheila was saying. "Why is it nobody knows how to dress anymore? You can't wear that crap on the set of a national television show. I don't care if nobody is going to see you. You look like a load of shit exploded in your pants. Do you have an IQ? Did some college actually take you? Did you graduate?"

Olivia arrived at the door of the room they had designated as their "office." It was actually the old house keeper's office back when this had been the house of very rich people who lived with what Sheila would call "style." Sheila herself had no style. At the moment, she was wearing enough black spandex to put the entire Olympic gymnastics team in mourning. The little girl with her — one of the second assistants, Olivia thought — was wearing a bright blue and green horizontally striped minidress. She looked like an awning in distress.

Olivia cleared her throat. "We do have work to do," she said.

"I was getting work done," Sheila said. "Little Miss Fat Ass here was being incompetent. Nobody has any brains anymore. Have you noticed that?"

"I'll deal with *Good Morning America,*" Olivia said to the awning.

The awning sniffed, and nodded, and then hurried away. Olivia and Sheila both watched her go.

"Cow," Sheila said. She said it loudly enough to be heard in the hall.

Olivia sat down in the nearest chair. "You shouldn't do that to the assistants," she said. "We need them. There's an awful lot of necessary but mindless work that has to be done on a show like this, and you don't want somebody like me wasting my time doing it. You can't go on *Good Morning America.*"

"Of course I can. They asked me. Who is it, these days? Paula Zahn? God, but that woman is a brainless twit. Where do they get the people they put on these shows, anyway? It's like they think all of America is made up of mental defectives who want nothing but mush with their coffee. Not that that's too far off the mark, mind you, but you'd think they'd at least try to look as if they gave a damn about something or the other —"

"You can't go on *Good Morning America* because the assumption throughout the media is that we staged that little mess last weekend. Staged it for publicity."

"Did we?"

"No," Olivia said.

"We should have," Sheila said. "It's worked like a charm, hasn't it? Why should I care what they think about it? Let them think it. I'm the woman they love to hate. So what? That's good. Let's go on *Good Morning America* and really let them have it. By the time I'm done with them, they won't be talking about what's-her-name anymore."

"According to Janice Ledbedder, her name is Emily."

"Is it Emily? Have the police found out? Why aren't we counterattacking here? The police aren't doing their job."

"The police are doing the best they can. At the moment, they also think you're the most likely explanation of Emily and her gun. Not that you inspire hatred, but that you hired her. And if they decide to make that their working assumption, you could be in a lot of trouble. It's not like it was thirty years ago, you know. They arrest people who cause phony incidents —"

"You just said we didn't cause it."

"We didn't."

"Well, then." Sheila was pacing. Sheila was always pacing. Sheila never stayed still. "If we didn't cause it, I've got nothing to worry about. Which one is Janice Ledbedder?"

111

"South Dakota."

"I remember. And there was the other one. What's the other one?"

"I have no idea what you're talking about," Olivia said.

"Yes, you do," Sheila said.

Olivia looked down at her clipboard for a moment. A moment later, she looked up, and Sheila Dunham was gone. She took a deep breath. The back corridor on the ground floor didn't matter, but everywhere else in this house there were cameras, running twenty-four seven. That was the point of a reality show. You filmed everything, and then you took all the footage and edited it down until it made good television. The problem was, none of that footage ever really disappeared. It showed up everywhere. It showed up on YouTube.

Olivia left the clipboard on the desk and got up. She could hear Sheila's footsteps pounding down the hallway, and then the sound of that swinging door. She hurried a little. It didn't take much. Sheila was easily winded. That was because Sheila had never been able to really quit smoking.

Olivia made it to the swinging door just in time to see Sheila disappear upstairs. She hurried out into the foyer. It was a big foyer with a chandelier, just the kind you'd expect

112

a robber baron to have. Olivia took the steps two at a time and caught Sheila on the first landing.

"You can't do this," she said. "You're being filmed, right this minute. It will get out. You can't keep —"

"Shut the hell up," Sheila said.

Olivia knew that look. Olivia would have said that Sheila was having a brainstorm, except that brainstorms were something else these days. Sheila had reached the landing for the second floor. Olivia was keeping pace, but it didn't seem to matter.

Sheila went down the second-floor corridor and threw open a door. It was barely eight o'clock in the morning, and they'd had a late night. They'd had that silly dinner. Olivia never did understand why they always had that dinner, why a dinner with servants should be one of the tests of whether a girl could be a "superstar." What the show meant by "superstar" was "paparazzi bait." Those people could barely eat with utensils, for God's sake.

The first room was the wrong one. The two girls in it both sat up in bed and looked confused, but Sheila was out in the corridor again in a flash. Olivia was beginning to feel winded. Sheila was panting as if she were about to have a heart attack.

"Sheila," she said.

Sheila tried the second room on the same side of the hall. Two girls again sat up. One of them slid back down under the covers and hid her head. They were the wrong girls.

"Sheila, for God's sake, there are cameras running," Olivia said.

Girls were beginning to stick their heads out into the hall. Some of them were even coming out to look around. None of them was the one Sheila wanted, and she went on opening doors.

She looked drunk, Olivia had to admit it. When they saw the film of this, they were going to assume she was drunk. She was reeling. There had to be something wrong with the woman.

They were almost to the end of the hall when Sheila found the right room. Olivia tried to grab onto her arm, but it was no use. Sheila went barreling into the room and ripped the covers off the girl in the bed nearest the door. It was the wrong girl. Sheila crossed the room and ripped the covers off the other girl. She took them off in a single sweep, and then tugged again and again until they fell in a heap on the floor.

Grace Alsop was curled almost into the fetal position but entirely exposed to the air. Sheila grabbed her arm and pulled her right off the bed to the floor.

"Get up," Sheila said. She was so angry, she had gone brick red in every part of skin that was showing. "Get up. Stand up. You filthy little whore. You don't think I know what you are? You don't think we'd all guess?"

Grace was getting up, favoring one of her arms and wincing. "What do you think you're doing?" she said. She should have demanded it, but it didn't come out that way.

"Wellesley my ass," Sheila said. "And don't you dare pretend there's anything wrong with you. You want a broken arm? I can give you a broken arm. I can give you a broken head —"

"For God's sake," Olivia said.

Sheila advanced on the now-standing Grace, grabbed the top of her sleep shirt, and ripped. The front cloth came away from Grace Alsop's body in ragged tatters.

Olivia grabbed Sheila's arm. This time, Sheila did not resist.

"You can't do this," Olivia said. "You have to realize you can't do this."

"She's a spy," Sheila said, perfectly calm.

"You don't know that," Olivia said.

"Her father is the entertainment news director for Fox." Sheila was still calm.

Olivia thought Sheila was much worse when she was calm. "Her name isn't Alsop. It's Harrigan. She doesn't go to Wellesley. She doesn't go to college at all. She's twenty-eight. I knew she looked old."

"You hurt me," Grace said.

Sheila leaned forward and grabbed Grace's wrist — Grace Harrigan, Olivia told herself. But she knew the girl was Grace Harrigan and not Grace Alsop. She'd discovered that information herself. That was the only reason Sheila knew it. Sheila would never do any of her research on her own.

Sheila jerked Grace toward the door to the hall and then out of it. By now, all the girls were there, or nearly all of them, standing as close to the walls as they could get and trying to figure out what was going on. Sheila pulled Grace out where they could all see her. The entire front of Grace's sleepshirt was gone. She was standing there, to all intents and purposes, naked.

"Traitor," Sheila said.

And now her voice was gone. Just gone. It had that tinge of crazy that was not anger and not calm and not hysteria — that was nothing Olivia understood, but that was recognizable.

"Traitor," Sheila said again.

Some of the girls were crying. All of them

had their arms wrapped around their bodies as if that would shield them from something.

"Traitor," Sheila said again. "Bitch. Whore. *Cunt*."

Grace whirled around. "Nobody calls me a cunt," she screamed. "Don't you even try."

Sheila grabbed Grace's wrist again and spun her around.

Then she lifted one Nike-trainered foot, flexed it back, and punched it directly into Grace Harrigan's backside.

Grace seemed to lift off the ground half a foot before she first stumbled onto the carpet and then went flying, face down, with a thud.

2

It was Janice Ledbedder who had not come out of her room when the fuss started. She had stayed, instead, lying very still in her bed, hoping that Sheila Dunham would not come back to see if everybody had gotten up and gone into the hall. Janice didn't think that would happen. She watched the show every week, every season. She watched it when it was on Oxygen and A&E in those marathon all-day season-complete runs. She knew how it worked. There were always a couple of these explosions. They happened in the house, like this one that had happened to Grace. Or they happened on set and as an official part of the show. Or they happened away from the cameras, in a parking lot somewhere, so that the only way the world knew about them was that they turned up on the entertainment news Web sites, or because somebody had a camera phone.

Janice checked the Web sites just as much as she checked the television. There wasn't really a lot more to do in Marshall, South Dakota. She was not especially "cute," as people said there — they never talked about pretty, or beautiful. The standard for being attractive in high school was definitely "cute." It was nonthreatening, and it didn't sound as if whoever had it was trying to be something other than what they were. "Trying to be something you're not" was the biggest sin in Marshall, as far as Janice could tell. It had once made her wonder about all those people who *were* on television. All of them looked like who they were trying to be — but it was impossible to work out. It really was. Maybe it didn't matter if you were uppity if you were somebody who deserved to be uppity. Maybe it was just people from South Dakota who didn't deserve that, and that was why she had never seen anybody who "acted uppity" and still had friends. Janice definitely had friends.

The noise in the hall had stopped. No, the screaming had. There was a soft, dull murmur that was girls talking in low voices, but Janice was sure that Sheila Dunham had to be gone. Janice couldn't see what she could possibly do to cause Sheila to go into one of her patented fits, but the longer she was in this house the more she began to think that nothing had to cause it. Sheila Dunham just had fits. If you were handy, you were it.

The problem was, Janice wasn't particularly "smart," either. She wasn't stupid. She didn't run around saying dumbo things about, well, stuff, the way some people did. It was just that she wasn't much interested in books and reading, which meant she hadn't gotten a good score on the SAT tests. That was the big thing about getting into a college. Janice got very good grades, but other people also got very good grades, and those people got better scores on those tests. The SATs. The ACTs. Some people could get out of Marshall, South Dakota, just by going away to school. When they went away to school, they never came back again.

Of course, just wanting to get out of Marshall was "uppity." There was that.

Janice got out of bed. Her robe was lying over the back of the chair next to the bed. Each of the beds in each of the rooms had its own chair next to it. Janice put her robe on. It was pastel blue and had a little clutch of kittens embroidered at the place where a breast pocket would be. She rubbed the embroidery a little and frowned. She'd heard a lot about diversity, and about how people thought differently and lived differently and liked different things depending on where they were from and what kinds of family they had, but she'd never entirely believed it before she came here.

She thought about putting on her slippers and decided against it. None of the other girls wore slippers except for Coraline Mays, and Coraline was obviously just as clueless as Janice was herself.

She stepped out into the hall. The girls were mostly sitting on the floor, except for the black one, that Andra Gayle. She was leaning against one of the walls and looking murderous.

"I don't think she can actually get away with touching you," one of the seated girls was saying.

Janice wracked her brains and came up with a name: Linda Kowalski. Linda Kowalski was Catholic and had a rosary she kept on her bedside table. Her roommate was a girl named Shari Bernstein, who was Jewish and came from somewhere in New York that was not New York City. Janice felt rather proud of herself for remembering all of that.

She worked her way down the row to her own roommate, who was not hard to find. This was a girl named Ivy Demari, and she had white-blond hair with an electric green streak in it. Janice thought you could probably have found Ivy on the moon.

"What's going on?" Janice whispered.

"I don't know what's going on," Grace said. Her face was still red. "Miss Dahl was just telling me not to go anywhere, and then she left herself, and now I don't have the faintest idea what I'm supposed to do. I'm not giving that vile little bitch another chance to kick me."

"Oh, Grace," Coraline said.

"She's a bitch and worse," Grace said. "And I'm not going to watch my language about it, either."

"This is what's going on," Ivy whispered.

Then she grabbed Janice's hand and squeezed it. Janice had been a little worried about Ivy at first, but it had turned out that Ivy was actually Very Nice, even though she had tattoos.

"I meant it about not being allowed to

121

touch you physically," Linda said. "I don't think I've ever seen that on this show, or on any reality show —"

"The contestants do it," Shari said. "They get into fights sometimes."

"The contestants, yes, well," Linda said. "But Sheila Dunham isn't a contestant. You could sue her."

"You could if you aren't really a spy," Shari said. "I mean, if you're really a spy, you could sue her, but you might not win. If you see what I mean."

"Of course I'm not really a spy," Grace said.

"Is your father really that guy she was talking about?" another girl said. Janice had to work at it a little, but she came up with a name: Mary-Louise Verdt.

Grace shifted a little on the floor. She was sitting down with her left leg stretched out across the hall carpet. Janice could see bruises starting to emerge on her thigh.

"Yes," she said finally. "My father really is who she said he was. But I'm not a spy. I haven't talked to the man for six years, for God's sake. I barely talked to him when I was still living at home. And Wellesley, my foot. I did go to Wellesley. I even graduated."

"They can throw you off the show for lying about things, I think," Coraline said. "We all had to sign that form, do you remember, promising that everything we said was true and we promised it on pain of perjury and that kind of thing."

"We did sign such a paper," Alida Akido said. "I remember."

"We signed a lot of papers, but I didn't read them," another girl said — that was Marcia Lee Baldwin.

"There are so many of us," Janice whispered to Ivy. "I have trouble keeping them apart."

"There are only fourteen of us now," Ivy said. "There were thirty, four days ago. More."

"I know. But I still get confused."

"Half of them have changed their names, you watch," Ivy said. "Or worse. It happens every season."

"I didn't change anything," Janice said.

It was true, too. She hadn't changed anything. She had just left some things out, like how she wasn't . . . ever first. She was popular enough, but never first. She looked a little sideways at Ivy and wondered what Ivy had been back where she was from. Somehow, she just couldn't imagine Ivy on a cheerleading team.

"You don't understand the real problem

here," Grace said. She was now getting very carefully to her feet. "It isn't being thrown off the show or not. Who gives a flying damn? It's what's going to happen next. I wonder which one of you is going to put this up on YouTube."

"Why would any of us put this up on YouTube?" Coraline said. "And how would we manage it?"

"Cell phone video," Shari said.

"And if one of you don't do it," Grace said, "then one of the crew here will. There are cameras everywhere, haven't you noticed? They're filming us all the time. One way or the other, this thing is going to be on the Internet by the end of the day, and it's going to be everywhere, and I mean everywhere, by the end of the week. Courtesy of my father."

"Your father is going to show a tape of this everywhere in the world?" Mary-Louise Verdt sounded confused.

"No, you rank idiot," Grace said. "My father being who he is means other people are going to show this to the world. It doesn't matter if I'm going to be sent home right this minute or not. I'm going to be made a complete and utter idiot. Which was the point."

"You know, I've thought that, too, sometimes," Coraline said. "That it's all done on purpose. You know, to make more drama."

"Oh, for God's sake," Grace said. "Of course it's all done on purpose. I mean, it's Sheila Dunham we're talking about here. It's not like she's Tyra Banks. The world doesn't worship the ground she walks on. She wouldn't have any career at all anymore if she didn't behave like a complete asshole in public and on unpredictable occasions. It's what she does. No wonder that silly little blond girl tried to murder her."

"Oh, do we know that's what it was about?" Coraline asked. "Emily, I mean. Was Emily a contestant on the show? I thought I'd seen all the shows and I don't remember her."

"But she looked familiar, didn't she?" Mary-Louise said. "I remember thinking that when I saw her. She looks very familiar."

"Maybe she was on the show for just a little while and then she got booted off, and she was wearing makeup, you know, or clothes, different things," Coraline said. "I'll admit I don't always remember the girls who go home first. I mean, they're not on very long and —"

"Oh, for God's sake," Grace said again. She was standing all the way now, but still leaning against the wall for support. Janice thought that that bruise on her thigh was going to be nasty. "Would you people please wake up? This is a game she plays, and you're all getting suckered into it. All of you. I'll bet you anything that Emily didn't try to murder her at all. I'll bet you it's a setup. That's what they're saying on the news."

"We're not supposed to watch the news," Coraline said.

"Oh, for God's sake," Grace said.

Then she stomped off toward her own bedroom, limping but obviously furious.

Janice watched her disappear through her bedroom door and then another girl, Suzanne Toretti, disappear after her. Suzanne looked scared to death.

Janice turned to Ivy. Ivy was looking at her fingernails.

"I didn't realize it would be so tense," Janice said. "I guess I didn't really think about what it would be like at all. I just thought it would be something to do. Something that wasn't just staying in South Dakota. If you know what I mean."

Ivy got up and held out a hand for her. "Of course I know what you mean," she said, "but Grace has a point. Sheila Dunham probably does do these things on purpose. And it's a good way to get yourself killed. Don't you think so?"

"I don't think anybody would actually kill her," Janice said.

"They'll just want to," Ivy said. "We can change the name of the show. We can call it *Wanting Sheila Dead*."

Janice giggled and allowed herself to be led back to her room, where her clothes were carefully hung up on one side of the closet and her slippers were still sitting side by side under her bed. She wished she could be sure that she would never be the one that Sheila Dunham was yelling at, but nobody could be sure of that.

Sheila Dunham even yelled at the girls who won.

FOUR

1

There had been a murder on Cavanaugh Street once, years and years ago, and Hannah Krekorian had been suspected of committing it. Gregor remembered that almost as well as he remembered moving back to the street after his first wife died. Cavanaugh Street was a place where odd things happened, but the odd things were almost never bad. Donna Moradanyan Donahue decorated things for holidays when she wasn't too pregnant to stand on stepladders. She'd once turned the entire brownstone building where Gregor lived — and where she had lived herself before her marriage — into a gigantic Christmas package, complete with a bow. She'd decorated the street for Gregor's and Bennis's wedding, too, although she'd had several helpers for that one, and it had included long lines of white ribbon running down the sidewalks.

It was a good thing John Henry Newman Jackman was mayor of Philadelphia. If there had been a stranger in that office, Donna would have been arrested and fined on a regular basis.

There was nothing decorated up and down the street now, although it was close to Easter. At least Howard Kashinian hadn't dressed himself up as the Easter Bunny this year. Even John Jackman hadn't been able to keep Howard for getting arrested for that one, although it had been mostly a matter of the police thinking they'd discovered a peculiarly flamboyant pedophile. The truth was, Howard was no more a pedophile than he was a decent attorney. He was just an idiot.

There was enough rain to prompt banalities about Noah and his flood. Gregor made his way through it, holding an umbrella very carefully over his head, and went down the small, clean alley to the back of Holy Trinity Armenian Christian Church. When they'd rebuilt here after the old church had been destroyed, they'd been careful to have everything done exactly right. The "alley" looked like one of those small pedestrian paved streets in London, and they didn't leave its maintenance to the city. They hired a firm to come in and clean it and the two courtyards at each end of it, and another firm to dig it all out of the snow, when the snow came.

Gregor went into the courtyard and saw that Father Tibor's apartment was lit up as if it were midnight. The apartment above it, being empty, was dark.

Gregor rang the bell and waited to be let in. He had no idea why he did that, since Tibor didn't actually expect him to, and Tibor also never kept the door locked. Gregor had talked to him about that a million times, but it did no good.

Tibor came to the door and opened up. Gregor put his umbrella down, shook it off, and dropped it into the umbrella stand just inside the door.

"I have them all here, Krekor," Tibor said. "And I have all the papers I could find on the kitchen table. Watch the books. I made the stack the night before last and I meant to put them away, but I forgot."

The books included the usual collection: *Areopagetica* by John Milton; Dan Brown's *Angels & Demons;* something in Greek. Gregor was careful going around them.

"I wish we'd find somebody for that apartment upstairs," he said. "I don't like it sitting empty. I know it's not the usual sort of thing, but there's always a danger of getting squatters in there. Or worse."

"We're not going to get squatters in," Tibor said. "And if we did I think it could be argued that we had the responsibility to serve them. That is what a church is for, Krekor, not just a beautiful liturgy but to help us live as Christ lived. That is more books, Krekor. Be careful."

There were indeed more books, dozens of them, stacked against the wall between the small dining room and the kitchen. There were books stacked on every wall. The parishioners of Holy Trinity had built this apartment particularly for Father Tibor. They had put built-in bookshelves on every available inch of wall space, including in some of the bathrooms. It hadn't been enough. There would never be enough wall space for Tibor's books. He read everything — in six languages.

Tibor swung back the door to the kitchen and Gregor went through to find the three Very Old Ladies sitting together at Tibor's kitchen table, drinking coffee that looked like black mud and probably had enough caffeine to keep the entire United States Army awake for a year. They had brought their own coffeemaker. Gregor could see it sitting on Tibor's kitchen counter next to the microwave, which was virtually the only kitchen appliance Tibor could operate without setting it on fire. On the other hand, Tibor had set the microwave on fire once. Gregor remembered it. Gregor wondered which of the Very Old Ladies had brought that coffeemaker from Yerevan, and which of her grandmothers it had once belonged to.

The women looked up when he came in, but they didn't stand. Gregor got the small folder he'd been carrying out from under his arm and dropped it on the table. Then Tibor motioned him to a chair, and he sat.

"I will make you some coffee, Krekor," Tibor said.

Mrs. Vardanian looked skeptical. "Better have some of ours. That stuff he makes tastes like dirty water."

Gregor looked into Mrs. Vardanian's small cup. Black mud was putting it mildly. The stuff was — Gregor didn't know what. Alive, maybe.

"I don't think my blood pressure can take it," he said. He opened the folder in front of him and looked at it. He didn't have to look at it. He'd spent the morning talking to the police, and the hospital, and David Mortimer, and he knew everything he was about to say.

"Well," he tried. Tibor put a cup of something down in front of him. Tibor's coffee did taste like dirty water. On the other hand, it wouldn't actively kill him. "First," Gregor tried again, "you might already know, Mrs. Mgrdchian is not dead. She wasn't dead when we found her, and she's not dead now."

"Is she conscious?" the smallest of the three Very Old Ladies said.

"Of course she isn't conscious, Marita," Mrs. Vardanian said. "If she was conscious, he would have said so. And he wouldn't have needed to talk to us. Isn't that so?"

"Ah, sort of," Gregor said. "Even if she was conscious, she might not remember anything. And there could be other reasons to want to talk to you. The police are definitely going to want to talk to you, eventually."

"I don't see why they don't want to talk to us now," Mrs. Vardanian said.

"Well," Gregor said, "at the moment, there's no real proof that a crime has been committed. We found Mrs. Mgrdchian unconscious, but the woman was very old, and you said she'd been reclusive for years. She could have been in poor health —"

"We're all in poor health, Krekor," Mrs. Vardanian said. "We don't go passing into a coma in our front foyers and having strangers in the house in the meantime. Who was that woman? Do they know what she was doing there?"

"No," Gregor said. "She says her name is Lily, but we know that from the other day. She's not saying much else that's making any sense. They're having a hard time identifying her —"

"DNA," the fat little Very Old Lady said.

"Oh, Kara, don't be ridiculous," Mrs. Vardanian said. "The world isn't made of episodes of *CSI*. Why in the name of God would the police department have samples of this woman's DNA?"

"Fingerprints then," Kara Edelakian said.

"Ah, yes," Gregor said. "There's always fingerprints, but the police haven't been able to come up with a clean set. Lily's — I suppose we'll have to call her Lily — Lily's fingertips are badly damaged. The best guess at this moment is that she's a homeless woman. The homeless often have hands that have been significantly damaged. It comes from being out in the very bitter cold for a long time —"

"It comes from putting your bare hands on metal in the very bitter cold," Mrs. Vardanian said matter-of-factly. "Then when you try to pull them away, the skin tears. You don't have to treat us like a pack of virgins, Krekor. We've all been around long enough not to be surprised by life."

"And we watch television," Kara said helpfully. "And not just *CSI. Law and Order.*"

"Yes," Gregor said. "Well, you do have to understand that real police departments can't actually do most of the things you see on *CSI.* I mean, they sort of invent technology . . ."

"I have the parish records, Krekor," Tibor said.

Tibor pushed a little stack of papers across the table, and Gregor looked down on them. He made out the name "Mgrdchian," and the names "Sophie" and "Viktor." Everything else was in Armenian.

"Well," Gregor said.

"There isn't much here," Tibor said. "I know I don't have the same training you do, and I know it would be better if you could actually read these on your own, but I don't see what you'd find. Viktor Mgrdchian came to the United States when he was six. Sophie Karnakian came when she was four. That was the same year. Their families came right here to Cavanaugh Street. They married when Viktor was nineteen and Sophie was seventeen. Viktor was in the Army then. There was one child, born dead, about six years later. Viktor was a tailor. He died when he was only fifty-six of a heart attack at work. And that's it."

"Brothers and sisters?" Gregor asked. "For either of them?"

Tibor nodded. "Sophie had two sisters, Leia and Marietta. Leia died in a flu epidemic when she was three and a half years old. Marietta never married and died a few years ago —"

"Eleven," Mrs. Vardanian said. "We went to the funeral. That was the year before Father Tibor came. It wasn't much of a funeral."

"Did Viktor have family," Gregor said.

Tibor searched through the papers. "Two brothers," he said. "There was Marco and Dennis. Both younger than he was, both married, and then they left the street. Left the state, I think. This must be where the niece comes in, or whatever she is, Krekor. It must be the daughter of one of the brothers."

"There was only the one?" Gregor asked.

"We're not sure," Tibor said. "We've been talking about it. The boys moved away, you see, and they never came back except for the funerals."

"Were they back for Marietta Karnakian's funeral?" Gregor asked.

"Not for Marietta's, but they came for

Viktor's," Mrs. Vardanian said. "I remember distinctly. The brothers came, Marco and Dennis, and they brought wives. Sophie had a dinner, you know, afterward, for people to come to. It's custom. But they didn't come, the brothers."

"Sophie said they didn't feel comfortable," Marita Melvarian said. "Only I don't think that was the word she used. But she said something about how they didn't know us anymore, and —"

"No," Mrs. Vardanian said. "Dennis came, and Dennis's wife. They didn't stay for long, but they came. She was Armenian. It was Marco and his wife who didn't come. She wasn't Armenian. I remember that. They weren't married in the Church."

"I think they weren't married in any church," Kara Edelakian said in a hushed little voice. "I think they were married by a justice of the peace. Can you imagine that? How could anybody do something like — *ouch.* You didn't have to kick me, Viola. And Krekor wasn't married just by a justice of the peace, he was married right out here in front of the church, even if it wasn't in it, so it isn't the same thing."

Gregor cleared his throat. "The problem," he pointed out, "is to find out who this woman was, this Lily, who was in Sophie

137

Mgrdchian's house. Even if it turns out that there was no foul play of any kind, and I'm not expecting any, there's still the problem of this woman and how she came to be there. Did any of you recognize her? Could she have been the wife of one of the brothers?"

"She couldn't be an Armenian wife," Mrs. Vardanian said. "You saw her, Krekor. She didn't look Armenian at all."

"But she didn't look familiar to any of you," Gregor said.

"If she had, we wouldn't have called you in the first place," Mrs. Vardanian said. "We came to see you because we didn't know who she was. And she was in that house for a very long time. Days and days."

"Almost two weeks," Mrs. Edelakian put in.

"You keep changing the time frame," Gregor said.

"We weren't really keeping track," Mrs. Melvarian said. "We were just watching her. And at first we just sort of saw her around, you know, through the windows, and —"

"You're going to make Krekor think we peep into people's windows," Mrs. Vardanian said.

"Well, we do peep into people's windows," Mrs. Edelakian said. "We have to, don't we?

Nobody talks to us anymore. We're just the Very Old Ladies."

"The point" Mrs. Vardanian said, "is that that woman was there for a while. And then we didn't see Sophie anymore. And that was a few days ago."

"If Sophie Mgrdchian had been in that state for several days," Gregor said, "she'd be dead. Dehydration alone would have killed her, I'd think. Did you tell me the other day that you'd knocked at the door?"

"Of course we'd knocked at the door," Mrs. Vardanian said. "What do you take us for?"

Gregor had an answer for that, but he wasn't going to say it out loud. "What happened when you knocked?"

"Nobody answered," Mrs. Vardanian said. "One day we went and knocked and knocked, and it was as if nobody was home."

"But somebody was," Mrs. Edelakian said. "We could hear someone moving around."

"One person or two?" Gregor asked.

"I couldn't tell," Mrs. Edelakian said.

"It was one," Mrs. Vardanian said. "Sophie might not have been as badly off then as when we found her, but I'd bet anything she was completely . . . completely —"

"Incapacitated," Mrs. Melvarian suggested.

139

"That woman did something to her," Mrs. Vardanian said. "I know it."

Gregor sighed a little. "First, let's find out who the woman is," he said. "Then maybe we'll have a better idea of what was going on in there for the last couple of weeks. And once we know that —"

The sounds of "Louie Louie" burst into the room.

Gregor put his hand in his pocket and pulled out his cell phone.

" 'Louie Louie'?" Tibor asked.

"Bennis set it as my ring tone for her. She sets all my ring tones," Gregor said. He answered the damned thing — this one slid instead of flipped opened; he didn't understand why phones couldn't just act like phones.

"Yes?" he said.

"You'd better come back as soon as you can," Bennis said. "There's a woman in the apartment who says she's not going to leave until she talks to you."

2

It was still raining when Gregor went back across the street and down the block to his own apartment. He came in the front door and saw that old George Tekemanian was out for the day, again. Old George was as old as the Very Old Ladies, or older. Lately, Gregor had thought he was looking tired, or maybe worse.

Gregor stopped in the hallway for a moment and looked at old George's door. There was that little I'M AWAY! sign on it that made Gregor convinced that George was trying to get himself robbed. George would have said that he was only attending to what was important. His great-niece had made him that sign, in kindergarten. It had pink Teddy bears on it, and if you lifted the flap there was a smiley face and in big green letters, HAVE A NICE DAY!

There ought to be some law against doing that to children in kindergarten, Gregor thought. But of course, it was too late to do anything about old George's great-niece. She had to be in high school by now.

He climbed the stairs toward his apartment and thought again about a point Bennis kept on making. It would be a lot better for both of them, especially if they intended to stay on the street for the rest of their lives, if they found someplace that didn't automatically require them to climb stairs as soon as they came in the front door. The problem was that there were no empty renovated town houses left on Cavanaugh Street. Old buildings became empty and people bought them and fixed them up, like Lida Arkmanian had done to the place across the street, and Donna and Russ had done with their place near the end of the neighborhood. Nothing was coming empty on Cavanaugh Street very soon, and the one place that was already empty was . . . ah . . .

"Too much of a project," Gregor said out loud, as he reached what had at first been Bennis's landing.

Bennis had occupied the second-floor apartment while he had occupied the third; they had knocked them together and put in yet another staircase. Bennis was standing just outside their door now, looking at him.

"What did you say?"

"I said that the old Zaroubian place is too much of a project," Gregor said, reaching her. "I was thinking of your thing about finding a house. Are you all right? Who's this person who's shown up?"

Bennis looked behind her, but there was nobody standing in the doorway, and there was nobody to be seen beyond it in the apartment.

"Her name is Olivia Dahl," Bennis said. "And she's, well, she's Sheila Dunham's personal assistant. Or something. I'm really not too clear on the title. And I know you said you didn't want to talk to them, Gregor, but it's really not my fault. Bobby gave her my address and she just showed up."

"I'll talk to her," Gregor said. "You should try talking to the Very Old Ladies. Or Tibor should. They seem to be determined to find a murder whether there is one or not."

"You mean there isn't one?"

"Well," Gregor pointed out, "nobody is dead. There's that. And the last I heard from the hospital, there was no evidence anybody could find of foul play. Where did you put this Dahl woman? And how do you spell her name? Doll? Like those Barbie things?"

"Dahl, like the guy who wrote *Matilda*," Bennis said.

Gregor had no idea what *Matilda* was, but he followed Bennis into the second-floor apartment. The apartments in this building were all the same, except for old George's on the ground floor. They each had a small foyer, and then beyond that a large living room with a window that overlooked the street. To the left and through a door was a kitchen large enough for a table to eat at. To the right and down a hallway was the bedroom. At the end of the hall that led to the bedroom was a bathroom.

Olivia Dahl was in the living room, sitting on the couch with her back to them. The room was very neat and impeccably dusted, because it was not the one Gregor and Bennis actually used. When they'd first knocked the apartments together, they had intended to use it, to make the public rooms on this floor and private ones upstairs. It just hadn't worked out that way, except for now.

Olivia Dahl was a very thin, very straight middle-aged woman with hair that had probably been dyed blond but didn't look it. When Gregor and Bennis came in, she turned a little on the couch and smiled at him. It was, he thought, a mechanical smile, a mark of courtesy and not emotion.

"Mr. Demarkian?" she said, standing up and holding out her hand as he came around the furniture into the room itself.

"It's Ms. Dahl, Bennis tells me," Gregor said.

"Just Miss," Olivia Dahl said. "I get a little crazy with all that trendy nonsense. I sent you a letter last week."

"You sent me a letter four days ago," Gregor said. "By messenger. And I answered it. Also by messenger. I'm sorry you're having trouble on your television show, Miss Dahl, but this really isn't my kind of thing. I generally work as a consultant to police departments."

"On murder cases," Olivia said. "Yes, I know. Would you hear me out, please? We've

144

got a rather unusual situation."

"It really wouldn't make any difference," Gregor said.

"That's because you think we staged the whole thing," Olivia said. "Oh, I've got my contacts, too. But even if I didn't, I'd know that was what you were thinking, because it's what everybody is thinking. But I can one hundred percent guarantee it isn't true."

"You can?" Gregor asked.

"Don't look like that," Olivia said. "Yes, I can. Mr. Demarkian, if we were going to stage something like that, I'd have to be the one to stage it. Do you know why? Because I'm the only one organized enough to pull it off. Even to pull it off badly. Sheila couldn't do it herself. Not only is she addled most of the time, and drunk part of it, but she's got no sense of discretion and she's completely incapable of keeping her mouth shut. As for the other judges — well. The other judges. Sometimes I think they made it a requirement in the eighties. If you wanted to be a celebrity, you had to have an IQ in single digits."

"Damn," Bennis said. "I always kind of liked Pete Waldheim."

"Oh, Pete is all right," Olivia said. "But sometimes I think Deedee Plant really is a plant. I mean vegetation. I've known broccoli better able to produce linear thought. And as to Mark and Johnny — whatever. Neither Sheila nor any of the twits we have on that panel was capable of putting something like this together."

"Possibly," Gregor said. "But you've admitted yourself that you were, and it wasn't put together all that badly. There may be a lot of rumors running around that you staged this thing, but as far as I know, nobody's been able to prove it. And nobody knows who this mystery girl is. Or do they?"

"No," Olivia said. "No, they don't. Although, it's really odd. She looks so familiar, and I can't put my finger on why. I thought she might have been a contestant on one of the shows, an early one, maybe — somebody who didn't make the house. But I've looked at all our records, and I can't find her."

"Do you even know what her name is?" Gregor asked.

"One of the girls who is in the house this cycle says she talked to her, and the girl said her name is Emily," Olivia said. "It's not all that unusual a name, but we've only had three Emilys even at auditions, and I called around and found all of those. And she's — well, I don't know how to put it. She's sort of like wallpaper. She just fades into the background. I can't imagine that she'd make an audition tape good enough for us to call her in for an interview."

"She's not on your interview list, either, I take it," Gregor said.

"No, she isn't," Olivia said. "As far as I can figure out, she just came to the building on that day, stood in line, and walked right in. I realized once the trouble happened that it wouldn't even be hard. You came into the Milky Way Ballroom through the front doors, you went up to a desk and gave your name, you got your waiting room assignment, and then you went there to sit. But there wasn't really any security. All she had to do was not bother to go to the front tables, to just sort of drift off to the halls on the sides and find a room to sit down in. There was such a crush of people, nobody would have noticed."

"And you're contending that nobody did," Gregor said.

"There really was a crush of people," Olivia said. "And there is all the way along. You go from your interview room to the ballroom itself. We had it tricked out with curtains. You sat in a little waiting area until it was time to talk to the panel, then you went through those curtains and talked to Sheila and the rest of them. But there were always five or six girls waiting to be interviewed. All she had to do was sit down in one of the chairs. And then, you know, when nobody was looking, she could follow a girl leaving the interview for the room with the first round of contestants in it. I mean, I counted the girls, but this one girl was out of the room in the bathroom and so my count came out all right but it shouldn't have. I'm sorry I'm not making much sense."

"You're making perfect sense," Gregor said. "I'm not sure I believe it. You're saying that anybody could just have wandered through into the competition, being filmed all the while —"

"Oh, yes," Olivia Dahl said. "We've got film. We've got a lot of it. The police have it for the moment."

Gregor waved this away. "You're trying to tell me you had no security at all, on a show hosted by a woman who is notorious for being a world-class, first-rate bitch on wheels, who gets death threats on a regular basis —"

Olivia blushed. "Everybody gets death threats," she said. "You can't be a celebrity in this country today without having some people decide they want to send you mail saying they want to kill you. There's never been a credible death threat against Sheila in spite of the way she behaves. Or maybe because of it. The woman is a complete loose cannon. Maybe even the crazies are afraid of her."

"Are you afraid of her?" Gregor asked.

"No," Olivia said. "Mr. Demarkian, I'm very good at what I do. I get a dozen offers a month to move. I could go anywhere if I wanted to. If she fires me, I'll be in another job before the night is over. But she isn't going to fire me. I'm the only one who knows how to keep the whole thing moving. And she's getting worse."

"What does that mean, worse?"

Olivia shrugged. "She's going off like a bottle rocket more and more often. It used to be deliberate. I'd know when the crap was coming, because I'd be able to see her thinking about it. She's not thinking about it anymore. She just seems to explode. This morning, she did something I'm pretty sure is going to get us sued by at least two people, and may get her arrested for assault as well. And it's on camera. Of course it's on camera."

"I don't actually know what you want with me, you know," Gregor said. "I'm not a private detective. I don't follow people. I consult with police departments on murders. You don't have a murder, and what you do have isn't the kind of thing I deal with. The police will do a good job of finding out who this young woman is and why she shot at your boss."

"Yes," Olivia said. "Well. The thing is . . ."

"What?"

"I'm pretty sure there's going to be a murder if I don't do something to stop it," Olivia said. "And I don't mean that Sheila's going to murder somebody."

FIVE

1

Andra Gayle had a roommate named Marcia Lee Baldwin, who made her very uncomfortable. Maybe the truth was that any roommate would have made her uncomfortable. Even somebody who was just like her, who was from her own kind of neighborhood, who had her own kind of history — but it was impossible for Andra to accept the idea that anything like that could happen. Girls with her kind of background and her kind of history did not end up on *America's Next Superstar* unless they had somehow managed to overcome all the signs of being who they were. It wasn't that the show was prejudiced against black people. There had been two black winners and three black runners-up over the course of only nine cycles so far. It wasn't that the show was prejudiced against people whose families were nothing like the *Leave It to Beaver* sort

151

of thing. What Andra thought the show was prejudiced against was ghetto, by which she meant a way of talking, and a way of behaving, that was so natural to her she was still having trouble convincing herself that people could be any other way. And yet, that was something she'd known before she came here. That was something she had worked on long and hard when she'd been making her audition tape.

The problem with this particular arrangement — with this spectacular house on the Philadelphia Main Line, which was a place only rich people had lived in forever — was that there was no place within walking distance that she could get to to do anything useful. If she looked out the windows she saw grounds, huge wide swathes of them, all green and wooded with no buildings anywhere, and no roads. There was a front drive, which was not only paved but, according to Marcia Lee, was made especially so that it melted any snow that fell on it. Andra would have really liked to know how that worked. It sounded impossible. The drive didn't seem to go anywhere, though. It went around in a circle in front of the front doors and then it went off through trees. Andra supposed there had to be a road out there somewhere. But she didn't think there would be stores and public phones and the other elements of real life.

"I don't see what you're worried about," Marcia Lee had said, when Andra had first started to get antsy after that blowup between Sheila and Grace. "She pulls these things all the time. You can't take it seriously. And things like that with Grace are almost certainly staged."

"Staged?" Andra said.

Marcia Lee was a tall girl with very red hair and the air of having done everything and seen everything and known everything that anybody would ever want to. Before this morning's craziness, she had been closest to Grace, because she and Grace had been the only ones who could talk about what good times they had had in places like Paris. Andra was not unused to girls who had been to other countries. There were girls back home who had moved there from the Dominican Republic and Ecuador and places like that, and who sometimes went "home" to visit their relatives for a funeral. That was different than this. Marcia Lee and Grace seemed to have gone to other countries just because they wanted to. They didn't have relatives there. Andra didn't know what to make of this yet. She also knew she couldn't keep up with it.

Marcia Lee just stood there, looking impatient. "Staged," she said, a little more loudly than she usually talked, as if Andra were deaf or retarded. "They do those things on purpose to get good television action for the show. They need the drama. Then they can put the clip on a commercial and it looks like all kinds of things are happening, and people watch."

Andra considered it. "Grace is upset. And Sheila Dunham punched her. She pushed her down on the floor."

"Well, of course Grace is upset," Marcia Lee said. "I'd have been, too, if it were me. But it's her own fault. She had to know that the show was going to look into the backgrounds of all the girls that made it into the house. Why did she lie? I'll bet she'd have had a better chance of ending up right where she is now — I mean in the house, you know, not in trouble — anyway, she'd have had a better chance of ending up here if she'd just been honest about who she was. I'd bet Sheila Dunham would just have loved to have that man's daughter on this show —"

"Why?" Andra said. "I thought she hated him."

"Oh, she does," Marcia Lee said. "She hates him because he's always airing stuff on Fox News about how awful the show is and how badly done it is and how lame it is and how nobody should watch it. Actually, I heard it was more complicated than that. It's like some kind of a vendetta. Sheila got him fired from NBC, or wherever he was last time, and it took him a couple of years just to find a job and he had to sell his apartment. That's the apartment where Grace grew up. Anyway, I'm probably getting this wrong. Grace told me a few things, but I didn't realize at the time that she was talking about her own father, and there it is. There are a lot of people who hate Sheila Dunham. No wonder somebody tried to shoot her at casting."

Andra wandered out into the hall. The girls who had been lounging around there were gone. Andra headed for the big formal front staircase. This house was like a palace in a movie. The staircase curved. The ceilings were incredibly high. The rooms were big. The foyer looked like people should be standing in it wearing ball gowns and gloves that went all the way up to their shoulders. It made Andra twitchy. It really did.

The other girls all seemed to be in the big living room at the front — but it wasn't called a living room, and Andra couldn't remember what it was called. She walked past it, trying not to make any noise. She wanted a telephone, or maybe a television. She wasn't sure. There was nobody for her to call. Her mother almost never had the phone service working, and if she did, she'd been so massively stoned that she wouldn't be able to make sense anyway. She'd just start in again on that whine about wanting a little money to make sure old Mama didn't starve. And Andra had to admit it: Old Mama really was starving. There was no getting around the cheeks that sucked in like deflated balloons and the ribs that poked out. The problem was that it was all the drugs and it didn't matter how much money she gave her. Mama didn't eat, and what she did eat came right off with the cocaine she took when she had more than her usual in folding cash.

There was a big dining room with a big table and — Andra counted — twenty-four chairs around it. There was a room up front that looked like somebody's office, with a desk and books and a little sort of half-statue of somebody sitting on the mantelpiece. All the rooms in this house had fireplaces. Even the bedrooms had fireplaces. There was a phone on the desk, but it looked like something in a play. The desk looked like something in a play, too. The phone was big and black with old designs all over it, and a dial that turned instead of buttons. The desk had skinny little legs that curved.

Andra went over to it and picked up the phone. There was no dial tone. Maybe it wasn't a real phone. Maybe it was just for decoration. Andra hated the way they tried to keep you from contacting anybody in this place.

She went over to the bookshelves on one side of the fireplace and looked at the spines of the books. "Aristotle," one of them said. *"Nichomachean Ethics."* Andra looked on the shelf below that and found "Jane Austen. *Pride and Prejudice.*" That made her feel a little better. She knew about *Pride and Prejudice.* That had been a movie, with Keira Knightley. She'd even tried to see it. She'd had to go forty blocks to find a movie theater that was playing it, but she had liked the commercials so much. She'd liked the women in big dresses that went down to the floor and the way everybody was so polite to each other all the time. In the end, though, she hadn't been able to sit through it. She hadn't been able to figure out what was going on. It was all so slow. There didn't seem to be a point.

She turned away from the bookcase. Did

people actually live in this house? If they did, where were their television sets? Anybody who had a house like this would have to be rich. If Andra were rich, she'd have at least thirty television sets, all big ones, the kind that hung on the wall. She'd have a better carpet than this, too, something that didn't look so worn. She might keep the house the same otherwise.

She turned to go, back out into the foyer, in search of other halls, other rooms. She wanted to call somebody. She wanted to call the weather line, if that was all there was. She wanted to talk to somebody outside of this.

She looked up and saw that there was somebody else in the room, just inside the door, that girl with the weird hair, Ivy. Whenever Andra heard the name "Ivy," she thought about Poison Ivy. Poison Ivy was a character in a movie, one about Batman. It was only after she'd seen that movie half a dozen times that a teacher in school told her that there was a plant called poison ivy, and if you touched it you got a bad rash and itched.

This Ivy did not look like poison, just very odd. Her hair was odd, and the clothes she wore were odd, too. They always seemed to have stripes and arrows and patterns on them, and to glitter a little.

"Hi," Andra said. She wasn't sure what she was supposed to do now. There was no rule she knew of that said they couldn't be in the other rooms of the house, but she still felt as if she'd done something wrong.

"Hi," Ivy said. "We're all in the living room. And we've got stuff, you know, like coffee. Why don't you come join us?"

"I was just looking around," Andra said.

"I know. I looked around, too, yesterday. It's a great house, don't you think? But it's stuffy. That's the kind of people who must live here. Stuffy people."

"I was wondering if people lived here at all," Andra said.

"Oh, they do. Or they sort of do. The house belongs to this guy who is a descendant of the old guy who built it in the first place, this guy who was big in building railroads back before there were cars or planes or anything. And he's got sisters and brothers, I think. But nobody spends a lot of time here anymore, because there were about three murders in the house about ten years ago."

"Murders?" Andra said.

"Yeah, the guy who owns the house, his father was killed in here, in this room. And then one of his sisters was killed upstairs in one of the bedrooms. I've been trying to find out which one, but I haven't been able to. I think it would be neat to live in a room where somebody was murdered, don't you? Maybe their ghost is still haunting the place, and you could talk to her."

"Ah," Andra said. That didn't sound good at all.

"Come on and join us," Ivy said. "It's better when we're all together, and you don't want to be out of too many of the shots they use for the show. Grace is having a public fit, but she's got the right, under the circumstances. If I was the first one Sheila Dunham pulled her crap on, I'd be hysterical."

Andra looked around. People really lived here, but they didn't have television sets. She would have to file that one away somewhere and consider it later.

"Marcia Lee," she said, "my roommate, she says that Sheila Dunham got Grace's father fired from some job he had and ruined his life."

"Not Grace's father," Ivy said. "Grace's father is older than Sheila Dunham and he's been a big deal in entertainment news for years. No, it was some guy on NBC when Sheila was still on the *Today* show. He was really young and she unloaded all over him and he got kicked off the show, and then he couldn't ever find another job in the business and he just disappeared. It's a famous story. If it had been a couple of years later, he would have been okay, because by then everybody knew she was crazy, but there it was. Don't you ever watch, you know, *E!* or things like that? It's not like any of this stuff about Sheila Dunham is a secret."

"Right," Andra said.

"Come on over and have something to eat. I think we're supposed to go somewhere and film something in about half an hour. It would have been earlier if it hadn't been for the thing with Grace. And Grace hasn't left, by the way. She's staying put and holding her ground. This ought to be interesting."

"Yeah," Andra said.

She was fairly sure it was the wrong thing to say, but it was the only thing she could think of. She looked around the room again. She couldn't imagine the people who lived here. It wasn't like on *Cribs,* where there were big beds that revolved under mirrors and game rooms with all the game systems you could think of, and home theaters that even had places next to the seats for soda and popcorn. It wasn't like anything Andra had ever seen or heard of in her life.

But the real problem was that her name was not Andra Gayle and she had lied to

Sheila Dunham, and before this morning it hadn't occurred to her what a terrible problem that could be.

2

Coraline Mays knew the way this show was supposed to work. The easiest challenges were supposed to come first, so that the people with the least potential to succeed could be sent home early. Being sent home early was the thing she worried about the most. How incredibly embarrassing would it be, to have just unpacked her things and to be filmed packing them up again? And then there were the things people would say at home, about how stupid you had been even to try. You could say anything you want about how hard it was just to make it into the group of fourteen who got to live in the house. The fact was that nobody at home really counted any of the girls who *didn't* make it to the house. There were the four-teen. That was your competition.

Coraline had been half sure that there would be no filming at all today, after that fuss about Grace. She'd been even more sure that Grace would be sent home before the competition even began, but that hadn't happened, either. Coraline could remember one season, cycle seven, where a girl who had been chosen to be part of the fourteen hadn't been able to participate, and one of the other girls from the competition had been brought in. Then that girl had ended up being eliminated early, so maybe it just went to show. Coraline wasn't sure what it was supposed to show. It was just the kind of thought that came to her. She thought about her family, too, and the people at her church, who all said they were praying for her.

Coraline's roommate was a girl named Deanna Brackett, who had come as something of a relief. Deanna was a lot more like the people Coraline was used to. She was even from the South — well, from Atlanta — which meant she had an accent that was at least a little soothing to Coraline's ears. Ivy Demari ought to have had a Southern accent, too, being from Texas, but she was too much of a punk. Or whatever you called girls who had tattoos and green hair. She was too much of a something. She sounded wrong.

The little house bell had gone off, and now all the girls in the living room were looking around as if they expected somebody to come in and tell them something. Even the black girl was doing that, and mostly she just looked angry and tough.

"What do you think is going to happen now?" Coraline asked Deanna.

Deanna got down close to Coraline's ear. "Remember, it's all about inside the house and outside the house. Any time you have to go outside the house, you have to be perfect. Even if it's just on the patio or in the yard."

"I don't think they call it a patio here," Coraline said. "I think they call it a terrace."

"Don't you love it, though?" Deanna said. "I don't care what they call it. I like those little pillar things that come just up to my knees with the lions on them. It must have cost the Earth for somebody to have built a house like this."

Coraline made a little, noncommittal noise. She wasn't going to say anything again about how whoever had built the house was some kind of criminal. She had said that the first time, and then it turned out that "robber baron" didn't mean that somebody was actually a robber. It was a term for people in the nineteenth century who had made huge fortunes from the railroads and from oil — legitimate things, businesses, that everybody was supposed to do.

Grace had stared right down the bridge of her nose at Coraline. "Don't they make you go to school back in Podunk, Arkansas?" she'd said.

And Coraline had had to cross her hands behind her back just to keep herself from slapping the girl. She hadn't been upset at all that Sheila Dunham had decided to go after Grace first, and it didn't matter to her what Grace's real last name was. It served her right. It was just like everybody at home said. They were all stuck up, all those people from the east, and especially the ones from New York.

There was a sound in the foyer, and one of the girls — the black one with the odd name — went to the doorway of the living room to see what was happening. A second later, she stepped back, and Mark Borodine and Johnny Rell walked through the doors. Coraline thought of the two of them as something like Siamese twins. They went together in her head. Mark was the gay guy you almost couldn't tell about. Johnny was the gay guy there was no mistaking. It all came down to the same thing in Coraline's mind. There were boys like this at home, but they didn't stick around long after high school.

Mark clapped his hands and smiled. He had a fake tan that looked sort of painted on, rather than actually part of his skin.

"Well now," he said. "The weather outside is awful, as you can probably tell. It's been raining for hours. But you know what? When you're a superstar, the weather doesn't change to accommodate you. Your first job is always going to be, being camera ready under any and all circumstances. So. We're going to take you into the town of Bryn Mawr for lunch, but you've got to get yourself there without giving the paparazzi a photograph that will embarrass you all over the tabloids. You've got exactly three minutes to get upstairs, get into hair and makeup, and make it out to the limo in a state fit to be photographed in. There will be photographers in places you won't even notice when you're going out to the car, and there will be more when you get to the restaurant. This is your first challenge. The girl who does the best will get two hours tomorrow afternoon with one of the biggest and most successful makeup artists in the business. Are you ready?"

Girls clapped. Girls yelled. Girls screamed. Coraline had seen it on the show. She didn't understand it.

"Get ready," Johnny Rell said. "One. Two. Three. *Go.*"

Somebody screamed again. Everybody rushed for the doorway at once. Coraline didn't stop to wait for Deanna. They were always telling you that this was not a place to make friends. This was a place to fight to win. Coraline was not very good at that.

Everybody started up the stairs at once, too. They were like a herd of stampeding bison, and once they got upstairs to the hallway leading to all the bedrooms they were even worse. Coraline raced past that black girl and past Grace Whoever-she-was and ran into the room she shared with Deanna. Her clothes were all hanging up carefully in the closet. It made her crazy. She never got dressed this fast. She always consulted with somebody, and took a long time choosing between things. She always asked her mother.

"Not too fancy," she said, under her breath.

"What?"

Deanna was in the room, too. They were both standing in front of the same closet.

"Nothing too fancy," Coraline said. "You see them on television, you know, going to lunch places. If they go to some big event like the Oscars, they're all dressed up, but when they go out to lunch they just wear stuff. Jeans. T-shirts. Nothing fancy."

Deanna stared. "You're right," she said. "You're absolutely right."

Coraline knew she was right. She had a good pair of jeans, her one really expensive pair, from Calvin Klein. She put those on and then went through her T-shirts to find the one that fit the best. It was hard to know what to do. She had an expensive T-shirt to go with the expensive jeans, but the expensive T-shirt didn't fit all that well. She finally grabbed a bright red one that said COKE — THE REAL THING! on it in swirly letters. It covered her like paint.

Coraline raced to the vanity table. She didn't wear a lot of makeup under ordinary circumstances. She didn't think she needed to. That would work here, too. These people wore enough makeup not to look bad in photographs, but not enough to look like clowns. She put on a pale lipstick and then some gloss over it so that her lips shimmered. Then she got up and started running again.

She got to the downstairs foyer just before Deanna and just after the black girl, who looked like she was participating in a freak show. She had her hair frizzed out beyond belief and enough kohl around her eyes and mascara on her lashes so that she looked half dead. Coraline backed away a little and bumped into the Asian girl.

"I don't understand how she ended up in

168

the house at all," the Asian girl said. "She isn't going to win this competition. You can see that she isn't."

Coraline made a strangled little noise. "Most of us aren't," she said. Which was true.

The Asian girl made a little noise and turned away. Coraline found herself next to Ivy Demari again. She told herself that it was really all right. Ivy was odd looking, but she was very nice. It was better to be next to her than to Grace.

Grace was standing right near the front door, so that anybody who came through them was sure to see her. She looked defiant.

"Do you think there's going to be another fight?" Coraline asked Ivy.

"With Grace?" Ivy shook her head. "Sheila's had Grace on a platter already once today. She won't do it again to the same person."

Coraline shrank back a little.

It was just at that second that the front door opened, but instead of the limo driver, it was Sheila Dunham herself who came in. Coraline shrank back yet again. Sheila Dunham was such an *unpleasant*-looking woman. She was too thin, in the wrong way. And her mouth always turned down.

And she stalked.

Coraline sucked in air.

"Take the earrings off," Sheila said to Mary-Louise Verdt. Mary-Louise put her hands up to her ears and unfastened her big gold hoops.

Sheila went past Grace without stopping. Coraline could hear the collective sigh of relief when it came. She was pretty sure she participated in it.

Sheila went past three more girls, looking them up and down. She stopped at Janice Ledbedder and walked around her. Then she moved on. Janice looked ready to faint.

Coraline was feeling a little better than she had. This was not too awful. There was no screaming. Sheila didn't act like a crazy woman all the time. This looked like it was going to be one of her calm periods. If only they could get out the door and into the limousine. If they could get this challenge started, Coraline was sure she'd be just fine.

Sheila inspected Andra Gayle, but didn't say something. Still, Coraline thought, you could practically see the contempt on her face. Sometimes, on the show, Sheila reduced girls to tears just by looking at them.

Sheila came up right in front of Coraline, and Coraline stopped breathing. She looked good. She was sure she did. She had double-checked her hair and her makeup. She had been careful about her clothes. She did not look overdone. She did not look sloppy.

Sheila seemed rooted to the spot. Coraline felt her looking up and down, up and down. Maybe she wouldn't like the shoes. Coraline was wearing cork-soled sandals. You saw celebrities wearing cork-soled sandals all the time.

Then Sheila put her hand up, grabbed the neck of Coraline's T-shirt, and ripped, just the way she had ripped at Grace this morning. The effect was worse. The shirt came away in so many pieces, Coraline had nothing to hold up against herself.

"The only logos we wear on this show," Sheila Dunham said, "are mine."

SIX

1

Policewomen were never called "matrons" anymore, as far as Gregor Demarkian knew, but it was a matron who greeted him in the lobby of St. Mary's Hospital when he came in to meet the doctor who was treating the mysterious Lily. Except, Gregor thought, that Lily wasn't really mysterious. She was just sad, and the things about her that did not fit the sadness — the fact that she was meticulously clean — did not add up to enough to make even a lame episode of *American Justice*. Gregor thought most episodes of *American Justice* were lame. He'd been interviewed on the show several times — and on *Cold Case Files* and *Forensic Files* and *Snapped* as well — but when he sat down and viewed the show as it was finally put together, it seemed to him that the writers and producers were working too hard to make it like a golden-age mystery.

Of course, he hadn't known that at the time. It was only recently, when he'd started reading Agatha Christie, that his mind had made the connection.

The woman waiting for him was middle aged, a little thick around the middle, and wearing one of those old-fashioned uniforms with a jacket and a skirt. He supposed there was no reason why she shouldn't be. There were probably plenty of variations on the standard uniform available to women on the force. It was just that he hadn't seen a policewoman in a skirt in decades.

She stood up when he came through the sliding glass doors and held out her hand. "Mr. Demarkian," she said. "I was hoping I'd recognize you. The mayor said I would, but I'm not really that good at recognizing people. I'm Billie Ormonds."

Gregor shook her hand. "I'm Gregor Demarkian. You threw me off a little. I didn't know that policewomen still wore skirts."

Billie Ormonds looked down at her knees. "Most of us don't. Slacks are just easier to manage. But some of the clerical workers do. And people like me, who end up dealing with the public. Do you mind being thought of as the public?"

"As far as I know, nobody's hired me," Gregor said. "Have you seen the woman who was in the house, the woman who calls herself Lily?"

"I'm attached to the investigation. Yes, I've seen her. She's in the hospital wing of the jail at the moment, although I don't know how long we're going to be able to keep her there. Or anywhere. We don't have any evidence that she's done anything wrong."

"I was thinking that myself."

Billie sighed. "It's an odd thing. There's this other woman, the one upstairs here —"

"Sophie Mgrdchian."

"Ah," Billie said. "That's how you pronounce that. Yes. There's Mrs. Mgrdchian, who is obviously in some distress. But as far as we know, she's in her eighties. Distress happens at that age. And there's nothing to say that this Lily woman wasn't invited into that house. It's a mess, really. If Lily was aware enough to have a lawyer, she'd certainly be out of jail already. The best we've been able to think of up to now, is to ask a judge to hand her over for a full-op four-day psych observation. I'm pretty sure we can get that done, in spite of the fact that the Legal Aid attorneys are going to land on us at any minute. But that's going to be four days, and after that —" Billie shrugged.

"So how's Sophie Mgrdchian?"

"Ah," Billie said again. "That's the other

problem."

"Is she worse than she was yesterday?"

"Not that I know of," Billie said. "Neither better nor worse, last time I checked. But the doctor. The reason I wanted you out here is that I thought you'd like to talk to the doctor face to face. The doctor is a little nervous. That's about the best way I can put it."

Gregor thought that almost anybody working in a hospital would have to be a little nervous. There was sickness everywhere. There was death everywhere. There was a lot of expensive equipment that could go wrong at any second, along with the hundred and one other things that could go wrong.

Just looking around this lobby made him think that he ought to be nervous. This was the front lobby, not the emergency room. Nobody was standing around bleeding on the carpets. Even so, there were people in wheelchairs, and people looking strained, and one small woman sitting in a corner with her face in her hands, crying silently and unceasingly.

"I know," Billie said. "I hate hospitals. It's like they're the one place you can go where you can't get away from the fact that we all die. Even funeral parlors aren't that bad. Or cemeteries. In funeral parlors and cemeteries, it's like it's all happening to other people. It's like it has nothing to do with you."

"Well, it's all happening to other people here," Gregor said.

"Only for the moment," Billie said.

She waved him toward the long bank of elevators, and Gregor followed. She was, he thought, right. Maybe it was a function of the fact that everybody had been in a hospital once or twice by the time they were middle aged. Children were in to get their tonsils out. Women were in to have children. Men landed in the emergency room because of accidents at work or at home. It was easy to think that a funeral parlor or a cemetery was just somewhere you would visit as a guest, and not as the center of attention. With hospitals, it wasn't so easy.

The elevator was very wide and very deep and very tall and had doors on two sides, although only the ones on their side opened. It was spotlessly clean, too, but it wasn't empty. Right after they got in, a woman got in whom Gregor only noticed on second glance was a nun. He liked his nuns traditional, in long habits and veils. This one was wearing a pants suit with a gold cross pinned to the lapel and a little half veil attached to the top of her head. It made her look like one of the help in an old British movie about the aristocracy.

"Right along here," Billie said, when they reached the third floor. "She's in the wing. It's kind of a trek. I've asked Dr. Halevy to meet us there in about three minutes. She's usually pretty prompt."

Gregor threaded his way through what felt like empty hallways, wide corridors with deep carpeting and doors, but no people that he could see. St. Mary's was not one of the expensive hospitals in the city. It was, in fact, the one that took in the vast majority of the uninsured, since it was subsidized by the Archdiocese. Gregor had a sudden vision of the present Cardinal Archbishop of Philadelphia, and then another of those nuns in the pants suit.

"Here we are," Billie said.

She opened a heavy swinging door, and behind it Gregor found the people he had been missing up to now. There was a wide curved desk that was the main anchor for the nurse's station. Behind it stood another nun in a pants suit, except hers was a standard nursing uniform and she wasn't wearing a veil of any kind. There were also two more women, also in uniforms, probably not nuns.

"It's too bad about the nuns," Billie said suddenly. "They used to be able to staff this entire hospital with Sisters of Mercy — well, almost the entire hospital. Nursing staff. Even some of the doctors, lots of the clerical people. The nuns worked for ten dollars a month and the medical bills were low or nonexistent to anybody who came through the doors and couldn't pay for it. And then suddenly there were no more nuns."

"I know somebody who can spend a fair amount of time talking about that," Gregor said. "She's an — extern sister, I think it's called. For a Carmelite monastery out on Hardscrabble Road."

"Oh, I know that one," Billie said. "I've seen them. It's like watching an old movie."

The nun at the nurse's station looked up and saw them. She came out from around the desk. "Officer Ormonds," she said. "This must be Gregor Demarkian."

"That's him," Billie said.

The nun had no sense of humor, and she wasn't interested in introducing herself. "Dr. Halevy is in with the patient. I've asked her to take this meeting into a conference room. There's one at the far end of the hall. Mrs. Mgrdchian is stable, but there's always the problem with comatose patients that you don't know what they're able to hear.

We like to think that they're just dead to the world, so to speak, without actually being dead, but many of them can hear everything that goes on around them."

The nun was pumping down the hall as she talked, and Gregor and Billie were following her. Gregor was getting a little breathless. The nun stopped.

"Here is is," she said. "We've got her alone down here until we're sure of what the situation is. We don't want to upset other patients if there needs to be a police presence. Please don't stay too long in the room, and please don't discuss the particulars of the case — the police case or the medical case — where she can possibly hear you. Even if you think she can't hear you. Is that clear?"

"Of course," Billie said.

The woman was chirping. Gregor almost laughed.

The nun looked dubious, then turned around and headed back down the hall. Billie opened the door to Sophie Mgrdchian's hospital room.

"Old bat," Billie said cheerfully. "She didn't decide to give Mrs. Mgrdchian a private room and neither did the hospital. We insisted on it. Come in and meet Dr. Halevy."

Gregor walked into the hospital room and looked around. It was a small room, but big enough to hold several chairs as well as Sophie Mgrdchian's bed. Sophie lay on her back with her head on a pillow and the top half of the bed raised just a little. There was a tube in her arm, but nothing else. Gregor was a little surprised. He'd expected a lot more technology.

A tall woman looked up from Sophie's bedside and then came around to greet them. Dr. Halevy was as middle aged and thick as Billie Ormonds, but her hair was pulled back tightly on her head, and she was wearing a stethoscope.

"Mr. Demarkain," she said. "Right on time. You have no idea what a relief that is. Hello, Billie. It's good to see you again."

"Actually," Billie said, "she wishes she'd never have to see me again. But that's only because she hates police work."

"I don't hate police work," Dr. Halevy said. "I hate crime. You'd think with all the pain and suffering in the world, people would refrain from causing it when it wasn't necessary. And it isn't necessary, pretty much ever, as far as I can tell."

"Police have to hurt suspects sometimes," Gregor started.

Dr. Halevy waved this away. "You know

what I mean. I'm not talking about the police." She gestured back to Sophie. "She's all right for the moment. The nurses have orders to check in on her at least once very fifteen minutes. Let's go out in the hall for a moment."

"I thought there was some kind of conference room," Gregor said.

"There's a conference room if you want it," Dr. Halevy said, ushering them all out into the corridor, "but I don't really know if we need one. I mean, I've got only one thing to say, and it doesn't mean anything, if you believe Billie here. It can't be used in court, or something."

"It just doesn't tell me anything," Billie said mildly.

"What is it?" Gregor said.

"What it is," Dr. Halevy said, "is that I have absolutely no idea what happened here. Not one. I've got no idea why this woman is unconscious or how she got that way. I've done all the usual tox screens. Nothing. We've checked heart and lungs. Nothing. We've checked for cancer. Nothing. There's no sign she's ever had a stroke. There's no sign she's ever had a heart attack. There's no sign of *anything at all.* It's like voodoo."

In an Agatha Christie mystery, what was happening to Sophie Mgrdchian would be discovered to be a secret poison — or maybe not so secret, because in spite of the clichés, Dame Agatha didn't really go in for the more esoteric stuff. She'd have thought of something else, something closer to home. Gregor could not, for the life of him, imagine what it would be.

Instead, he found himself walking down City Ave after his talk with Dr. Halevy, passing the edge of St. Joseph's University and thinking that he'd soon be at the place where City Ave went to hell after dark. For all he knew, it might go to hell in the daytime, too. He ought to get a cab and get back to Cavanaugh Street.

Instead, he got out his cell phone. He had to be careful with it. For the first six weeks he'd had it, he hadn't been able to pick it up without "launching the browser," which apparently meant getting on the Internet. From his phone. Here was something else Dame Agatha hadn't had to contend with. Still, Miss Marple would not have objected. Miss Marple believed in accepting change and embracing progress, one way or the other.

He was standing on City Ave, thinking

about Jane Marple as if she were a real human being. Tibor was getting to him. Tibor thought of all fictional characters as human beings, even if they were hobbits.

Bennis had set up his speed dial list. All he had to do was remember the number he'd given to David Mortimer. Eventually, he gave up trying to remember and just looked at the list instead. The list was interesting. Bennis had given herself the number 3. She'd given Tibor number 1, and his doctor number 2. He'd have to talk to her about that.

He pressed down hard on the number 6 and then held the phone to his ear to listen to it ring. He got David Mortimer on the first ring, which meant that Mortimer did without an assistant. When had they stopped calling them secretaries and started calling them assistants?

"I'm wandering around in the city," Gregor told Mortimer, "and I was wondering if I could come over and talk about things for a bit. I've just been with Dr. Halevy."

"Ah," Mortimer said. "Yes, I talked to her this morning."

"Well, there's that," Gregor said. "And a few more things."

"Come on over. Maybe we can go to

lunch. I've been here since five-thirty and I'm dying."

Gregor put the cell phone back in his pocket. He didn't like the fact that phones didn't just ring anymore. He was less attuned to the modern than Miss Jane Marple.

Ack, he thought.

Then there was a cab, and he was raising his arm in the street and watching it slow down.

3

There was no murder, and therefore no murder mystery, and that mattered. But something was going on, and Gregor didn't like the way it felt, so he was here. Or something. Maybe he was just bored being without something professional to do.

Gregor watched the floors go by as the elevator went up and thought that he would have to poke his head in to say hello to the mayor before he left. He'd known John Jackman too long not to do that. Then the elevator stopped and the doors slid open, and David Mortimer was right out there in the hall, waiting for him.

"Mr. Demarkian," he said. "Come on back with me for a while. I've got some information printing out for you."

"As far as I can tell, there isn't any information," Gregor said. "At least there isn't
any from the doctor. Is there anything about
this Lily woman?"

"Not really." David Mortimer was moving
fast. Gregor watched offices go by, and then
a big office full of cubicles, and then a little
door at the end. Mortimer opened that door
and ushered Gregor into a space that must
once have been a biggish closet. It did not
have a window.

There was a visitor's chair. Gregor sat in
it. Mortimer sat behind the desk and looked
into the little tray of the printer.

"Here we are," he said, picking up a little
pile of papers. "And in case you're wondering, yes, this was indeed a closet. But the
mayor wanted his special liaison to have an
office, not a cubicle, so here we are."

"That's what your title is? Special Liaison?"

"Yeah. Personally, I think Mr. Jackman
just likes the word 'liaison.' You've known
him forever, haven't you?"

"Something like that." Gregor did not say,
"He dated my wife before I did," because
he found that idea uncomfortable.

Mortimer placed the papers on the desk
as close to Gregor as he could get them.
"We've done a preliminary search for the

two brothers," he said, "given the information you've given us. And for the niece, I think you said she was. So far, we don't have much, but then we don't have much, if you know what I mean. We've asked for a search warrant so that we can go into the house and look through the papers there to find some clue to where the rest of the woman's family is, but it's harder to get warrants like that than you'd think. There are privacy concerns, and legal concerns, and constitutional concerns. You weren't really serious when you suggested that we just let this, um, this Mrs. —"

"Vardanian," Gregor said.

"Vardanian," Mortimer said. "You didn't really mean we should turn a blind eye to her going into the house and rooting around?"

"No," Gregor said. "Not really. But she suggested it, and I thought I should pass it along. She's — maybe I should say understandably concerned."

"Yes, well," Mortimer said. "Look. If this Mrs. Mgrdchian were any younger, we'd probably have homicide detectives assigned to the case already. Not that there's been a homicide, but we don't really know that there hasn't been an attempted one. This whole thing gets odder the longer it goes on. We did check the public records, and we have birth data on Sophie and Viktor Mgrdchian and draft information on Viktor and his two brothers, plus records of the baptism, but not the birth, of a Clarice Ann Mgrdchian, who seems to have been Marco's daughter. But Clarice Ann couldn't be Lily. She's too young by nearly thirty years."

"And you don't know where she is?"

"We've got a couple of people working the Internet," Mortimer said, "but it's not as easy as you think, especially when you don't really know where to start geographically. And we don't know. Those women you sent us to are very sharp, sharper than I expect to be at their age, but they don't really know anything. Seeing somebody at a funeral more than a decade ago isn't —"

"Yes, I know," Gregor said. "What about Lily herself? I understand that the thing with the fingerprints isn't really all that unusual, but —"

"It's not unusual for homeless people," Mortimer said. "They burn themselves. They cut themselves. Sometimes accidentally and sometimes on purpose. We run into it every winter when the cold hits and we have to try to identify the one or two who always die. Our problem here, of course, is that this Lily woman didn't seem to be homeless. She was too clean —"

"Yes, I thought about that," Gregor said. "Maybe Sophie Mgrdchian saw her homeless and took her in."

"Was Mrs. Mgrdchian like that?" Mortimer asked. "Because I'm not saying it's impossible, but I am saying that it's unlikely. Homeless people tend to be scary for reasons other than the ordinary citizen's prejudices. A lot of them are alcohol or drug addicted, and addicted people are volatile and unpredictable. A lot of them are mentally ill, and they're even more volatile and unpredictable."

"That's what we're assuming here, aren't we? That Lily is mentally ill?"

"I guess. But she's not mentally ill the way homeless people are usually mentally ill. She's not belligerent. She comes with us when we ask her to. She obedient and mild mannered and not at all violent. She wouldn't last half a day like that living on the street, not most places in this city. And I'll tell you what. We've never picked her up before."

"Picked her up?" Gregor asked.

"For causing a public nuisance, or something like that. We do keep records when we have to send the police to get homeless

188

people out of stores or other places where they cause disturbances. A lot of them use the libraries in the winter, and if they stay out of the way and don't get loud or smell too bad, we don't bother them. The librarians don't want us to bother them. But some of them go into libraries and bring up porn on the machines and, uh, well —"

"Masturbate," Gregor said.

"Yeah," Mortimer said. "That. They do that. Not the women, usually, though. Or they smell so bad it isn't possible to get near them. Or they start shouting and threatening people. Mostly people who aren't there, but still. And we've never picked her up for anything like that. Of course, if she was as clean and as quiet as she is now, we wouldn't have been asked to pick her up, but then she couldn't have been homeless. She'd have had to have someplace to go to wash."

"Have you checked the shelters?"

"All of them, and the temporary housing organizations, too. She hasn't been at any of them. This Lily of yours might have been a homeless person, but if she was, she wasn't homeless in Philadelphia."

"I can't see Sophie Mgrdchian taking in a homeless woman off the street," Gregor said. "I didn't know Mrs. Mgrdchian personally, except maybe back when I was twelve, but I know these women. I can see them baking all night and passing out bread to people they think need it, but I can't see them taking in strangers."

"My point exactly."

"So," Gregor said. "I guess there's nothing to do but wait for the results of the new set of tests Dr. Halevy has ordered. I asked her if she thought we were going to find foul play, and she wasn't able to give me an answer. I asked her if she knew what was wrong with Sophie Mgrdchian, and she couldn't answer that, either."

"It's probably going to end up being something natural, or an accident," David Mortimer said. "But take that stuff. It's all the test results we have on Sophie Mgrdchian, plus all the search results so far on Lily. If you can make something of them, we'd be glad of the help. I'm sorry we're not being more efficient."

"You're being fine," Gregor said.

He picked up the papers, and looked at them, and frowned. There really was nothing here. He wished he had something concrete in the old-fashioned sense, like a bullet hole in the ceiling. Then he put the papers down on the desk again.

"Could I ask you a favor?" he said. "Could you get me some information about an incident in Merion."

"Merion?"

"I think that was where it was. *American's Next Superstar* seems to be filming its new season at my wife's childhood home, and back last weekend there was a shooting at something the show was doing in Merion."

David Mortimer looked happy. "I know what you're talking about. A girl we think is called Emily tried to shoot Sheila Dunham in the middle of some filming they were doing, or something. Oh, I can get you a lot on that one. And it's even got interesting parallels. I mean, this Emily woman isn't talking, either, last I heard."

Seven

1

Alida Akido had had no idea that it would be as hard as this to live with other girls in the house, or that she'd be so close to killing one of them because she just couldn't stand the stupid endless chatter anymore. The one she wanted to kill was not Andra Gayle, who didn't actually talk much — probably because, when she did, she sounded like a rap record or an actress playing a drug-addicted whore on *Law & Order.* No, the girl who was driving Alida crazy was her roommate, Mary-Louise Verdt.

The situation was being made worse by the fact that Mary-Louise seemed to think, *because* they were roommates, they had to do everything together.

Right now, they were sitting side by side in the limousine, and Alida wanted to tear the hair out of her own head. At least it would cause a scene. At least it would mean that Mary-Louise would stop talking.

"This means Coraline won't have any film from the challenge," Mary-Louise was saying. "That's fatal, it really is, especially at this point in the competition. I mean, it's not like they've got days and days of film to judge by instead?"

"Oh, I know," Janice Ledbeddder said. "Wasn't that awful? And don't you worry about it? I mean, Sheila Dunham is, well, she's like this all the time, isn't she? Or at least she seems to be, on television. Any one of us could be next."

"At least we'll all be at the challenge," another of the girls said. Alida wracked her brains and came up with a name: Linda Kowalski. Linda roomed with a girl named Shari Bernstein, and as far as Alida was concerned, they might as well be twins.

Shari was fluffing her hair in a mirror. It had been teased out beyond belief. "There's always somebody who gets left behind at the beginning," she said. "It's never the first person to actually go home. Even Grace hasn't gone home."

They all looked at Grace on the far end of the car. She was talking to Suzanne Toretti. She didn't seem to have heard them.

"It won't be Grace, either," Shari said. "Don't you see? It's got to be a surprise, and Grace and Coraline wouldn't be surprises. Everybody would be expecting them. It's got to be somebody the audience expects is going to stay forever, or maybe even win. Otherwise there wouldn't be any drama."

"I just hope we're not going to have to do another of those debriefing interviews, or whatever they call them," Mary-Louise said. "I really hated the one I had the first day. I mean, you never know what you're saying, do you? And they can do things with the tape so that when they show you on television, you look like a complete idiot. That's just what I need, everybody watching at home and seeing me look like a complete idiot."

"At least you didn't have to do one about how you were knocked out at the end of casting and didn't get into the house," Janice said. "I hate those. I leave the room when they come on. I won't even watch them. I mean, just how embarrassing does that have to be? Everybody in the world knows you tried, and everybody in the world knows you failed."

"My mother says you can't be afraid of failure if you're going to succeed," Linda said. "She says everybody who succeeds fails a lot at first, and then they pick themselves up and just go on with it. But I'm glad I didn't have to do one of those interviews, either. I think they're so sad."

The car was pulling up to the curb on a street that looked too quaint to be real. This would be the center of the town of Bryn Mawr, Alida supposed, although she had the impression that most of Bryn Mawr was like where they were living now, big houses on big estates laid back across wide lawns away from the roads. Still, it was interesting. This was supposed to be one of the richest towns in America. Alida liked the look of rich towns.

"Oh, look," Mary-Louise said. "There they are. The photographers."

"The paparazzi," Shari Bernstein corrected her.

Alida looked in the direction Mary-Louise was pointing. They were there all right, half a dozen men with cameras, half hiding in the doorway of the shop next door. In a real celebrity situation, there would be hundreds of them. They would fill the streets and stop traffic. Alida supposed that these people had been hired, and that there wasn't enough money to hire enough of them. It did not look to her like much of a challenge.

The driver stopped the car's engine. The girls all hesitated, wondering what they were supposed to do next. Alida thought she was sure. Celebrities didn't open the doors of their own limousines. They had drivers to to open the doors. She folded her hands in her lap. Down at the other end of the car, Grace Alsop and Andra Gayle were gathering up their things.

The driver came around and opened the door closest to the curb. Shari Bernstein was closest to the door. She got out first, and when she did the photographs rushed up to her, screaming at her to turn to look at them, and snapping pictures all the while. Shari ducked her head and raced for the door to the restaurant.

Linda Kowalski was next. By now, all the girls were looking out of the car windows, watching the performances as they came by. Grace looked very thoughtful, and that was important, because Alida thought Grace was her only real competition.

Mary-Louise went out next, and Alida almost laughed out loud to see that performance. First she ran. Then she seemed to lose her way, then she skidded and fell. When she got up, she had dirt all along the side of her little black dress. She rushed toward the restaurant door and lost a shoe. She turned around, found the shoe, picked it up, and rushed some more.

Alida was next. She got her umbrella from the floor where she had left it when she first got into the car. She stepped out of the limousine in that swiveling way her mother had taught her would not expose any part of her that she did not want people to see. The photographers rushed her as they had rushed all the others. She opened the umbrella directly into their faces and walked — not ran — to the restaurant's front door. She was inside and out of the range of the cameras in no time at all.

Mary-Louise was standing near the reception desk, crying softly into a napkin somebody had gotten her from someplace. Alida ignored her. Other girls were coming in: Janice Ledbedder, looking out of breath; then Ivy, Grace, and Suzanne; and then Andra and Marcia Lee. It took a while for all thirteen girls to enter the restaurant.

Alida moved closer to Grace. "They're all so pathetic," she said. "They don't look this pathetic on television, do you know what I mean?"

"They're edited for television," Grace said.

Alida shrugged. The restaurant door opened again and the judging panel came in, or some of them did — there was Sheila Dunham, and Mark Borodine and Johnny Rell, but not the other two. Alida had never had much use for gay men, but the entertainment business was full of them, and she supposed she'd have to tolerate them.

Sheila was walking up and down in front of them. Alida wondered if she took drugs. She was always so extreme, so angry and hyperactive. She did seem to have managed to make it into the restaurant without a hair out of place or an inch of stocking wet.

Alida watched as Sheila stopped in front of Mary-Louise Verdt and looked her up and down. It really was very hard not to laugh in these situations. It really was. Mary-Louise looked terrified. She also looked like she'd been wrestling in mud.

Alida could feel all the girls holding their breaths. They were waiting for Sheila to do something outrageous and violent, as she had already twice that day.

Instead, Sheila just said, "Go home."

Mary-Louise's tears welled up yet again. "Excuse me?" she said.

"Go home," Sheila said. "Get back in the car. You're out of this challenge. No decent restaurant would allow you in looking the way you do."

"I slipped," Mary-Louise said, and now the tears were coming down hard and fast. "I — they just all ran at me and so I was running to get away, and I slipped."

"I don't care what you did," Sheila said, "you can't come into the restaurant like that. Go back and sit in the car. You're out of this challenge."

"But I can't be," Mary-Louise wailed.

"Get out or I'll have you taken out," Sheila said, and then she turned her back on the crying Mary-Louise, and looked down the line at the other girls.

Alida didn't know why she expected the next target of Sheila Dunham's gaze to be herself, but she did. She was not surprised that Sheila stopped in front of her. She was not afraid, either. She knew she looked good. Unlike most of the rest of these girls, she had clothes that really suited the occasion. She was wearing Betsey Johnson and Gucci, not knockoffs from Kmart and JC Penney. Her hair was good, too, sleek and styled and combed, jet black and falling to her shoulders. She didn't have too much makeup on. She wasn't wearing too much jewelry.

Sheila Dunham said, "Do you think that was smart, what you did out there?"

"I'm not sure what you mean," Alida said.

"Holding the umbrella in front of your face. Do you think that was smart?"

"I think it successfully prevented the photographers from photographing me,"

Alida said.

"And you think that's what you want to do?"

"I think that's what most celebrities do," Alida said. "They try to avoid the paparazzi if they can."

Sheila leaned in, far enough so that Alida couldn't help smelling her breath. It was very bad breath.

"Wrong," Sheila said. "You've got to be a star on the level of Brad Pitt to want to avoid the paparazzi. That's just something you say when reporters ask you, because you don't want to sound like a jerk. When you're a celebrity on the way up, or a celebrity who isn't known for anything but being a celebrity — well, then you need the paparazzi as much as they need you. More. Do you know what people like Paris Hilton do? They make deals with these guys. They make a point of being easy to photograph at least some of the time, because not to be photographed is not to exist. Not to be photographed is not to be famous."

Alida took a deep breath. There was nothing to say. There wasn't even anything she wanted to say.

Sheila stood back. "So," she said. "I watched all your performances. And we'll have the pictures at judging, to back this up. But I know right away who has won this challenge. You need to be seen and photographed in a way that makes you look good. Some of you did all right. Some of you did not do so well. Some of you were hopeless, like what's-her-name out in the car. But Johnny and Mark and I have talked it over, and the winner of the challenge is —"

Alida stood very still. She wouldn't be the winner of the challenge, so she assumed that Grace would be. If Sheila hadn't sent Grace home, then Grace could not be out of the competition.

Sheila made a flourish with her arms and announced, "Andra!"

The word bounced across the restaurant foyer like a Ping-Pong ball.

Andra Gayle squealed and jumped up and down, and did all those other things winning contestants loved to do in front of the cameras.

Alida nearly spat.

2

Ivy Demari was completely astounded that she hadn't been the subject of one of Sheila Dunham's patented on-camera rages — almost as astounded as she was that she'd managed to make it into the house at all. No matter what she had told Dennis at home, she hadn't really thought that *America's Next Superstar* was her thing, except perhaps in the sense that the casting always contained one or two freaks. She certainly looked like the freak in this particular group. She was the only one with visible tattoos. Grace had a small Chipmunk on her left buttock, but she didn't have the buttock on display. She was the only one with hair that wasn't a normal color for hair, too. Even her mother had warned her about that one before she came. Still, Ivy thought, you had to be yourself. She really hated all the normal colors for hair.

They had been ushered into the restaurant, which was very small and empty of all other patrons. That didn't seem like the best way to do this. Ivy could see that regular, ordinary people probably could not be included in a day like today. You'd have to chase them around and get them to sign releases in case their faces showed during one of the shots you wanted to use for television. In real life, though, there would be lots of other people in the restaurant besides the celebrity of the moment, and the celebrity of the moment would have to find a way to deal with them. Ivy almost wished she had agreed to go to those clubs where a bouncer kept watch at the door and only let in the people he thought would "count." Dennis always wanted to go to those clubs, even though he wasn't sure of getting in. Dennis always wanted a lot of things.

They were being shown to a table near the back window wall that overlooked a little waterfall. They were all trooping along like girls in line at summer camp. Ivy let herself be seated in the chair that looked directly outside. Then she heard Janice fall into the chair to her right, as thick and breathy as if she were collapsing.

"Oh, whoosh," Janice said. "Can you believe that happened to Mary-Louise? She's one of the nicest girls here, too. Not catty, like so many of them. It's like any of us could mess up at any time, and then what would happen? We'd go home, that's what would happen."

Then there was the thing where so many of these girls lived and breathed the show, and nothing but the show. Ivy looked up as Grace Alsop and her roommate Suzanne Toretti took the other two chairs at their table. Grace looked the way she had always looked, Sheila-attack or not: like one of those girls' boarding-school girls who didn't talk to anybody who wasn't on her cotillion invitation list. And Ivy knew cotillions. They did cotillions in Dallas.

"You could have come out if you'd wanted to," Ivy's mother had said, at around the time Ivy was making the audition tape she'd sent to the show. "Do you know why you do things anymore? Do you care?"

"It's a chance to see a part of the country I haven't seen before," Ivy had said.

"If you want to see a part of the country you haven't seen before, use your American Express."

"It's a chance to do something I haven't done before, then."

Her mother had put her coffee down on the kitchen table and sighed. "It's a chance to get away from Dennis without having to hurt his feelings straight on, and you know it. I warned you it wasn't going to work out when you started dating him. You've got more ambition than that."

Ivy had wanted to point out that she wasn't using any ambition she might have had, but she hadn't. She got along with her mother. She got along with her father, too. It made her the odd man out at most of the places she liked to frequent.

"Tell me if the Wicked Witch of the West is advancing," Grace said. "The last thing I need is another surprise."

"She's off at a table with Andra and that

Chinese girl," Janice said.

"You can't call Alida Chinese," Suzanne said. "She'll bite your head off. I don't think she's a very nice person, do you? I mean, she's terribly snobbish, and she's — she just doesn't like anybody. She doesn't just relax and talk."

"I wish you'd stop saying things like that," Grace said. "You know they're taping everything we say. And filming it. You're going to get us stuck in some segment where we sound like first-class bitches, and I'm going to be there as much as you, even if I don't go along with it. She's probably just nervous. It's probably her culture or something."

"You know what I heard," Janice said, leaning in a little. Ivy wondered if she imagined that this would mean that no microphone could pick up what she was about to say. "I heard that Sheila Dunham had a daughter, only now the daughter doesn't talk to her anymore. She's on drugs, or something. She ran away from home. I don't remember."

Ivy sat up a little straighter. That was odd, she thought. She'd heard that story, too. And there was something —

But Grace was going on. "That's an old story," she was saying. "It was all over the

205

news at the time. The daughter had a drug problem, and she'd been picked up for shoplifting a couple of times and the next time it happened, she was going to go to jail, so Sheila had her put in one of those youth facility things, you know, the ones that are practically like jails."

"A private jail?" Janice looked confused. "Is that legal?"

"It's not in this country," Grace said, "but they have them on islands in the Caribbean and things where it is. They take the kid's passport when he shows up and then they make everybody get up at the same time and go to sleep at the same time and eat meals at the same time. And if you don't behave they throw you in solitary. You can look it up on the Internet if you don't believe me. A lot of really rich parents put their kids in places like that when they think the kids are out of control. So anyway, Sheila put her daughter in one of those, and the daughter managed to escape, somehow. Anyway, nobody has ever seen her since."

"But I don't understand," Janice said. "Is it a jail? Or is it rehab? What?"

"It's both those things." Grace shrugged. "I barely talk to my father as it is, but if he'd ever done anything like that to me, I'd have found a lawyer and sued him over it.

Although you can't really do that, I think, when you're a minor your parents can do pretty much anything they want to you until you're eighteen."

"No," Janice said. "That's not true. You can call the authorities and charge them with child abuse. I know that's possible."

"They aren't going to charge someone like Sheila Dunham with child abuse," Grace said. "And they're not going to do it for sending her daughter off to some place that says it's a psychiatric facility. I don't know if you've noticed, but they don't take children away from rich people almost ever."

"What about Britney Spears?" Janice asked.

"What about her?" Grace said. "They didn't take the children away from her and put them in a foster home, did they? Their father sued for custody and he got it, but it isn't the same thing. Anyway, Sheila's daughter disappeared. Maybe she went to live with her father. I don't know who that was. Nobody knows. Somebody Sheila was married to when she first started working, I think. Nobody ever talks about her. Which makes me think she really did disappear. It's just the kind of thing the tabloids really like."

The waterfall really wasn't a waterfall. It

was the turn wheel of an old mill, placed in the river in such a way that the water should have turned it as it passed through. Ivy wasn't sure why the wheel wasn't moving. She wasn't sure of the name of the river, either. She didn't think there was a major river that went through Bryn Mawr, Pennsylvania, but then she was only sketchy at geography. It was other things she was good at.

"A girl who got herself thrown out of history class in the eighth grade by throwing *Brandenburg v. Ohio* in the face of her history teacher is not going to be happy for life with a guy whose highest ambition is to have really neat body art," her mother had said.

"I like really neat body art," Ivy had said, but she hadn't gone on with it, because of course her mother was right.

Janice poked her in the arm. "Ivy? Are you all right?"

Ivy shook her head. She wondered what compromises you had to make to become "accomplished," as her mother had put it. She didn't like the idea of making compromises at all.

"Sorry," she said. "I was thinking about the Kennedys."

"You mean the political Kennedys?" Grace said. "Why?"

"It was Jacqueline Kennedy Onassis I was really thinking of," Ivy said. "When we came in here, I thought that it wasn't very realistic, putting us in an empty restaurant without other people in it, because in real life, celebrities eat with everybody else —"

"Not really," Grace said quickly. "They go to places that keep most people out."

"Most people, not all people," Ivy said. "And lots of times they go to places that are stuff ed with people. That's why you get all those awful stories about people like Britney Spears and Lindsay Lohan. But then I remembered about Jacqueline Kennedy Onassis."

"What about her?" Janice said.

"They used to clear places for her," Ivy said. "When she was still married to Onassis. If she wanted to shop, you know, they'd send a team of people in and they'd clear out the entire store if they had to, and then she'd come in and shop. And at Vail, too, they'd clear an entire slope. There are celebrities who live in a sort of bubble."

"Well, I know something else celebrities do," Grace said, "and I'm going to do it. I don't see I have anything to lose. If I'm not the first person eliminated this week, I'll be shocked out of my skin. Are they letting us order things?"

"I don't know," Ivy said.

She looked around. The waitresses were working their way through the tables, holding out menus, which did make it seem as if ordering was on its way. The menus did not look like they could be the ones the restaurant used most of the time, since they were only two sides of a single piece of laminated cardboard. Maybe it was the kind of place that served very small portions of everything to women who couldn't eat anything and still maintain the weight they wanted to be for social occasions.

Ivy tried to think. She didn't really know what she was doing here. She didn't know if she wanted to win the competition, or just get some air time on television, or if she was just wasting time generally and, as her mother said, letting Dennis down gently. And other people's private lives weren't her business. But still . . .

She looked around the room. Sheila Dunham had left Andra's table and gone on to another one, this one with only three girls at it. She looked so old up close like this, and so tired, and so unhappy. The lines in her face were all hard, and all the wrong kind.

"I'm sure she's had absolutely a ton of plastic surgery," Janice said, leaning in close.

"She always looks so bitter. Did you ever notice that?"

"Did you ever wonder why we're all here, trying to be just like somebody who's so bitter?" Grace asked.

"We all think we'll do it better when we do it ourselves," Ivy said, but that wasn't what she was thinking about. She was thinking about that first day, when that girl had stood up and fired that gun at Sheila Dunham's head.

At least, that was what Ivy thought had happened.

The waitress had arrived at their stable. She took Suzanne's order first, something with chicken and French words in it.

Then she turned to Grace.

Grace put the menu on the table.

"I'll have steamed broccoli on a bed of white rice," she said.

Ivy paid attention. The waitress looked startled.

"We don't actually have —" she started.

Grace waved her away. "I'm sure the kitchen can make it up for *me*," she said.

EIGHT

1

Things moved faster these days than they used to. There were cell phones, and computers, but Gregor thought the real reason was that there were so many more people. When Gregor had first started working, businesses had put up HELP WANTED signs in their windows and taken in almost anybody who walked in off the street. There was a lot of work and too few people to do it. Or maybe it had only seemed that way, because women had stayed home and done their own laundry and housework, and that had left the field of paid employment look more open.

Actually, Gregor had no idea what his mind was nattering on about. It was the kind of thing he thought about these days. Maybe that was getting older. Maybe that was getting married again. What it probably actually was was the fuss with the court-appointed attorney. In Gregor's day, most court-appointed attorneys half slept through their cases. Now there were kids fresh out of law school who took being a court-appointed attorney as a crusade.

He got out of the cab in front of the Wilson Deere Memorial Hospital and looked around. The woman on the phone had sounded very young, almost too young to have graduated from anything. There was nobody waiting for him at the door, so he went inside. Here was something that had not changed. The interior landscape of public mental hospitals was as grim and terrifying as it had always been.

The big ground-floor foyer had linoleum on the floors and walls the color of pale pea soup. There was a male attendant at the front desk. The desk was behind a cage of barbed wire. Weren't the inmates all upstairs and restrained by orderlies? Maybe people came in off the street and threatened the staff, for whatever reason.

The young woman he was waiting for was standing near the elevators, looking through her briefcase. There were no chairs to sit down in. There were no magazines to read while you waited. Gregor thought of Olivia de Havilland in *The Snake Pit,* and then he thought that this young lawyer wouldn't have the faintest idea who Olivia de Havilland was.

Gregor went up to the elevator. "Excuse me," he said. "My name is Gregor Demarkian. I'm looking for LeeAnn Testenaro."

"Oh," the young woman said. She dropped the briefcase, looked at it for a moment, and then picked it up. "Oh," she said again. "Excuse me. Yes. Mr. Demarkian. I'm Lee-Ann Testenaro."

Gregor held out his hand. In his youth, men did not offer their hands to women. They waited for women to offer their hands instead. It all seemed unnecessarily complicated for this time and place.

LeeAnn took Gregor's hand and shook it. Then she dropped it and looked at her briefcase again.

"I don't mean to look this disorganized," she said. "It's just that I'm not used to this kind of thing. I mean, our usual case, in Legal Aid, is of some kid who robbed a liquor store or got so incredibly stoned on something that he wandered into a police station and puked all over the desk sergeant."

"Did that really happen?" Gregor asked.

"Oh, yes," LeeAnn said. "And you wouldn't believe how hard it is defending

214

people who do things like that. It's as if they wanted to go to jail. You can't get them to shut up. We're up on the fourth floor. They're expecting us."

"Good," Gregor said. He punched the elevator button and the doors opened directly. The elevator was gray and ugly and metal. There was no carpet on the floor.

"It's awful, isn't it?" LeeAnn said. "We don't do anything to make life easier for these people. Do you know who ends up in here, most of the time? Homeless people. A lot of them are genuinely mentally ill. A lot of them are just addicts, but they can get very out of it and seem mentally ill. I spent all last winter getting dozens of them committed for four-day observations."

"You did?" They had gotten into the elevator together. It was heading upward. It creaked. "Why?"

"Because it keeps them out of the cold," LeeAnn said. "I know this isn't the kind of thing I'm supposed to think, and I know why the courts did it, but I don't think I've ever found anything so stupid as that bit where you can't involuntarily commit somebody who isn't a danger to themselves or others, and then you define being a danger as not actively going after people with an ax. Aren't they a danger to themselves when

215

they're too paranoid to go to a homeless shelter when it's minus six outside?"

"You really don't want to make it too easy for people to be socked away against their will," Gregor said. "We make that hard even when they have gone after people with an ax."

"I know," LeeAnn said. "I know. I know all the arguments. I just get fed up." The elevator stopped and the doors opened. "Here we are. It's just as bad as downstairs, isn't it? Can you imagine being depressed and being committed to a place like this?"

Gregor did not think the fourth floor was as bad as the lobby, because it was full of people, and the people made it feel less dead. There were plenty of nurses up here, and plenty of patients, and not all the patients looked comatose.

"They've got them on so many meds, they're like zombies," LeeAnn said. "Give me a minute here."

She went up to the nurse's station and talked with one of the women there. Then she came back, nodding. "They'll bring Lily down in a second. She's got a room at the far end of the hall. We can go in here in the back."

LeeAnn led Gregor into a small side room. It was painted pale pea soup green, too, and the floors were still linoleum, but there was a table with three chairs and the chairs had padded seats. Gregor wondered when she had time to acquaint herself with all this. She couldn't have been Lily's attorney for more than a day.

"Under the usual circumstances, I wouldn't let you talk to her," LeeAnn said. "You do work with the police, and the police are not our favorite people. But there doesn't seem to be a crime here. At least not yet. And it isn't as if she could say anything that's likely to be admissible in court."

"When I saw her, she seemed to be pretty disoriented."

"She's that, yes," LeeAnn said.

"Maybe she has some kind of medication that she needs to have adjusted."

LeeAnn looked into her briefcase again and came up with a small sheaf of papers. She looked through them for a while and shook her head.

"She had one of those plastic pill organizers on her when she was first brought in to the police station," LeeAnn said. "There wasn't much of anything in it except a diuretic and some vitamins. There wasn't even any blood pressure medication. They did a workup when she first came here and her blood pressure was a little elevated, so they're giving her something for it. But there weren't any psychotropic drugs, or anything that would be likely to cause this kind of mental disorganization."

"A plastic pill organizer means that somebody must have prescribed pills for her," Gregor said.

"Of course," LeeAnn said. "But there was just the organizer, as far as I can tell. The police didn't find the actual prescription bottles. Which is too bad, really, because if they had, we'd have some clue to who she was and where she came from. I'd give a lot to be able to talk to her regular doctor right now."

"You don't find it odd," Gregor asked, "that she's got a pill organizer full of pills, and she's very clean, both in her body and her clothes, and that even so all her fingertips are so damaged that the police couldn't get a clear fingerprint reading from them?"

"Odd?" LeeAnn said. "Why? A lot of people have that sort of damage to their fingertips. I mean, you might not deal with them, but I do, all the time, they mess them up — freeze them to pipes, burn them accidentally on matches, and —"

"And those people are not only mentally ill, but homeless," Gregor pointed out. "But we've just pretty much demonstrated that whoever Lily is, she couldn't have been a homeless woman."

"Ah," LeeAnn said. She considered it. "Maybe this other woman, the one in the coma, maybe she was being a Good Samaritan and —"

"Taking in a stranger? That's so unlikely as to be impossible. But even if it wasn't likely given Sophie Mgrdchian's character, the fact is that in order to get a pill organizer full of pills, Sophie would have had to take Lily to a doctor. And that would have taken time, time for an appointment, time for the prescriptions to be filled."

"Maybe they went to the emergency room."

"Did the police find evidence of Lily having been to an emergency room?"

"No," LeeAnn said. "And they did check, at least preliminarily. It's in my notes."

There was a sound at the door. Gregor and LeeAnn both looked up. A woman in a nursing uniform was leading Lily in, leading her by the hand as carefully as if she were a kitten with a broken leg.

"Come over here and sit down, dear," the woman was saying, patting Lily's hand over and over again as she said it. "Just come over here and sit down. These people want to have a little talk with you."

Lily allowed herself to be led to a chair. Then she sat down and looked from one of them to the other. She put her hands up on the table and folded them.

"I wish you wouldn't do these things," the woman in the nursing uniform said. "I do realize there are legal issues here, and we'd all like to know who this woman is, but you disrupt her entire routine. You make her more disoriented than she already is."

Lily leaned forward. She was smiling.

"I'm not disoriented," she said, in a perfectly clear and lucid voice.

The three of them turned to stare at her. It was, Gregor thought, the oddest thing. It was as if they had been looking at a statue, and the statue had ended up being a real person who moved. There was a change not just in the expression on Lily's face, but in the way she held her body and the tilt of her head. Even her spine was straighter.

"Is there something wrong with the whole bunch of you?" Lily demanded. "Can any of you talk? Because I wish one of you would. I'd like to know where the hell I am."

It was LeeAnn who moved first. "Maybe we ought to clear the room," she said. "I'm this woman's lawyer, and I want to make sure that there's nothing said here —"

"You're my *lawyer?*" Lily said. "Why do I need a lawyer? And where is this place and what am I doing here?"

"Clear the room," LeeAnn insisted. "Lily, please, stop talking until I can make sure —"

"My name isn't Lily," the woman said. "Whatever made you think my name was Lily?"

"You told us your name was Lily," Gregor said. "Yesterday, when we found you in the house of a woman named Sophie Mgrdchian. Do you remember anything about that at all?"

"I will not have you asking her questions," LeeAnn said, now positively frantic. "And I don't want you answering them, either. I'm your attorney, and —"

"Of course I remember being in Sophie's house," the woman said. "I've been staying there for two weeks. She's my sister-in-law."

2

A cab was pulled up to the curb right in front of the hospital when Gregor walked out, and the driver was willing to go to Bryn Mawr. That was the only reason Gregor went to Bryn Mawr at all, and it surprised him that he did. Not all cabs were willing to go out to the Main Line. Of course, not all times found Gregor more than happy to pay the asking price, either.

He sat in the cab and put his head on the back of the seat, trying to think. There would be no talking to Lily — no, to *Karen* — any time soon, and he could hardly blame LeeAnn Testenaro for that. He probably should have called Bennis and told her what had happened. The problem was, he didn't know what he would say. That scene had been so bizarre, and so completely improbable, that —

He thought back to yesterday when he had first seen Lily. There she had been in Sophie Mgrdchian's foyer, smiling and babbling like someone in a trance. He tried to picture it in his head exactly as it had been. He hadn't thought to question the authenticity of it at the time. That was partly assumptions. He was on Cavanaugh Street in the presence of a harmless-looking old lady. You didn't usually assume that harmless-looking old ladies would fake dementia. And what would they want to fake dementia for? He'd talked to the police and to the doctor who was looking after Sophie Mgrdchian. They didn't know what had happened to her, or why she persisted in her coma, but they weren't suggesting that anything had been done to get her that way, either. They'd checked for all the usual things and found nothing.

Part of the reason he had not questioned Lily's dementia, though, was that it had not felt fake at the time. It frustrated him that he was not able to just recreate the scene in his head. It hadn't felt fake at the time, so that meant that, if Lily was acting, she must be a good enough actress to convince non-experts and distracted people. Later, though, she had been in the presence of experts and of people who were devoting their whole attention to her. They hadn't spotted a fake, either.

They were out of the city now, and on those long roads that wound through big houses and wide stretches of lawn. It had been a long time since Gregor had been out here. It had been nearly a decade since he'd been at Engine House. He couldn't remember what that first night had been like, either. He did remember he'd met Bennis then, and John Henry Newman Jackman, now mayor of Philadelphia, when he was just an investigator for the Bryn Mawr police.

Gregor got out his phone and looked at his speed dial list. He knew that the point of putting people on speed dial was so that he could call them just by tapping a single number and not worrying about looking them up, but he could never remember which number was tapped for who. He found Tibor and held that down, hard. Then he put the phone up to his ear and waited.

"Yes," Tibor said.

Tibor answered the phone the way people did in Italy and Greece — *Pronto! Embross!* — but never in Armenian, so Gregor had always wondered. Gregor identified himself and then ran down the story of the day.

"So," he said, "where we're at the moment is where this woman claims to be Karen Mgrdchian, the wife of Marco Mgrdchian, who she says died last year. Is there any way we can check any of that out?"

"I'd think the police would be better at checking it out, Krekor," Tibor said. "Don't they have ways to run down identities, and things like that?"

"I was thinking of other kinds of checking out," Gregor said. "There's got to be a church, right? People of that generation went to church."

"Yes, Krekor, there could be a church. But what church? This woman's name, Karen, that is not Armenian for that generation, or even for yours. Maybe she was not a member of our Church. Maybe she and her family went to another church. That's very common, the family goes to the wife's church."

"I thought you said that there was a marriage certificate. That they got married on Cavanaugh Street."

"Ah. Krekor, I'm sorry. I don't remember. I can look."

"Thank you," Gregor said. "Would you? And there's a daughter, I think, to that marriage. I should have paid more attention when the Very Old Ladies were talking. I didn't really think this could be anything like a crime —"

"You think now that this is a crime, Krekor? Why do you think it is a crime?"

"I don't know," Gregor said. "I can't put my finger on it. And I may be crazy. But I'd like to get it all checked out. The best thing would be if we could find the church they went to in, where was it, Ohio, I think, if we can find that church and find out if they know anything about them. About the two of them. The couple. No," Gregor thought. "The best thing would be to find the daughter."

"All right, Krekor, I will look through the parish records. Maybe I will find something."

"And maybe you can ask Bennis to do one of those Internet searches for obituaries of Marco Mgrdchian. Maybe for the last eighteen months, say, to make sure she isn't being careless about the time. I want to know what he died of."

"Krekor. The man must have been around eighty."

"Yes, I know," Gregor said. "But we all do that, don't we? That was in one of the Agatha Christie's you gave me. *A Caribbean Mystery.*"

"What was?"

"The fact that we don't tend to pay too much attention when somebody dies, if we think it's to be expected that he died. The old, you see. The very sick. We're not surprised. We don't look too closely."

"I am no longer sure that Agatha Christie was such a good idea."

"You have to get past the fluffy," Gregor said. "All the villages and the costume party constables and that sort of thing. If you can ignore all that, the woman had some good ideas. And this is definitely a good one. I want to find that church, I want to find that obituary, and then I want to talk to the police in whatever town it is. I didn't get much information at the hospital, because Karen Mgrdchian's lawyer had me out of the room as soon as she could. You can hardly blame her. That's her job."

"No, Krekor, you can hardly blame her.

You do not want to talk to Bennis yourself?"

"I'll talk to her when I get home. I'm in a cab."

"In a cab coming home?"

"It's a long story," Gregor said. "Would you mind going ahead with all of that? There's just something — I don't know."

"All right," Tibor said. "But possibly you should make the cab bring you home. I don't like the way you sound."

Gregor closed his phone and put it back into his pocket. They were way out into the suburbs now. The first time he had come out here, Bennis's father had sent a car for him, complete with a driver in livery. It was incredible the way some people lived, right through inflation and taxes and all the rest of it. Bennis had shown him a picture, once, of her coming-out party — the real one, not the public cotillion that was apparently just for show. There was the terrace and the back lawn decked out in lights, and two bands, and a champagne bar. Bennis was wearing an ice blue dress and a necklace that looked like it should have come with bodyguards.

Gregor wondered what had happened to the necklace. Bennis had not inherited it, because Bennis had not inherited anything. There had been a little something from her mother, but that was all.

227

The cab was slowing down. The driver opened the privacy shield and said, "Is this it? Engine House?"

The name ENGINE HOUSE was engraved on a plaque bolted into a rock next to the tall gate. It had once been engraved directly onto the stone, but erosion had taken care of that. The house was close to a hundred and fifty years old. It was a little unnerving to think that there were houses in America like that.

"This is it," Gregor told the driver.

The gate was open. Gregor wondered if that was usual, either for Bobby Hannaford or for these television people. Gregor watched as long columns of trees went by on either side, towering up into the air and blocking out the sky. It was an already dark day. It felt spooky. He'd witnessed the effect at night. It was spookier.

They drove up into the roundabout in front of the front door and stopped. Gregor got out and handed the driver what felt like all the money in the world. The driver handed Gregor a business card.

"Call me if you have to get back," he said.

Gregor thanked him and put the card away. The ride had cost an arm and a leg, but it had gotten him where he wanted to go. He had to make allowances if he didn't want to drive himself and he didn't want to ask Bennis to drive him. He never wanted to drive himself. He thought it must have been five years since the last time he'd tried it. He never wanted Bennis to drive him, either. She thought of speed limits as minimums and brakes as largely unnecessary.

He looked around. He could hear the cab retreating up the drive. There was a black limousine off to the side, in the direction of the garages. There was still rain coming down. The house felt empty and looked it, but he knew that didn't mean anything. Houses this large often felt and looked empty when they weren't actually full of people.

He pressed the doorbell and waited. The door was opened a few seconds later by a very young girl who looked as if she had been crying. Gregor didn't think she was a maid. She wasn't dressed for it. She wasn't acting like it, either.

"Excuse me," Gregor said. "I've come to see a Miss Olivia Dahl."

All of a sudden, the door was pulled back in a jerk and Olivia Dahl was standing there, looking a little disheveled and completely wild.

"My God," she said. "It's Gregor Demarkian. I can't believe it. I really can't believe it. Get out of the way, Coraline. What do you think you're doing?"

Olivia Dahl grabbed the crying girl and jerked her out of the way. Then she grabbed Gregor Demarkian by the wrist and pulled him into the house.

The foyer was full of people, most of them young girls, many of them hysterical. Gregor wondered why he hadn't heard any of it when he was standing on the step.

Then a tall, thin, black-haired woman walked up to him and grabbed his lapel. "Get in there," she said. "What's the good of you anyway, if you can't prevent something like this? Don't you see somebody's trying to kill me?"

"For God's sake, Sheila," Olivia said.

"Somebody is trying to kill me," Sheila Dunham said. "That's the truth. It really is. Do you honestly think that anybody cares about whoever that is? And what's she doing out, anyway? She was in jail. She was supposed to stay in jail. How do you live with yourself if you let dangerous criminals out in public when you're supposed to keep them in jail?"

"Sheila, make sense," Olivia Dahl said. "This is Gregor Demarkian. He's not part of the police department. He's —"

"One of these filthy little whores is trying to kill me," Sheila Dunham said, "and you're all standing around talking about it."

"It's over here," Olivia said, pulling Gregor toward the right of the foyer.

That was when Gregor Demarkian got the oddest feeling of déjà vu. There was the door to the study. There was the study. When they opened the door to the study they would find a man on the floor in front of the fireplace, his head bashed in with a bust of Aristotle, his wheelchair pushed back a little toward the desk.

But that was not, of course, what they did find. Olivia opened the door and there was no man and no wheelchair and no bust of Aristotle.

There was a small, thin blond girl lying across the stone hearth.

She had been shot at least three times in the chest.

■ ■ ■ ■

PART II

■ ■ ■ ■

It is never right to do wrong.
                    — G. K. Chesterton

ONE

1

By the time the police arrived, Gregor Demarkian had managed to get himself past the point where he felt that he was living in one of his own nightmares. He even called Tibor to talk about it, twice.

"I can't call Bennis," he pointed out. "I mean, she wanted me to come out here and talk to these people about what happened in Merion, but you'll notice she didn't come out here herself. She never comes out here. I thought, after Bobby got the house back — well, I thought with childhood memories, and that kind of thing. But it didn't happen. She hates it out here."

"This is not surprising, Krekor," Tibor said. "Her father was murdered there. It doesn't matter that it was many years ago now."

"I know," Gregor said. "And I also know that unless Bobby Hannaford committed

235

this murder himself, the weird correlations have to be just coincidence. The study. The body in front of the hearth. It's still very unnerving. And I don't like the fact that she's going to hear about it. And she *will* hear about it. She can't keep herself off the news shows."

"She will be fine, Krekor. Bennis is not an irrational woman. Are you going to investigate this murder that is there now, then?"

"I don't know," Gregor had said.

And he didn't know. He really didn't. He had forced all the people from the show into the hall and left the room untouched, but not until he had walked around the body once or twice. He had always been glad that he had not been the kind of law enforcement agent that has to deal daily with the results of violent death. By the time his unit of the FBI had come in on a case, the bodies were in the morgue or buried, and he had only pictures to look at. Still, he knew how to study a corpse if he had to, and he had looked over this one.

The three entry wounds were unmistakable. Gregor didn't know enough about pathology to know if those would turn out to be the only ones, or if somebody had pumped God-only-knew how much lead into this tiny young woman. There were the three, and he could see, just by looking around, two of the bullets, both lodged in the wall next to the huge fireplace. He walked around the room a few times. He thought that whoever had done the shooting had done it from the direction of the delicate French secretary near the tall arched windows — whoever had done the shooting had been *all the way inside* the room, and not standing in the doorway.

He went out into the hall and looked around. Some of the young women had left, he presumed to go upstairs to their rooms and lie down, but most of them were still milling about, as were Olivia Dahl and Sheila Dunham. Except that Sheila wasn't milling as much as she was pacing, and wasn't upset as much as she was furious. That might be just her way. Gregor had known people who could only show upset as anger.

"I want to know what's going on around here," Sheila was saying, stalking from one end of the broad foyer to the other. "This is ridiculous. Why is that girl even here? And don't tell me I should call her a woman. All that crap went out in the eighties, and she's not a woman, she's a damned twit. And she's here."

Olivia made a sour face and shrugged in

Gregor's direction. "I'm sorry," she said. "It just occurred to me. You've been here before, haven't you? You've investigated another murder in this house."

"That's right," Gregor said.

"I should have realized. I'm sorry I didn't think of it to begin with. It was a long time ago, wasn't it?"

"Over a decade," Gregor said.

"And it was somebody you knew — your wife's father, or something like that."

"My present wife's father," Gregor said. "I hadn't met her at the time. Well, I met her in the course of that investigation."

"I should have realized," Olivia said again. "I do remember that case, and when we decided to rent this house for the show, I looked into it. You have no idea the kind of nonsense we have to put up with with all of this. I had to make sure I could fend off any paranormal phenomena —"

"What?"

"Not real paranormal phenomena," Olivia said. "But the girls, you know, they get — I don't know how to explain how they get. But I wanted to know enough about what happened here so that if one of them decided she was seeing ghosts, I could head it off at the pass. And of course I talked to Mr. Hannaford about it. He hasn't ever seen any ghosts. At least he says he hasn't. And I don't believe in them."

Gregor looked back toward the study. "Do you still not know who that is?" he asked. "She doesn't look familiar to you in any way?"

"Really. She does in a way, but it's not anything I can put my finger on," Olivia said. "I suppose it's just possible that she sent in an audition tape at some point or the other and I just don't remember it. We send back the ones we aren't interested in if they come with a self-addressed stamped envelope. We throw away the ones that don't. But I do know she was never in consideration for casting, because we keep copies of all of those."

"And you've looked through them all?"

"Oh, no, I couldn't," Olivia said. "For one thing, I don't have them. They're on file back in California. But there aren't that many of them, and I'm sure I would have remembered."

"What's not that many of them?"

Olivia looked at the floor. "We ask three hundred people to interview," she said. "I know that sounds like a lot, but it really isn't. We routinely get over ten thousand tapes when we put out a call for them. Of course, we didn't get that many at first. In the first couple of seasons, we were really straining to find girls to cast, in some ways. We could always have just taken whatever we happened to get, but those first two years there weren't necessarily enough girls we thought were plausible. So in those days we went out looking for girls. We went to malls. We went to small towns and set up shop in the local theater. There aren't as many theaters on Main Street anymore as you'd think there'd be."

"I suppose it would be safe to say that this girl wasn't from those first two seasons, because those you might have remembered." Gregor didn't know if this would be true, but he knew it was what Olivia believed, and he wanted to move forward. "What about the girl herself. Is she a plausible candidate? *Could* she have been invited to an interview?"

Olivia looked back to the study door. Everybody was avoiding it. The girls who were still downstairs were either in the living room or sitting on the stairs. Sheila Dunham was still stalking. The two gay men Gregor had been told were judges were leaning against the wall next to the front door, looking tired.

Olivia looked away. "I don't know," she said. "She was certainly pretty enough. I remember thinking that the first time, in the first incident, back in Merion. Pretty is a consideration. Beautiful would be better, but it's unusual to find really beautiful girls who haven't figured out how to make that work for them without us. Really beautiful girls have options, if you know what I mean."

"Yes, I do."

"When we get the really beautiful ones, it's usually because they're from very small towns. Rural South Dakota. Godforsaken places in Wyoming. But she wasn't that kind of beautiful. She was pretty enough, though. It would have depended on the audition tape. You have to do more than look good to work on television. You have to have some kind of spark, and the camera has to like you. Some girls are too stiff, and some of them are just too retiring. They fade into the background."

"Is that what this one did, fade into the background?"

"Well," Olivia said, "she must have. I know we talked about what happened in Merion, but it was very odd. This girl must have just walked in with the rest of them and skipped the sign-in table. It just didn't occur to me that anybody would bother. To be interviewed, you had to be on my list. In order to be on my list, you had to check in at the table. Just doing what this girl did and wandering off to sit in one of the waiting rooms wouldn't get you, well, it wouldn't get you anything —"

"It got her access to Sheila Dunham," Gregor pointed out.

"Oh, I know it did," Olivia said. "But I wasn't watching for that. It did occur to me that some girls might try to sneak past the sorting system and get interviews when we'd rejected their tapes, so we had a rather elaborate system worked out to make that impossible. And this girl seems to have drifted in, gone to a waiting room, then went from station to station and just blended in with the crowd. Some of the girls remember seeing her, on and off, and didn't think anything of it. Why would they? It was a huge casting call."

"And in the room where this girl took a shot at Sheila Dunham," Gregor said. "How many people were there?"

"There were thirty girls — well, thirty-one, with this one — and Sheila and the judges and the camera people, and that kind of thing. We were filming. Those would have been the first group of girls that would get air time during the show. The usual procedure is to pick those final thirty, then run a few of what we call challenges, then whittle those down to twenty, then run a few more challenges, then whittle those down to fourteen. It's the fourteen who come here and live in the house. Or whatever house we have. And usually we do it all in two days. That day when we pick them, and then the next when we do the challenges. Except, of course, we couldn't do it that fast this time. The police were involved."

"So you did what?" Gregor asked. "What happened to those original thirty girls?"

"We put them up in a hotel for three days," Olivia said. "It cost an arm and a leg. Sheila was livid. But we just couldn't go directly to filming with all the trouble. Eventually the police got whatever it was they wanted, and we got a day to film and sort and do the first big eliminations. And then we moved out here."

"With fourteen girls."

"That's right."

"What happened to the sixteen who didn't make it?"

"They went back to wherever they're from," Olivia said. "That's how it works. You compete, and if you're eliminated, you go home. In the meantime, we get a lot of film of you talking, we do on-camera interviews, we have cameras filming everything almost all the time, and we edit that footage and use it on the show to punctuate the challenges and things. Sometimes I think we could skip the entire thing and go directly to eliminations. It's eliminations that the audience likes to see."

"When you say you're filming them all the time, what do you mean?"

"Oh, we've got stationary cameras everywhere, running nonstop," Olivia said. "We've got them in the bedrooms, in the kitchen — there are two here in the hall; if you look up you'll see them. The whole point of a reality show is to have as much raw, unscripted footage as you can, and this is a reality show in spite of the fact that it's also a kind of game show. Sheila says it's a game show for women, because women like all the drama."

Gregor looked around. There really were two cameras in the foyer, fixed up near the ceiling and pointing down. He saw another one near the ceiling on the landing to the stairs.

"Are there cameras in there where the body is?" he asked.

2

David Mortimer did not show up at Engine House by accident, or by epiphany. Gregor called him as soon as he realized what a royal mess of jurisdiction he was about to get himself into. The police arrived first, with sirens blazing and lights whirling, as if this were an inner-city neighborhood instead of one of the quietest and most discreet in the county. Gregor waited by the door to the study until the tech crews had come in.

"I didn't want people wandering in and out," he said to the taller of the two plain-clothesmen who came in.

He didn't want himself wandering in or out either. It was bad enough to look into that room. There is always something wrong about a dead body. It never looks as if it were sleeping. Then there was the blood, everywhere, blood that Gregor hadn't noticed at first. The bullets had gone through her and out the other side. There was blood not only on the carpet and the wall and some of the furniture, but on the ceiling.

When David Mortimer arrived, Gregor had left the professionals to their work and gone to wander around the hall by himself. He was familiar enough with this house to make the walk difficult. It is always hard to observe properly when you know what you expect to see. Even so, he didn't think there was anything to see. The foyer was, as always, broad and high ceilinged and highly polished. Whatever else was wrong with Bennis's brother — and he thought a lot was wrong with him — he obviously kept up the house. The people belonging to the show were less easy to read. The two judges, Mark and Johnny, both looked a little sick. Sheila looked as if she wanted to hit somebody. The girls were mostly crying, except for one Asian girl who seemed to be almost as angry as Sheila herself. Only Olivia Dahl was behaving the way Gregor expected the bystander at a murder scene to behave, and he had the feeling that she was doing it from force of will.

Mortimer did not arrive in a police car with the sirens blasting, but he did arrive in a car that was driving very fast, too fast to negotiate the Engine House drive with anything like equanimity. The car screeched to a halt behind half a dozen police cars and Mortimer got out of the back. Gregor found himself wondering if he'd had a lot of trouble convincing his bosses that he needed a car and driver to get out to Bryn Mawr, or if John Jackman's office had simply assumed it. Whatever it was, Mortimer took the front steps two at a time and then fairly sprinted through the foyer to the murder scene.

He was back in a moment with the tall

plainclothesman in tow.

"Gregor Demarkian," he said, "this is Detective Borstoi. Len Borstoi, Gregor Demarkian."

Gregor held out his hand. He was thinking that his life was about to be a nightmare of competing police forces. He wondered who had handled the attempted murder in Merion.

"I've heard of you," Borstoi said.

Gregor made a noncommittal noise.

"I thought you only worked for police departments," Borstoi said.

"I do only work for police departments," Gregor said. "As a consultant, usually."

"Are you working for a police department now?"

"I'm not working for anybody." Gregor glanced toward the study. By now, most of the people going in and out were doing lab work, collecting fibers, taking pictures, sampling blood. "There's been an, ah, incident. Back in Philadelphia, where I live. Anyway, I was looking into that when Miss Dahl here asked me to look into the shooting in Merion last weekend. But I said I wasn't interested. And then —"

"What?" Borstoi said.

Gregor shrugged. "Curiosity, I guess. I thought I'd come out and talk to her. I investigated a murder in this house once. A long time ago."

Borstoi gave him a long stare. "Did you solve it?"

"I helped to solve it. John Jackman was the detective on that case at the time. John Jackman who's now the mayor of Philadelphia."

"Did he solve it?"

"I think both of us sort of contributed something," Gregor said.

"Look," Mortimer said. "The mayor —"

"He's not my mayor," Borstoi said, "and I don't understand what business he's got messing around in this. This is a reality show going on here?"

"Yes," Gregor said. "*America's Next Superstar.*"

"Oh, that one," Borstoi said. "My wife loves that one. I can't stand it. This girl was one of the contestants?"

"Definitely not," Olivia Dahl said, suddenly thrusting herself into the conversation. "She was pretty enough, but she was just too — it was almost as if she didn't have a personality."

Len Borstoi seemed to consider this. "If she's not a contestant," he said reasonably, "what's she doing here?"

Gregor took a deep breath and explained

248

the whole thing as far as it could be explained: the shooting in Merion during casting, the girl's arrest and subsequent release, presumably on bail.

"But I don't know that much about it," Gregor said, "because I really was not investigating it. I was just sort of wandering around poking into things because I was bored, and later I was doing it because I was frustrated. I only came out here because I thought I'd talk to Miss Dahl here and get my mind off other things."

"Nobody knows how she got here," Olivia said. "Nobody has the faintest idea. She didn't bring a car. There isn't an extra car parked anywhere that I saw, anyway. And besides, if she had a car, the police in Merion would have been able to figure out who she was. There would have been a registration, or a rental agreement. Instead, all we know is that she told one of our girls here that her name is Emily, and then — well, you'd have to talk to the Merion police about then."

"Which of the girls?" Borstoi said. "Which one did she talk to?"

"Janice Ledbedder," Olivia said.

"Is this Ledbedder girl here?"

"Of course she's here," Olivia said. "She's either in the living room or upstairs. Some of the girls went running up to their rooms after we found the body. They were upset. Do you want to talk to Janice Ledbedder?"

"Yes," Borstoi said.

Olivia looked at him, and then at Gregor, and then at David Mortimer. Then she turned around and headed for the living room.

Borstoi was staring at the floor. Gregor realized what it was that was bothering him. He wanted Len Borstoi to be doing something with his hands. You didn't smoke around crime scenes these days. Most police departments frowned on officers smoking on the job at all. Maybe Borstoi should have had a lollipop in his mouth, like Telly Savalas on that old television show.

"It wasn't a Greek name," Gregor said.

Len Borstoi gave him the kind of look police detectives like to give people they think are probably crazy.

"*Kojak,*" Gregor explained. "It was a television show that was probably before your time. The detective was supposed to be Greek, but Kojak isn't a Greek name. I wonder if they'd have made that kind of mistake these days."

"I don't think we really have to go into a jurisdictional war here," David Mortimer said. "Whether we like it or not, pieces of this thing seem to have happened in different townships. We can't just ignore the pieces just because they didn't all occur in one place. I'm sure the Mayor's Office would be glad to —"

"Why don't we just leave the Mayor's Office out of it?" Len Borstoi said. He looked toward the study. "Does anybody know what happened here? You came, Mr. Demarkian, and you discovered the body —"

"No, I didn't discover the body. It had already been discovered. I came in through the front door and there were people milling around. The door to the study was open and the body was inside."

"Were there any people inside?" Borstoi asked.

"No," Gregor said, "not when I first saw the room, but I'd be very surprised if there hadn't been some traffic in and out beforehand. It's natural, really, to go up to a body and see if it's really dead. There's always the chance that there's something you can do about it, some help you can give, or that if you called an ambulance you could revive them."

"But this body was dead," Borstoi said.

"As a doornail, as the saying goes," Gregor said. "I knew it as soon as I saw it. But I'm used to seeing dead bodies. These people aren't."

"And you don't know who she is?"

"No," Gregor said, "and the impression I get is that none of the people here do, either."

"But the Merion police will know," Len Borstoi said.

"You'd think," Gregor said. "I really mean it when I say that I haven't been investigating this. All I know I heard from Miss Dahl, the woman we were just talking to, and the last I heard, this girl wasn't talking. At all. To anybody. She was just sitting in jail and keeping her mouth shut. More than that must have happened or she wouldn't have been released, but I don't know about it. I don't think anybody here, including me, even knows her real name."

"She gave a false name?"

"I couldn't tell you. She did apparently tell this girl she talked to, Janice Ledbedder, that her name was Emily. Whether that was true or not, I have no idea. Whether Ms. Ledbedder is remembering correctly or not, I also have no idea. But there is one thing you ought to be aware of."

"What?"

"This is a reality show," Gregor said. "If you look up toward the ceiling, you'll see that there are cameras mounted practically everywhere. They film these girls twenty-four seven. They film everything they do."

"Really?" Borstoi said.

He looked up at the foyer ceiling and spotted two of the cameras. Then he went to the door of the study and looked around.

"There seems to be only one in there," he said, coming back. "But it is aimed at the door."

There was a sound on the stairs. They all turned to look. Olivia Dahl was leading a sobbing girl by the hand, practically tugging her to get her to come downstairs.

"It's not the end of the world, Janice," she was saying. "It's just Mr. Demarkian, and the Bryn Mawr police. You talked to the Merion police without going to pieces."

Two

1

Janice Ledbedder had never seen a dead body before today, and she was already sure she never wanted to see another one. She'd known it was a dead body, too, as soon as she'd set eyes on it. It didn't look at all like anything she'd seen in the movies or on television. It didn't even look like the pictures of the real dead bodies she had seen on shows like *Cold Case Files* and *City Confidential.* It was unmistakable even so. She had come running into the house, laughing a little because it was fun to try to outrace the rain. She had skidded a little in the foyer. Then she had started to take off her jacket, and when she'd done that she'd turned, and there it had been, right near the fireplace, where anybody could see it.

Now she came down the stairs, being led by Olivia Dahl. She could see a lot of men standing in the foyer, and to the left of the stairs, where the study was and the body was, there were people going in and out in with strange equipment and things on wheels.

One of the men standing in the foyer was somebody Janice had seen before — Gregor Demarkian, who was some kind of important detective, and who was sometimes interviewed on those true crime shows. She didn't know if she was pronouncing his name right in her head. She thought she could get away with not actually saying it as long as he was right here. The other girls were standing in the doorway to the living room — or most of them were. Janice looked around for Coraline and didn't see her.

Miss Dahl got out of her way at the bottom of the stairs. Janice walked up and looked at the two men. Miss Dahl nodded.

"This is Janice Ledbedder," she said. "Janice, this is Detective Borstoi. He's with the police. The taller one is Gregor Demarkian. He's —"

"He's a detective, too," Janice said quickly. "I've seen him on television."

"Maybe we could find somewhere to go," Miss Dahl said. "It's such a huge house. There must be an empty room you could use somewhere."

"I don't think it's necessary at the moment," the man called Borstoi said. "I'm just trying to get some kind of feel for what happened here. It's Miss Ledbedder?"

"Yes," Janice said. She would never correct a police officer to make him call her Ms., even though she knew she was supposed to. At least, Ivy had told her she was supposed to.

"You found the body," Detective Borstoi said.

"What?" Janice said.

"You found the body," Detective Borstoi said. He had that endlessly patient tone in his voice that people got when they thought Janice was being stupid. She wasn't being stupid, though. She wasn't being anything like stupid. He leaned in toward her a little. "You were the first person to see the body," he said.

"Oh," Janice said. "Well. I mean. I don't know."

"Maybe we should say that it was Miss Dahl's impression that you found the body," Gregor Demarkian said. "You were the first person into the house after you all got back from wherever it was you were —"

"It was a challenge," Janice said. "That's kind of like a minicontest. I mean, if you don't watch the show. We were supposed to leave the limousine and get photographed by paparazzi, and then we were supposed to have lunch at this place and then they'd see how we handled it. Andra won."

"Excuse me?" Detective Borstoi said.

"Andra won," Janice said again. "She won the challenge. She did the best. Anyway, that's where we were."

"And then you came back to the house," Detective Borstoi said encouragingly, "and you were the first one inside, and you found the body."

"I was the first one inside," Janice said. "But I don't know if I found the body. I mean, the body was already there. The girl. Emily. That's what she said her name was. I met her in line the first day, the day of the interviews. Casting."

"And she told you her name was Emily," Detective Borstoi said.

"Well, she did, but she could have been lying," Janice said. "And as for today, I was the first one through the door, but we were all pretty much together, and she was there next to the fireplace and already dead. But the house wasn't empty when we got home. There were people here. The people who clean and stuff and some of the crew. They were already here. And Coraline was already here, too, because she didn't go."

"Who's Coraline?" Detective Borstoi asked.

Janice heard Coraline's sniffling before she saw Coraline. Coraline must have been at the back of the pack in the living room. Now she came out into the foyer and looked at Mr. Borstoi and Mr. Demarkian. Her eyes and nose were red. She looked like she'd been crying for hours.

"I'm Coraline," she said. "Coraline Mays."

Janice didn't think she'd ever realized just how thick Coraline's accent was.

"You were in the house all day?" Detective Borstoi asked.

Coraline nodded. "I didn't go on the challenge. I was supposed to go, but when we all got downstairs and we were waiting for the limousine, Sheila came in and looked at us and she — she didn't like what I was wearing, so —"

"She ripped her T-shirt right off," Janice said. "Sheila Dunham ripped Coraline's T-shirt right off, I mean. It was really dramatic. And then she said Coraline couldn't go, and then the rest of us went."

"And you stayed," Detective Borstoi said.

Coraline nodded. "But I wasn't downstairs. I went up to my room to change, because my shirt was all ripped up and anybody, well, anybody could see . . . So.

And then when I got up there I just felt awful, so I laid down for a minute just to see if I could calm down, and I must have gone to sleep. The next thing I remember is somebody screaming her head off, and then I got up and ran downstairs."

"And that was you screaming?" Detective Borstoi said.

"It might have been," Janice said. "But everybody else got in just after I did. I mean, it wasn't like I was alone in the foyer for more than a second or two. They all came running in from outside. And I remember seeing the body and going to the study door and then I think I did scream, but I think somebody else screamed before I did, only I'm not sure —"

"And by the time I got all the way down the stairs, everybody was screaming," Coraline said. "And people were crowding into that room and crying and, I don't know. But I went to the door and looked in, and then somebody sort of bumped me from behind, and then I'm not sure. Some people went over to the . . . the body. They went and looked at it."

"I looked at it," Olivia Dahl said. "I had to. There was no way to know from the doorway if the girl was still alive. And somebody called nine-one-one."

Janice saw Detective Borstoi and Mr. Demarkian both look at the room together, and then at each other.

"I really didn't know who she was," Janice said. "I mean, I did talk to her that first day when we were waiting in line, but she didn't say much. She didn't say anything at all really, except for her name when I asked her. I sort of talk a lot when I'm nervous. But I'd never seen her before that time and I hadn't seen her since, you know, until this. She was just sort of there and then she wasn't there and then, you know, whatever."

"Did you by any chance see where she went after you and she parted, that first day in Merion?" Mr. Demarkian asked. "From what I've been able to understand, all the girls were waiting in line, and then they were let into the Milky Way Ballroom, and there was a sign-in desk, and you went there —"

"That's right," Janice said. "We went to the desk and gave our names and there were people with clipboards who told us where to go."

"Do you remember this Emily stopping at the desk?" Mr. Demarkian asked.

"I really don't," Janice said. "I don't remember anybody. Oh, except for Ivy. She's one of the girls who made it into the house. But everybody remembers Ivy because she's white-blond and she has a neon green streak in her hair, so it's hard not to notice. But I was so nervous, and I was trying so hard to go to the right place and not make a mistake, I really wasn't paying much attention."

"What about here, today?" Mr. Demarkian asked. "Was there anybody in the foyer when you came in?"

"Oh, no. Not that I noticed."

"Could you hear anybody moving around?"

Janice shook her head. "It all happened really fast. It really did. I came in, and I left the door open when I did because everybody was right behind me. So I could hear the rain, and I could hear the other girls, and I could hear one of the judges, Johnny Rell. I could hear him talking. I couldn't make out the words but I knew it was him. And then everybody else started coming in right behind me. So if there was something quiet going on someplace, you know, if somebody was dusting somewhere or something, I probably wouldn't have heard it."

Gregor Demarkian looked out over the sea of girls crowding in the doorway to the living room.

"What about the rest of you?" he asked. "Did any of you see or hear anything?"

There was silence.

"Did any of you touch the body in any way?" Detective Borstoi said.

Janice was sort of surprised to hear his voice. He had faded into the background when Mr. Demarkian was talking. Maybe that was why Mr. Demarkian was the great detective, and Janice hadn't heard of Detective Borstoi at all.

The girls in the doorway were all murmuring, but they were all murmuring "no." Janice tried to remember if that was right — surely, if somebody had touched the body, she would have seen it? Maybe not. She was still feeling a little sick, and she was finding it hard to remember anything.

"It's like my mind is all jumbled up," she said to Mr. Demarkian. "I'm not usually a scatterbrain, but I can't seem to remember when things happened or in what order. I just saw the body and — but I knew it was dead. I knew right away. I don't know why. I think somebody shot her. There were red holes in her chest."

"And you could see that from the door?" Detective Borstoi asked.

"I could see it in the mirror," Janice said, and suddenly it all started to make sense to her. "That's what happened. That's what I forgot. I got into the foyer and I looked into the study because the door was open. You know, not because there was anything for me to do, or anything like that, not that I was doing it deliberately. I just sort of did it because the door was open, and I was there. And then I saw the body near the fireplace and my head sort of jerked back, and then I saw the same thing in the mirror. There's a big mirror tilted over the fireplace and I could see the body in that, and there were big red holes in her chest."

Detectives Borstoi and Mr. Demarkian looked at each other. Then they both walked over to the study door and looked inside. Then they came back.

"Interesting," Mr. Demarkian said.

Janice thought the entire day had been entirely too interesting, but that was something else.

2

Grace Alsop had waited patiently, while all those people were in the house, to be pointed out and exposed. She'd expected Sheila Dunham, at least, to have told that Gregor Demarkian person who her father was, and what she was assumed to be doing in the house and on the set. Of course, Grace only had the vaguest idea of what it was Sheila thought she was doing. She'd told the entire truth when she'd said that she hadn't spoken to her father in years, but even if she had, what could she get for him by being a contestant here? It would be different if she were some kind of investigative journalist, or if she wanted to write a book about her experiences on a reality show. As it was, all she wanted was a diversion for a few weeks, and a chance to see if she'd be any good at it. She'd been at loose ends for a while. She had an excellent education. She was bright enough. She knew what she liked and what she didn't like. She just couldn't get herself to focus on any one thing for any period of time.

Maybe that was the real reason she had had so many fights with her father, and why she had stormed out of their apartment in New York the way she had. Maybe it had nothing to do with Fox News and the political causes it championed, or the Republican Party and the way it was behaving about . . . about . . . Grace couldn't remember what it was she had objected to. She knew it wouldn't be hard to find objections. She objected to most of what the Republican Party did, just because it was the Republican Party.

There was still yellow crime-scene tape across the door to the study. It was the first thing anybody saw when they were coming downstairs. There was a uniformed officer standing guard at the study door. That would only last for twenty-four hours, and only that long just in case the police wanted to come back and look things over again. Grace thought they'd looked things over well enough. There had been dozens of them, and so many test tubes, she'd thought she was in a remake of some old Roger Corman horror movie.

Dinner was due to begin at seven o'clock, as usual, in the big dining room. Most reality shows that put contestants together in a house left them to cook for themselves. This one provided breakfast, lunch, and dinner in the dining room, and served and cleared, as if they were all training to be Jacqueline Kennedy instead of Paris Hilton. At least, Grace assumed that what Sheila Dunham was looking for was somebody like Paris Hilton, or maybe Tara Reid — somebody who would make a big splash in the tabloids and be photographed drinking until she fell over or was caught in a hotel room with somebody else's husband.

Did anybody know what a superstar was anymore? Michael Jackson had died. The television stations went insane over it, sending camera crews to stake out the front of the house even though nothing was happening there, doing tribute show after tribute show. At least Jackson had had talent. You could see that in the way he danced in his old music videos. What about Anna Nicole Smith? All she'd ever done was to be very pretty and take her clothes off to prove it. Then she'd gained a lot of weight and lost it again.

Every bedroom in this house had its own bathroom. Grace was sitting in hers, looking at her face in the big mirror. It was absolutely the wrong house for this show. It was a house for the old-money rich. There were nice things here, but they were subtle things. There were none of the things the contestants on this show would think of as necessary to people who had a lot of money. There wasn't a single large-screen, wall-hanging TV. In fact, as far as Grace could tell, there was only one TV, and it was downstairs in a little room near the kitchen. Grace wouldn't be surprised if only the servants were expected to use it.

Her hair was a mess. Her makeup was smeared. She washed the makeup off and ran a brush through her hair. She didn't wear makeup most of the time. At college, nobody had. That was one of the great things about going to a women's college.

She leaned close to the mirror and checked out her eyes. She wasn't going to cry over Sheila Dunham.

She got up from the little vanity stool and went out into the bedroom. Her roommate Suzanne was sitting on one of the beds, and Ivy Demari and Mary-Louise Verdt were sitting on the other. They all looked up as Grace walked in.

"Mary-Louise is hiding out from Alida," Ivy said. "And since I couldn't blame her, I came in, too."

"Are you hiding from anybody?" Grace asked. She didn't actually like Ivy. Ivy made her nervous. Grace knew she was fifty IQ points to the good on most of these girls, but not on Ivy. And that made her feel worse than useless.

Ivy and Mary-Louise were on Suzanne's bed. Grace couldn't even ask them to get off. She went to her own bed and shooed Suzanne a little to the side. Then she sat down herself.

"I'm not running away from anybody," Ivy said. "Janice is in something of a state, but she's talking to Coraline. Come to think of it, Coraline is in something of a state, too."

"Well, I'd be in a state if I was Coraline," Suzanne said. "I'd be in one if I was Mary-

Louise, too. You hear all these things about the way Sheila Dunham behaves, but you don't really believe them until you see them yourself. Or she does them to you. You've got to wonder how much more of that stuff there's going to be before all this is over."

"There's going to be a lot of it," Grace said. "Don't you people understand? I keep saying it, but nobody listens. It's not real. She stages those things. It makes good television. They get hundreds and hundreds of clips, and then they use the ones that look the most dramatic."

"I wonder if they'll use any of the clips of the murder," Ivy said.

"Do you honestly think they have clips of the murder?" Grace said. "If they had those, they'd have given them to the police."

"They did," Ivy said. "At least, Olivia Dahl let the police take something out of the security camera in the study. I saw them. You know, this whole thing could be over in a day. Maybe the camera got a picture of it."

"The camera doesn't point that way, does it?" Grace asked. "I thought it was aimed at the door. It wouldn't see anything that happened in front of the fireplace, would it?"

"It might catch the reflection in the mirror," Ivy said. "And the mirror's funny anyway, didn't you notice?"

"Funny how?" Grace said.

Ivy shrugged. "It's tilted, I think. I didn't get much of a chance to really look at it. But it had to be tilted, because I could see the body in it when I was standing at the door, and the only way I could do that is if it was tilted a little ways down. That Gregor Demarkian noticed it, too. I saw him."

"I think Janice noticed it," Mary-Louise said. "I think she said something —"

Grace brushed it all aside. "Even if the mirror was tilted, I don't see what difference it would make. Maybe it just is that way. Things don't always hang straight. If you leave anything hanging on a wall for long, it's more likely than not to become messed up one way or the other."

"I think it's terrible to think of it," Mary-Louise said. "That girl. I wonder what she was doing out of jail. I thought they'd arrested her."

"They did arrest her," Grace said. "I saw it in the newspaper. They do bring the newspapers in here every day for a reason. You could look at them."

"Well, if they arrested her, I don't understand why she was out," Mary-Louise said. "And I don't understand why she was here. I mean, how did she even know where the house was? This house, I mean. It's not like it was a hotel, you know. It's a private house. Did the show put the address on the Internet or something?"

"I don't think they'd do that," Ivy said.

"Exactly," Mary-Louise said. "So what was she doing here? And how did she get here? And why is she dead, come to think of it. I mean, she shot at Sheila Dunham, that I understand, but today somebody must have shot at her, and none of us even know who she is."

"It's like a murder mystery," Suzanne said. "I hate murder mysteries. *Murder, She Wrote* and all that kind of thing. They're really boring."

Grace got off the bed. "Well, if there really was camera footage, then the police will look at that and know who was in the room. And that will be that. I don't really care who she was."

"I heard Olivia Dahl tell the police and Gregor Demarkian that she wasn't a contestant. A former contestant, I think I mean," Ivy said. "Anyway, nobody remembers her turning in an audition tape or anything like that."

"You mean she just came in out of the blue and decided she wanted to kill Sheila Dunham?" Mary-Louise said. "Maybe just from watching her on television? That's creepy."

"Things like that happen all the time," Grace said. "There are stalkers. Anytime anybody is even a little famous, there are always crazy people who follow them around. It can't be helped."

"Makes you wonder why you want to be famous," Mary-Louise said.

"I don't want to be famous," Grace said. She went to the closet. She had clothes there for dinner, but she didn't really feel in the mood for dressing up. She didn't see why she should have to, either. If you were a superstar, you could do what you wanted. She found a peasant-smocky gold dress with little cornflowers across one shoulder, and chose that.

"Isn't it a little odd to try out for this thing if you don't want to be famous?" Ivy said. "I mean, unless you go home the first week, just being in the house will get you a little famous. People do watch this show."

"I really have to get dressed," Grace said. "If the rest of you don't mind."

Ivy stood up and stretched her legs. "I'm as dressed as I'm going to get. It's been a long day."

Mary-Louise got up, too. "I just don't want to go back to my room and listen to

271

Alida talk about how awful we all are. All of us. And she really hates Andra, and Andra won the challenge. She's not going to be able to shut up."

"Come along to my room and I'll save you from Alida," Ivy said. "Janice won't mind. She likes company."

Grace stood with the dress in her hands and watched them go. Then she went over to the door and made sure it was shut.

Suzanne was still sitting on the bed, but this was Suzanne's room as well as hers. She couldn't make a fuss about that.

Grace laid out the dress and looked at it. This really would be enough for dinner tonight, and if Sheila Dunham didn't like it, she could do what she wanted. Grace wouldn't even mind being eliminated first, the way this was going.

What she did mind was the idea of that security camera in the study. She kept forgetting that there were cameras everywhere.

It really was not a good omen, though, that there had been a camera there, and that whatever was on it was now in the hands of the police.

THREE

1

Gregor Demarkian did not like to be involved in things he was not officially involved in — that was a convoluted way of putting it, but he knew what he meant. It was one thing to be paid by police departments to consult on difficult cases. He liked that, and even in his days at the Bureau, he had never been one of those men who liked to bemoan the depravity of all things human that he was forced to confront in his work. He knew very well that not all human beings were depraved, or anything close to it. Most of them were good enough for the lives they lived. They weren't great saints, like Augustine or Aquinas or Frances. They weren't great sinners, like Hitler or Stalin or even Jeffrey Dahmer. They were just people. In living every day, they made the small but necessary decisions that kept the whole enterprise going: get up and go to work, do your job, pay your bills, help your friends, contribute a little to charity, pick up your garbage when it drops on the ground.

David Mortimer had given Gregor a ride back into Philadelphia proper. He would have dropped Gregor at his own front door, but that wasn't what Gregor wanted. It was getting late, although not quite dark, not yet. Spring was well under way. Gregor had Mortimer drop him off on City Ave and started walking. He got onto the campus of St. Joseph's and walked some more. He liked city college campuses. He liked the fact that they did not look pristine and sealed off from real life.

He didn't want to go home, right this minute, that was all. And apparently he didn't want to go home because he was thinking of human beings. In his experience, plenty of human beings did more than the minimum to keep things going. They organized food drives for the holidays. They volunteered in food banks and homeless shelters, and at literacy schools that taught new immigrants how to speak English and pass the citizenship test.

Gregor always found it odd to realize how much work it took just to do the minimum, though. He found it odder to realize how little slacking off could land you and everybody else in a very bad place. He thought he was being obscure again, but he probably wasn't. If he had walked the other way on City Ave, he would have landed in the middle of a place where too many people did too little of the minimum.

If I keep this up, I'm going to go crazy, he told himself. He sat down on a bench and looked around. The college was in session. There were students everywhere, and too much traffic on the roads. The real problem was going home to face Bennis. The two of them did not talk often about the way they had met, or what it had led to. Every once in a while, Gregor would think that the whole past thing was about to blow up in his face. Then the crisis would come and go, and it would be as if it had never happened, at least as far as he could tell. It had been several years now since that long weekend when the murderer of Bennis's father had gone to the gas chamber. Bennis had barely talked to him about it at the time, and she hadn't said a word to him about it since.

The bench was cold. It was colder than the air around it. That was the trouble with spring. The days were warm enough. The evenings got cold, and now it was marching toward evening. It was raining, too, although not as badly as it had been a few hours ago. Gregor's jacket was soaked through, and he hadn't noticed it. So was his hair. This was very bad. He wasn't stupid enough to believe that a marriage had to be an absolute meeting of the minds, with no secrets withheld between both parties. He had his secrets, and he was sure Bennis had hers. That was what happened when two people married in late adulthood.

But there was something wrong with a situation that required him to get pneumonia on a college campus bench rather than go home and talk to his wife.

It would have been different if he'd had an affair. Or if she had.

What was he thinking about?

He got out his phone, found his speed dial list, and called the cab company. He promised to be out on City Ave in less than a minute and a half. It really was interesting, the numbers Bennis had thought to put on his speed dial list.

He got himself off the bench and went to the road. He looked at his watch. It was nearly six. This would be rush hour traffic on the road. It felt like it. The rain started to come down harder. Had he had an umbrella when he started this day? He couldn't remember.

The cab came, and pulled up to the curb, and stopped. Gregor got in and gave the driver his address. Cavanaugh Street was not an obscure part of the city. It was even featured in the newspapers every once in a while, with the Ararat getting restaurant reviews and the Ohanian's Middle Eastern Food Store being listed as a good place to get things like olive oil and grape leaves. These days, the street probably showed up on television as well, as the place where a woman had been found in a coma.

Gregor suddenly realized that he had no idea if there had been any publicity at all about what had happened in Sophie Mgrdchian's house. It made him feel even odder than he already did. It wasn't like him not to know that kind of thing.

The cab pulled up in front of the five-story brownstone where Gregor and Bennis had the second and third floors. Gregor paid the man and got out and looked around. The street was mostly deserted. The lights had come on in the church and in a couple of the storefronts, in spite of the fact that it wasn't totally dark. In another hour, the Ararat would start filling up.

Gregor climbed the stairs to the front door and let himself in. Old George Tekemanian had the door to the ground-floor apartment open and was sitting in it, playing with a gadget that seemed to be shooting little arrows of light every once in a while, to no purpose Gregor could see. Old George was in a wheelchair these days, but he was as sharp as always, and his nephew Martin had paid to put in a ramp so that he could go in and out. Martin had paid for the motorized wheelchair, too. Martin's wife Angela had stopped making noises about a nursing home.

Gregor went to where George was and looked at the gadget.

"What is it?" he asked.

"It's a light saber," old George said. "Martin's son Michael gave it to me for my birthday. It's a miniature light saber, that's what. I've got to remember to say miniature. I can fight the Empire with it."

"Empire?"

"*Tcha,* Krekor. In *Star Wars.* How can you not know about *Star Wars*? We had a *Star Wars* party over at Father Tibor's back around Christmas. He's got all the DVDs."

"So you're sitting in the doorway fighting the Empire?"

"No, Krekor. I'm sitting in the doorway waiting for Lida and Hannah to come get me. We've having dinner together at the

Ararat tonight, and I'm supposed to speak Armenian to the Very Old Ladies. I keep telling them that the Very Old Ladies aren't as old as I am, but they never listen. Lida and Hannah, I mean. They never did listen. Not even as children."

"No, they didn't," Gregor said.

"You ought to take an interest in things," old George said. "You ought to get a hobby. It's this running around thinking about criminals that makes you look the way you do."

Gregor let that one go, and made his way upstairs. Now that the apartments were knocked together, he could have gone in on the second floor, but he didn't want to. He went up to the third floor and let himself in there, into the foyer of what he thought of as his own apartment. This did not make any sense, and he knew it. They were married. There was a stairway between the two floors. It was their apartment.

On the other hand, the third floor had the areas they used — the kitchen they cooked in, the living room they watched television in. The second floor held mainly the spaces Bennis herself needed for privacy, like a room to write in.

Gregor took his jacket off as soon as he got through the door and hung it on the coatrack. It was an ordinary suit jacket, not some kind of outerwear, and it dripped. He looked at the little puddle of water forming underneath it and then left it there. Bennis could have a fit about what he was doing to the hardwood later.

He went into the living room and looked around. It had been tidied up. It had been tidied up entirely too well. Bennis didn't tidy. There was the sound of water running in the kitchen. He went through the room and through the swinging door into there. Bennis was standing at the sink, filling a coffeepot.

"So," she said, not turning around when he came in. "I've been watching television."

Gregor sat down at the kitchen table. One of the great advantages of his marriage was the fact that, with Bennis in the apartment, he no longer had to make coffee for himself. Bennis wouldn't let him make coffee for anybody.

"It was your idea I talk to the people from the reality show," he pointed out. "You knew they were renting Engine House."

"Yes, of course I knew it," Bennis said, getting the top back on the coffeemaker and plugging it in. She turned around to face him and leaned back against the sink. "I feel like a complete idiot, if you want to know the truth. It's been more than a decade since all that happened. If you'd asked me yesterday, I'd have told you I was over it. Or over the worst of it, if you know what I mean."

"People don't usually get over it," Gregor said. "I think it changes people, the first time they see a dead body. Any dead body. I think it's worse when the body is somebody they know, and worse yet when it's violently dead. You can't honestly expect to be 'over' the sight of your own father's dead body. Especially considering the shape it was in."

"I didn't like my father. And he had no use for me."

"He was still your father," Gregor said. "And it was still a shock."

"If you feel like this about every dead body you've seen," Bennis said, "then I don't know why you're not in an insane asylum."

"You get more used to it over time," Gregor said. "And the dead bodies I see are almost never of anybody close to me. We don't talk about all that, you know. I don't know if we should, but we don't. If you ever do want to talk about it —"

"No," Bennis said. "Really. I don't even talk to my brothers about it. Christopher called, by the way, when he heard the news.

And yes, it's already been on all the networks and the cable news stations. Or I think it has. It's Sheila Dunham, I suppose. She's a draw for the press."

"She's a piece of work," Gregor said. "Did your brother Bobby call? Or Teddy?"

"Nobody knows where Teddy is at the moment," Bennis said, "which is par for the course. And of course Bobby didn't call. This is Bobby we're talking about."

"It's just that there's something I need, and I don't want to ask you for it."

"What do you need?"

The coffee was going crazy. Gregor watched Bennis turn around and take a pair of mugs out of the cabinet next to the sink.

"I need to sit down with somebody who was there at the time — at Engine House when your father died — to help me go over what the scene looked like when we found the body."

"Ah," Bennis said.

"I really don't want to ask you to do that," Gregor said. "I'm not an idiot. I know that you won't be all right with it."

"But you are an idiot," Bennis said. She put the coffee mugs on the kitchen table. "You don't need to talk to anybody. You can do better than that. There are pictures."

"Well," Gregor said, "yes. But I'm not sure —"

"The *City Confidential* TV program," Bennis said. "There were pictures of the study, and my father's body, and that silly bust of Aristotle — anyway, I think they were still pictures and they were in black and white, but they were there. We watched that together. Don't you remember?"

"I remember that we shouldn't have watched it," Gregor said. "Or you shouldn't have."

"It doesn't matter now. Tibor's got the complete set of all those *City Confidential* and *American Justice* and *Snapped* things you've been in. All of them. On DVD. All you have to do is go over there and get him to play them for you. It'll be a lot better than talking to my brothers. Christopher won't remember much, and Bobby will embellish what he does know, and if you could find Teddy, he'd just lie."

2

Gregor Demarkian did not call ahead to make sure Father Tibor was at home. Father Tibor was always at home at this time of the evening, unless he was having dinner in the city, and if that had been the case, he would have mentioned it at breakfast.

Gregor walked up the street toward Holy Trinity Armenian Christian Church, crossed in the middle of the block, and then made his way down the alley and to the back where Tibor's apartment was. This was a new apartment, just as the church was a new church, both having been rebuilt only a few years ago. The alley had been spruced up, too, and decked out in security lights. The whole thing reminded Gregor of those little side streets in London where traffic was no longer allowed to go.

Gregor made his way into the courtyard and knocked on Tibor's front door. Overhead, the second-floor apartment that had been built in the hopes of finding Tibor a priest assistant for the church was still empty, dark and a little forlorn looking. It was not shabby, because the women on the street made a point of keeping it up, but it still looked wrong.

Tibor opened the door and stood back to let Gregor in. The little front foyer was full of books, stacked one on top of the other against the wall, just as the foyer in the old apartment had been. The books were cleaner now, because with the new apartment the women's auxiliary had insisted on hiring a housekeeper. This was not altogether a happy thing — it wasn't just the foyer that was full of books stacked against the walls — but this apartment was at least more comfortable for Gregor to sit in, and he was grateful for that.

"I take it Mrs. Flack wasn't in today," he said, waiting for Tibor to close up.

Tibor shrugged. "She was here this morning, but I've finished putting everything back. Why is it that she can't understand that Jacqueline Susann belongs with Aristotle and Augustine belongs with Stephen King?"

"I haven't the faintest idea," Gregor said.

Tibor led the way into the living room. It was a much larger living room than the one in the old apartment, but it already looked cramped. Gregor sat down in a big overstuffed armchair, then immediately stood up again. He felt around in the cushions and found *Last Exit to Utopia* by Jean-François Revel.

"Oh, thank you," Tibor said, taking the book. "I was looking everywhere for that. I must have left it on the chair. Mrs. Flack wouldn't put it there, would she?"

"It doesn't seem like her kind of thing."

"She must have missed it. Maybe I'm wearing her down. It's hard enough to keep track of the books in here when I don't have somebody moving them around, but with

Mrs. Flack." Tibor shrugged. "I spent forty-five minutes last weekend trying to find my copy of Irenaeus to use in the homily, and she'd put it on a bookshelf in the bedroom. In the bedroom. The church fathers do not belong in the bedroom."

Gregor was afraid to ask where they did belong. He didn't put it past Tibor to say the breadbox, or the refrigerator. He stretched out his legs and put his head back.

"Have you been watching the news today?" he asked.

Tibor sat down, too. "Yes, of course, Krekor. The murder in the house where Bennis grew up. But it isn't her family there now. She said that the other day. It's somebody her brother has rented to."

"A reality TV show," Gregor said. "Do you remember the first time we ever met?"

"Yes, of course, Krekor. How could I forget?"

"That was when Bennis was still living in Boston, before she bought the apartment on the street. And she bought it because we were all here, because she'd met us when —"

"Yes, Krekor, I know. When her father was murdered in that house and when you solved the case."

"That's when we all met John Jackman,

too. It's odd the things you forget."

"I haven't forgotten any of it," Tibor said. "But then, you know how it is. I have less on my mind than you do."

Gregor sat forward. "Yes, well," he said, "here's the thing. I went to that house today on a whim. I was talking to the people dealing with Sophie Mgrdchian, and this woman, Karen we know now her name to be . . . or she says it is. Never mind. I get tangled. But that was it. I was feeling tangled and frustrated, so I got in a cab and paid the price of a trip on the space shuttle to get out to Bryn Mawr, and when I got there there was a body — there was a body right where the other body was."

"What?"

"It was right where the other body was. I told Bennis it was in the study, and it was, but it was more than that. It was laid out in front of the hearth just like old Robert Hannaford's body was when I first saw it."

"And it was the same?" Tibor said. "This girl, she had her head —"

"No," Gregor said. "No head bashed in, no bust of Aristotle to do it with. There were three visible bullet holes in her chest. Which isn't official, by the way. I haven't been hired by anybody at the moment. I don't have access to official information. It looked like three bullet holes from what I could see. But the whole thing was wrong. It was just wrong. And I can't quite put my finger on why."

"Do you usually put your finger on things that quickly?" Tibor said. "Of course there is something wrong that you should have noticed, Krekor. That's how a detective works. You told me that. Agatha Christie told me that."

"Bennis says you have DVDs of the episodes I've been on for things like *City Confidential.*"

"Yes, Krekor, of course. I have all of them. Do you want to see them?"

"I want to see the *City Confidential* episode about the murder at Engine House. How do DVDs work? Can you pause them the way you could the VHS tapes, so they stay still on one frame and you can look at it?"

"Of course, Krekor. You want to see just one frame?"

"I want to see the picture the police took of Robert Hannaford's body on that floor. There is a picture like that. I remember it."

"All right, Krekor. You will give me a minute and I will find it. In the meantime, you will tell me what is going on with Sophie Mgrdchian."

"Nothing much is going on with Sophie

Mgrdchian," Gregor said. "I talked to her doctor. She gave me a list of the medications Mrs. Mgrdchian was taking. They didn't amount to much. A lot of vitamins. Some painkillers for the rheumatoid arthritis. One of those medications to help with high blood pressure. The police even had the stuff analyzed. There was nothing in it that could cause a semicoma, or whatever is wrong with her. And the two women have been separated for days. Lily — Karen — whoever it is, can't be feeding Sophie Mgrdchian some kind of voodoo poison when she doesn't have any access."

"Voodoo?" Tibor said.

"Something Dr. Halevy said," Gregor said. "That Sophie Mgrdchian's condition is practically like voodoo."

"So what will happen to, what shall I call her, Krekor? Mrs. Mgrdchian? If she is Marco Mgrdchian's wife —"

"Widow," Gregor said. "At least, as far as I could tell before her lawyer got me out of there. At the moment, nothing is happening to her. She was bound over for a four-day psych evaluation, so she'll be in the hospital for a four-day psych evaluation. After that, it's anybody's guess. I can't see that they're going to be able to hold her. There isn't actually any evidence that she did anything

289

to Sophie Mgrdchian. If she really is the sister-in-law, there's no reason not to think that it's probable she was invited in. Then the two of them had some kind of physical breakdowns, or something, coincidentally at the same time —"

"Tcha," Tibor said. "Everybody in this country always assumes that when someone is old, it only makes sense that they have physical breakdowns. Look at the Very Old Ladies. They could probably walk to Washington, D.C., from here if they had a good reason to. Being old does not necessarily mean that you are falling apart."

"For most of us, it does," Gregor said.

Tibor had been paging through a big black carrying case for DVDs. There were hundreds of them all placed in clear plastic pockets, one after the other, page after page. Now he had stopped on a particular page and was tapping through the possibilities.

"This one, I think," he said, taking a DVD out of one of the pockets. "I should label these more clearly, but most of them have all the information you need on the disk itself, so there doesn't seem to be a point. Have you met this woman, this Sheila Dunham that everybody talks about? Is she as awful as they say?"

"She's very rude," Gregor said. "But I

wasn't all that impressed. I've met rude people before."

Tibor put the DVD in the DVD player, fiddled with his television set, got a blue screen, then got the DVD to play. It was a really magnificent television set, and a really magnificent set of equipment to go with it. When the parish had replaced Tibor's apartment, they had defined the word "replaced" the way most people would define "upgraded."

Tibor had the DVD started. He held up a remote and stopped the action. "Here is what we can do," he said. "We can go through the scenes as if they were still pictures, and you can tell me the one you want me to stop on to look at. Will that work?"

"I think so," Gregor said.

Tibor sat on the couch, aimed the remote at the set, and started clicking. It was like watching somebody turn the pages of a photo album. There were pictures of Bryn Mawr, the self-consciously "quaint" downtown, and the wide roads winding through the estate areas. There were pictures of Gregor himself, and of various members of the Hannaford family. It took a while to make it through to what he wanted to see. Then, there it was, on the screen.

"Wait," Gregor said. "Go back to the last one."

Tibor obligingly clicked again, and the screen was filled with a black-and-white photograph of the last murder scene in Engine House, a picture of Robert Hannaford's dead body lying across the hearth.

Gregor wasn't looking at the body. He'd seen the body up close and personal when it had been lying on that hearth for real. Instead, he looked up the photograph at the big mirror over the fireplace. He sat forward. Then he sat back. Then he sat forward again.

"I knew it," he said.

"Knew what?" Tibor asked.

Gregor's phone began to beep in the way it did when he got a text message. He pulled it out of his pocket without looking at it.

"I knew you couldn't see the body in the mirror," he told Tibor. "Today, you could see the body in the mirror. I saw the body in the mirror. But when Robert Hannaford's body was in the same place, all you could see was stuff on the opposite wall of the room."

"This is important?" Tibor asked.

"I don't know," Gregor said, looking down at his phone and clicking the little button that would allow him to read the text message.

He expected it to be from Bennis, wanting to know what they were going to do about dinner, but it wasn't.

MEET ME 745 AM DEXMALI CITY AVE, the message said. *IT'S ABOUT THE GUN. DAVID.*

Gregor tapped his fingers on the arm of his chair. He hated text messages. David Mortimer should have called.

FOUR

1

Olivia Dahl was not afraid of Sheila Dunham's rages, even when they were public rages. She'd been with this circus long enough to realize that the rages were always at least half calculated. Even when they seemed to be both spontaneous and off the wall, there was some part of Sheila's brain working in the background there, little hamster elements among the synapses making the world go round. The image was so compelling, Olivia was having a hard time getting it out of her head — Sheila's skull full of hamsters, all furiously pumping on wheels.

At the moment, Olivia was mostly worried about getting the legal pads placed on the table in front of the chairs where Sheila expected the other judges to sit. It was a ridiculous gesture. The judges were not corporate heavyweights or government heads of departments about to attend a meeting that would change the lives of thousands of people forever. They were just a small collection of D-list celebrities whose careers were long over, trying to look both important and unintimidating for a television audience that didn't care about them in the least.

Olivia knew the numbers that were important to this show. She knew them even better than Sheila did, and Sheila was surprisingly coherent on the subject of numbers. What the viewers of this show wanted to see was the eliminations, which girl would go home this week, who would be caught on camera crying or fuming as they dragged their bags into the night.

Olivia had not been in favor of renting Engine House for this show. It was a wonderful place; she understood why rich and reticent people had lived here. But that was the thing, wasn't it? The people who had lived here were the kind of rich people who had no interest in being famous. That was why they'd tucked themselves out in the country where almost nobody was likely to drive by.

All the pads were on the table. Next to each pad were two ballpoint pens and a water glass. Three carafes of iced water were standing on trivets in the middle of everything. The tablecloth was gone. This was not a conference room. It was the Engine House formal dining room. Dinner parties had been held here, and in the distant past there had been dinner parties with a hundred people at them. Olivia thought that would have been something to see.

Sheila was standing near the baize door to the kitchen, leaning against the wall just next to a portrait of a woman in a gauzy long dress. She was not having a fit or a meltdown. She was just standing there.

"I don't like this picture," she said. "Do you? It looks like she's wearing a prom dress instead of a ball gown. I hate prom dresses."

"I think it was the style of the time," Olivia said.

"I hated the prom, come to think of it," Sheila said. "But then, nobody asked me. I had to ask a boy I knew from drama club, and you know how that kind of thing works out. He's some kind of enormously important gay rights activist in San Diego now. Did you go to your prom?"

"We've been through this," Olivia said. "I went to my prom with a boy I'd dated since the seventh grade. He went off to college. I went off to secretarial school. That was the end of that, and there isn't anything interesting about my life since. How could there have been? I've been working for you for nearly twenty years."

Sheila pushed off from the wall and pulled out the chair she was supposed to sit in for the meeting. It was at the head of the table. It couldn't have been anywhere else. She sat down.

"It's a long time, twenty years," she said. "Don't you ever want to get up and go someplace else? Take another job? Take a vacation?"

"I took a vacation once," Olivia said. "You had a nervous breakdown in O'Hare Airport and I had to come back."

"You didn't like coming back."

"I don't like a lot of the things you do," Olivia said. "We got all that straightened out a long time ago, too. We don't have to like each other to work together. I like this job. I like the perks it brings. You wouldn't know how to break anybody else in. We go on with it. I should get the judging panel. If we wait much longer, Deedee's going to be too drunk to stand up. She's not doing all that well even now."

"Do you know who that girl was, the one that died in the study today?"

Olivia was looking down the table again, counting the pads and water glasses. "No," she said finally. "I don't. I didn't know who she was back at the Milky Way Ballroom. It doesn't matter who she was."

"It must matter to somebody," Sheila said. "She must have family, or friends, or people she worked with. She wasn't a hooker, or a bum. You could see that by looking at her."

"Maybe she was mentally ill," Olivia said. "A lot of people walk around mentally ill without being diagnosed until they finally do something too odd to ignore. Maybe this was *her* too-odd thing."

"She also didn't kill herself," Sheila said.

"Didn't she?" Olivia said. "Did the police tell you that?"

"The police didn't tell me anything," Sheila said. She was sitting aslant in the chair, stretching out her legs under the table. "They didn't tell anybody anything. Your Mr. Demarkian didn't, either. But I did overhear things."

"She must have killed herself," Olivia said. "Why else would she be dead? None of us knew her. Why would any of us want to kill her?"

Sheila picked up the ballpoint pen and twirled it through her fingers. "I thought you were going to get that Mr. Demarkian to look into all this for us."

"I'm trying, Sheila. He doesn't usually

work for private individuals. He works for police departments as a consultant. He does take private cases sometimes, if he's interested in them. So I've got my fingers crossed, and I'm going to get in touch with him tomorrow."

"Good," Sheila said. "Because I think he's the only person who might actually get this through your thick skull. And your skull is thick, Olivia. You're an excellent assistant, but your mind works at the speed of molasses."

"Is that supposed to mean something? Or are you just insulting me for the hell of it?"

Sheila sat forward. "That's supposed to mean that I do know what you're trying to do, and you aren't going to get away with it. That wasn't Mallory on that study floor. Believe it or not, I haven't been completely cut off from Mallory all these years."

"Haven't you? And I didn't think it was Mallory."

"No, I don't think you did," Sheila agreed. "But I think you expected me to think so. Or maybe you just expected me to suspect. But I saw Mallory only last year. I know where she is. I know what she's doing. I know what she looks like."

"I thought the two of you didn't speak."

"We don't," Sheila said. "You don't have

to speak to someone to see them. What I want to know is who that girl is, because no matter what you say, I think you do know. I think you have to know."

"Don't be ridiculous," Olivia said.

Suddenly, she was having one of her rare fits of anger. It wasn't very useful, getting angry at Sheila Dunham. It didn't make a dent, and Sheila was too good at using it against you. Still, this made Olivia furious, and it was all she could do to stop herself from taking one of those pitchers of ice water and pouring it over Sheila's head. Wouldn't that be something for the camera footage? There were a good six cameras in this dining room. They'd catch the whole thing, and there would be YouTube videos for a month.

Olivia looked down at her clipboard. Counted nothing in particular, just to give herself a chance to calm down, and then said:

"Why don't you sit still for a minute and I'll get the others."

It was not a question. Olivia did not expect an answer. She went to the door on the other side of the room, the one that led to the living room, and opened it. They were all out there in a little cluster, milling around and eating little finger things that

Olivia had had put out on a tray. That was whistling in the dark. She'd hoped that if there was enough food, Deedee's trips to her pocket flask would have less effect than usual.

It hadn't worked. Deedee Plant rarely ate anything, because she thought that would keep her from getting fat. She was a middle-aged woman, though, and she looked it, thick around the middle even without having gained any significant weight. She didn't have the money for personal trainers and liposuction. Either that, or she spent all the money on the pocket flask.

Olivia looked up and across the living room and saw the yellow crime-scene tape still up across the study door. There was a uniformed policeman sitting on a chair just outside it. She had no idea how long that was going to stay up or when they would be able to get back to their lives. She did know that none of it would interrupt the filming. They had no time to allow themselves to be interrupted.

Olivia stood back and held the door open. "Come right in," she said. "Sorry to call on you all in the evening like this, but we have some things to discuss. I've got water waiting if anybody wants it."

"It's a terrible thing," Deedee Plant was

saying to Johnny Rell. "Somebody dead and right here. Right on the set of the show. And it's funny, too, isn't it? I'd have thought that if there was a dead body on *America's Next Superstar,* it would have been Sheila."

"Everybody wants Sheila dead," Johnny said. "That's why she's going to live forever."

Down at the far side of the dining room, Sheila was still sitting in her chair. She was leaning back in it and stretching out her legs. And she had gone back to twirling the pen through her fingers. Olivia did not like the look on her face, or the way her body moved.

Something was coming. Olivia knew it. She always did.

2

It was Ivy Demari's idea to listen in on the meeting, and some of the other girls were not happy with the idea.

"Of course I want to know what's going on," Grace said, "but I'm already in trouble. This will get all of us in trouble if we get caught. And you know what she's like. You must know what she's like."

"Everybody knows what she's like," Alida said. "I don't see any reason for putting ourselves in jeopardy for nothing that concerns any of us. We didn't know this girl. She wasn't even cast in the show. She was just some crazy person looking for public-ity."

Ivy looked out at the group of them, spread out in the hall outside their bedroom doors. There were still fourteen of them, and would be for another week. They should have been spending the evening doing individual camera interviews to be used in the show to break up the action. None of them looked like they were competing on a reality show that required them to be glam-orous. None of them looked entirely dressed.

Ivy tried to think of a way to put it. "Here's the thing," she said. "It's not just that that girl died here, it's who killed her. Because somebody must have killed her."

"Don't be ridiculous," Alida said. "She committed suicide. I heard Miss Dahl say so."

"Olivia Dahl may have said so," Ivy said, "but it isn't true, and if you think about it, you'd know it isn't true. I looked into that room. I could see the body and I could see it again in the mirror. She had three holes in her chest."

"So?" Alida said.

"So," Grace said, "people who commit suicide don't usually shoot themselves in the chest?"

"Well, usually is usually," Alida said. "That doesn't meant it couldn't happen."

"It couldn't happen three times." Ivy was trying, trying very hard, to be patient. She was not Grace, or Alida. She didn't look down on these girls because so many of them seemed never to have gotten a good education, even on the elementary level, or because they were from places that weren't very sophisticated. Still, she thought, you'd expect they'd be able to think their way out of a paper bag.

"Look," she said. "If this girl had managed to shoot herself even once in the chest, the pain would have been excruciating. She'd almost certainly have dropped the gun. She wouldn't have been able to shoot herself two more times. And then there's the issue of the gun, too. If she shot herself, the gun would be there, in the room, wouldn't it? Did you see any gun?"

Nobody said anything. Grace and Alida looked angry. They always looked angry. The rest of the girls looked miserable.

"The gun wasn't there in the study," Ivy said. "I stayed as close to that Mr. Demarkian as I could, and I heard him talking with one of the police officers. The gun wasn't there where the body was, so somebody must have taken it away. Somebody murdered this girl, whoever she was. Somebody murdered her while we were all out."

"But it wasn't me," Coraline said suddenly. Then she burst into tears. "It wasn't me. It really wasn't."

"I didn't say it was you," Ivy said.

"I know you didn't," Coraline said. "Nobody says it, but they've all got to be thinking about it. The police and everybody. I mean, I was here. I was in the house the whole time. I didn't go to the restaurant."

"You were here," Alida said.

"But I've got no reason to want to kill anybody," Coraline said. "I didn't even know that girl. I wasn't even one of the people who talked to her at casting. And I thought she was in jail, anyway. We all thought she was in jail."

Ivy closed her eyes and counted to ten. She opened her eyes again. This was really very simple, and they were all wasting time.

"You were here but you were upstairs," Ivy said. "You didn't hear anything because — well, because you can't really hear anything in this house. It's huge, and the walls are all six inches of plaster instead of drywall or whatever it is that modern houses use. And we don't know about the gun, you know. It might have had a silencer. That would explain why none of the staff heard anything —"

"None of the staff heard anything because they were all out back smoking cigarettes." Alida made a face. "I've seen them. They all go out in the back courtyard near the garages and smoke. Anytime anybody is not looking."

"I guess," Ivy said, "but it still comes back to what I said. She was here, and somebody murdered her here. Either she found out that we were here and came on her own, or somebody told her where we were and asked her to come. We can't just ignore the fact that somebody murdered her. And that means it's really important for us to know what's going on down there at that meeting."

"Why?" Grace demanded.

"Maybe they're going to cancel the season," Mary-Louise said. "Do you think they would do that? There's been a death. That's a big thing. Maybe they just won't want to go on with it."

"They'll go on with it," Ivy said. "It's expensive to do something like this. If they don't do the season, they don't make the money they're expecting to make, and they'll still have to pay all these bills. I'm not worried about them canceling the season. I'm worried about what they're going to do about the murder — oh, I don't know. Security measures, maybe? More background checks for the bunch of us? Guards?"

"Do you have something to worry about from a background check?" Alida asked.

"No," Ivy said. "I don't. But there's another consideration that none of you seems to have thought of. She was murdered here. Maybe there's somebody here right now —"

"It doesn't have to be somebody here right now," Coraline said frantically, bursting into tears again. "It could be somebody from the outside. It could. Somebody could have come in and done it, somebody who has nothing to do with the house and nothing to do with the show. Maybe somebody just snuck in here and —"

"Oh, for God's sake, make sense," Grace said. "You're such an idiot. Really. Of course it has to have something to do with the show. It's always about the show. It's at casting. Now it's here. Why would that girl have been at casting and here if it hadn't anything to do with the show?"

"Maybe somebody is just using us," Janice

Ledbedder said. Ivy felt sorry for her. She was so obviously working hard to say calm, and to sound reasonable. "Maybe somebody who knew the show was going to be filmed out here, maybe they convinced this girl to come, and then they called her out here. I know, they could have said they were somebody from the show, and told this girl that there was a place —"

"And then what?" Grace demanded. "Then this girl got to casting and decided to shoot Sheila Dunham because there wasn't a place? Where did she get the gun? She had a gun at casting, in case you don't remember."

"Maybe," Mary-Louise Verdt said, "maybe she *was* somebody who didn't get called in for an interview, and she was upset about it. That would work, wouldn't it?"

"It would work for the shooting at casting," Ivy said, "but it doesn't make so much sense with her getting murdered here. If she was a girl who sent in a tape and didn't get asked in for an interview, I could see her coming in and shooting Sheila Dunham because she was angry about it. I can even see her coming out here to try it again once she got released from jail. What I can't see is somebody shooting her once she got here."

"Maybe it was self-defense," Janice Led-bedder said. "Maybe she came out here, with a different gun, I guess, because I don't think the police would have given back the gun, would they? Anyway, maybe she came out here and somebody found her in the library and she tried to shoot them and —"

"And now we've got two guns," Ivy said.

"I'm sorry," Janice said.

"The thing is, it just seems so sensible, doesn't it?" Ivy said. "A lot of people want Sheila Dunham dead. She's such a terrible woman."

"True," Grace said.

"Look," Ivy said. "At the very least, they're likely to discuss what they know about what the police are doing at that meeting. All we have to do is to go to the end of this hall and use the attic access. I've already scouted it out. You go up, then you go over to the left a little, and then the ceiling is lower and you sort of have to go down, and you end up in this little space right above the kitchen, which is right next to the dining room. And there's a vent."

"You don't even know if you can really hear anything from there," Alida said.

"There are a lot of vents," Ivy plowed on. "If we all go, we can team up and listen at all the vents, and some of us can go a little farther in the access space. It could even be me. I wouldn't mind crawling. Then we'd be right there, and we'd be able to hear at least something. And that would give us some idea of what's going on around here."

"Well, I'm not going to do it." Alida said. "The rest of you can all jeopardize your chances of winning this competition if you want to, but I've never been that stupid."

"She can't throw us all off the show at once," Ivy said. "If we all go together, we'll be pretty safe."

"We'll be nothing of the kind," Alida said. "You know what she's like. We'll all get in trouble at once, and then she'll pick one of us to unload on. Well, it's not going to be me. I don't care what the police are thinking."

Alida stood up, and turned her back to them, and marched back to her room. She did not slam the door, but she closed it with such a determined *click* that she might as well have.

Mary-Louise, who was Alida's roommate, blushed. "Sorry," she said. "She's always like that, really. She's always angry all the time."

Ivy looked from one girl to the other in the hall. There were still so many of them. The schedule called for two weeks of filming before the first elimination, in order for the crew to get in enough individual interview time and challenge time to give themselves some backup in case one of the later weeks got a little thin. Over time, some of these girls would become more sophisticated. Some of them just needed a chance to get away from home, to be on their own at last. Ivy wondered if she should tell them the other thing that had occurred to her, and decided that, no, that wouldn't be helpful.

But it was always a possibility. There was a girl dead. They didn't know who she was or where she came from, but that wasn't really comforting. Ivy knew that if they didn't know those things, they also didn't know why she was dead. And if they didn't know why she was dead, they didn't know why somebody wanted to kill her. And that meant, of course, that they didn't know that there wasn't somebody out there who still wanted to kill one of them.

Ivy stood up.

"Come on," she said. "We can at least find out something about something. It'll make us all feel better."

"Until Alida turns us in," one of the girls in the crowd said.

Then somebody giggled, and somebody

else started to cry.

Ivy thought her head was about to explode.

3

Andra Gayle did not think her head was about to explode, but she was cold all over, and feeling sick, and nothing she did could make it go away. She was not like these other girls. She had seen dead bodies before. In the neighborhoods were she had grown up — and there had been so many neighborhoods, she found it hard to keep them straight in her mind — dead bodies were a fact of life. Dealers got into turf wars, or just got tired of some guy stiffing them for the money they were owed. Users got frantic because they had no money to buy dope. There were always old people around. Old people were easy to hit when you wanted to pick up a little cash. The Korean grocery stores were less easy to hit, but they had more money.

The rest of the girls were making their way to the attic access place on the landing, and for the moment, Andra was following them. She was not as interested as they were in knowing what the police were doing. She did not trust the police. She did not trust that other detective, the one who wasn't the police, which was something she just couldn't figure out. These girls did not understand how things like this worked. It wasn't hard to get a gun. It wasn't hard to get a dozen guns. If you had the money, you could pick up anything you wanted on any street corner in the Bronx on any day of the week. Even if you didn't have much, you could get something, although it was usually something foreign that wasn't made very well and jammed.

Once, when Andra was six years old, she had gone with her mother to a neighborhood where all the houses had been abandoned. She hadn't understood that at the time. She had only known that the houses all looked empty. They had gone up to one of the empty houses and gone inside, and her mother had talked to a man for a long time. Then her mother had grabbed her by the wrist and pushed her in the man's direction, and then —

But there was no "and then." Andra remembered what had happened. She remembered exactly, and she remembered that that was the split second when she knew she was going to do something else with her life, that she was going to get up and get out some day. She did not think about the "and then" unless she had to, to keep herself motivated.

What she was thinking about now was what had happened after the "and then." The man had pulled her dress back down over her body and then pushed and shoved her until they got to the front door. Then he'd opened the door and had almost thrown her down the steps to the street. Andra's mother was there, sitting on the bottom step of the stoop, so high she couldn't keep her head up.

"Fuck it," she'd said, looking at Andra up and down. "Nobody killed you. You're all right."

Then there was the sound of a car in the street, and Andra looked up just as something rackety and loud pulled up to the curb. It was full of people, and the radio was on so loud it hurt her ears.

Then one of the doors popped open, and there was a noise, and suddenly there was something right there on the sidewalk in front of her — a dead body, a huge dead body, a man who had to be a million feet long, with his throat cut and the blood pouring out of him.

Andra's mother had looked up, and blinked, and said, "Fuck it."

FIVE

1

There was a message from Dr. Halevy on Gregor's voice mail when he got up the next morning, and it was just the kind of message that was likely to put him in a bad mood for the rest of the day.

"I'm very sorry I couldn't take your call when it came in," she said. "I was hoping you could answer the same question. We don't know who Sophie Mgrdchian's regular doctor was. The police couldn't find any information that would help us. We know what medications she is taking regularly because she had one of those plastic pill organizers on her when she came in. As I said before, it wasn't much. Arthritis, high blood pressure — she's in pretty good shape for a woman her age, or she was, or we think she was. If someone you know has information on her doctor, though, we'd appreciate it."

Gregor sat on the arm of the couch and looked at his cell phone. Nothing was likely to put him in a good mood today. He went back into the bedroom and shook Bennis awake.

"Wake up," he said. "Listen to me for a minute."

Bennis sat up in bed. She was one of those women who looked good woken out of a sound sleep. Gregor wondered what the evolutionary adaptability of that was. Then again, he didn't.

Bennis turned on the light and looked at the clock. "Are you all right? Are you not feeling well? Should I call nine-one-one?"

"I want to know if you know how to get into Sophie Mgrdchian's house."

"What?"

"Well," Gregor said reasonably, "there must be a way. I've lived on this street long enough to know that none of you has the sense God gave a squirrel when it comes to security. It's not like you hire outside experts to make sure your places are impenetrable. There must be a way to get into that house."

"It's four o'clock in the morning."

"I have an early meeting downtown."

"But why do you want to get into the house?" Bennis asked. "I mean, what's the point? That woman isn't back yet, is she?"

"No, and I don't know if she's coming back. I don't know what's going to happen to her once they let her out of the hospital. I had a voice mail overnight from Dr. Halevy."

"Who is —"

"The doctor who's treating Sophie Mgrdchian at the moment," Gregor said. "I called her to ask if she knew the name of Mrs. Mgrdchian's doctor. She didn't. Mrs. Mgrdchian had a pill organizer on her when she was brought in. That's how the hospital knows what medication she's taking. Other than that, they don't have a clue. Apparently, the Very Old Ladies don't, either."

"Oh," Bennis said. "I remember that. When the paramedics were here. They asked around, but nobody knew who Mrs. Mgrdchian's regular doctor was."

"It's absurd," Gregor said. "You'd think the whole pack of them would have some Armenian guy they'd been going to forever. That's how they do things most of the time. Dr. Halevy said the police couldn't find any information that would help, which means they must have looked. But there has to be something. There has to be an address book. There has to be a refrigerator magnet. Or a cell phone."

"You think Sophie Mgrdchian had a cell phone?"

"Why not?" Gregor said. "I have a cell phone. Old George Tekemanian has a cell phone."

"You have one because I gave it to you, and old George has one because his nephew gave it to him. As far as we know, Sophie Mgrdchian didn't have any family in the area."

"She has that niece."

"Who isn't in the area," Bennis said, "and if she was, she'd have come forward by now, wouldn't she? And if there's a reason why she wouldn't — oh, never mind, Gregor, I'm getting confused. Aren't we going to get into trouble going into the house by ourselves at four o'clock in the morning?"

"I don't see who we could get into trouble with. It's not a crime scene. There's no family in the vicinity. Sophie Mgrdchian is in the hospital and needs our help, so if she wakes up and decides she's mad at us for looking through her house, I'd say we have a defense. Do you know how to get into that house?"

Bennis sighed. "We could climb through a window," she said. "I'm surprised somebody hasn't done that already. Really, Gregor, if you could just wait until *daylight*."

But Gregor didn't want to wait until daylight. He was the closest he'd ever been to being completely fed up.

2

It was surprisingly cold in the dark. Gregor found himself thinking that he had never understood weather. He should have put on a jacket other than his suit jacket. He should have dressed in something other than a suit. Bennis sometimes said that the only clothes he owned were suits, and that he sat on the sand in Jamaica in wingtips and a tie.

Gregor thought about his honeymoon, which had been very good, really, with the house borrowed from friends and the privacy and the utter lack of feeling like he wanted to kill somebody. It was the kind of thing that would make a sane man want to retire, but sane men didn't retire because work was bothering them. Sane men retired because work was boring them. He was not bored. He was just exasperated.

"There's a reason," he said, as they chugged down the street, past the dark church, past Lida Arkmanian's town house, past the closed-up Ararat. "There's a reason I work as a consultant to police departments. It's one thing when the police ask for your help. And even then, there are going to be a lot of people who aren't happy with you. But when the police haven't asked for my help, everybody is mad at you, it's virtually impossible to get information in any coherent, cohesive, or complete way, and —"

"But I thought the police *did* want your help," Bennis said. "I mean, they've certainly been asking for it. And it's not even as if we know there was a crime here. You're the one who said it was just as likely that there was a perfectly innocent explanation for everything and it would all turn out to have been just . . . um . . . I think you said 'unfortunate.' "

"I know what I said," Gregor said. "I've changed my mind. And it wasn't those police I was thinking of anyway."

They had reached Sophie Mgrdchian's house. It was close to the very end of the neighborhood. In the block just past it, Cavanaugh Street became a different kind of place — emptier, dirtier, less comforting. Gregor looked up at the tall facade, at the stone steps leading up to the front door. The place looked haunted.

"I remember this building from when I was growing up," he said. "Three families lived here, but that was the good news. That was far fewer than in most of the others.

There was a boy here named Mikail. He was my brother's age. He died in Korea the same week my brother did. I can remember the funerals."

"She lives here all by herself now, doesn't she?" Bennis asked.

Gregor nodded. "I don't know when that happened. I don't know when most of the transformation of the street happened. I wasn't living here then. I suppose a spare key under the doormat isn't likely."

"There isn't a doormat," Bennis said. "What police were you talking about, if you weren't talking about these?"

"The Bryn Mawr police," Gregor said, climbing the steps to the front door very carefully. There was no light on over the door, of course. It was still too early in the year for there to be dawn before six. "Maybe the Merion police, too, for all I know. I haven't talked to any of them yet. But there I was, right in the middle of this guy's murder investigation, and he did not want me around. Do you ever feel like life is spinning completely out of control?"

"Not lately," Bennis said.

"There are dozens of people involved in these two things," Gregor said. "There are police officers and witnesses and suspects and it's more like Cecil B. DeMille than

The Thin Man. A cast of thousands. And none of it makes sense."

"It's not going to do us much good just standing here in front of the door," Bennis said. "Why don't we go back home and wait until daylight, and then you can call that guy from John Jackman's office and maybe he can get the police to let you in. At least that would make a certain amount of sense."

Gregor got some tools out of his pocket — his file, his miniature wrench. "Burglar's tools," the police always called them, but they were ordinary items that anybody might have around a house. He was fairly sure the door would not be bolted. There was nobody inside to bolt it. He tried fiddling with the lock for a while, but it didn't budge.

"Do you actually know how to do that?" Bennis asked him.

"No," Gregor said. He looked around again. "What about a back door?" he asked. "Do these houses have back doors?"

"Of course they do, Gregor. There's an alley back there where they keep the garbage cans between pick-up days. Do you think the back door is going to be any easier?"

"I think Sophie Mgrdchian was an old woman," Gregor said. "I think the back door might just be open."

Bennis made a noise. Gregor ignored her. He went back down the stairs and around to the side of the house. In some places, the sides of the houses were right up next to each other, with no space in between. In others, there was a small walkway. He picked the wrong side the first time. The second, he found a walkway so narrow he almost thought he was going to have to go through it sideways.

"I hope you've got your phone," Bennis said. "I can just see us getting trapped in here."

They made it through to the back, where the space was much larger, but also much darker. There were actually lights back here, but not on Sophie's house. The house across the alley had one trained on its own back door, and the houses to either side seemed to have light coming from them one way or the other. Gregor found the back door and went up to it. It was locked.

"Well, that didn't work out," Bennis said.

The locked door was behind another door, a rickety one with screens. Gregor propped that back with a rock he found in the alley and went to work with the file. It was too bad that trick with the credit cards didn't often work.

"Both of these things," he said, working

away, "are wrong. They're just wrong. I saw two bodies lying on the floor this week, and both of them were wrong. Sophie Mgrdchian wasn't technically a body, since she wasn't dead, but it was still wrong. And the body of the girl at Engine House — well . . . all right. That one I know for certain was staged."

"How do you know it was staged?" Bennis asked.

"Because the mirror on the wall was tampered with — listen to me. How do you tamper with a mirror? Never mind. That mirror usually sits flat against the wall. Somebody changed it so that it was leaning just slightly forward, just enough so that the body could be seen in it from the doorway. And the only reason to do that was to make sure that whoever saw the body had it drilled into their heads that the body was where it was as it was."

"Okay," Bennis said. "But Mrs. Mgrdchian? Why do you think that was staged?"

"I don't know," Gregor said. He got the file between the door and the door frame. He thought he might have splintered some wood.

"Do you think this woman, this sister-in-law, or whoever she is, do you think she did something to Sophie Mgrdchian when she was out cold?"

"I think," Gregor said, "that there should have been an address book in this house. Sophie Mgrdchian is an old woman. Old people have doctors, pharmacists, maybe physical therapists. They've got all kinds of people keeping them going. And they don't have the kind of memory to hold it all in their heads. They'd have to write it down."

"So we're going to find the address book?" Bennis said.

"No," Gregor said, as the door popped open under his hand. "We're going to search through the house and discover that no address book is here. Because it isn't here. If it had been, the police would have found it."

"And this required coming out at four in the morning?"

"I couldn't sleep," Gregor said.

That was literally the truth.

3

Gregor arrived at Dexmali thinking he should have known better. Even on City Ave, a place with that kind of name was likely to be a shining example of the New Philadelphia. Gregor had very little use for the New Philadelphia. He understood that time did not stand still. He understood that having a metropolitan area full of "creative class" types — who in the name of God ever took "creative class" seriously, besides Richard Florida — anyway? — was better than being Detroit, a city that was dying out from under you. On the other hand, creative class types seemed to come along with pretentious art and precious enterprise. Nothing could be named Joe's Diner anymore, unless it was a forties-retro shining chrome dining car that served things like Macaroni and Cheese Florentine.

Gregor didn't understand what people ate anymore. He really didn't. He liked large slabs of meat, preferably called Porterhouse, and big flat fried potatoes. He didn't want McDonald's and he really didn't want Macaroni and Cheese Florentine. And if a cheese was made from a goat so rare it only lived on a single Himalayan mountain, he thought they should all just leave it all alone. If the goat was a Buddhist —

He was very tired. He was very, very tired. He should not have gotten up in the middle of the night, no matter how urgent it had seemed. He should be sitting in the Ararat right this minute, bribing Linda Melajian to bring him bacon and sausage when Bennis's back was turned.

Gregor could see David Mortimer sitting

at a table near the back, against the wall. The tables were plain and serviceable, but there was a menu in the window. That was not serviceable. It included something called a "rose hip omelet."

Gregor went in and looked around. There was no seating hostess, which was not surprising. There were not that many patrons. This was not a good area for the New Philadelphia. There were lots of college kids, but not the kind of college kids who ordered rose hip omelets.

Or quiche with feta cheese and violet petals, either. He was not making this up. That was the special, and there was a picture of it, along with a description of it, on a chalkboard on an easel at the very back of the room.

Gregor went to David Mortiner's table and sat down. Mortimer seemed to be eating a whole wheat burrito with vegetables that looked like they had been invented for a Roger Corman movie.

"I thought it was a good idea," Mortimer said. "You know. Get away from the usual thing. Also, I'm watching my blood pressure, and my cholesterol. You know how it is."

"Um," Gregor said.

A young woman came over without a

notepad. That was something else that was endemic in the New Philadelphia. The restaurants all thought there was something wrong with waitresses carrying note pads. The young woman did have a menu, but Gregor wouldn't take it.

"Coffee, please," he said. "I don't suppose you have hash brown potatoes and breakfast sausage?"

"Oh, yes," the young woman said. "We have hash browns with rosemary, cooked in olive oil. And we have three kinds of breakfast sausage: turkey sausage with sage, vegetarian sausage with —"

"How about pork sausage, sort of spiced up?" Gregor asked.

"Oh, yes," the young woman said. "Of course. We use thirteen different spices —"

"That's all right," Gregor said. "Why don't you get me the hash browns, and the pork sausage, and whatever kind of coffee you have that comes black and heavily caffeinated."

"It's fair trade coffee," the waitress said.

"Fine," Gregor said.

David Mortimer watched the young woman retreat. "Fair trade is a tremendous deal to a lot of people," he said. "They don't like to think they're contributing to the oppression of peasants in Latin America. It's

328

actually very good coffee."

"If you want to make sure you're not contributing to the oppression of peasants in Latin America," Gregor said, "you're going to have to do a lot more than buy coffee from self-consciously virtuous co-ops. In fact, buying from the co-ops might not be a good idea to begin with. I've had absolutely no sleep. I've just broken into a house in the dead of night. I'm completely out of patience. I hope this is important."

Mortimer looked nonplussed. "Why did you break into a house in the middle of the night? And whose house did you break into? Are we going to have to do something about that to keep you out of trouble?"

"It's nice to know that John Jackman thinks he has to keep me out of trouble," Gregor said. "And I broke into Sophie Mgrdchian's house looking for her address book. As to why I did it in the middle of the night, I was royally annoyed and I couldn't sleep. I didn't find an address book, by the way. And that tells me something."

"Does it?"

"Yes," Gregor said. "It tells me that you should tell the police and the mental hospital to find some excuse for keeping that woman locked up. And no, I'm not sure why yet. But I'm sure."

329

Mortimer took a deep breath. "I'm not sure we can do things like that," he said.

"No," Gregor agreed. "You can't. What did you want to talk to me for, and why did you want to talk to me out here, instead of just having me come into your office? It's not like the mayor's people aren't used to seeing me."

"Yes," Mortimer said. "Well. Here's the thing. This is sort of under the table."

"You're doing something John doesn't want you to do?" Gregor asked. "You probably shouldn't do that. He's not known for being lenient with employees who —"

"No, no," Mortimer said. "The mayor knows all about it. That's why we're here. He suggested it."

"John Jackman suggested a restaurant called Dexmali?"

"No," Mortimer said. "The mayor suggested that we get away from my office and from any of your usual places, and meet somewhere where nobody would be looking for us. Not that I know who would be looking for us, but you see what I mean. I have some information. Some of it comes from the Merion police, and they're fine with it. They're willing to talk to you all you want. The other comes from the Bryn Mawr police, and they're —"

"Not willing to talk to me," Gregor said.

"No," Mortimer said. "Not at all."

"Well, why should they be?" Gregor said. "I haven't been hired by them. Len Borstoi is probably a very good cop with a very good record. Why would he want to look like he couldn't solve his own cases without outside help?"

"You did say you wanted information about what was going on with the reality show people," Mortimer said. "And now that there's actually been a murder — well, the mayor thought you'd like to be kept informed. If you see what I mean."

"Sure," Gregor said. "That's keeping me up at night, too. Why can't they just bring you a cup of coffee in this place? There aren't more than three other tables with people at them. What is it you think I want to know?"

"It's the gun," Mortimer said. "This girl, the one called Emily, who supposedly shot at Sheila Dunham last weekend at the Milky Way Ballroom in Merion —"

"Supposedly?"

"Well, I guess she did," Mortimer said. "Forty or more people saw her aim the gun and pull the trigger, and lots of the ones close to her heard noise. But here's the thing. We took two shells out of the wall

331

behind where Sheila Dunham had been standing, and — well — neither of them came from the gun the girl had."

"Ah," Gregor said. "Yes. All right. That would make sense. Let me tell you something. You took a few shells out of the body, or, rather, the study at Engine House, after the murder yesterday. And those shells matched the shells that the Merion police found in the wall at the Milky Way Ballroom."

"Well, we didn't do anything," Mortimer said. "The Bryn Mawr police did. But yes, that's it exactly. How did you know? Or did you guess."

"I suppose I guessed," Gregor said, "but it wasn't a very hard guess. It's the only way it would make sense really. Have you ever read any Agatha Christie?"

"No," Mortimer said. "I can't say I have."

"I've got a friend who really likes Agatha Christie novels," Gregor said. "He's been on me to try them for years. I kept resisting him, but then he had a bunch of them sent down to Jamaica while I was on my honeymoon, and there they were, so I read some of them. She was a very smart woman. You wouldn't think so, but she was."

"I don't know that I'd ever thought about it," Mortimer said.

"One of the things she's constantly stress-ing in the Hercule Poirot novels," Gregor said. "And yes, I do know about *The Inquirer* constantly calling me the Armenian-American Hercule Poirot. It used to annoy the hell out of me. Anyway, one of the things she's constantly stressing, or Hercule Poirot is, is that you have to pay attention to what actually happened."

"Well, that makes sense," Mortimer said.

"It makes sense, but most of us don't do it," Gregor said. "Take Sophie Mgrdchian. What actually happened?"

Mortimer looked confused. "We don't know that yet, do we? She's still in a coma and nobody is completely sure why?"

"We found her on the floor of the foyer of her house, in a coma, yes, and with this woman who says she's Karen Mgrdchian, widow of Sophie's brother-in-law, Marco, there with her. And Karen Mgrdchian, when we found her, said her name was Lily and seemed very disoriented. So far so good? That's what actually happened."

"Yes, all right," Mortimer said. "So what?"

"So that's what we should be concentrat-ing on, and not the seven thousand things that might possibly have been the reason that brought Karen Mgrdchian to that house. Because that's the other thing we know. Karen Mgrdchian's fingertips have been destroyed. That's a fact. Isn't it?"

Mortimer looked more confused than before. "It's a fact, yes, but from what I understand, it's fairly common for something like that to happen —"

"To homeless people," Gregor said. "That's because they try to get warm around pipes and things and sometimes they catch hold of some metal that's too cold and they rip the tips of their fingers off. But if this woman is Karen Mgrdchian, she isn't a homeless person. Or at least, she shouldn't be. She's from, where — Cleveland? I can't remember off the top of my head. She's not from Philadelphia. Right?"

"Right." Mortimer now looked completely dazed.

"Well, if she was homeless, she wouldn't have had the money to get here, and she probably wouldn't have done all that well hitchhiking. I mean, we're not talking about homeless for a couple of days. Homeless people don't lose their fingertips when they've been out on the street for a couple of days. It takes a while for them to get disoriented enough and desperate enough to do the kind of stupid thing that makes that happen. So, I feel pretty confident in saying that this woman was not homeless.

So why are the tips of her fingers such a mess that we can't get accurate fingerprints?"

"I don't know," Mortimer said.

"Well, that's the question, isn't it?" Gregor said. "Those missing fingerprints, that's what actually happened."

The young woman had come back to their table, carrying a tall mug of coffee in one hand and a plate in the other. The plate was thick white stoneware and very plain. She put the coffee down, and Gregor tried very hard to ignore the single coffee bean floating on the single mint leaf at the top. She put the plate down, and Gregor just stared.

The hash browns looked all right, but the sausage seemed to be shot through with little threads of blue and green and gold.

Gregor had no idea what they were.

SIX

1

Mary-Louise Verdt resented the idea that they were all supposed to go on as if nothing had happened, that they were supposed to film interviews today and do a challenge in spite of the fact that there was yellow crime-scene tape across the study door and somebody they were living with was probably a murderer. *Murderess* — there weren't really a lot of men around here, were there? *Murderess* was what they would have called it on those *Masterpiece Theatre* shows her mother liked to watch. Mary-Louise felt a little odd about the fact that she hadn't felt as if she ought to call her mother. Even when the murder had happened, and she knew it would be on the news all across the country, she had had to be shooed onto the phone by Olivia Dahl, who seemed to be convinced that something awful would happen if they didn't all call home at once.

Mary-Louise checked herself out in the mirror and tried to ignore Alida Akido in the room with her. Most of the time, with Alida, Mary-Louise tried not to think the things that immediately came into her mind. She wasn't used to "diversity," as they called it here. In her small-town high school, there were a couple of black girls, but that was it. She'd never met an Oriental person before. She corrected herself, in her mind this time, which was good. She'd actually said "Oriental" out loud their first day in the house, and she'd thought Alida was going to rip her head off. "Asian" was the word she wanted. Mary-Louise had no idea if it was part of being Asian, this furious anger all the time, and the withering disdain for almost everybody. It wasn't nice, and Mary-Louise had been brought up to believe that the most important thing in the world that anybody could be was nice.

Of course, virtually nobody was nice here. Mary-Louise had noticed it right away. People were catty, as her mother would say — bitchy, as they'd say on television. People were always talking about each other when they knew they'd be overheard, or that the conversation would get back to the person. And then, of course, there were the interviews, the one-on-ones, where they were asked very specific questions about other people in the house and were expected to answer them "honestly." Somebody told somebody who told somebody. That was how Mary-Louise had found out that all her clothes were "hick."

She looked into the mirror again. She was wearing her best going-out dress, because today they were going to do a challenge where they were supposed to be interviewed on television. They had to handle themselves and a hostile reporter, and later the tape of them doing that would be played back for everybody and they would be "critiqued." Mary-Louise hated "critiques." She didn't understand what the point was. If you'd made a fool of yourself in public, wouldn't it be nicer if everybody pretended that it hadn't happened? Maybe it was true that nobody ever pretended that nothing had happened if you were famous, because if you were famous and did something to make yourself look ridiculous, somebody could sell the story to a magazine.

Mary-Louise's dress had a ruffle thing around the neck and down the front, and then it sort of flounced. This was very common at home, but here, nobody wore dresses like that. Here, they wore dresses like the one Alida had put on, very sleek, and mono-colored, and cut high on the leg. Of course, Mary-Louise's dress was also cut high on the leg, but the skirt was so wide and swishy it looked as if it were going to fly up into the air with the first wind. It was a good thing she had no intention of going commando.

Mary-Louise leaned very close to the mirror, as close as she could get. She thought she was wearing too much eye shadow. She wondered if she had time to take it off and put on some that was less . . . obvious. She thought of the girls in her town in their prom dresses. The prom dresses were almost always made out of chiffon, and they always flounced, and the girls always wore their hair twisted up high on their heads and hairsprayed into sculpture.

Mary-Louise thought she was wearing too much lipstick, too. She ran her tongue over her lips. It didn't help.

Alida had come up behind her, looking annoyed. "So," she said, "I don't see what any of you accomplished. You went crawling through the air ducts, or wherever it was —"

"It wasn't anything like that," Mary-Louise said. "It was just a little attic kind of place, except part of it had a really low ceiling."

"I don't care what it was," Alida said. "You did it. You were up all night. And what was the point? You didn't get any information that I could see. And you all could have been thrown out of here on your ears."

"Ivy is right," Mary-Louise said. "They wouldn't throw that many of us out at once. They couldn't do that and still film the whole show. It would cost them too much money."

"You don't know what you're talking about," Alida said. "You listen to Ivy and you think she knows something. They could have slated you all for elimination right on the spot and taken a few weeks to do it. Why not? None of you get it. It's really pathetic. You all think this is the Girl Scouts or something."

Mary-Louise had, in fact, been a Girl Scout. She didn't know whether this would be considered normal or stupid by the girls in the house. She hadn't thought about mentioning it before now. She sat back on the vanity chair with its rickety wire backing and started to gather up her things.

"I can't believe you're going out like that," Alida said.

"It's the best dress I own."

"And you didn't think about getting anything special for the show? It's a show.

You're trying to play a part. You're not really being yourself, no matter what they say in the interviews."

"There wasn't any time to buy any clothes," Mary-Louise said. "We got to casting, then we got put in the top thirty, then that got pared down to twenty, then that got pared down to fourteen, and then we came here. All in one day. I don't even know if there were any stores where we were."

"I don't mean you should have bought a dress after casting," Alida said. "I mean you should have bought some things before you ever came out here. You should have at least considered the possibility that you'd end up in the house and come prepared."

"I think it's a very bad thing to assume you're going to win something like that," Mary-Louise said. "There were hundreds of girls trying out. How could I know I was going to get into the house?"

"Honestly," Alida said. She backed away from the mirror. Mary-Louise had to admit that Alida looked very nice, almost wonderful. She was all lines and angles anyway, and the short black dress that didn't look like it was much of anything when it was on the hanger, just straight lines and arm and neck holes — *Well,* Mary-Louise thought, *it did look wonderful on.*

"Sheila Dunham's prowling around in the hallways," Alida said. "She's going to pounce on us and try to make us lose our cool. She's a joke, really. If she hadn't done this, she wouldn't have any career left at all."

Mary-Louise did not think that Sheila Dunham was a joke. She thought about being eliminated from the last challenge and blushed.

"The spying wasn't for nothing," she said. "I mean, we did find out a few things. We found out that the show was going to go on filming in spite of everything. And we did hear that the police hadn't found the gun. I wonder if the gun is still in the house somewhere. They searched practically the whole place. I wonder if somebody has the gun and, you know."

"I know what?" Alida asked.

"Well," Mary-Louise said. "You know. Maybe somebody has the gun because she wants to kill somebody else. Maybe this is all part of a plot. Or maybe it's a serial killer who's killing off contestants for *America's Next Superstar.*"

"That girl wasn't a contestant on *America's Next Superstar,*" Alida said. "Nobody knows who she was. You'd better hurry up or you'll be late, and you know what they're like when you're late. At least this time you won't have to go outside. You won't be able to fall flat in the mud again."

Mary-Louise didn't say anything to this. She waited until Alida left the room. Then she went to the windows and looked out. Their bedroom overlooked the front drive, which was full of equipment vans and vehicles she didn't recognize. It was still raining. It seemed to do nothing but rain and rain and rain out here, and then it rained some more.

She ran her hand up and down the ruffle on her dress and then headed for the hallway herself.

2

Coraline was the first person downstairs this morning. She was standing all by herself in the foyer when the camera people started setting up. She sat down on the bottom step and watched them all get to work. On her left was the study. There was yellow crime-scene tape across the door, and a police guard, but the door was open. Coraline did not understand that. She would have had the door closed, just because the room would remind people of what they had seen the day before. Coraline could not make herself forget it. She had thought about it all last night, lying in bed, and when she had gone to sleep, she had dreamed of it. She didn't understand it. It had not looked real when she first saw it. When she remembered it, it had looked entirely too real.

"I don't think you're going to have to worry about it," she'd told her father on the phone yesterday afternoon. Olivia Dahl had insisted that all of them should call home right away, so that their families heard about it first from them and not from the television news. "I don't think I'm going to last very long."

"I don't believe it," her mother said. "I don't believe there's another girl there who can hold a candle to you. Unless you mean they're going to get rid of you because of your faith. I know about that kind of thing. Think about Carrie Prejean."

It had taken Coraline more time than it should have to remember Carrie Prejean, but it had come to her. She was the woman who couldn't be Miss USA, or somebody like that, because she had come out against gay marriage. Actually, that incident was a little hazy in her mind. Coraline didn't pay as much attention to the news as her mother did, and she didn't like to watch the Fox cable news station, because everybody seemed to be yelling at everybody else most of the time.

"I don't think you should get discouraged," her mother had said. "We're all so proud of you just making it onto the show, and we know you're going to make a difference in the lives of the girls you meet. Most of them have no idea what it's like growing up in a Christian home, or living the life of a Christian lady. It's so much better than anything they're used to. You'll see. You'll bring one of them to the Lord, and you won't even know it."

Coraline stretched out her legs and tried to see if she could figure out what was going on in the living room. It looked like a jumble of wires and lights and cameras. In a way, her mother was right. She did think that the life she had grown up with, the home that was always clean, and where her parents were still married to each other and didn't fight; the Sundays at church, teaching Sunday school and then coming in at the end of the service with the children, to hear the sermon and to sing; the fact that she never had to think twice about whether her period was late or to cry for hours because some boy she'd thought she was in love with had ditched her for another girl — there was a lot of it, a lot of the ways her life was different from, say, Grace's life, or even Janice's. She had already figured out that she probably was the only virgin here. She was probably even the only one who wanted to be a virgin.

She wondered who that girl was, the one who had died. Was she saved? Was she in Heaven now, or in Hell? Maybe God had a special procedure for people who were murdered, or who died very young from cancer or car accidents. Maybe there really were ghosts. Coraline looked a little to the left and saw that the blood was still there on the carpet and the far wall. There was so much of it, she could tell even from this far away.

The police officer at the door did not look at her. He never looked at anyone.

Coraline heard a door open at the back of the foyer. That would be somebody coming in from the kitchen or the utility rooms. When they were first in the house, Coraline had gone searching around with Janice, just looking at things. She had never seen a house like this before, and neither had Janice.

"It's like an English country house in a murder mystery," Coraline had told Janice, thinking of her mother's *Masterpiece Theatre* evenings.

And now it was an English country house

in a murder mystery. How odd was that?

There was no mistaking the sound of those footsteps in the hall. Nobody on Earth walked the way Sheila Dunham walked. Coraline would have been able to pick out that sound in a crowded airport. She wished she was in a crowded airport. She wished she was anywhere but here. If Sheila made her go upstairs and change, she would have a fit.

Sheila didn't seem to see her on the stairs. Coraline held her breath. When you saw Sheila up close, she was nowhere near as glamorous as she looked on television. She was old, for one thing. Coraline had heard that she'd had a million dollars' worth of plastic surgery, and she didn't have wrinkles, but she just looked wrong. Her skin didn't look like skin, and it was sort of dull, as if it weren't really alive. Her eyes were worse. Her hair looked brittle enough to snap off if somebody pulled at it.

It was hard to know what to do. Did she want to cough or do something to make herself known, or just pretend not to be here, so she didn't startle Sheila? Coraline looked down at her dress. It was the dress she'd worn this year to the roast beef dinner, the one the church held to raise money for missions. She'd been a hostess at that dinner. The dress was the only thing she had ever bought at Anne Klein, and she still couldn't believe what it had cost.

Sheila stopped in the doorway to the living room. Then she turned and looked Coraline right in the face. Coraline let herself breathe again. She'd done the right thing. Sheila must have known she was there all along.

"Where are the rest of them?" Sheila asked.

"I don't know," Coraline said. "They were still getting ready when I came down. Maybe they're still getting ready."

"I'm not letting anyone into the challenge who's late," Sheila said. "I don't care how many of them I have to disqualify. You're the Christian one, aren't you?"

"I'm a Christian," Coraline said. She didn't want to say she was the only one. That wouldn't be right. There might be another Christian girl here. Maybe she was trying to hide it, because she was afraid that it would end up getting her eliminated. Coraline did not think that would be right, but she knew people who did that kind of thing.

Sheila was looking her up and down. "How old are you?" she asked.

"I'm eighteen."

"You didn't lie about that to get on the show? You aren't really sixteen?"

"No," Coraline said. "Why would I lie about that?"

"People lie about their ages all the time. God, you're insipid looking. And you're young. Not that that ever hurt anybody. How long do you think it's going to take you to grow out of it?"

"To grow out of what?"

"The religion thing," Sheila said. "People grow out of it. I grew out of it. It gets to the point where you just can't stand the stupid anymore. Then you wake up one day, and you can't believe you ever took any of it seriously. Which is a good thing, if you don't mind my saying so, because that way you aren't making yourself crazy about going to Hell all the time. Do you expect to go to Hell?"

"Nobody goes to Hell if they're saved," Coraline said.

"Right," Sheila said. "And once you're saved, you can slaughter babies in the middle of church on Sunday and you still can't go to Hell. I love religion. It's not just stupid, it's disgusting."

"It's not the Christians who are slaughtering babies," Coraline said. Her neck had begun to feel stiff. Her arms had begun to ache.

"Oh, I know what we're going to ask you about," Sheila said. "Let's see how that looks on an interview tape, why don't we? Slaughtering babies and murdering queers."

"I'd never use a word like —"

"Oh, of course you would," Sheila said. "You just wouldn't use a word like that in front of somebody you know doesn't agree with you. And don't tell me a Christian would never murder anybody. Think about Matthew Shepard."

"The men who killed him weren't Christians," Coraline said. She was finding it hard to breathe. She was finding it hard to talk.

"Nobody's a Christian if you don't like what they do. I know how that works," Sheila said. Then: "Those camera people in that room have got less than three minutes. Then I'm going to start pulling the plug."

She leaned over Coraline until Coraline could smell the mint on her breath. "I really hate you people, do you know that? You can't mind your own business. And you're idiots."

Then she straightened up and went away. Coraline did not notice where.

The foyer felt very hot, and she wanted to cry.

Grace Alsop noticed Coraline crying on the stairs, but she didn't stop to ask what it was all about. Coraline's makeup was running. She'd either have to run back upstairs to fix it, or allow herself to be filmed as a mess. Grace had already put Coraline down as somebody who was going to be leaving early. There had been the incident with the T-shirt yesterday, and now there was today, and the tears.

Janice was hopping around, trying to calm her nerves by chattering nonstop. Grace thought Janice might always chatter non-stop.

"I heard Alida say that it could have been on purpose," Janice said. "You know, that thing with the T-shirt. Coraline could have worn that T-shirt on purpose because she knew she'd be disqualified from the challenge and get to stay here while we were all out, and that would mean she could meet that girl and kill her."

"She couldn't know she would be barred from the challenge," Grace said. "And she couldn't have known that about the T-shirt, either. I don't remember Sheila Dunham ever caring about logos before."

"Ivy says it's a legal thing," Janice said. "You can't use other people's logos on your show without their permission. It's a — it's a trademark thing."

Grace was fairly sure Janice had no idea what a trademark was.

"Anyway, that's what Alida said," Janice said. "I've got to admit, I don't much like Alida. She's angry all the time, and she really thinks she's special. I'm glad I don't have to room with her like Mary-Louise."

"Mmm," Grace said.

Suzanne was just coming out of the living room, looking flushed. If Janice hadn't been talking so much, Grace would have been able to hear how the interview was going.

"I wonder what they're going to ask us about in there," Janice said.

Grace was about to tell her that they would ask her anything they thought she wouldn't want to answer, but she didn't have a chance. Olivia Dahl had come out into the foyer and called her name. Grace got up and smoothed down the sides of her skirt. She was wearing a suit, the kind of suit she had worn to her serious job interviews. It did not matter that she hadn't gotten a job.

The living room was a complete mess of wires and lights and cameras. Grace threaded her way through them to the middle of the room. The furniture had been rearranged a little to place two wingback chairs in front of the fireplace. There was a fire lit there, too, although it did not seem to be putting out any heat. There was a fireplace in almost every room of this house.

One of the wingback chairs was occupied by a small blond woman Grace vaguely recognized from one of those E! "news" shows. She ran the possibilities through her head, but couldn't come up with a name. Sheila Dunham was sitting just past the cameras on the couch. None of the other judges were there. Grace was beginning to realize that the other judges were almost never there. Deedee Plant seemed to be kept on ice somewhere to be brought out only for elimination panels and group pow-wows like the one last night. Now there was somebody who couldn't have killed that girl last night: Deedee Plant was so plastered so much of the time that she couldn't aim the liquor into a glass, never mind a gun at anybody.

Olivia Dahl was back. She shooed Grace into the empty chair before the fire. The fire really was not emitting any heat. It had to be a gas fire, or something else artificial. Sheila was leaning far forward on her chair.

"My God, you look like a dyke," she said. "Are you a dyke? Is that what we haven't figured out yet?"

"If you're asking if I'm a lesbian," Grace said, "the answer is no."

"You're the one who went to Wellesley, aren't you? That's still all women. I thought all those places were full of dykes."

Olivia was looking at her clipboard. "You've got the notes there," she said to the small blond woman. "She's going under the name Grace Alsop —"

"Her real name's Harrigan," Sheila said. "Her father does entertainment news for Fox. He's a right royal prick, too."

Since Grace actually agreed with this, she let it go. Olivia hurried away, and somebody said "Action."

The small blond woman turned to the camera and smiled. "Good evening! This is Deirdre Damien with *Entertainment News Tonight,* and I'm here with the latest winner of the phenomenally popular reality show, *America's Next Superstar*! Our guest beat out literally hundreds of other girls just to make it on air, and then she beat out another thirteen to take home the top prize. Here's Grace Alsop, and I'm very excited to have her!"

Deirdre Damien, Grace thought. What a name. She turned to the camera herself. It was very important not to leave dead air.

Not ever.

"Good evening, Deirdre," she said. She smiled.

"Well," Deirdre said. "Let's start at the beginning. Your name isn't really Grace Alsop, is it? That's your stage name."

"That's right," Grace said. "My original name is Grace Harrigan."

"Well, now," Deirdre said. "There are some people, quite a lot of them really, who say you changed your name so that people wouldn't know that you're your father's daughter. Your father is the entertainment news director for Fox, isn't he?"

"That's right," Grace said. "But I don't think I was hoping nobody would know. It isn't a hard thing to find out. I was just hoping to be judged on my own merits and not because my father is important in the industry."

"Was it his importance in the industry that bothered you," Deirdre said, "or the fact that Fox is known to hire only very bigoted people to work for it? Is your father a homophobe?"

"What?" Grace said.

"Or maybe it's race," Deirdre said. "I know a lot of people at Fox are supposed to favor a return to segregation. Didn't your father once say that President Obama looked like a monkey with a Harvard accent?"

"Not in front of me, he didn't," Grace said. Somewhere in the back of her mind, she was trying desperately to think. She had expected to be accused of being a spy. She hadn't expected this. She had no idea where this was going to go.

"A lot of people are concerned that America's most popular reality show has thrown up a winner who may not be open to the aspirations of all Americans," Deirdre said. "I'd like to know what you're going to do to make sure that people know you aren't really like that. Do you intend to do some outreach? Some community service? Maybe you'd be interested in dating an African American man."

Grace had been watching entertainment news all her life. She knew that it never threw up interviews like this one. It didn't even come close.

"Actually," she said, "I've got something else I'm working on at the moment. I don't know if you know it, but there was a murder during our filming for this show."

Deirdre looked confused. Grace shot a look at Sheila Dunham. Sheila was sitting far forward on her chair. Her hands were knotted together. They looked like claws.

"I'm committed," Grace said, "to proving that the police and the public are wrong. I've started a crusade to prove that Sheila Dunham did not murder that girl, and that she'd never kept her in a house in Malibu as a slave."

SEVEN

1

It was the lack of sleep, Gregor thought, that was making him behave so . . . erratically. It didn't sound to him like the right word. He emerged onto City Ave like a night flying bat suddenly thrust into daylight. Everything looked too bright, even though it wasn't bright at all. It wasn't raining, but there were clouds covering the sky, black ones, promising even more rain. He didn't used to be subject to insomnia. Even during his earliest days at the Bureau, he had been able to sleep at night. There were people who thought he was a little odd that way. How could you sleep after you'd pulled the body of a kidnapped twelve-year-old out of a back-road ditch at four o'clock in the morning? How could you sleep when you knew there were children missing, girls dead in basements, piles of paper supposed to be full of leads piling up on your desk and falling off it in the night?

The FBI handles more than one kind of crime, and when Gregor had first joined it he had signed on to work on the financial stuff. That made sense, because in those days special agents were expected to be either lawyers or accountants, and Gregor had been an accountant. It would be better to say he had trained as an accountant, at the Harvard Business School. He'd never actually worked as one. Still, given his background, he had expected to be put to work on organized crime and fraud investigations. Instead, he had found himself working on kidnappings. He could still remember going home on the night he had received his first assignment — going home to his first wife, Elizabeth, and being completely astonished at what he was expected to do.

"I think it sounds better than bank fraud," Elizabeth had said at the time. "At least there's a human element to it. It isn't all numbers."

Elizabeth was buried in an Armenian cemetery in Philadelphia. Gregor went there once or twice a year, even now. He had, however, stopped doing that thing he had been so addicted to just after she had died. He didn't talk to her anymore, aloud or otherwise. He couldn't remember when he had stopped doing that. It was before he had started seeing Bennis with any seriousness, he was sure of that, but it might have been quite a bit before. Bennis seemed to know that they had been seeing each other long before he had become aware of it.

He was really very tired. Too tired to be where he was, walking along a street, in the middle of the morning rush, with traffic everywhere. He was getting too old for this. There had been a time in his life when he had been able to stay awake for a couple of days at a time and still function. He could get by for a couple of days more with just a few half-hour catnaps here and there. Now he had to sleep for eight hours and roll carefully into the day just to be coherent, and he hadn't done anything like that this time. He'd even woken Bennis from a sound sleep. She'd probably gone back to bed after he'd left, after first going to Donna Moradanyan Donahue's house and complaining about the entire night.

He was in a neighborhood he did not recognize. It was not a bad one. There were stores, and none of the storefronts were boarded up. There were places to eat, mostly pizza and Chinese food. Gregor remembered growing up in Philadelphia. There had been pizza and Chinese food even then, but there had been more little hole-in-the-wall diners that served always exactly the same kind of food: hamburgers; cheeseburgers; diet plates. The "diet plates" were always the same, too. They consisted of a single hamburger patty without the bun, a little collection of lettuce and tomato, and a big round scoop of macaroni salad thick with mayonnaise. Some diners had a variation that included the macaroni salad and the lettuce and tomato, but that substituted a big round scoop of tuna salad — also full of mayonnaise — for the hamburger patty. The tuna salad had had as much mayonnaise in it as the macaroni salad. Had anybody ever really thought she could lose weight by eating that kind of thing? Gregor's mother hadn't been the kind of woman who had tried to lose weight. It was the girls he grew up with who were worried about that, and he'd never seen any of them eating in a diner.

He came to a little open area in front of a small collection of stores that had been set just a little back from the sidewalk. He really had no idea at all where he was. He couldn't even remember why he'd wanted to walk instead of take a cab. The little open area had two stone benches in it. One of the benches was taken up by an old woman with six or seven layers of clothing and the rest of her things in black plastic garbage bags piled in a shopping cart. Gregor sat down on the other bench and wondered where all the bag ladies got their shopping carts. The shopping carts were always in good repair. He couldn't imagine that they were sold down at the Goodwill store. The bag ladies had to take them from supermarket parking lots, and they had to be good at it, because these days the supermarkets locked them up in chain guards that cost twenty-five cents to open. On the other hand, it was only twenty-five cents. Even a bag lady could come up with that much at least some of the time.

He got his cell phone and his notebook out of his jacket pocket. He looked up to see a woman standing behind the plate-glass front window of one of the stores, staring at the bag lady and looking furious. It had to be difficult for shop owners. It was a public space, after all. They couldn't just ban parts of the public because they didn't like them. Gregor wondered what they did do, and then what the bag ladies did when they were finally told to move along.

He looked through his notebook until he found the number he wanted. He tapped it into his phone and put the phone to his ear to hear it ringing. He missed the sound of phones ringing. These days people had ring tones, which weren't tones at all, but entire musical per for mances, often annoying.

I'm getting to be an old fart, Gregor thought. Then somebody picked up on the other end of the line and said, "Ormonds."

Gregor got a picture of Billie Ormonds in his mind and almost smiled. "Gregor Demarkian," he said. "I just talked to David Mortimer. I thought I'd better call you."

"Why?" Billie said. "Is the office of the mayor about to try to get me fired?"

"Not that I know of. Listen, I'm sorry if I sound a little incoherent. I haven't had any sleep. Something occurred to me in the middle of the night, and then I couldn't let go of it."

"I do that sometimes," Billie said.

"The police searched Sophie Mgrdchian's house," Gregor said. "I'm right about that, aren't I?"

"From the notes I got, you were there."

"Yes," Gregor said. "Yes, I was. But here's the thing. I've talked to Sophie's doctor, the one she has now that she's in the hospital. Who is not her regular doctor —"

"We don't know who her regular doctor is," Billie said. "We did try —"

"I'm sure you did," Gregor said. "But you

didn't find any information on one, which is really very odd. There should have been an address book in that house, or refrigerator magnets, or a little stash of business cards. Old women like Sophie Mgrdchian don't keep things like that in their heads. I don't suppose you checked for a cell phone."

There was silence on the other end of the line. "You know," Billie said slowly. "I don't know if they did. Not everybody has a cell phone, and —"

"Yes, right, and old ladies aren't likely to," Gregor said. "Let me apologize again. I really am running on fumes here. I broke in to the house."

"What?"

Gregor was just tired enough to wonder if that was the only response anybody in Philadelphia was ever going to have to his breaking in to Sophie Mgrdchian's house.

"It made me feel thirty years younger," he said, "and I told David Mortimer about it this morning. I kept thinking about all this, and it kept bothering me, so I broke in to the house at four or five this morning and looked through it myself. There was no address book. There were no refrigerator magnets except the plastic fruit kind. And I didn't find a cell phone. And all that's not possible."

"I see what you mean," Billie said.

"It occurs to me," Gregor said, "that you could check her bank, and that might tell you if she had a cell phone. There would be records of payments, at least if she was paying her own bills. Some of the older people on Cavanaugh Street have things like cell phones and cable that they don't pay for, because they've got children or grandchildren who pay for them instead, but from what I can figure out about Sophie, she wasn't in contact with her family, she didn't have children of her own, and she doesn't seem to have seen this niece of hers for a long time. So if she had a cell phone, she paid for it herself. You could find that out from the bank. The cell phone company would have had records of her calls. You could probably get the name of her regular doctor from that."

"Very good," Billie said. "I'm beginning to feel like an idiot here."

"Even if she didn't have a cell phone," Gregor plowed on, "she certainly had a landline. I saw it. The landline company would have records, too. Sophie must have called her doctor at some point in the last three months. She's an old lady. They call their doctors."

There was a little pause on the other end of the line. "She didn't have insurance," Billie said finally. "We checked with Medicare. There's no record of her. If she has a doctor, she's paying out of pocket."

Was it possible that Sophie Mgrdchian didn't know she was eligible for Medicare? Wouldn't her doctor have told her? Gregor wished his head would clear.

"If she paid out of pocket, she'd almost certainly have written a check," he said. "There would be records of that at the bank, too."

"Good thinking," Billie said.

"This doesn't make sense," Gregor said. He tried to remember what Dr. Halevy had told him, and couldn't. He looked in his notebook and found mostly squiggles. "Listen," he said. "Dr. Halevy said they found a plastic pill organizer on Sophie when she was brought into the hospital. Did she by any chance give you a list of the medications that were in it? I'm pretty sure she gave me one but I can't —"

"I've got it right here," Billie said. "Motrin — I think that's ibuprofen. Levatol — that's a beta-blocker, for high blood pressure. Lipitor. That's to lower cholesterol. Bayer low-dose aspirin. Amoxicillin."

"What's amoxicillin?"

"It's an antibiotic," Billie said. "It's a very common one. They give it to people with ulcers, sometimes."

"Did she have ulcers?"

"I don't know," Billie said.

"Neither do I," Gregor said. "But you're telling me she had a pill organizer with all this stuff in it, and at least two of those prescriptions are expensive. Did she have enough of all that stuff, the full doses you'd be likely to expect? Or was she skimping?"

"I don't know that, either," Billie said.

"I think we have to find out," Gregor said. "Because Sophie Mgrdchian was not a rich woman. She wasn't poor, and she wasn't destitute, but she wasn't rich. And if she has no insurance, not even Medicare, and she's getting all those pills over the counter, then — I don't know what then. But if she had enough and she didn't seem to be skimping, then it's imperative that you find some way to hold Karen Mgrdchian as long as possible. I've got to find a cab."

"We've got another day," Billie said. "You'd have to come up with something a lot more concrete for us to be able to hold her after that."

"Yes," Gregor said. "I know. I've got to get a cab. I'll call you again when I get home and when I've had some sleep. You need to check with the police in wherever it is that Marco and Karen Mgrdchian lived. And you need to do this all fast. And I'm being no help at all."

Billie was making fluttery little protests about how much help he was being when Gregor hung up, and then a cab appeared in the street, miraculously free.

2

By the time Gregor got out to Bryn Mawr, it was raining again, and he was cold. It was not the weather that was cold. Even with the rain that had gone on all week, the temperatures had been suspiciously warm. Television weathermen talked on and on about the risk of infectious disease from "near subtropical conditions." Gregor doubted that this was anything like near subtropical conditions — in fact, considering that he was just back from Jamaica, he could practically guarantee it — but he couldn't complain about freezing to death, which was the problem he often had in Philadelphia. No, his cold was something else. His cold was lack of sleep. He got that way sometimes at night these days. It was how he knew he should have gone to bed half an hour earlier.

The gates were not closed at Engine

House this morning, and there were no police cars in the drive. Gregor asked the cabbie to go right up to the front door steps, and then proceeded to pay him the kind of money he would ordinarily have spent on a small kitchen appliance. The intelligent thing to do would have been to know in advance that he wanted to come out here, and either call for a cab appointment ahead of time with one of the companies that offered fixed rates, or gotten somebody from Cavanaugh Street to drive him. Bennis wouldn't come out to Engine House, so that probably would have left Donna Moradanyan Donahue, who was usually busy. Still, he could have asked.

He got out of the cab and looked up at the house. He really couldn't expect the cab to wait. He had no idea how long he would be. He walked up the steps to the front door and knocked. Nothing happened, although he could hear people from just on the other side of the door. He tried the knob and it turned. He pushed in the door and looked in on the foyer.

The foyer was packed with people, and there were people on the stairs and in the living room as well. The yellow crime-scene tape was still up across the study door, and there was a policewoman there now when there had been a policeman before. That meant that the police were either not finished with the room, or that Len Borstoi wanted to come back to it. Gregor understand that last thing. He'd always liked coming back to crime scenes himself. It was the kind of thing a federal officer almost never got the chance at.

Nobody was paying any attention to him. He walked in and among the girls as they milled around, and among the other people, too, people he hadn't seen the last time he was here. There were dozens of young men moving equipment around. Gregor had no idea what most of the equipment was for. There were young women with clipboards, all of them looking anxious and rushed.

Gregor stopped right outside the living room doorway and looked in. One of the contestants was sitting on a wingback chair, talking to a woman sitting on a couch. They were both in front of a fireplace and the fireplace was lit. Off to the side, Sheila Dunham was standing, leaning against a long table that was backed up in front of another one of the couches. It was a massive and old-fashioned living room, full of overstuffed furniture and knickknacks of every possible variety. Had there really been an era when women of "taste" had wanted to own a dozen porcelain angels?

The girl in the wingback chair looked like she was going to cry. Gregor ran the names he remembered through his head and came up with one: Mary-Louise Verdt. Somebody came up behind him and leaned in close.

"They keep changing where they sit," the voice said. "First they have the interviewee in the chair, and then they have the interviewer in the chair. I think it's just to make us feel as uncomfortable as possible."

"I think it's to make us cry," somebody else said.

Gregor turned around. The first girl who had been whispering in his ear was the one with white-blond hair with a neon green streak in it. The other was the girl named Janice Ledbedder, who had talked to the murder victim on the day of the auditions in Merion.

The girl with the neon green streak in her hair smiled. "Ivy Demari," she said. "I used to be Ivy Demaris. We went over all this yesterday."

Olivia Dahl came flying out of the living room with the clipboard clutched to her chest. "Will you all just stop it?" she demanded. "This is not a movie we're on. We don't get to rerecord the sound later. And it's expensive and annoying to get rid of white noise when we don't have to. So if you please, will you all just shut up — oh, Mr. Demarkian."

"I can shut up," Gregor said.

Olivia shook her head violently and headed back for the set. Gregor could see Mary-Louise Verdt on the couch, wringing her hands the way the mothers of good boys gone bad always did in thirties-era movies. Janice Ledbedder was right: Mary-Louise looked ready to cry. If she didn't cry, she was going to jump off the couch and run away. Gregor didn't think he had ever seen anybody so uncomfortable.

All of a sudden, the woman on the couch stood up, and people in the living room started fussing around. Mary-Louise left the wing-back chair as if she had been launched from it, pushing past the men with their cameras and almost running out into the hall.

"Oh," she said, reaching Janice and Ivy. "Oh, my God. That woman is such a — she's such a —"

"Oh, I know," Janice said. "And they look into your life and they find out everything, and then she just comes along and socks you with it. She was hitting me with my boyfriend right up to the very end —"

"They didn't have to dig hard for that

story. You've told all of us a dozen times about how your boyfriend dumped you for another girl," Ivy said.

"I know, I know," Janice said. "I'm sorry if I keep talking about it. But it worked . . . But it worked out all right. We both sent in tapes for this, and I got asked and she didn't. And I'm going to be on television for at least a week, right? I mean, I'm in the house, so I have to be on television at least until the first elimination."

"Wouldn't that suck?" Mary-Louise said. "Going home on the first elimination. That's got to be the worst feeling. I'd almost rather not get on than get on and go home first."

"Oh, people are always saying things like that," Janice said. "And then they're saying the opposite two minutes later. We're all here."

"Who goes next?" Mary-Louise asked.

Ivy shook her head. "You were the last one," she told Mary-Louise. "They're cleaning up. Can't you see."

Gregor looked into the living room with the girls. They were indeed cleaning up. Men were packing equipment away or just moving it around on wheels. The woman who had been playing the interviewer was standing next to Sheila Dunham, talking and looking dissatisfied. Olivia Dahl was checking things out on her clipboard.

Olivia came back into the foyer. "I'm sorry, Mr. Demarkian, we're just doing a little work around here. I wish you'd called. I could have given you a better time. We're going to be another ten or fifteen minutes, I'm afraid."

"That's all right," Gregor said.

Olivia started shooing the girls. "Come on now. We're going to film one of Sheila's pep talks, and then you're all off for a couple of hours. No, Janice. Don't go upstairs and get changed. You're supposed to look 'come as you are.' "

"I just have to go to the bathroom," Janice said. "I'll only be a second."

Olivia rolled her eyes. Then she raised her voice and said, "Get into the living room, please. We've got to set you up. It's a bigger room than the study. We've got to make sure we get the shot. I'm going absolutely crazy. What do the police want around here? The body is gone. I mean it's really gone. There's nothing more to find here. Why can't they go away and let us have access to that room again?"

"It's probably procedure," Gregor said, fully aware that he'd said nothing of any importance whatsoever.

Janice came hurrying back down the stairs, from where Gregor presumed the bathroom was. Olivia started checking things off on her clipboard. Then she raised her voice and said,

"Mary-Louise? Mary-Louise, for God's sake."

"I'm right here," Mary-Louise said, coming from the direction of the front door. "I was just getting some air for a second. I feel like I'm going to faint. But it's raining again."

"Of course it's raining again," Olivia said. "Into the living room. Into the living room, all of you. I think we're going to have Sheila in the chair in front of the fireplace. We'll have you people in front of her — Ivy, sit on the couch. You make a good focal point. Alida, too. Grace, I know you don't want to be right in front of Sheila anymore, but she's not going to have a fit at you on camera —"

"She always has a fit at people on camera," somebody said.

"Yes, all right," Olivia said, "I meant she isn't going to do it during a scripted sequence, and this is a scripted sequence. All right, if Grace won't sit on the couch, why don't we have Shari and Linda. That will work. You're both small. If the rest of you could just stand right behind the couch, stand up so that we can see you. We're going to have only the one camera again, so make sure you're all visible. We'll be shooting you from a little far back, because the focus here is going to be on Sheila. If you'll just move in a little closer —"

Gregor moved in a little closer, too. He even came into the living room, although he knew better than to get too close to what they were doing there. He scanned the crowd of girls behind the couch. Olivia Dahl had told him yesterday that there were fourteen of them, fourteen girls who had been chosen to move into Engine House and begin the real competition. He tried counting them now, but they were moving around too much. Olivia was moving with them.

"Stand still, for God's sake," she was saying. "Stand still. Why can't any of you ever stand still? Janice, come closer to the back of the couch. You're shorter than Suzanne. Marcia, the same with you. Faith, I want you farther back. You're as tall as a flagpole. Brittney —"

They were milling around a lot. They were. Gregor's head was spinning. He tried to make himself concentrate. The girls kept shifting in and out. They were all nervous.

There was a sudden hush, and then a light directly on Sheila Dunham. From this distance, she looked more regal than sad. Gregor couldn't see the lines on her face, or the tightness where the plastic surgery had tried to fix them.

"Ladies," Sheila said. Gregor supposed there was nothing she could do about that voice. It was harsh and flat and angry, and always would be.

"Ladies," Sheila said again. "You have just completed the last challenge you will have this week before the judging panel, and an elimination. You know that there will be an elimination every week while you're here, and that when a girl is eliminated, she has to pack her bags immediately, and go home. We'll have a car waiting at the door for you when the time comes. We'll take you directly to the airport. We'll have plane tickets waiting, if you need them. If you live closer than that, we'll do something else. Olivia will handle it."

The girls all laughed. Gregor had no idea why they were laughing.

"So," Sheila said, "this is to put you all on notice. Every one of you signed a contract when you came here, promising to reveal nothing about what went on in the show until after the show is aired. We're not stupid. We do realize that some of you come from small towns and that your casting for this show was big news there. If you go home early, the papers in those small towns will probably have something to say about it. What we care about is that you do not under any circumstances talk to reporters, or anybody else, about what you have seen and done here. We don't even want you to confirm your elimination. If you're asked — and you will be asked — just say that you've signed a contract not to talk until the season has aired, and keep your mouth shut. Because if you don't, if we find that you've given an interview, or put up information on your blog, or on Facebook or MySpace or wherever, if any of that happens, we've got lawyers from here to Sunday and we will sue you. And we're good at it. That goes double for any video you may have taken while you were here, or any you get your hands on. Any of the video we've taken ourselves belongs to us. Any you've taken, you've taken illicitly and in violation of your contracts, since you're not allowed to have video cameras here, or still cameras, or even your cell phones. Revealing what has gone on in this house before it airs is like telling somebody who done it before they've read a murder mystery. It makes the entire exercise futile. And I won't have it. Am I clear?"

The girls all seemed to nod in unison. Gregor looked across the big clustered knot of them. They all looked very somber.

Sheila stood up. "But none of you should be thinking about elimination now," she said, making her voice deliberately and, Gregor thought, unbelievably peppy. "Right now, you should be thinking positive, and keeping in mind — one of you is going to be *America's Next Superstar*!"

The girls all started jumping up and down at once, thrusting clenched fists in the air and yelling "hooo!" at the top of their lungs.

And right in the middle of it all, two shots rang out.

■ ■ ■ ■

Part III

■ ■ ■ ■

The past is always to some extent a
fiction of the present.
— David Bentley Hart

ONE

1

He got them all out into the hall. He got the doorway to the living room blocked off as best he could, meaning not really blocked off at all. There was no door to it, as there was a door to the study, but the policewoman was still there. She'd come running when she heard the shots, and then she'd gone running back almost immediately. The chaos was almost complete. The girls were running all over the place, screaming and crying. He'd seen that sort of thing on TV, but never quite like this. The policewoman held her post and kept looking suspiciously everywhere. Gregor turned back to look at the living room and saw the gun, lying right out in the middle of everything, right next to the couch.

He went across the foyer and got the policewoman.

"I'm sorry to bother you," he said, "and I

know you're supposed to stay put, but I need a witness. There's a gun lying on the floor in the living room, on that Oriental carpet right next to the big couch they have set up in front of the fireplace. All I want is for you to just see it."

The policewoman looked at him doubtfully, and frowned. Then she turned around, closed the study door, and came with him across the hall.

"Right there," Gregor said.

"Yes, I see it."

"It looks to me like a thirty-eight," Gregor said. "You wouldn't happen to know if the bullets that hit the wall at the Milky Way Ballroom were from a thirty-eight."

"No," the policewoman said.

"Well," Gregor said, "I can practically guarantee you they will have been. And I can practically guarantee you that that's the same gun. But that's not the point now. Did you call this in and get them to send somebody out?"

The policewoman looked puzzled for a moment. Then her face cleared. "Oh," she said. "Did I call headquarters? Yes, I did. They're sending somebody."

"With sirens blaring, probably," Gregor said.

The policewoman went back to her post.

When she did, she opened the study door again. Gregor took note of it for later, because he was too tired to work it out now. He sat down on the staircase, four steps up from the bottom, and got out his phone.

It rang six times before Bennis picked it up. Gregor suddenly realized that she must have been asleep.

"Hello?" Bennis said.

She had definitely been asleep. Gregor took a deep breath. "I'm sorry to wake you. I didn't think."

"It's all right. Are you all right?"

"I just thought of the phrase 'shots rang out.' I mean, not just. It must have been a good fifteen minutes ago now."

"Shots? Where are you? Who's shooting at you?"

"I'm at Engine House. Nobody is shooting at me. Somebody was shooting at Sheila Dunham. At least presumably."

"Are you hurt? Is somebody else dead?"

"I'm not hurt, and nobody else is dead. Nobody is so much as injured. I'm a little dizzy. I think it's from lack of sleep."

"Are the police there?"

"Not yet."

"Did you call them?"

"There's a policewoman on duty at the crime scene from yesterday," Gregor said.

"So I suppose that means that the police are here, except there's just one of them. But there are others coming because she called them. Am I making any sense here at all? I'm too old to stay up all night, and I'm about ready to pitch the kind of fit everybody else in the world gets to pitch and I never do. And in about two or three minutes, Borstoi is going to come running through that door, and all I'm going to get out of it is to be stared at. Remind me never to listen to you again when you say you just want me to do something to keep busy."

"I never said anything of the kind."

"You meant it. I don't think I'm completely recovered from Jamaica."

"I think I'm going to call Donna and have her go out there and get you," Bennis said. "If the police are as fed up with you as you say they are, you're not going to be able to do anything there anyway. She can bring you home."

"I can call a taxi."

"It costs a million dollars," Bennis said. "Which makes me wonder. How did you get out there to begin with?"

"I called a taxi," Gregor said.

"Oh, for God's sake. I'm going to go get Donna."

The connection went dead. Gregor looked

at the phone and sighed. He didn't like cell phones in general, and he really didn't like this thing where people could hang up on you and all that happened was no sound at all. He closed the phone — it slid up and down, sort of like the old iPhone case, but not, and it was green — and put it away in his pocket.

If he'd been more awake, he would have kept his eye on the door to the living room. He hoped the policewoman was doing that, and he knew Olivia Dahl was, although that was not a perfect solution. Gregor thought Olivia Dahl was probably in his top five possible suspects. The policewoman did, however, seem to be doing what he had asked her to, so he let it go.

Then he looked up and Sheila Dunham was standing next to him, just at the other side of the stair railing. She was not yelling or screaming. She was not posing for a camera, or for a fan line at a red-carpet event. She was just standing there, and the first thing Gregor thought was that she looked very old.

He blinked a couple of times. Sheila Dunham was not old. She was younger than Bennis by about a year, but she looked a hundred and three.

"Hello," he said.

"Somebody shot at me," she said.

"Theoretically," Gregor said.

"What's that supposed to mean?"

"That's supposed to mean," Gregor said, "that if I had shot at you from a distance of, what was it, maybe six feet? Anyway, if I had shot at you from that distance, I'd have hit you."

"So she has bad aim. And I suppose that 'she' is legitimate. There wasn't anybody there but women."

"There were men on the crew," Gregor said. "I assume some of those men must have been at the Milky Way Ballroom."

"They all were," Sheila said. "We hire crew for the run of the season, absent their doing something to get themselves fired. Which doesn't happen very often, and hasn't happened this year. Not everybody in the entertainment industry is crazy. The tech people tend to be very — well. Down to earth."

"Right," Gregor said.

"You didn't answer me," Sheila said. "I said somebody shot at me. You said theoretically. I asked you what you meant."

Gregor took another deep breath. It was all he could do not to yawn. Hell, it was all he could do not to fall asleep.

"Well," he said, "they didn't hit you. And

they were close. Even the tech people, as you call them, were reasonably close. They might have been as much as ten feet away from you. But whoever it was not only didn't hit you, he or she didn't even hit anything that could have hit you."

"What?"

"The stone hearth," Gregor said. "If the bullets had hit the stone hearth, they would have bounced off. And a ricochet of that kind would have done some damage. It could have hit you. It could have hit one of the girls sitting or standing in front of you. It could have broken a window. But there was no ricochet. I would have heard it."

"If you don't mind my saying so, Mr. Demarkian, it doesn't look like you're in any shape to hear anything at all."

Gregor nodded. "You're right. I'm a complete mess this morning. I couldn't sleep last night. But I do this for a living. And a ricochet is a noticeable noise and it's not usually quiet. There was no ricochet. When the police get here, they'll find the bullets in the walls, maybe, or in the painting. There's a painting over the fireplace in there, isn't there?"

"I don't remember."

"It doesn't matter," Gregor said.

He looked around the foyer. All the girls

seemed to be there. All the tech people were there. All the administrative assistants with their clipboards were there. This was, Gregor thought, the show in its entirety — but, no. The judges weren't there.

"Why is it," he asked, "that the other judges never seem to be around?"

Sheila looked at the crowd. "They don't need to be around," she said. "Why would I want them to be around?"

"Aren't they supposed to be judging things?" Gregor said. "Don't they have to watch the girls do, what do you call them —"

"The challenges."

"Right. Don't they have to watch those and then judge them? Isn't that the point?"

"They watch video," Sheila said. "Everything the girls do officially, and a lot of what they do unofficially, is taped. We play the videos back in judging and they vote on that."

"And do their votes count? If they wanted to eliminate a girl you wanted to keep, or if they wanted to keep a girl you wanted to eliminate —"

"I get to do it my way," Sheila said. "It's one of the perks of being not only the star but the producer. I own this show — lock, stock, and barrel. It isn't even leveraged. We had to borrow money the first two cycles, but since then we've been doing fine. We've got a cash basis accounting system. You have no idea how cheap it is to do one of these shows. Or how much money they make."

"All of which, I presume, is good."

"Of course it's good. It's better than good. People got stupid. Writers and actors and producers. I don't know what it is about some people. Most people, really. It's as if they can't count." Sheila came around to the front of the stairs and sat down. She now looked not only old, but tired. "They got — everybody wanted more money. The unions wanted more money. The stars wanted more money. The producers wanted more money. But it's a different world now. Not so many people watch television, and when they do, they can watch hundreds of channels. They don't always go to just a couple. The old broadcast channels are absolutely dying. The cable channels have fragmented audiences. Nobody has the kind of share they did in the sixties. So they can all want more money, but that doesn't mean they can get it."

Gregor was suddenly interested. "But you didn't want more money? I thought you just said that a show like this made a lot."

"Of course it does," Sheila said. "It makes

a lot because it doesn't spend a lot. For one thing, I don't have to pay actors. The girls don't get paid. They're considered contestants on a game show. So that eliminates one big huge budget problem. There doesn't need to be a writer, never mind an entire room full of writers. That eliminates another budget problem. And then, due to the nature of the thing, we can save money on down the line: no expensive sets, no costumes because the girls bring their own clothes, an absolute ton of time filmed on stationary cameras plugged into walls that don't even need a cameraman to run them. Fifteen years from now, the unions are going to fall apart. People want to work."

Out in the distance somewhere, there was the sound of a siren. Gregor and Sheila both looked toward the door at once.

Gregor stood up. "I'd better get ready for this one," he said.

Sheila Dunham stood up, too. She was right below him, and although she was tall, she wasn't a match for his own six feet four. She retreated down the stairs and watched him come after her.

Then she leaned very close to him and said, "It wasn't Mallory. That girl in the study. Olivia wants me to think that was who it was, but I've seen Mallory just last year. It wasn't Mallory."

Gregor had no idea who Mallory was. The police sirens were right up to the front door. He stood still in the middle of the foyer and waited for the trouble to start.

2

Len Borstoi was the first through the door when the police came in, and he didn't bother to knock. Gregor filed that away for later. It was probably against two dozen laws and a mountain of court cases. Borstoi was followed by two uniformed officers, both of them with their guns drawn. Gregor's head hurt. The girls did what they could be expected to do when they saw the guns. They screamed and started running around the foyer. The girl called Coraline was sobbing. The one called Janice who had tried to go to the bathroom before was jumping all over the place as if her underwear had been invaded by ants.

Another siren started coming up the drive. Gregor looked up and through the open front door and saw that it was an ambulance. He wanted to sit back down and go to sleep.

The policewoman who was charged with guarding the study came up to Len Borstoi and said something to him, too quietly for

Gregor to hear — but then, Gregor was not trying to hear. Borstoi went to the doorway of the living room and looked in. Then he went into the room. Gregor moved just enough so that he could see what the detective was doing. He was staring down at the gun on the carpet. Then he was walking around the room. Then he was walking up to the wall around the hearth. The living room was huge, and he walked all around that, too.

He came back into the foyer, and Gregor looked him straight in the face. "If you don't mind," he said, knowing that the man minded, "I'd like to know where the bullet holes are."

"The bullet holes," Borstoi said.

"They've got to be somewhere," Gregor said. "They didn't hit anybody. They didn't ricochet. And don't ask me how I know. I know a ricochet. Did they go into the furniture?"

Len Borstoi was still staring at him. Gregor thought that this was the worst part about his incredible tiredness. The very air around his head felt as if it had texture. Everything pulsed a little. Everything glowed.

"I know you think I shouldn't be here," Gregor said, "but I am here, and I think I know a couple of things. It couldn't hurt to listen to me, and if you want to, I'll absolutely promise to act as if I had nothing to do with it. Hell, I always prefer to act as if I had nothing to do with it."

"The press likes to write as if you had everything to do with it," Borstoi said. "The Armenian-American Hercule Poirot. The master detective showing all us poor dumb slobs how it's done."

"I'd be willing to bet just about anything," Gregor said, "that the gun lying on the carpet in there is the gun that fired the shots at the Milky Way Ballroom. You may not want to talk to me, but the Merion police are apparently not so close with information. The gun the girl was holding at the Milky Way Ballroom wasn't the gun that fired the shots there. It wasn't even loaded with live ammunition. When the Merion police got the bullets out of the wall, they were bullets from a different gun. Then, when you got the bullets from yesterday's murder to the lab, they turned out to be bullets from the same gun. And now, I'm pretty sure that the gun lying in there is the gun in question. In fact, it has to be. Nothing else makes any sense."

Len Borstoi was looking at the ceiling over both their heads. "How did you know about the bullets from yesterday?" he asked.

Gregor shook his head. "I've got people in and around the city of Philadelphia who tell me things like that," he said. "I've got some kind of minder over in the Philadelphia Mayor's Office who's got even more people to tell him things like that. The bullets that hit the wall at the Milky Way Ballroom and the bullets that killed that girl yesterday were from the same gun, and, like I said, that gun in there is probably the gun in question. I'm not trying to get publicity at your expense. I'm really not. I'm just bumping up against — things."

Borstoi was still not looking at him. Gregor thought he might be looking through the door of the study. It was hard to tell.

"Did these people hire you?" he asked, waving his hand around to indicate the present company.

"No," Gregor said. "They did ask me to look into things, but I didn't make them any promises, and I didn't agree to be hired. I don't usually work for private individuals. I consult for police departments. That way I'm not stepping on people's toes and I can't be charged with hindering a police investigation."

Borstoi looked back at the door to the living room. "All right," he said. "Consider yourself attached to this investigation. I'll get you paperwork later. My bosses all think you walk on water, in case you're interested."

"I don't walk on water," Gregor said. "I'm just less distracted than most police officers. I only work on one case at a time."

Borstoi looked at Gregor for the first time. "Come with me," he said.

And suddenly, Gregor had a second wind. Or a fourth one. He had no idea how long he'd been this tired. The two uniformed policemen were rounding up members of the cast and crew of *America's Next Superstar.* The policewoman was sticking to her post.

Gregor followed Len Borstoi through the living room door. The gun was still lying on the floor. The crime-scene people would pick that up and bag it later. Gregor looked around. There were no signs of bullets in the plaster wall around the fireplace. There were no signs of bullet holes in the couch. Borstoi pointed at the floor, and Gregor saw them — just two, right there, dug into the hardwood.

"She had to be aiming down," Gregor said.

"She?"

"Sheila Dunham had a point," Gregor

said. "Everybody around her was female. There was the crew, but —"

"You don't think it's possible for the crew to have wanted to kill Sheila Dunham?" Borstoi asked. "From what I hear, everybody on the planet wants to kill Sheila Dunham."

"Maybe," Gregor said, "but the crew wasn't here yesterday when that girl was found dead. At all. They were at some restaurant in downtown Bryn Mawr. I suppose one of them could have remained behind, but my guess is that he'd have been noticed. If you've listened to the girls, you know that one of them was left behind, but she supposedly went upstairs where she couldn't hear anything. So she could have committed the murder, or one of the girls in the cast could have committed the murder at the last minute, by running in when they were about to take off —"

"Did anyone do that?" Borstoi asked.

"At least three of them did," Gregor said. "The Asian girl called Alida came back for her umbrella. The one called Suzanne came back for her purse. Janice came back to go to the bathroom. And then there's when they came back."

"Do you think that's likely? First in the house?"

"No," Gregor said. "Well, maybe. It's hard to get the timing straight. But there were no judges here today, so that leaves the judges out. Did you ever get that Emily girl to talk to you?"

"It wasn't me," Borstoi reminded him. "I have talked to the Merion police. They brought her in. She gave her name as Emily Watson, got an attorney appointed, and just shut up. Then when it turned out that she hadn't actually fired any bullets, and her gun wasn't the one that did, well —"

"There was nothing to hold her on."

"Something like that," Borstoi said.

Gregor walked over to where the bullets were and knelt down. He was not a lab technician, or a forensics expert, but he didn't need to be one for this. The bullets were buried deep in the wood. It wasn't that somebody had fired at Sheila Dunham and missed. It was that somebody had fired at the floor. He stood up and backed off.

"Well," he said.

"I know," Borstoi said. "And I know there are cameras in this room, security cameras, and there were cameras filming what was going on here. But I get the feeling we're going to be in the same shape with this as we were with the murder yesterday."

"The security camera didn't do any good?"

"It had been turned off," Borstoi said. "Or, to be specific, it had had its wires ripped out at the wall."

"There were live cameras in here today as well," Gregor said.

"Yes, there were," Borstoi said, "but I don't think they're going to be any more help than the stationary ones, and you don't think so, either. Do you walk on water? Do you have any idea of what's going on here?"

"Well," Gregor said. "There is one thing. And I'm not trying to sound conceited. There's the mirror in the study, the one on the wall above the fireplace there."

"What about it?"

"It's been moved. Specifically, it's been allowed to lean very slightly forward. I've been in this house before, you know. My wife grew up here, and when I was first back in Philadelphia —"

"Oh, the Hannaford thing. I remember. I was still in a uniform then."

"I went and looked at some of the pictures of that. The mirror always hung flat against the wall. When you looked into it, from whatever part of the room, you could see a lot of things, but you couldn't see what was right under it on the hearth. But yesterday, the first thing I noticed was that you could see the body on the hearth in that mirror, at least if you looked at it through the doorway. And the body had been — how should I put this? It was as if it had been arranged."

Len Borstoi looked impressed. "That's very good. It had been moved. How did you know that? Or was it one of your sources of information?"

"No, it was a guess," Gregor said. "I just assumed that it was highly unlikely that the second murder I should see in this house would end up damned near replicating the first one."

"You mean, you think somebody arranged the body so that it was in the same position as the body of old Mr. Hannaford?"

"Well, it's like I said. That, or a really incredible coincidence."

"And the mirror?"

"So that I couldn't mistake what I saw. So that from far off, as soon as I looked at the scene, the first thing I'd notice was the resemblance."

"All right," Borstoi said. He looked half amazed and half amused. "Was there a point in doing that kind of thing? Why would anybody want to go through all that trouble?"

Gregor looked at the wall, and the floor, and the ceiling. He looked at the bullets embedded in the hardwood.

"I think," he said, "the idea was to take my mind off whatever was actually going on there. To distract me from the obvious."

"And what's the obvious?"

"Well," Gregor said, "the most obvious thing is that Sheila Dunham is not dead."

TWO

1

The other girls were avoiding her. They had been avoiding her since yesterday. Coraline had taken a long time to come to that conclusion, but now she found it inescapable. Only Janice was being nice to her, she felt, and that was probably because Janice was nice to everybody. She couldn't help it.

The yellow tape was coming down from across the door of the study. Police were walking in and out of the foyer. People in lab coats had gone into the study again and then come out, and now people in lab coats were in the living room. That Gregor Demarkian person had left, fetched by a girl who looked young enough to be his daughter and who drove the kind of car Coraline had only heard about. It was a tangerine orange two-seater convertible Mercedes-Benz.

Janice had explained it. "That's not the

woman it belongs to," she'd said. "I've seen a picture of the woman it belongs to in magazines. She's some kind of writer, I don't know. I never could read much, you know what I mean? Anyway, she's his wife now, and she's a lot older than that. She must have loaned the car to whoever that is."

Coraline didn't really care who it was. She had gone into the interview with the police and Mr. Demarkian feeling like she was about to be arrested at any moment. She was the one who was in the house all yesterday afternoon. She could say she was in her bedroom, crying her eyes out over Sheila Dunham and her torn T-shirt, but there was no way to prove that. And if she had been in the house, shouldn't she have heard the shots? Of course, the gun could have had a silencer, but she hadn't heard anyone talking about a silencer. She'd been listening, too.

She thought it had been wrong for her to come here. It was all well and good for her mother to talk about providing a Christian inspiration, but this was not a Christian place. Most of the other girls didn't even like Christians, and when Coraline tried to provide a Christian inspiration, they told her she was a bigoted jerk. They'd only just started, and she'd already found it easier to sit still and keep her mouth shut.

When the police had asked to talk to her, Coraline had gone into the living room and sat down on a chair across from the fireplace. The room was so large, police technicians could be working on it at one end and interviews could be going on at the other, and nobody got in anybody else's way.

"Show us where you were standing," Gregor Demarkian had said.

Coraline had looked around and blushed. Of course, she'd been standing right there at the end of the couch, just a little behind Faith Stackdopole, who had the silliest name she'd ever heard. But she'd wanted to stand behind somebody. She'd wanted to be where Sheila Dunham couldn't see her. And that, of course, had been the wrong decision. The gun had been there. Right there. When it was all over, Coraline had seen it lying on the ground.

"I was right behind Faith," she'd said, as carefully as she could. She was trying so desperately not to seem guilty. "And in front of me to my left was Suzanne. And next to me and behind me was Janice. And I was thinking that if I wasn't so afraid of Sheila Dunham, I'd have been able to sit on the couch, and that would have been better. You could see the girls on the couch. On camera, I mean. They're the ones who are going to get noticed when the show airs."

Coraline had no idea if the show would air now that there had been a gunshot, but maybe it would. Maybe that would make "good television." People around here were always talking about good television.

"Could you tell where the gunshot was coming from?"

All right, that was true. There had been no silencer today. The gunshot was very loud. Everybody had heard it.

"It just happened," she had said, threatening to break into tears again. "It just did. We were all sort of jumping up and down, and yelling 'yay' and 'dynamite,' and that kind of thing. We were all just making noise. And then there were those sounds, you know, and everybody stopped."

"Everybody stopped completely? They stopped moving around as well as talking?"

"Well, no," Coraline had said. "There was a lot of moving around. And then, you know, people were making noise. And other people, people from the crew, were running around. We all thought somebody had been hurt."

"But nobody had been."

"No. No. That was a good thing. I hate it

here. I want to go home. I didn't think it would be anything like this."

Now Coraline stood in the door of the study and thought that she had completely lost track of who had asked her which questions. She knew one was Detective Borstoi and one was Mr. Demarkian, but she wasn't paying attention to either of them. She'd just wanted to cry, and to go to her room and hide, except that she wasn't sure she was welcome in her room. Last night, her roommate, Deanna, had gone down the hall to talk to people and never come back.

Coraline went into the study and looked around. There was still blood in places. There was blood on the hearth, and on the wall, and on the ceiling — only a little of it on the ceiling, just a drop or two. She went to the mirror and looked up at it. It did tilt a little forward — who had she heard talking about that? Somebody. If you looked at the back of the mirror you could see there was something like a ribbon there, or two ribbons, and the mirror was hanging on them. Coraline didn't think anybody had done anything about the mirror on purpose. If that was how it was fastened to the wall, it would be easy for it to just come loose a little and let the mirror hang forward. Maybe it would come so loose that the mirror would crash to the ground, and then there would be shards of glass everywhere.

What Coraline really hated was this thing where they were none of them ever allowed to call home, except for the limited call they got to make to their families after the murder. They couldn't have their cell phones. They couldn't use the phone here except in the evenings, and then there was only one, and all of them had to share it. It was impossible to get any time for a really good talk.

She walked around the room again. She looked up at the mirror again. She looked at the floor. There used to be two carpets on the study floor, Oriental ones like the ones in the living room, but the carpets closest to the fireplace had been taken away. There were still bloodstains on that, too.

Coraline heard a sound and looked up. She was starting to get supersensitive to sounds. It would make her look guiltier if anybody noticed.

Ivy was standing in the doorway to the study. "Are you all right?" she asked.

"I'm fine," Coraline said.

She revised her impressions in her head. Janice was not the only one who was being nice to her. Ivy was being nice, too. The problem was, she didn't like it when Ivy was nice to her. There was that hair. There was that tattoo. Back in Southport, only guys got tattoos, and only guys who weren't nice. Ivy could ride with a motorcycle gang when she was back home. For all Coraline knew, Ivy could be a prostitute.

"They're going to put a buffet out in the dining room," Ivy said. "You ought to come and eat something. People really aren't ostracizing you, no matter what you think."

Coraline thought about telling Ivy about Deanna, and how Deanna didn't want to sleep in their room anymore, but she wasn't sure Ivy would understand. Janice would understand. Janice was almost like the girls she knew at home, and so was Mary-Louise, although neither one of them were saved. Didn't anybody get saved outside the South? Maybe the people who got saved outside the South just knew more about television and things like that, and didn't try out for shows like *America's Next Superstar.*

"Coraline?" Ivy said.

Coraline looked back up in the mirror. It wasn't tilted much forward. If you weren't looking for it, you wouldn't notice that it was tilted at all. Nobody would have done something so small on purpose.

"Coraline," Ivy said again.

"I'm coming," Coraline said.

She didn't want to. She wanted to go back upstairs and cry some more. She wanted to call her mother and leave the house and go back home.

She had no idea what she could do and what she couldn't do without making herself look guiltier and guiltier, because from what she'd heard them talking about this morning, she seemed to be the only person in the house who could have killed that girl.

2

Janice knew that a lot of the girls were trying to keep their mouths shut when they were talking to the police, but she didn't see the point. It was exciting, all this. It was much more exciting than she had expected it to be, and she had gone over and over the possibilities in her head before she came to the auditions. This was going to be the most famous season of *America's Next Superstar* ever. Everybody on the planet was going to watch it, because they'd want to see if they could tell which one of the girls was trying to kill Sheila Dunham. It would be even better if nobody was arrested, because then there would be suspicion everywhere. People would not only watch, they would watch closely. All the girls would be famous in no time flat. Janice Ledbedder wanted to be famous.

Most of the girls were trying to pretend they didn't know anything about crime, too, but that was even sillier, in Janice's opinion, than trying to keep their lives a secret. She had no secrets in her life. Everybody in Marshall, South Dakota, knew she loved to watch all those true-crime shows on television. A lot of the girls liked to watch them, too, and if they didn't they had mothers who liked to watch.

"I saw the one about the murders at Margaret's Harbor," Janice had told Mr. Demarkian when she'd been called in to talk to him and Detective Borstoi. "They made a *City Confidential* about that and an *American Justice,* too, and there was stuff on it on *Forensic Files.* I think maybe that was because of all the celebrities. Everything's more interesting if there are celebrities, don't you think?"

"I don't think," the police detective had said.

Janice ignored him. "They did the one that happened here, too," she said. "It was the first thing I thought of when I heard the name of the house. I mean, I wouldn't have known it was the same place, you know, because all those pictures of the outsides of big houses look alike. But then somebody said the name and I knew. And I'm not the only one. Mary-Louise knew, too. She'd even looked it up on the Internet."

"Looked up what on the Internet?" Mr. Demarkian said.

"Looked up the house," Janice said. "The first night we were here. We aren't allowed to have Internet, really, but there was a computer in one of the offices downstairs and we didn't know we weren't supposed to be in there, so we were using it. We were IM-ing, if you want to know the truth. It's terrible, being stuck up here without being able to talk to anybody practically ever. Anybody outside, I mean. We're really not allowed to. So we did that and we looked at pictures of the house and talked to people, except I didn't talk to anybody because, you know, nobody I knew was on."

"Tell us where you were when you heard the shots," the detective said.

Janice took a deep breath and brightened right up. This really was exciting. Nothing like this ever happened in South Dakota. There was crime there, but it was the kind of crime that would make anybody bored.

"I was standing behind the couch in the back row," she said. "Not that there were really rows, if you know what I mean. It's just that even though the couch is big, it isn't big enough to have ten girls strung out in a single line behind it, so we were all sort of squished together. I had Coraline in front of me to my right, a little, and then in front of me to my left a little there was Deanna Brackett, Coraline's roommate."

"And who was to either side of you?" the detective asked.

"Faith Stackdopole on my right, more up front, and Suzanne, I think, on my left. I'm not really sure about that. We were all just sort of moving around until the last minute."

"Did you hear the shots when they happened?" Mr. Demarkian asked.

"Well, of course I heard them," Janice said. "I mean, they were very loud. I'd have to have heard them."

"Do you know what direction they came from?"

Janice shook her head. "No. No, they were just there. Just sort of everywhere, if you know what I mean. I thought they were close, but they would have to be close, so I don't see that that's any help. Really, it was just — well, we weren't expecting it, were we? And then everybody starting yelling and running around, and somebody got off the couch — that Shari girl, I think. And she was jumping around and yelling, and so was everybody else."

"There's a police technician over there," the detective said. "She's set up to test your hands for gunshot residue. I'm obliged to tell you that you do not have to agree to take such a test without a lawyer, but —"

"Oh, I don't mind," Janice said. "This really is exciting, isn't it? Do you think they'll do an episode of *American Justice* on this one? It would be so wonderful if they did. Then maybe I'd be on two television programs instead of one. They could interview me the way they do, you know, with a backdrop of justice scales or something, and then the person talks about what it felt like to be there."

"Well," Gregor Demarkian said.

"Oh, I know," Janice said. "You have to solve it first. But you will solve it. I know all about you. So that's all right. I just wish you'd do it soon, so that everybody could stop stressing about it. I mean, there's one of us here who killed somebody, and we don't even know why. Maybe they'll kill somebody else."

"That's true," Mr. Demarkian said.

"Nothing like this ever happens in South Dakota," Janice said, "and nobody from Marshall ever gets famous, either, so this is going to be the biggest thing in years.

Everybody in town's going to want to talk to me when I get home, and they'd have wanted that even if I'd just gotten on the program."

"I'm sure," the detective said.

They weren't very friendly, either of them, but Janice didn't mind. She was just racing at the mouth, that was all. She'd like to be one of those people who could keep her cool no matter what, but she wasn't, and that was that.

Afterward, she wandered around in the dining room and looked at the food on the "sideboard," which seemed to her to be just the bottom half of a hutch, but people here used different words for everything. They ate different food, too.

She wondered if Coraline was going to come in to eat.

3

Grace Alsop was also wondering if Coraline was going to come in to eat, but she had more practical reasons in mind.

"They tested all of us," she told Alida and Suzanne, "and they didn't find gun residue or whatever it is they were looking for on any of us. They didn't find it on Olivia Dahl, either."

"Well, it couldn't have been Olivia who

did the shooting," Alida said. "She was standing at the back there, not where we were. The bullets wouldn't have been in the wood that way if she'd shot the gun —"

"Right, and then she'd have had to get the gun around to the side of the couch," Suzanne said. "That was where the gun was found, between us and Sheila Dunham."

"It was a little to the side," Grace said impatiently. "And anybody could have dropped it there. We were all running around acting like lunatics. None of us was noticing anything. Anybody could have dropped a cannon on that floor and we wouldn't have seen it."

"I was sitting on the couch," Alida said. "I couldn't have dropped it anywhere. I was sitting down."

Grace thought she was going to scream. "All right," she said. "You were sitting on the couch. It probably wasn't anybody sitting on the couch. I agree. But Coraline wasn't sitting on the couch."

"Oh, don't start that again," Alida said. "She didn't have any of that gun stuff on her hands any more than the rest of us did."

"No, she didn't," Grace said, "but that doesn't necessarily mean anything. She could have been wearing gloves."

"Did you notice her wearing gloves?" Suzanne asked.

"No, I didn't," Grace said. "And I'd guess nobody else did, because nobody said anything. But it wouldn't have been hard. Wearing gloves, or holding something that would protect her hand from the gun stuff. It wouldn't have been that hard, and it wouldn't have been hard for her to hide it — especially if it was gloves, or just one glove. It wouldn't have been hard for her to hide it somewhere."

"Where?" Alida demanded.

"In the couch, maybe," Grace said. "Or, you know, anywhere. It's a huge room. She didn't have to hide it where we were. She could have put it anywhere."

"They'd have found it by now," Alida said.

A couple of the other girls had come up to listen. Grace saw Deanna, and Mary-Louise, and Janice, and Linda. They all looked wide-eyed and excited, as if this was some kind of murder game made for TV and completely unreal. They didn't seem to understand that someone was dead, somebody else might end up dead before it was all over, and somebody was almost certainly going to jail. This being Pennsylvania, somebody could be going to a lethal injection.

"Look," Grace said. "In the first place,

Coraline is the only one of us who could have done it. She was the only one here when the murder happened —"

"You don't know that," Mary-Louise said. "You don't know when it happened, I mean. Maybe it happened when we all got back."

"How?" Grace asked. "Think about it. We got back. The doors to the limo opened. We all piled out and came rushing into the house in a big wad —"

"I wasn't first," Mary-Louise said quickly. "There were already people in the hall when I got there."

"There wasn't even a full minute between the first person going into the house and the rest of us going in," Grace said. "There wasn't time enough for anybody to commit a murder. Coraline was the only one who was here. If it isn't Coraline, then it isn't any of us. And the crew didn't stay behind, either. They came to the restaurant to film us."

"She makes me feel creepy," Deanna said. "I know she's my roommate, and we're supposed to get along, but —"

"Why would she kill somebody she didn't even know," Linda Kowalski asked. "I mean, we didn't know this person, right?"

"Coraline could have seen her before," Grace said. "We don't know who this girl was or where she was from or anything. And the police don't know, either. She could be anybody. She could be somebody Coraline knew back home."

"What was she doing here?" Suzanne asked.

"I don't know," Grace said. "How am I supposed to know? The girl was whoever she was. It doesn't matter. The police will find out eventually."

"Maybe Coraline is one of those serial killers," Mary-Louise said. "There are women serial killers. They just go around killing people. Except, you know, mostly it's about sex."

Grace wanted to do more than scream. She wanted to jump around and hit somebody. These girls were all such idiots. They really were. They couldn't think straight to save their lives, and they couldn't actually reason their way through a problem for anything at all.

"Listen," she said. "The fact is, she's the only one who could have done it, and she's the only one I can think of who might have had a motive. I think she's trying to wreck the show."

"Why would she want to wreck the show?" Janice asked. "Don't be silly, Grace. She's just as much involved in the show as any of the rest of us."

"She may seem like she is," Grace said, "but she's one of those born-again people, isn't she? They're all a little off-balance, if you ask me, and a lot of them are violent. They get crazy. That's why they believe in God."

"Oh, come on," Mary-Louise said. "I believe in God. Everybody believes in God."

"I don't," Grace said, "and not everybody believes in God in the same way. Some people believe in God and they're very sensible about it. But the born-again types aren't sensible about it. They're fanatics. I think she's trying to wreck the show. I think she thinks it's sinful, or something, and she's trying to shut it down."

"By killing somebody none of us knows and who wasn't even supposed to be in the show?" Linda Kowalski said. "And anyway, that other girl had a gun, didn't she? At the Milky Way Ballroom? There were shots and she was there holding the gun, and that was why the police arrested her."

"Well, guns can be planted," Grace said.

"In somebody's hand?" Ivy said.

Grace hadn't heard her come in. She didn't think anybody had. They all turned to look at Ivy's green hair streak and then looked away again. Grace didn't like any of the girls in this competition, but the longer they lived together, the more the one she liked least was Ivy Demari. It wasn't just the tattoos or the weird hair. It was the attitude.

"Guns can be planted," Grace said again. "They can be. And I don't know about in somebody's hand, but that's still not to say the gun wasn't planted. After all, they let that girl out because the gun she was holding wasn't the one that fired the shots they got out of the wall at the Ballroom. I heard that police detective talking to Gregor Demarkian about it."

"We're all hearing entirely too much about what the police detective said to Gregor Demarkian," Ivy said, "and you've got to stop this now. You've got poor Coraline on the edge of a nervous breakdown as it is. I can't get her in here to eat something, and she should eat something. She's going to collapse."

"Good," Alida said. "Let her collapse. Let them send her home. Get her out of here. Then I can go back to sleeping at night."

"She could do it again," Deanna broke in. "The next victim could be any of us."

Grace thought Ivy was going to slap somebody. "Why would it be any of us?" she asked. "It's Sheila Dunham somebody has been firing guns at. It's Sheila Dunham somebody wants to kill. And no, I don't think that somebody is Coraline, and neither do any of you."

"Speak for yourself," Grace said. "I think that somebody is Coraline. And wanting to kill Sheila Dunham makes even more sense. It is a religious thing. Sheila Dunham has to represent the worst kind of cultural depravity as far as somebody like Coraline is concerned. She probably looks like an agent of the devil. Maybe Coraline thinks she can wipe out depravity and sin and get us all back to God if she just gets rid of Sheila Dunham."

"And the other girl?" Ivy asked.

"Sheila Dunham has a daughter," Janice said suddenly. "I heard about it. They don't talk to each other anymore. Maybe the girl who died was Sheila Dunham's daughter, and —"

"And what?" Ivy said.

"Oh," Janice said. "I don't know. I'm sorry. I don't think Coraline did it, either, you know, because, well, she isn't that kind of person. She's very nice."

"For God's sake," Grace said.

Ivy took a plate from the stack on the sideboard and started loading it with food. "I'm going to take this to Coraline," she said. "She's sitting out on the stairs. She doesn't want to go into the living room and she really doesn't want to go into the study. I think the entire pack of you are first-rate bitches, I really do."

"Somebody has to make sense in a situation like this," Grace said. "Somebody has to do something to protect us from getting hurt, and the show doesn't seem to give a damn. I think they ought to post a guard in here to make sure she doesn't go off her nut again and kill somebody else."

"I think that if anybody dies, it's going to be you," Ivy said, "and I'm going to do the killing."

Then she took the full plate, and a fork and a knife, and marched out of the dining room.

Grace watched her go, and the rest of the girls watched with her.

It didn't matter what Ivy thought. Grace knew as much as she needed to know about what was going on around here now.

THREE

1

For Gregor Demarkian, Len Borstoi's announcement that he was to consider himself hired, or on the case, or whatever the man had said, felt unreal. That was not how he was hired to consult on cases. First there was a letter, or a fax, or a phone call from the chief of police or the mayor. Then there was a discreet little talk about money. Then there was the advance prep, lots of paperwork with forensic reports and detective logs scattered through it. This was more like the sort of thing that would happen in dreams, except that Gregor never had dreams about work. His dreams always had to do with Bennis and Elizabeth meeting, sometimes for lunch, sometimes in the afterlife. He'd talked to Father Tibor about that once, but neither one of them had been able to come up with a satisfactory explanation.

"You love both your wives," Tibor said. "You hope that if they met, they would get along."

In the dreams, Bennis and Elizabeth always did get along, but Gregor wasn't sure they would have if they'd met in real life. They were opposites in ways that weren't supposed to matter much, but always did: Bennis had grown up rich on the Main Line while Elizabeth had grown up poor in a tenement in a poor neighborhood in Philadelphia; Elizabeth had been very traditional about marriage while Bennis had treated marriage like a poison she'd be lucky if she managed to escape; Elizabeth had believed in women being homemakers and Bennis had the career from hell.

Of course, they had both gone to Vassar, about ten years apart, so there was that. But maybe not. Gregor himself had gone to the University of Pennsylvania for his undergraduate work, and he could remember better than he liked to, the divide between the live-at-school, come-from-Ivy-League-families crowd and the students who, like him, commuted from home and had really large scholarships.

It had been years since Gregor had thought so much about Elizabeth, who had died of cancer before he'd ever moved back to Cavanaugh Street. He didn't really know why he was thinking about her now. He was married again, yes, and just back from his honeymoon — but it wasn't like that was a sudden thing. He'd not only known, but been practically living in Bennis's lap for years. Thoughts of Elizabeth had never bothered him before.

Donna pulled Bennis's car to the curb in front of Gregor's building and cut the engine. "I've got to go put this back in the garage," she said. "Can you believe that Bennis spends three hundred dollars a month just to keep this thing in a garage?"

"If it was mine, I'd probably put it in a vault," Gregor said. "It's not the kind of thing that blends into the background."

"Oh, I know," Donna said. "And I know it's supposed to be silly to have a car like this when you live in the city. But it's a lot of fun to drive."

"Why don't you get one?"

"Well," Donna said, "I've got a son and a daughter. And there are going to be tuitions."

"True," Gregor said.

He looked up and down the street. When he'd first moved back here, Donna had had a habit of decorating the entire neighborhood for any holiday that came up. She'd once wrapped the entire building in which he lived — and where she then had the top floor floor-through apartment — in shiny stuff and a bow that made it look like a Christmas package. With this last pregnancy, she seemed to have given that up. He was sorry to see that go.

"I miss the decorations," he said. He sounded abrupt even to himself.

Donna laughed. "You're not the only one. I've just got a lot to do these days. Maybe I can convince the youth group to help me out and we can decorate for the Fourth of July. That's not too far away. Listen, Bennis is up there practically hanging out of the window. She's very worried about you."

"I know she is," Gregor said. "There's really nothing to be worried about."

Donna gave him the kind of look that said she didn't believe him for a minute, and Gregor got out and started walking up the steps to the building's front door. He was light-headed, but that was just exhaustion. What bothered him was that he still felt the nagging half panic that had bolted him awake at four o'clock in the morning, but it wasn't strong enough to keep him in gear. He wanted to sleep, and he wanted to sleep even though he felt that something awful was about to happen any second now, and that he was the only one who could stop it.

He let himself into the foyer and saw that the door to old George Tekemanian's apartment was closed and locked. He supposed George was out somewhere with Tibor or Lida and Hannah or somebody. If there had been something wrong, if old George had gone to the hospital or had an accident or any of that kind of thing, Donna would have known and told him.

Gregor started climbing the stairs. There were a lot of them. If he had owned this entire building, instead of one of the apartments in it — two, if you counted the one Bennis owned, since they were married now — he would have put in one of those little elevators.

He got to the second-floor landing feeling winded. He got to the third-floor landing feeling dead. He now had old George on his mind as well as everything else.

"You look like hell," Bennis said. She was standing in the doorway of their apartment, holding the door open. "Have you had any sleep at all? Are you crazy?"

Gregor went through the door and into his own foyer. He took off his suit jacket and dropped it on the floor. He never dropped clothes on the floor. He heard Bennis come in behind him and pick it up. He kept on walking into the living room, made his way to the couch, and sat down. Or lay down. It was hard to tell which. He had half sprawled across it. He didn't think he could move again.

Gregor heard Bennis close the door, and then her footsteps as she came into the room. She was standing right behind him. He could feel it.

"Do you want me to make you some coffee?" she asked him.

"No," Gregor said. "Definitely no coffee. I've had enough coffee."

"I could make you milk and honey," Bennis said. "I'd like to say that was what my mother made me when I couldn't get to sleep, but you knew my mother. It wasn't the kind of thing she did. On the other hand, it is the kind of thing Lida does, and she told me all about it."

"I just need to relax for a minute," Gregor said.

Bennis came around the couch and sat down on one of the chairs. She was a beautiful woman. She had been a beautiful woman when he first met her, and she would be a beautiful woman if she lived to be a hundred and six. That was because there was no part of her beauty that was dependent on age. She was not beautiful the way that, say, somebody like Christie Brinkley was beautiful, with that perky blond evenness that indicated an age of twenty-five, and looked strange ever afterward. Bennis's face was angular and strange. It looked like nothing else on earth. It also worked.

She leaned closer to him and said, "Is there something wrong? Is there something I should know about? I think I always worried that if we ever actually got around to doing it for real —"

"We got around to that part years ago," Gregor said.

"I meant getting married." Bennis made a raspberry. "I was always worried that it would freak you out. That we were all right being not-married married, but we wouldn't be all right being actually married."

"Not-married married," Gregor said. His eyes were half closed now. "That's a good way to put it."

"So I thought I'd ask," Bennis said, "whether the way you're behaving has something to do with me. Because you're behaving like a lunatic."

Sleep was a foreign country, but Gregor was right there, at the border. He could see the little guard station and the little guard. He could see the gumdrop houses and cotton-candy mountains. This was the silliest line of thought he could remember himself having in all his life.

He forced his eyes open. "It's not you," he said. "It's time."

"What?"

"I'm in the middle of two things, and they're both sensitive to time," Gregor said. "There's only a short amount of time, and if we don't get them right then something bad is going to happen. Well, it is definitely in the one case, and it could be in the other."

"Which case?" Bennis asked.

Gregor made himself sit up just a little. "Sophie Mgrdchian," he said. "She's still lying in a hospital bed, but they've been through just about everything they can think of, and it's been, what, two days? And they don't have any reason why she should be in practically a coma. So they can't hold this woman —"

"Karen Mgrdchian," Bennis said. "That's Sophie's sister-in-law, isn't it? Didn't you tell me that?"

"She says she's Karen Mgrdchian," Gregor said, "but I'm pretty sure she isn't. In fact, I know she isn't. But I can't prove she isn't, and nobody can prove that anybody did anything to Sophie Mgrdchian to put her in the state she's in, so there we are.

The court handed this woman over for a psychiatric examination, but that's limited to four days. By the end of the week, they're going to have to let her out of there, and if they do, I'd be willing to bet she'd find a way to kill Sophie Mgrdchian in no time flat. Either that, or Sophie will die of whatever this is before she ever leaves the hospital."

"Isn't that odd?" Bennis asked. "I mean, Sophie Mgrdchian is in the hospital, away from this woman. If she was being poisoned, or something, shouldn't she be getting better? With nobody around to poison her anymore?"

"There is that," Gregor said. "And, of course, that's one of the reasons why it's going to be nearly impossible to hold this woman calling herself Karen Mgrdchian after the observation order. Especially now that she's acting like a perfectly normal human being. But she can't be Karen Mgrdchian. She just can't."

"Why not?"

"Because she destroyed her own fingerprints," Gregor said. "And I've been telling that to everybody who would listen since this thing started. And what I hear is that lots of people destroy their own fingerprints accidentally. But Bennis, you know, they don't, they really don't. I can't think of a single case among all the people I've known in my life. Not one. Junkies do it sometimes, if they're playing around with, I'm sorry, I can't remember the name — the gas in industrial-sized canisters of whipped cream. Nitrous oxide? Anyway, people who play around with those sometimes get their hands stuck to them and frozen solid and then the fingertips have to be cut off to get the canister off, but does this look like a woman who uses nitrous oxide?"

"The day we found her," Bennis said, "she was acting like she was on nitrous oxide."

"Yes, well, I still can't see it. Anyway, homeless people do it to themselves sometimes because they grab metal, a metal bar, a metal railing, they're just trying to steady themselves and it's freezing cold and they get their hands stuck, and then they pull them off and there you are. But ordinary human beings do not do that, and we all know it. And I'm sitting here trying to figure out what could possibly be causing Sophie's condition and what I could possibly say that would make the Philadelphia police look at this differently than they do, and I keep running up against brick walls. I told David Mortimer this morning about searching the house and not finding an address book or refrigerator magnets with doctors' names on them or a cell phone or anything. And Billie Ormonds said that from what the police have been able to figure out, Sophie Mgrdchian wasn't even on Medicare. How the hell could she not be on Medicare?"

"She didn't sign up?" Bennis suggested.

"The doctors would have signed her up," Gregor said. "Or their nurses would have. Doctors like to get paid. And she has to have been seeing doctors. You need doctors to get prescriptions. I need to convince them to go search that house."

"Sophie's house? Haven't they already searched it?"

"No, the other house," Gregor said. "The Mgrdchian house in wherever it is. Cleveland? I can't remember. That house."

"Why?"

"Because I'm fairly sure there's at least one body in the basement."

"What?"

"Maybe two," Gregor said. "In a worst-case scenario, maybe three. But that's getting ahead of myself. I've got to get some sleep."

"I can see that," Bennis said.

"Do me a favor," Gregor said. "Get my phone, and look at that address-book thing . . . Then there's Billie Ormonds." She spells it like Billie Burke, you remember, that actress who was Glinda in *The Wizard of Oz*. Tell her who you are and then tell her I need to talk to her, later this afternoon, as soon as she's got a minute to give me. I'd do it now, but I'm —"

"In no shape," Bennis said. "I can see that."

"See if you can't get an appointment for me to talk to her, to see her face to face, I don't know. Invite her to the Ararat for dinner or something. She's not a homicide detective. There isn't any homicide as far as anybody knows, and there isn't anything we know that could make it a suspected homicide, in spite of the fact that —"

"Don't go into all that again. You'll fall over."

"I'm okay. I'm fine. I'm getting up. Do that for me, if you don't mind. I've got to —"

"You've got to get at least a few hours of sleep," Bennis said. "I know. Go ahead."

2

Going to sleep was not always the best idea in the world. It wasn't always the second best idea in the world. Gregor threw himself out of his clothes and into his bed as if he

were diving into water. When he hit the mat-
tress, he thought he might have passed out,
but it was an odd kind of passing out. He
couldn't count the number of stories he'd
heard about people who were supposedly in
comas — or who really were in comas —
who could actually hear and see and understand everything that was going on around
them. He remembered the story of one
woman who had laid in bed day after day,
listening while her family and her doctors
and her nurses had all argued the pros and
cons of taking her feeding tubes out and
letting her "die with dignity." There was
some kind of a show on that one — Oprah,
maybe, although he wasn't sure. The woman
had written a book about her experiences.
The television shows had gone looking into
it all and found out that the phenomenon
was rare, but not vanishingly rare. There
were a couple of dozen people out there,
now alive and well, who had been through
the same thing.

Gregor wondered how many dead people
there were who had actually been just like
this comatose woman, who lived. The
woman had had one granddaughter who
was adamantly opposed to taking out the
feeding tubes. This granddaughter had
fought hard and long and managed to delay

the day, and then the woman had woken up. How many dead people hadn't had granddaughters like that, or anybody else who would keep them from being —

Killed off, Gregor thought. He understood the reasoning behind taking people off machines that did things like make their hearts beat and make their lungs work when those organs would no longer operate on their own. The coma patient, however, hadn't needed machines like that. Her heart and lungs had been working on their own. All she'd needed was food and water, delivered through a feeding tube.

Why was he thinking about these things now? Sophie was not on machines, either. Her heart and lungs were working. She only had a feeding tube. Nobody had suggested that they take it out. Could this woman — the woman calling herself Karen Mgrdchian — could she have the authority to demand it be taken out? If she was who she said she was, she would be one of only two existing relatives. The other one would be the daughter, who would be Sophie's niece. That assumed that the daughter wasn't in the basement, with her real mother.

This was getting worse than surreal. He had liked it better when there had been gumdrop houses and cotton candy mountains. He kept seeing things floating through the void, like the things in the tornado in *The Wizard of Oz* — it was like everything had a theme. He saw syringes and IV tubes and plastic pill organizers and latex gloves that changed mysteriously into beige-colored lace ones, stretchy beige-colored lace ones that —

Oh, Gregor thought.

He tried to force himself awake, but it didn't work.

3

It was Bennis who woke him finally, sitting down at the edge of the bed and shaking him by the shoulder. Gregor started to surface very slowly, and all the way up he was convinced that he had thought of something very important, and that he'd better remember it. He couldn't remember anything. His head hurt.

"Gregor?" Bennis said.

"Is it six o'clock already?"

Bennis cleared her throat. Gregor wondered if he'd ever actually said anything about waking him at six o'clock. He might not have. He turned in bed — he usually didn't turn at all in bed — he always slept on his left side, and forced his eyes awake.

"Sorry," he said.

"It's five, if you want to know the truth," Bennis said. "I've got a dinner appointment for you at seven with your Billie Ormonds person. I should be waking you up anyway. But that isn't why I'm here."

"You're waking me up," Gregor said reasonably. "So that is why you're here."

"The Very Old Ladies are in the kitchen," Bennis said. "I tried to get them to sit in the living room, but they weren't having any. They're making that kind of coffee . . . you know, Lida serves it sometimes, it's like mud and it can double as rocket fuel."

"Turkish coffee," Gregor said. "Except you never say Turkish in an Armenian neighborhood. Call it Armenian coffee. I need to take a shower."

"I agree, you do, but they're here. They climbed all those steps. On purpose."

"I don't suppose I could take a quick shower and then come out in my bathrobe."

"Somehow," Bennis said, "I'd guess the answer is no."

Gregor knew the answer was no, too. He waited for Bennis to stand up. Then he sat all the way up himself and swung his legs onto the floor. He was wearing nothing but boxer shorts, and he was willing to bet that if he looked in the mirror, he'd be a mess. He saw his clothes piled on the floor. They looked wrinkled and dirty. He didn't want to put them on.

"I am going to take a shower," he said. "I'm not going to put on fresh clothes when I'm like this. Give them something to eat and I'll be out in a minute."

"If I give them something to eat, they'll complain about how I can't cook," Bennis said. "And they're right, so I can't even tell them off about it."

"They'd only swear at you in Armenian if you did," Gregor said. "Fifteen minutes tops. Less than that. I'll be right out."

He was right out, too. He made sure by turning the water on full blast and cold. It woke him up, and it got even his hair washed in record time. He kept going over and over the dreams he remembered. They were jumbled up, and Terri Schiavo was in one of them. He did know what that one was about, though. He'd known that before he'd fallen asleep. It was the other things that were making him nervous. He remembered a tornado with things floating in it. He remembered the syringe, and the gloves, but the gloves were wrong.

He got out of the shower, toweled off, and went back to the bedroom. He took a fresh pair of boxers from the top drawer and found a clean suit hanging in the closet. He threw on a plain white button-down shirt, which was the only kind of shirt he ever wore. Bennis always complained that he dresses as if he were still in the FBI.

He got on socks. He thought about dispensing with the shoes. He thought the Very Old Ladies were going to notice. They always noticed everything.

He opened the bedroom door and stuck his head out into the hall. He could hear murmuring noises coming from the kitchen. He hoped Bennis was holding her own.

He left the bedroom, walked down the hall and through the living room, and went into the kitchen. The kitchen was "eat in," because there was no dining room. Sometimes he understood what Bennis meant when she said that the apartment was cramped.

The Very Old Ladies were sitting around the kitchen table, drinking coffee out of large mugs that were only half full. Gregor guessed that this had been Bennis's compromise with the fact that she didn't own any of the tiny little cups Armenian coffee was supposed to be served in. According to Bennis, Armenian coffee was not a beverage. It was a drug addiction.

There was an empty chair at the table. Bennis was standing up, leaning back against the sink. She looked a little dazed.

Gregor sat down. "Good afternoon," he said, as if it were the most ordinary thing in the world for these three women to have climbed three sets of stairs plus the stoop to sit in his kitchen. He suddenly wondered if they had elevators in their houses, or if they'd kept in shape all these years making their way up and down staircases that were difficult for much younger people to manage.

Viola Vardanian, made a face. It was a very sour face. "We've come to find out what is going on," she said. "We have tried to talk to the police officers, and they will not tell us."

"What police officers did you try to talk to?" Gregor asked.

"We went to the precinct, Krekor," Mrs. Vardanian said. "What did you think we would do. We went there, and we went to the hospital, and talked to Dr. Halevy. Nobody would tell us anything, because we are not next of kin."

"I think that's probably the law," Gregor said.

"They did ask us a lot of questions," Mrs. Melvarian said. Mrs. Melvarian was the small round one, the one that looked most like an Armenian peasant grandmother.

"Dr. Halevy especially asked us. And she expected us to answer."

"It's been hard to get information," Gregor said. "There doesn't seem to be anything anywhere to tell us, well, to tell us things. Who her doctor was, for instance."

"Yes, yes," Mrs. Vardanian said. "Dr. Halevy asked us the same thing. You should find Sophie's little book and use that. Although I don't think I've ever known her to go to the doctors. She doesn't like doctors."

"Doctors can be necessary," Gregor said. "What little book are you talking about?"

"Oh, her niece made it for her when she was in the fifth grade," Mrs. Edelakian said. It was more like gushing. "When the niece was in the fifth grade, I mean. It's beautiful, it really is. It's got pictures on the cover of it, all these pictures of Sophie and her family. Sophie herself, and Viktor, and Dennis and Marco and their wives, and Clarice, too. Clarice made it in her art class."

"Clarice is in fifth grade?" Gregor was confused.

Mrs. Vardanian snorted. "Of course she isn't. She's a middle-aged woman now, I would think. But Kara is right. She always used that one. She kept it in the little telephone table in the kitchen."

"I looked in the telephone table," Gregor said. "I looked in a big cedar chest in the living room. I looked in the night table next to her bed. I spent nearly three hours this morning going through every room in the house, I didn't find any address book, with pictures on it or not. I didn't find much of anything except very old lace and some copies of a magazine in Armenian."

"The police say this other woman is Marco's wife," Mrs. Vardanian said. "I don't believe it."

"We need to find out what doctor Sophie was seeing," Gregor said. "He or she might be able to tell us something about why she's still in a coma. If it is a coma. I get the medical terms confused, sometimes. We need to know why she's unconscious."

"Really?" Mrs. Vardanian said. "Maybe there isn't any doctor. Sophie wasn't sick. She was never sick. She didn't even get colds. And she didn't have the aches the way the rest of us do. She had a little arthritis, but that's to be expected, Krekor. People didn't always go running off to the doctor every time they have aches. There's no point to it."

"And it costs a fortune," Mrs. Melvarian said. "Even with the Medicare."

"She had to be seeing a doctor," Gregor

said patiently. "She had one of those plastic pill organizers on her when she was taken to the hospital. She had medications, and the only way you can get medications is by seeing a doctor. She had a prescription painkiller for the arthritis. She had one of those drugs that lower blood cholesterol. She had one of the ones that lower blood pressure —"

"She never had any such thing," Mrs. Vardanian said.

The other two Very old Ladies looked equal startled. "Oh," Mrs. Edelakian said, "Viola is right. Sophie couldn't have had blood pressure medicine."

"She really couldn't," Mrs. Melvarian agreed.

Mrs. Vardanian would have looked triumphant if she hadn't looked so disgusted.

"Sophie Mgrdchian," she said, "has *low* blood pressure. It's so low that once when she went in for a gall bladder operation and they gave her Demerol for the pain, when they did the blood pressure test they thought she was dead. Except that she was sitting up and talking, so she wasn't. Sophie Mgrdchian never took a pill to lower her blood pressure in her life. It would have killed her."

FOUR

1

The individual interviews were an important part of the show, just as they were an important part of any reality show. They were always filmed as if the girl being interviewed was talking by herself, as if nobody was asking her questions or even in the room. The trick was to convince the girls that nothing they said would be heard by the judges — and especially by Sheila Dunham — until the show was in postproduction and about to be aired. You didn't want the girls pulling their punches, or saying insipid little nicey-nice things because they were afraid of Sheila having one of her fits, or of being eliminated. You wanted them right there and pumping away, saying the kind of things that made viewers write in and call them bitches.

Olivia Dahl had the schedule for the individual interviews in her hand, on her clipboard, with everything else. She had called the interviewer, an outside film editor whose name she kept screwing up no matter how many times she wrote it down, and told him that he would have to come in and work, regardless.

"I know there's a lot going on," she'd said, "but we just can't get too far off schedule. We've got commitments to the networks. Try to think of a way to get them to talk about anything else besides the shooting."

Actually, Olivia didn't expect them to talk about anything else but the shooting. It wasn't the way this sort of thing went. She just wanted a reasonably calm and not particularly actionable set of interviews, because she was going to need a few for the second episode. With the first episode — the one where they picked the base fourteen — she always had a lot to work with, because there were interviews with the girls who failed as well as the ones who succeeded. She had thirty girls to choose from and more film than she needed. With the second episode, there were only the fourteen, and she got what she got.

The room they had designated for the interviews was called the morning room. It was at the far end of one of the wings, accessed by the main hall that ran in both directions from the back of the stairs in the center core of the house. Olivia had originally chosen this room because it was far away from the main action and therefore more likely to be private. She didn't want girls listening in on other girls. Now the main attraction of the morning room was that it wasn't a crime scene or anywhere near a crime scene.

She stood in the doorway and looked around. There was a fireplace here, but then there were fireplaces in most of the rooms of the house. Or there seemed to be. The ceiling was high. That was true of most of the rooms of the house, too. The crew had cleared out all the furniture that had been in here and substituted just two plain steel and leather chairs of the kind they sometimes used for conference rooms at businesses that didn't have enough money. It didn't matter, nobody was going to see the chairs. Olivia checked off all this on her clipboard, and then she turned around to see what Sheila Dunham was doing.

"Do you mean to follow me around all afternoon?" she asked. "Or are you seeking safety in numbers or something like that?"

"If I was seeking safety in numbers, I wouldn't seek it with you," Sheila said. Her black hair was pulled back so tightly on her head, it made her forehead look almost smooth. She still looked every day of fifty-six, and she was nowhere near that old yet. "No," she said. "I was thinking. Maybe we should come right out and ask them."

"Ask them what?"

"If they shot at me," Sheila said.

Olivia sighed. "They won't tell you if they did," she said. "And they'd have every right to scream bloody murder for their lawyers. And don't think some of them don't have them, or that some of them couldn't get them in a blink."

"Maybe," Sheila said. "But have you considered this? Somebody is shooting at me —"

"Apparently, two somebodies."

"Yes," Sheila says. "Doesn't that seem odd to you? Never mind. Somebody is shooting at me. She shot at me at the Milky Way Ballroom. She shot at me here. We've got to at least consider the possibility that she shot that girl in the study yesterday."

"There is no logical reason why the two things have to have anything to do with each other," Olivia said.

"There's a common-sense reason," Sheila said. "This isn't some murder mystery from the nineteen thirties. The chances that there are going to be two people running around crazy are pretty slim. There's a lot of non-sense happening, it's probably all by the same person."

"There were two guns," Olivia pointed out.

Sheila shrugged. "So what? The other gun wasn't even really a gun, as far as I understand it. I mean, it was a gun, but it didn't shoot anything. However that worked. And then the same gun that shot the actual bullets that hit the wall at the Milky Way Ballroom shot the girl who was killed here. My guess is, that's going to be the gun they found on the floor today. So maybe we should go with the flow."

"What's that supposed to mean?"

"Maybe we should have what's his name ask them," Sheila said. "Maybe we should have him ask each one of them if they were the ones who did it all."

"And you think one of them is going to confess to murder. On camera."

"Ask them if they shot at me then," Sheila said. "Leave the murder out of it. Yes, yes. I know you think we'll just get a lot of tearful denials, but will we? I mean, think about it. What is this girl doing? She's staging shooting incidents that will take place on camera. That seems to be the entire point of them. Both times, they've happened when we were actually filming for the show. So —"

"What?" Olivia said.

"So," Sheila said. "Maybe this is somebody who wants to be on camera. Maybe that's her entire point. Maybe she came here intending to pull the first little stunt if she didn't get cast, and then she made it into the final thirty, but she thought, oh, that that was as far as it was going to go. So —"

"The other girl wasn't in the final thirty," Olivia said. "That was my fault. I screwed up. And I'm sorry about that, Sheila, but it's a madhouse at casting and you know it. I did go into the room and count the girls —"

"But one of them was in the bathroom," Sheila said. "I know. I'm just telling you. We should ask them. We should see what they do if we put them on camera. And maybe we should dispense with what's his name. Maybe I should ask the questions this time."

Olivia thought she was about to get the mother of all headaches. This kind of absolute crap came up all the time. It was as if the woman had no sense of the way the business worked.

"For God's sake," Olivia said. "I could run this show a million times better if I didn't have you to worry about. I really could. I don't understand why you can't

451

ever — and I mean ever — learn the way these things are done. You can't interview the girls. They won't be candid if you do. They won't want to risk getting eliminated because they say something you don't like and they really won't want to risk having you have a screaming fit in their faces. We need these interviews to be good. It's how the audience gets to know the girls and how they follow the plotline. Please just go back to your room and keep out of the way for a while."

Sheila just smiled. "You," she said, "couldn't do any kind of show without me here. Like it or not, it's me people turn in to see, and it's me the networks are paying for when they buy the production. Whether you like it or not, no matter how stupid you think I am, I am the one thing essential here. And that's why I sometimes think that it's you doing all this nonsense. You're one of those oppressed, downtrodden types. Maybe you find it a relief to shoot at me."

"I couldn't have shot at you in the Milky Way Ballroom," Olivia said, ready to explode. "I was standing behind you at the front of the room. At least, learn enough physics to do a rough bullet trajectory in your head."

"You know what Aristotle said?"

Olivia didn't really believe Sheila had ever read Aristotle. She hung on to her clipboard and kept her mouth shut.

"Aristotle said," Sheila went on, "that some people are born to be subservient. It's their nature. I've always thought that that was a very insightful comment."

2

The word went around that Sheila Dunham was going to be at the individual interviews in person, and Andra thought she was going to faint. This experience had not been what she expected it to be, and she hadn't been here one whole week. It wasn't as easy to pass for something you hadn't ever had a chance to be. There were the things that she had expected to go wrong, like her voice. She knew she talked "ghetto," as people said. Even black people said it. She talked "ghetto," and she was supposed to talk like Tyra Banks, or Barack Obama. The speech thing was a dead giveaway. There were things she had not expected to go wrong, and that she didn't know what to do with. There was the thing with the anger, for instance. If people criticized her, she got angry. She blew up. She told them off. She got in their face. It was what you did. You never let anyone disrespect you.

But people here did not do that. People here stayed polite, almost all the time, and they never, ever, ever got physical. They didn't push each other. They really never had full-out fights. Andra had been in at least a dozen of those over the course of her life. One time, her forehead had been cracked by a bitch with a beer bottle. That had happened in a bar somewhere in the Bronx, and the police had been called, and she had been the only one arrested, because she had been the only one still there. She hadn't been able to go anywhere because her head was bleeding. The blood was getting into her eyes and making her blind. They took her to the hospital and got her bandaged up, and in the end they didn't arrest her. It wasn't against the law to have blood flowing into your eyes. There was nobody around to say she'd hit them, too.

Olivia Dahl came out into the hallway and called her name. Andra adjusted her tank top and rubbed her right ankle into the top of her left foot. Her clothes were wrong. She knew that, too. The other girls wore things that didn't fit too tightly on their bodies, and that weren't very bright in color. Grace, who was the classiest girl Andra had ever known, always looked as if she didn't have a real body under her clothes, and her clothes floated when she walked. The other girls walked differently, too. It had gotten to the point where Andra was afraid to stand up and go anywhere. She felt like she was a billboard screaming STREET HO! STREET HO!

But she had never been a street whore. That was the truth. It had always been number one on Andra's list of things she would never do.

Olivia was standing at the door, holding it back. Andra went in. She saw the plain black and metal chair at the other end of the room right away. There were lights beaming down on it. That was obviously where she was supposed to go. She tried to walk very slowly past where Sheila Dunham and the man from the interviews at the ballroom were sitting. The man who had done the interviews at the ballroom was sitting in a chair just like the one that had been put out for Andra. Sheila was sitting in something fancy in green upholstery. Andra had no idea why she was noticing any of these things.

Andra sat down. She couldn't see Sheila or the interview guy because the lights were right behind them, or something. When Andra looked in their direction, all she got was glare. She folded her hands in her lap.

"Let's start at the beginning," Sheila said. "Your name isn't Andra Gayle."

Andra felt her stomach clench. If she ever ate anything, she would throw it up. She never ate anything. That wasn't right. She never ate much. She didn't like most food.

"Ms. Gayle," Sheila said.

Andra made herself concentrate. "My birth name is Shanequa Johnson," she said, "but it's not right to say my name isn't Andra Gayle. Lots of people change their names when they go into show business."

"So Andra Gayle is your stage name."

"I guess." Andra didn't know what a stage name was.

"Why did you want to change your name?"

For a split second, Andra thought about spilling the whole thing right here: her mother the crack addict; the years of "and then" when she was a child; the bar fights; the sleeping in abandoned buildings. Now that would be a personal interview that would definitely make it onto television.

"I want," she said instead, "to be something else. To be someone else. To be something I wasn't born to be."

"And you don't think there's anything wrong with that? You don't think it's better to be yourself?"

"It depends on who 'yourself' is."

"According to our investigation," Sheila said, "you've been arrested at least a dozen times, all for acts of violence."

"They weren't acts of violence," Andra said quickly. "I didn't jump people or anything like that. I didn't go out and try to hurt people. It's — where I come from, if somebody disrespects you, you gotta do something about it. You can't just let it go. So I got into a few fights. I never hurt anybody bad enough to put them in the hospital, even. Not for overnight. I never killed someone."

"Did you ever own a gun?"

"No," Andra said. "That was my number two."

"Your number two what?"

Andra looked down at her hands. There was a barking noise from the other side of the lights. She looked up again. She was supposed to look at the camera the whole time. She couldn't see where the camera was.

"When I was growing up," she said, "I made a list. I made a list of all the things I would never do. I would never own a gun or live anywhere there were guns in the house. That was my number two."

"What was your number one?"

"I would never go out on the street and sell it," Andra said. She was sweating. She could feel the thick wash of it around her neck. It confused her a little, because she did not feel especially stressed. She was just sweating.

Nobody was saying anything. Andra hated the silence so much, she wanted to shout.

"It was what my mother did," she said finally. "My mother sold herself for as long as she could, and now she's too old and she just stays wherever. Home, if she's got one. She doesn't care as long as she's high."

"And do you get high?"

"No. That's number three."

"Did you shoot at me at the Milky Way Ballroom?"

"No, I told you. I don't touch guns."

"Did you shoot at me here?"

"No."

"Did you kill that girl who was found dead in the study?"

"No."

"Do you know who she was?"

"No," Andra said, and now she was just tired. "I didn't even get a good look at her at the casting thing. Everything happened so fast and then it was over and the police were there, and I was sort of nervous. But it didn't happen the way I thought it would.

They didn't, you know, search everybody, or arrest anybody, or whatever."

"And you were afraid of being searched?"

"No," Andra said, but she wasn't thinking about that.

She was thinking that it must be a very odd thing to live a life where you didn't just automatically expect the police to arrest you, if they were there and you happened to be around.

3

When Andra came out of the interview room, she almost looked like she was in tears. Mary-Louise was impressed. Andra always looked so tough that Mary-Louise didn't think she ever cried. Olivia Dahl, on the other hand, always looked either disapproving or furious, and she was looking furious now. When she called Mary-Louise's name, Mary-Louise came forward and did her best to smile.

"This shouldn't be bad," she said. "We don't get judged on this."

Mary-Louise wanted Olivia Dahl to say "of course not," or something like it. Mary-Louise really wanted to be sure. It was a little off-putting, the idea of having Sheila Dunham here. Sheila Dunham did a lot of yelling, and she'd already yelled at Mary-

459

Louise once.

Mary-Louise went across the room and sat down in the empty chair. She crossed her legs at her ankles and folded her hands in her lap. They had been instructed to fold their hands in their laps during interviews. You didn't want to wave your hands about, because if you did it made a distraction and the tape wasn't worth using. You wanted the show to use your tapes, because then you would get more time on the air, and the more time you got the more famous you would be. You had to let America get to know you. That had been in the lecture Olivia had given right before — well, before.

Mary-Louise smiled. She didn't know why she was smiling. She always smiled. It was something people did.

"So," Sheila Dunham said. "Your name is Mary-Louise Verdt, and you're from Holcomb, Kansas."

Sheila pronounced the name as "VerD."

"Actually," Mary-Louise said, "you say my last name as 'VerT'. As if the 'd' wasn't there."

"Verdt," Sheila Dunham said, pronouncing it wrong yet again. Mary-Louise let it go. She didn't want to embarrass anybody. "Tell me," Sheila said, "about Holcomb, Kansas."

Mary-Louise was ready for this. When she was first trying to get on the show, the little brochure they had sent her about how to try out had had a list of things that could help her chances, and one of them was writing an application letter that made her sound "interesting." Mary-Louise did not think she was a very interesting person, but she came from an interesting place, and she was proud of that.

"Holcomb, Kansas, is where the *In Cold Blood* murders happened," Mary-Louise said happily. "That was the murder of a whole family in their farmhouse in the middle of the night. Their names were the Clutters. They had a big farm, and a pretty big house, out in the middle of nowhere, really, and then one night this guy who'd worked as a hired hand for them came with another guy he'd met in prison and they robbed the house, and tied up the Clutters, and killed them. It was a really big deal."

"Was it?" Sheila Dunham said. "I don't remember hearing about it on the news."

"Oh, I don't, either," Mary-Louise said. "It happened before I was born. It probably happened before you were born, too. November 15, 1959. It was really famous at the time, but what made it more famous and the reason everybody has heard about it is that this writer named Truman Capote wrote a book about it. It's called *In Cold Blood.* There have been two movies made of it, and then another movie was made about Truman Capote that was sort of about it, about him writing the book about it, but it wasn't a very good movie. I mean, I tried to see it in the theater, but I couldn't keep my mind on it. It was one of those floaty movies, if you know what I mean."

"So this interests you? Murders?"

"Well, you know, it's interesting that it happened where I live," Mary-Louise said. "Holcomb is just a farm town, really. There are lots of them all over the state. They're not anything special. But we're special, because that happened to us."

"Do you play video games?"

"Excuse me?"

"Do you play video games," Sheila said. "You know —"

"Oh, no, I do know," Mary-Louise said. "No, I'm sorry. I didn't think for a minute. I like some games, sort of. I guess you can call them video games. I like Bookworm."

"What's Bookworm?"

"It's where you spell things and if the words aren't long enough, red tiles come down and they can make you lose. I'm pretty good at spelling."

"Do you like any other video games?"

"Not really," Mary-Louise said. "I mean, you know, I've got a computer at home, but my parents want me to use that for school. They don't like it when I just goof around with it. And a lot of the boys have those game systems things, like Nintendo, you know, but it's all just blowing things up, so I don't think that's very interesting."

"Why did you try out for *America's Next Superstar*?"

"Really?" Mary-Louise said. "Well, I guess I tried out for the same reason everybody does. Because I wanted to win. And because I wanted to get away from home. I mean, you can get away from home by going away to a fancy college, and my parents would probably have paid for that, but I didn't do all that well on the SATs. And, you know, it's not that I'm a great singer, or a great dancer, or anything like that. But you don't have to do all that, from what I can see. You just have to be a personality. And I've got a lot of personality."

"Did you expect to be cast when you were asked to come in and audition?"

"I didn't think I'd get asked to come in and audition," Mary-Louise said. "You really wouldn't have believed it when I got that letter. I went running all over the house, just screaming. And all my girlfriends were jealous. They really were. The girl who's cheer captain this year sent in a tape and didn't get asked. I laughed so hard, I thought I was going to explode. Not that she was a friend of mine or anything, or bad to me, you know how that goes. It's just that I'm not the kind of person who wins things, and there I was. It was wonderful."

"Did you shoot at me in the Milky Way Ballroom?"

"Oh," Mary-Louise said. "No. No, of course not."

"Did you see who did?"

"Well," Mary-Louise said, "I was standing in the middle of the crowd, you know, when you started talking. And after we heard the shots, I looked around and, right near me, there was that blond girl and she had the gun. But I thought that was a little funny, because I didn't hear anything. I mean, I was standing so close, I should have heard something. And then later one of the girls here told me that that wasn't actually the gun that fired any shots. I heard the shots today, though, when they went off. They were really loud."

"Did you know the girl who died?"

"The little blond one?" Mary-Louise said. "No, I didn't know her. I mean, I didn't know who she was or where she came from. But I'd seen her before, you know, in the Ballroom. And before that, too."

"Before that?"

"I was the first in line, so I didn't notice her in line, because she must have been behind me," Mary-Louise said. "But she was in the pink room, the same one with Grace. I know because I saw her come out of there and go to the place where the panel was. You know, the judging panel, where we all came and talked to you guys. Then they called my name and I went in and when I came out she wasn't there anymore. I have no idea where she went."

"Have you ever been arrested?"

"Oh, of course not."

"Have you ever owned a gun?"

"We've got a shotgun at home," Mary-Louise said. "It belongs to my father. He uses it because of the animals, you know, the ones that get into the yard."

"If I asked you which of the girls you would choose as the one who had been firing shots at me, which one would it be."

"Oh," Mary-Louise said. "That's easy. Everybody in the whole house says it's Coraline who's doing these things, and that it's Coraline who killed that girl, too. Grace says Coraline is a religious fanatic and she'd kill anybody for God, but it doesn't make much sense to me. Coraline seems like she's all right. Most of the girls do. It's that Ivy person who really makes me get the hives. I don't understand her at all."

FIVE

1

By the time Gregor Demarkian got to Sophie Mgrdchian's hospital floor, there were several uniformed officers and two homicide detectives as well as Billie Ormonds and David Mortimer already there. Dr. Halevy was also there, yelling at nurses in what sounded like Arabic. Gregor went to the door of Sophie's room and looked in. She still looked like she was sleeping.

Gregor went up to Billie Ormonds and tapped her on the shoulder. "So?" he said.

Everybody turned to look at him at once.

Gregor cleared his throat. "I take it I'm not crazy," he said. "I take it giving blood pressure medication to somebody without a blood pressure problem, or a low blood pressure problem, can cause what we've been seeing."

Billie looked back at Dr. Halevy and the nurses. "I don't think *they* even know what she's saying. She's livid, by the way. People didn't write things down on charts. People didn't double-check other people."

"The problem," Mortimer said, "is that this still won't get us what we want."

"Meaning an excuse to keep Karen Mgrdchian locked up," Billie said. "We've got homicide here now, and we can start treating this as an attempted murder, but the simple fact of the matter is that we can't really prove it was one. Sophie Mgrdchian had this other woman's pills in her own pocket — well, they're old ladies, aren't they? They could have become confused. They could have picked up one another's medication by accident."

"She's not Karen Mgrdchian," Gregor said. "She's the wrong type, if that makes any sense."

"That's not exactly enough to go on," Billie said. "And you've got the fact that this woman was in Sophie Mgrdchian's house. Her friends on the street say she wasn't disoriented or going into dementia —"

"As far as they know," Gregor said. "Sophie Mgrdchian hasn't been running around being social for years."

"Even so," Billie insisted. "You have to at least assume that the woman would have been able to recognize her own sister-in-law."

"No," Gregor said. "She hadn't seen the woman in decades. Literally decades."

"Again," Billie said. "Not enough to go on. She was in Sophie Mgrdchian's house. There's no evidence that entry was forced, and in fact we know it wasn't, because we know she was there for some days. Are you trying to say that this woman calling herself Karen Mgrdchian forced her way into the house and stayed there by — what? Threatening Sophie? But Sophie has been in and out of the house since the woman arrived there; she could have broken free any time. There isn't a child to be held hostage, is there? Or even a pet. And yes, I do know that sometimes kidnap victims end up collaborating with their kidnappers for all kinds of weird psychological reasons I can't understand, but there's no indication of that here."

"Didn't Bennis give you the message about looking in the basement for bodies?" Gregor asked.

"Well," Billie said, "she gave it to me, but I thought it was mostly metaphorical. Are you trying to tell me you know where bodies are buried?"

"I think so," Gregor said. "I'll admit, it's

mostly a guess, but I'm pretty sure it's only a guess about where, not about if. If I was the woman calling herself Karen Mgrdchian, and I'd killed the real Karen Mgrdchian, I'd have put the body in the basement. It's the most logical place, if I'm working alone and I'm an old lady. It's out of the way, so that the chances of a smell permeating the immediate area are slim for at least a while. And it's easy for me to get to and get done."

"I thought there was a daughter," Billie Ormonds said.

"There is," Gregor said. "I don't know anything about her. That's why I said it was a good idea to look for two bodies, or even for three. I know Marco Mgrdchian is dead, but not when he died or how he died. Assuming that was natural causes, though, and a bit back, that leaves the mother and the daughter. If the daughter was in the habit of coming over to the house, if she lived close by, if she was responsible and not sick or addicted in some way — then my guess is that you'd find two bodies in the basement and not one."

"Why?"

"Because the daughter hasn't called," Gregor said. "And even if she didn't have the numbers of the people on Cavanaugh

470

Street, if the address book at that house is missing as the address book is here, then there's the fact that she hasn't reported her mother missing. I've checked every source I can think of. I've looked on the Internet. There's no missing person's report on Karen Mgrdchian."

"Maybe," Billie said, "the reason for that is that Karen Mgrdchian isn't missing. She's here, and her daughter isn't worried about her because her daughter knows that she's here."

"If she was Karen Mgrdchian," Gregor said, "she wouldn't have done that to her fingerprints."

"It doesn't matter what she does to her fingerprints," Billie said, "there are no fingerprints on file for Karen Mgrdchian. We really did check."

"I'm sure you did," Gregor said, "but I'm willing to bet that there are fingerprints on file for whoever this woman really is. Because this is not some brand-new, supercreative secret plot. This is an old-time con game. And I'm going to be shocked if it turns out she's never been picked up for it before."

"You mean you think the woman calling herself Karen Mgrdchian has been — what? Convicted of murder?"

"No," Gregor said, "convicted of fraud, or, if not, then arrested for fraud. The only reason to destroy your fingerprints is that you don't want the police to be able to connect you with something you've already done, the only reason to destroy your fingerprints is because they're on file somewhere you don't want anybody to know about."

"People do sometimes destroy them accidentally, no matter what you think," Billie said.

"Not people like Karen Mgrdchian," Gregor said. "We need to pinpoint the place where this woman lived and have the local police go out there with a search warrant. And I'm sure they'll be able to get one. We've got an elderly woman, incapacitated under suspicious circumstances, and another elderly woman we've got reason to be suspicious of. They'll be able to find a judge."

"But you don't actually know what the address is," Billie Ormonds said.

"Someplace in or around Cleveland," Gregor said. "The Very Old Ladies seem to be convinced of that. That would be the best place to start. I'll ask Father Tibor, to go over the parish records again. They may have a mailing address, although I did have him look once before and he didn't come up with anything. I wonder what the story is there. Cleveland isn't all that far away."

"So?" Billie asked.

"Armenian families tend to stick together," Gregor said. "They visit for holidays. I don't know. Maybe they didn't get along, and after Viktor died, they didn't see each other because they didn't want to. I wish we had that address book. It would tell us a lot of things."

On the other side of the room, Dr. Halevy had stopped speaking Arabic and was onto English. She sounded beyond livid now, and possibly ready to do violence.

"The patient is old," she said. "We have all kinds of fancy terminology for it, but that's what it amounts to. The patient is old. We could have killed her. Didn't it occur to anybody, anywhere, that — never mind. Never mind. I want somebody in here twenty-four seven. I want her every breath monitored. And I want you to come and get me if she so much as sneezes."

Dr. Halevy broke away from the group of nurses, and came over to Gregor and Billie and the police. She was red in the face and short of breath.

"Yes," she said, "yes. Screwups happen in hospitals. They happen all the time. It's a scandal. But this is really egregious. One of those women over there said she thought the low blood pressure readings she was getting were normal, because Mrs. Mgrdchian is in a coma, and that's the kind of thing comas produce. Of course, very low blood pressure can *give* you a coma. She doesn't seem to have thought of that."

The two homicide detectives came forward and introduced themselves as Allejandro and Kennedy. Dr. Halevy said hello to everybody but didn't really take them in.

"What we need to know," Gregor said, "is whether or not this could have killed Sophie Mgrdchian if it had been done on purpose. If somebody had given her medication to lower her blood pressure when she didn't need it, could that have resulted in death?"

Dr. Halevy sighed. "You can kill anybody with any kind of medication," she said. "It's just that some things would take larger doses than others. In this case, it would have been mostly a matter of time. If this had gone on for another, I don't know, week or so, with the patient this elderly and somewhat frail — yes, it would have resulted in death. And as a murder method, it wouldn't be bad. It would be hard to pin down."

"How do you mean, pin down?" Billie asked.

"Well, you've probably all talked about it already," Dr. Halevy said, "but you know how people are with the elderly. The same way they are with children. If I was the doctor on the case, and I had an elderly patient who died from taking the wrong medication — well, I'd just assume there'd been a mistake, or an accident. That the patient had become confused or forgetful. Two old women in a house, both of them have pill organizers, one of them picks up the wrong one." Dr. Halevy shrugged.

"Exactly," Billie said.

"Except," Gregor said, "that this is an experienced con woman. I'll guarantee it. She made friends with the real Karen Mgrdchian, got all she could out of her, found out about Sophie and the chance that Sophie had something worth stealing —"

"Does she?" Billie asked.

"Well, she's got a house in one of the most expensive neighborhoods in Philadelphia," Gregor said. "And my guess is that you'll find it without a mortgage. She almost certainly had money, and social security income if nothing else. She wasn't starving. The house was in good enough repair. She must have been paying somebody for that, or for some of that. If Sophie hadn't lived in the same neighborhood she'd been in all her life, and if there hadn't still been people there who had known her for years, this woman would have been able to move into the house and take over. That's what she almost certainly did with the real Karen Mgrdchian. Moved in, took over the house, then either ran through the money or started to feel she'd be better off getting out of town. So, having heard about Sophie and her house from the real Karen Mgrdchian, she came out here."

"Just like that?" Dr. Halevy asked.

"I think we'll start looking for where this Karen Mgrdchian lived," Billie said. "We've got twenty-four hours, as far as I can tell, and then it's over. And I hate to tell you this, but as things stand, I'm not sure we can stop her from going back into that house. There aren't any relatives, you see, to say she isn't welcome there, and what she says is that she was invited in to live there permanently. Or, you know, that's what her lawyer said she said."

"That's all right," Gregor said. "Whoever this woman really is, she isn't interested in going back to Sophie Mgrdchian's house."

2

By the time Gregor left the hospital, it was pitch dark. There were still a lot of people

476

on the street, but most of them looked hurried. He walked a few blocks and tried to stay oriented. This was not a part of the city he knew well. The trouble, he thought, was that the two cases had so many odd similarities — women who claimed to be other people than they really were, for instance, and who simply stayed quiet and shut up and wouldn't say anything except to their lawyers. But that was a little thing. There was also the problem that both cases looked terribly complicated when they were really terribly simple —

No, Gregor thought. That was not quite right. The case of Sophie Mgrdchian actually looked simple when it was really very complicated. It wasn't complex. There was nothing complex about a con game. Of course, newspapers and magazines and television shows liked to call con games "elaborate," because that made them sound more plausible. Nobody likes to think he'd fall for the simplest and most obvious little lie. Everyone likes to think he'd see through the nonsense right away.

In real life, though, con games were absurdly, stupidly obvious, and people fall for them anyway. Bernie Madoff confidently tells his clients that he can get them 17 percent a year on their investments, year after year, good markets and bad — and virtually none of them go, "but that's impossible, there must be something wrong here." Then there was all that Nigerian nonsense, and the idiocies with "Australian lotteries" on the Internet. You go to your e-mail. You open one that announces that the writer has heard such wonderful things about you and knows that you are trustworthy, and therefore he's willing to pay you five million dollars to help him get his money out of Nigeria. All you have to do is send him $2,500 or so to pay the bank fees so that he can get the money out of the country.

The first time Gregor had heard about the Nigerian Internet scam, he'd been dumbfounded that *anyone, anywhere* had ever fallen for it. Did people really know so little about the way banks worked to think that this thing even began to make sense? And what about the people who fell for the same scam, except it's presented as the declaration that they'd "won" a lottery? Didn't it bother them that they'd never entered that lottery? There were lotteries in the United States. Surely, people knew that they didn't have to fork over money before they were allowed to pick up their prize? Weren't there enough specials on brand-new lottery winners that demonstrated at least that much? Gregor remembered a man in Pennsylvania only a few years ago, who had bought a lottery ticket with his last dollar. He'd been out of work for months and was living, with his wife and two young children, in his car. It had to be obvious that he hadn't been required to spend a couple of thousand dollars to get his money. If he'd had a couple of thousand dollars, he'd have had a place to take a shower.

What the psychologists said, when you asked them, was that people believed what they wanted to believe. Most of us would be happy to get five million dollars. Many of us desperately want the money. Then there are the very old, who may not always be thinking straight.

Gregor still thought that the phenomenon was bizarre. No matter how much you wanted to believe, there had to be some part of your brain that was telling you it was all a lot of crap. And that was the word for it. Crap.

He looked around to see where he was, and found he wasn't sure. It was a nice stretch of city, with a few small restaurants offering pizza and a few shops already closed for the evening. He went into one of the pizza places and looked around. There had to be dozens of places like this across the United States. There were a few, but only a few, wooden booths along one wall. There was a counter with a glass top and two big pizza ovens beyond it. Most of the business seemed to be in takeout and delivery.

Gregor sat down at one of the booths. It had started to rain again when he wasn't paying attention, and his hair was wet. He took out his cell phone and punched in the number 3, which is where Bennis had placed herself. He still didn't understand the logic of the numbers she assigned to speed dial. If it had been up to him, he'd have put 911 first and not worried about the rest.

Bennis picked up and asked him where he was.

"Give me a minute," he said. He went up to the counter and looked at the menu. Then he read off the name of the place and the street address. "They sell slices. I thought I'd get myself some. Unless you haven't eaten."

"I've been picking all afternoon. I'm fine. Can you get a cab from there?"

"I could," Gregor said, "but I was hoping you might come get me. I need a ride out to Bryn Mawr."

"Gregor —"

"I know," Gregor said. "You don't go to Engine House anymore. I don't blame you. But I don't need a ride out to Engine House. I just need a ride out to Bryn Mawr. If I can set this up the right way, you can take me to the police station. And you can wait for me there if I do have to go out to Engine House. The trick, you see, is that you must always concentrate on what in fact happened."

"You're making absolutely no sense," Bennis said.

"It's Agatha Christie. I told you that Tibor gave me those books. I read them on our honeymoon. According to Hercule Poirot —"

"And you're the Armenian-American Hercule Poirot?"

"Don't be like that. I'll do something drastic. It's a good point. What you have to deal with is what actually happened. Not what you think happened, or what you think must be the case because it makes sense. You have to deal with what happened."

"I thought that was Sherlock Holmes. 'Once you eliminate the impossible, whatever remains, no matter how improbable, must be the truth.' "

"Not bad," Gregor said. "Come on out

and get me. I'll get something to eat. If I'm lucky, I'll talk to Len Borstoi and we'll be able to meet him at the police station. I don't think I could stand to pay another taxi for that ride. They charge you enough to buy a house. I don't even know if I've got enough money on me."

"I'll be right out," Bennis said. "Eat something. You're going to kill yourself with the way you've been behaving lately."

"I'll see you in a minute."

It would, Gregor knew, be more than a minute, and probably more than ten. He got up and went to the counter. There were three big pizzas back there, all available to buy by the slice. He asked for a slice of sausage and a slice of onion and mushroom, and waited patiently while the man in the white apron slid them onto a paper plate. Then he asked for a bottle of water, and paid.

Back at the booth, he set his food and water down and took his notebook out of his pocket. The case of Sophie Mgrdchian had looked simple but really been complicated — that is, it had actually been a con game and not just an old lady passed out on her own foyer floor. The case of *America's Next Superstar* looked complicated, but it was really entirely straightforward. It only seemed complicated because people kept insisting on making it make sense.

No, that wasn't the way to put it.

Gregor paged through his notebook and came to the page where he had written out the names of the girls and their roommates. He looked down the list and frowned:

Shari Bernstein and Linda Kowalski
Janice Ledbedder and Ivy Demari
Coraline Mays and Deanna Brackett
Grace (Harrigan) Alsop and Suzanne Toretti
Mary-Louise Verdt and Alida Akido
Andra Gayle and Marcia Lee Baldwin
Brittney Cox and Faith Stackdopole

Fourteen girls, each of them chosen from thousands of applicants across the country, and then chosen again from the thirty applicants who had been allowed to do an on-camera audition. Fourteen girls — but it didn't help, really, to know who roomed with whom unless he also knew the characters of the girls involved, and he only knew those sketchily. No, it wasn't who they roomed with that was the key. It was —

He shook his head. The pizza was passable, but not spectacular. The water made him wonder when it had become commonplace for restaurants to sell the stuff in bottles instead of just give it away in glasses. Fourteen girls, plus a fifteenth who was not on anybody's official list. She had not been asked to come in and audition. She had not been one of the thirty chosen for the on-camera auditions and the first on-camera elimination. She was just there, out of the blue, and if she had had a gun full of real bullets and disappeared afterward, that was all she would ever have been.

Fourteen girls, plus a fifteenth, dead in a room with a video security camera in it that apparently had been no use at all. If it had been, Len Borstoi would not be floundering around telling Gregor Demarkian he was hired.

He'd have to ask about the security camera. He'd have to ask about a lot of things. At the moment, he knew a couple.

He got out his phone and called Len Borstoi's cell number, a number he'd had now for less than ten hours. He was thinking that if he got Borstoi at dinner, or in bed, he would probably hear about it.

He got Borstoi at the station house. He knew that because he recognized the sounds in the background. Police stations sound the same everywhere.

"Listen," he said. "There's something you

need to do. Or to get the uniforms to do. And it had better be done sooner rather than later. Although I think it's probably already too late."

"Too late to find what?"

"A glove," Gregor said. "A single, small stretchy glove. It might be a latex glove, but I doubt it. For one thing, you can sometimes get fingerprints off the inside of latex gloves, although I don't know why I think our murderer would know that. What she's much more likely to know is that a latex glove would be a red flag. If it was found on her, it would immediately cause suspicion. And she would have to have had it on her today."

"We searched them all today," Len Borstoi said. "Don't you think you would have noticed a single glove?"

"No, I don't," Gregor said. "This afternoon, it would probably have been in her handbag. You've seen the handbags those girls carry around? They're the size of suitcases. And they've got everything but the kitchen sink in them. Makeup. Pieces of clothing. If one of your guys was poring through a huge bag like that, a single glove wouldn't look suspicious or like anything but one more bit of stray clothing shoved in the bag when she didn't know what else to do with it. And my guess is that her bag would have had a fair amount of stray clothing in it. And maybe more than one glove. What you're looking for is something stretchy that kind of contracts when it's off the hand, and not too noticeable a color. Maybe a beigy kind of thing, what they call 'champagne' in stores. And my guess would be that it's a lace thing, with mesh and little patches of stuff — I'm no good at describing women's clothing. There's this kind of stretchy lace they make gloves out of sometimes that has little appliqued things on it. Butterflies. That kind of thing."

"Oddly enough," Borstoi said, "I think I know what you mean."

"Yes," Gregor said, "well. This afternoon, she would have had it in her bag, but it's probably gone now. You need to search not just the handbags but the rooms. The bedrooms. I take it the video camera in the study didn't give you anything you needed."

"No," Borstoi said. "It had been disabled. And it had been disabled a long time before the murder. The last footage was from the night before."

"That's about right. The murder had to have occurred in the morning, the very early morning, before breakfast. You said the body had been moved —"

"Not from very far. There's a utility hallway —"

"Right behind, yes, I know. I suppose the body was left there for a while."

"We can't tell."

"All right," Gregor said. "Get somebody out there to look, or wait for me and we'll go out there together and look. I'm a little worried about what's going to happen if we don't work fast, but I'd like to talk to you if you're going to be at the station house for a while."

"I'm going to go and see if I can't get a search warrant," Borstoi said. "If you're coming right out, you shouldn't have to wait long for me to get back. The girls' rooms, and their handbags, looking for a glove."

"That's right," Gregor said. "And you're going to find that glove in the things belonging to a girl named Coraline Mays, and if we don't get there fast, I think she's going to commit suicide."

Six

1

The police arrived just as Janice Ledbedder was about to go into the interview room. She stood for a second in the hall to watch them pass. There were a lot of men in uniforms, and one of them stopped in front of Olivia Dahl to give her some paperwork. That had to be the warrant, Janice was sure. It made her more than a little nervous to realize that she didn't know what was going on. She had watched millions of those shows, the documentaries and the mini-documentaries, and the police shows, like *CSI Everyplace,* and she'd thought she had a good understanding of how a police investigation worked. It turned out she had no idea. The police were not like the police on TV, even if the TV said it was presenting something real, the way it really happened.

Olivia Dahl came back down the hall and found Janice standing in place, staring.

"Go," she said. "What are you waiting for? Sheila will have a fit. And you're the last one for tonight."

"What do you think they're looking for?" Janice said.

"I have no idea. They want to look through the bedrooms. I've sent them upstairs. Now go do your interview while I go upstairs and watch."

Janice went into the interview room. The lights shining on the chair she was supposed to sit in were too harsh. She was very nervous. She was as nervous as she'd ever been during the whole of this competition. She sat down and looked around. When they showed this on television, if they did, they would block out all the background and it would look like she was sitting in empty space. She didn't know why they did that, but they were not the only ones. She adjusted her skirt so that it came down almost to her knees and smiled.

"Are you all ready?" somebody asked.

Janice couldn't see who it was, but she knew it wasn't Sheila Dunham. She knew Sheila Dunham's voice.

"I'm fine," she said. "The police are here. I'm a little nervous."

"What are you nervous about?" Sheila Dunham asked.

"Well," Janice said. "I'm nervous all the time, I guess. I didn't expect to be on the show. I mean, I came to the audition and I had hopes, but I didn't think I was actually going to get chosen. So, you know, I'm still having a hard time getting used to it. And there are things."

"What things?"

"I didn't expect to get on," Janice said, "so I didn't make any plans for it. Do you know what I mean? I had to call my mother and tell her I was staying on, and that got her all excited. It was in the papers, you know, about me being asked to the audition."

"And has it been in the papers that you made it into the house?" That was definitely Sheila Dunham.

"I don't know," Janice said. "I haven't had a chance to really talk to anybody. If I was going to change anything about this, I'd change the thing where we're not allowed to make calls and we can't have our cell phones. It makes me really crazy not to be able to talk to anybody. I mean, I know that you're trying to keep it a secret, who gets into the house and who stays and who gets eliminated. But you see what I mean."

"Did you shoot at me this afternoon?"

"What?"

"Did you shoot at me?" Sheila's voice sounded very patient. Janice didn't think that was a good sign.

"I don't think anybody shot at you," she said, thinking it over. "I've been trying to remember it all day. I think somebody shot something, but I don't think they shot it at you."

"Why not?"

"Well, you know, it missed, didn't it?" Janice said. "And we were all so close. If somebody really wanted to shoot you, they would probably have hit you. I've been thinking that maybe they've been shooting at one of us. Maybe we have the whole thing wrong. But I could be crazy. I mean, I don't really understand how people like you live, if you know what I mean. It has to be really odd never to be able to go anywhere without people knowing who you are. I don't know if I'd really like that."

"Then you don't want to be *America's Next Superstar*?"

"Oh. Yes. I would. I mean, I'd like to win the competition. That would be a good thing. That would be in the paper."

"And that's what you want, to be in the paper, in, where was it —"

"Marshall, South Dakota."

"And you were the one who had a big

tragedy, or something, before you came."
There was a rustling of papers. Janice
wished she could see past the lights.

She didn't like Sheila Dunham. She really
didn't. The woman was old, and she was
nasty, too, with that way adults sometimes
had of acting as if everybody under the age
of thirty was a moron with a morals problem. Janice smoothed her skirt.

"I don't think I had a tragedy," she said.

There was a long pause on the other side
of the lights. "I remember," Sheila said.
"You're the loser. You're the one whose
boyfriend dumped her for her best friend."

Janice rubbed her hands together. This
was bad. A male voice from the other side
of the lights told her to sit still. You weren't
supposed to move around a lot during
interviews. It made it hard for the audience
to hear what you were saying if they were
concentrating instead on your jumping all
over the place.

"It wasn't like that," she said. "They're
very good for each other. And I don't
begrudge her, you know. She had a hard
life. She came from a very bad family. Well,
it wasn't a family, really. It was just her
mother. But her mother drank. Drinks, I
guess."

"So you didn't mind it? Your boyfriend

dumps you for your best friend, and you don't mind it?"

"I didn't like it. But I didn't think about it. And then I got this, and everybody in the whole place just thought I was wonderful for it. And you know, there was a sort of justice in it. She tried out, too. She didn't get asked to the audition."

There was more silence from the other side of the lights. Janice really couldn't keep her body still. She'd never been able to keep herself still. She talked all the time, and she was always moving. They made fun of her about that at school, and that was one of the things her boyfriend hadn't liked.

The papers rustled again. Sheila said. "Do you think it's a good idea, you telling that story to everybody you meet? You have told that story to everybody here. You've told it to me before. You've told it to the other girls. You mentioned it in the first interview you did, back at the Ballroom, before you were chosen to come to the house. Don't you think telling that story over and over again makes you look pathetic?"

"I don't know," Janice said.

"It makes you look pathetic," Sheila said. "It is pathetic. If I had a story like that in my background, nobody would ever hear it from me. Perception is everything. People will think what you want them to think. You want them to think you're a loser."

You want them to think you're a bitch, Janice thought, but she wasn't that crazy. She didn't say it. What she said instead was, "Yes, I can see that. I can see how that would be."

"Who do you think took those shots at me?"

That was better. Janice could breathe again.

"Oh," she said, "I don't really know. I don't think anybody knows."

"But they suspect," Sheila said.

"They make guesses," Janice said, "but I think it's all just talk. I mean, everybody wants to believe they know what's going on, so they pretend they do. But it's just talk."

"And who are they talking about?"

"I wouldn't like to say."

"You wouldn't like to, or you're afraid I'd bitch you out for being a rat?"

"I wouldn't like to say," Janice said again. She was feeling very short of breath. She wondered if everybody else had said it was Coraline they were all thinking of. She wondered if the police knew.

She just sat where she was, waiting for it to be over, saying nothing. That was the best she could do, and even that was so hard, she wanted to burst.

2

Ivy Demari had come to a decision. No matter how good a setup this was, no matter how far this entire project had exceeded her expectations, it was probably time to go. She hadn't intended to go. When she'd first come up here from Dallas, she thought she'd just keep a diary of the whole thing, and then see where that would take her, once she was — as she was sure she would be — eliminated before she got a chance to see the house.

She had been honestly surprised to find herself in the final fourteen, and even more surprised to find herself getting along well enough so that she wasn't always in fear of instant elimination. With the hair and the tattoo, she was sure she would hear from Sheila Dunham sooner rather than later. Ivy was a level-headed person, but she didn't take crap from anybody. She really wouldn't take crap from a has-been B-TV ex-star, whose only source of power was behaving as badly as possible in public.

Now she stood in the upstairs hall where the bedrooms were, and watched the police going through the rooms. The rest of the girls were out in the hall, too, except for the ones who were still downstairs. They had been told that they would not be allowed into their rooms until the search was over, but they all wanted to be right there on the scene, just in case. Ivy was sure none of them knew just in case of what, but maybe that didn't matter, either.

The police had already searched the room where Shari Bernstein and Linda Kowalski lived. They were just finishing up in the room Ivy shared with Janice Ledbedder. Janice was still downstairs. Ivy folded her arms across her chest and watched the men come back out into the hall, carrying nothing they hadn't had when they went in.

They headed for the room Coraline Mays shared with Deanna Brackett, and Coraline came up to Ivy and shuddered.

"I wish I knew what they were looking for," she said. "I wish I knew what was going on. Why would anybody kill that girl here? We didn't any of us knew her."

"Maybe Sheila Dunham killed her herself," Ivy said, but her heart wasn't in it.

"I hate it," Coraline said. "All this talk about who did it and who didn't do it. I used to like that kind of thing on television and, you know, sometimes in books, but I don't like it in real life. I hate it. People shouldn't make guesses when they don't know what they're talking about."

"Mmm," Ivy said.

Coraline turned away. "I guess you're not talking to me anymore, either. Nobody's talking to me. I hope they find out who killed that girl and arrest her. Or him. I hope they do it right away. Then maybe people will just stop looking at me."

Ivy had not stopped talking to Coraline. She did not think Coraline had committed a murder, but she didn't think anybody else really believed that, either. That was not what was going on. It was just that she couldn't concentrate on two things at once, and right now she was concentrating on the police.

Ivy let Coraline drift away and moved closer to the door to the bedroom where the police were. If she stood right there at the edge, she could see the action inside, or some of it. The men were going through the drawers of the dresser, one after the other. They were taking out every single article of clothing, unfolding it, shaking it out, then folding it up again. When they were done with everything in a particular drawer, they pulled it all the way out and turned it over and backward.

"Don't they already have the gun?" Grace asked suddenly in her ear. "What do they think they're going to find under or behind a drawer?"

"I don't know," Ivy said.

"I wonder if they have to clean up after themselves," Grace said. "Do they leave the room a mess when they go? What?"

"They've been putting the clothes back in the drawers all folded, up to now," Ivy said. "I expect they try to leave things the way they found them."

"Well, they can't, can they? Your things are never going to be the same after people have been pawing through them. God, this is really awful. I thought they searched the house the other day."

"Maybe they're looking for something they weren't looking for the other day."

"What? They've got the gun. Do they think they're going to find bloody footprints, or something? What's the point of all this?"

Ivy got closer to the door. The drawers were all back in their places. The clothes were all folded and put away. One of the men was looking through a jewelry box. Another of them was dumping out a makeup bag. Both of them were wearing those whitish-but-nearly-clear latex gloves that people wore on police shows on television.

Ivy shifted a little to get a better look.

They had to know they were being watched. They just weren't paying attention. The one looking through the jewelry box put the jewelry back and put the box on top of the dresser. Ivy found herself wondering who brought a jewelry box to a competition like this. Whoever it was must have brought it to the auditions without the faintest idea whether she'd be in the house or not. The one who was looking through the makeup bag put the makeup back into the bag.

"I can't believe this," somebody in the hall said.

Ivy didn't immediately recognize the voice, so she ignored it. As far as she knew, the police hadn't taken anything out of the other rooms they'd searched. That meant they hadn't taken her diary, which was a good thing. It would be interesting to know what they'd think if they read it.

On the other hand, they would almost certainly find it impossible to decipher her handwriting.

One of the men started to take the suitcases out of the closet. The other one sat down on one of the beds and opened the drawer to the night table. Then he stood up again and leaned over toward the bed he hadn't been sitting on.

"Here," he said.

"What?" the other one said.

The first one put his latex-gloved hand over the bedspread and then under it, moving carefully, inching along as if he would set off a bomb if he made any sudden movements. Then he made a sort of strangled noise and stood up. He was holding a little wad of beige something, crumpled up in his hand.

"My God," Alida Akido said, from right over Ivy's shoulder. "That's Coraline's bed. *That's Coraline's bed.*"

"What?" Coraline said.

The other girls had rushed the door by now. The policeman with the beige wad was holding it in the air. The other policeman was holding out a plastic evidence bag. The first policeman dropped the wad in and the second one sealed up the bag.

"They took something from *your* bed," Alida said, swinging around at Coraline. "It's you, isn't it? It's always you. We all told you to go away and leave us alone, and you wouldn't listen. Well, I don't want you here. I don't. And I'm not going to have it. They took something out of your bed!"

"What did they take out of my bed?" Coraline was in tears, again. "What did they take? There wasn't anything in my bed. I don't even keep my nightgown in my bed."

"Just stop it," Alida said. "Stop it. Nobody cares anymore. Nobody cares. You're just stupid white trash and we don't want you here."

"I want her here," Ivy said.

"Just shut up," Alida said. "I want this stupid, murderous bitch out of here right now. I won't sleep on the same floor with her. I won't eat at the same table with her. I won't look at her face again. And if she comes anywhere near me, I'll claw her to shreds."

3

Olivia Dahl was standing at the foot of the stairs when the police came down and went out the front door to their cars. There was a lot of calling back and forth, and what she thought was people on cell phones. Two of them came back in and asked to speak with her, but they didn't have much to say.

"Mr. Demarkian and Detective Borstoi are on their way," one of them said.

The other just sort of nodded, and Olivia felt as if she'd like to slap one of them. Was it really necessary for police to be this annoying? They had taken something from one of the rooms upstairs. She supposed it was whatever it was they had come to look for, because they didn't seem to be interested in

501

looking anymore. She went into the interview room and looked around to make sure that the crew was striking the set and packing away all the equipment. Then she came back into the hall again.

Sheila was standing near the bottom of the stairs, looking out the open front door to the police cars in the driveway.

"I take it they aren't leaving yet," she said.

"They said Mr. Demarkian's coming. Him and that detective, Borstoi, who was here before."

"This seems to have backfired," Sheila said. "You wanted to hire Demarkian, and now it seems the police have hired him. Or maybe not. I don't know what's going on around here anymore. Nobody tells me anything."

"I think this may be a good sign," Olivia said. "They found something. They were carrying something when they came downstairs. And I don't think they would have come back tonight like this if —"

There was sound from upstairs, and they both looked up. Olivia thought that what she heard was a scuffle, girls physically fighting, but then there was a high-pitched shriek, and she saw that the girls were all pouring out into the main hall from their bedroom wing.

"Get out of here!" someone was screaming.

Olivia tried to see through the clutch of moving girls, but it was impossible. Nearly all of them were there together and moving in a clump, except for Ivy, who was hovering around the edges of it all anxiously.

A moment later, Olivia realized there was somebody else at the edge, but she wasn't hovering. She was being pushed, and each time she was pushed she staggered a little and almost fell down.

"I didn't do anything! I didn't do anything!" Coraline screamed.

The crowd of girls surged at her almost in a mass. It was like watching bees swarm. Alida was right out in front of it and she had her hands on Coraline's side.

"Get out of here," she shrieked — yes, Olivia thought, that was the voice she had heard a second ago — "Get out of here and don't come back. Don't you dare come back. What's wrong with you? How sick are you? Nobody wants you here."

"I'm not going, I'm not going," Coraline screamed back. "You can't make me go. I'm not going."

"You're going now," Alida said, and this time, when she shoved, she shoved hard.

Coraline stumbled again, and fell, and

suddenly she was coming down the stairs, falling end over end like a rag doll, howling all the way, the tears streaming down her face in big wide gushes. Olivia rushed up the stairs to break the fall, and as she did the police came back into the house. Alida had not stopped advancing. She was marching downstairs, most of the other girls right behind her, and she was still shrieking.

"Die!" she was saying, "I wish you'd die! I wish they'd arrest you! Get out of here. Get out of here!"

"Wait a minute," one of the policemen said, grabbing Alida by the wrist. "Calm down. What do you think you're doing?"

The other policeman had rushed to Coraline and was now helping her up. "Are you hurt? Should we call an ambulance? Do you think anything is broken?"

"You'd better be damned glad she isn't dead," the first policeman said to Alida. "We're going to arrest you for assault, but we could be arresting you for murder. What did you think you were doing?"

"She's the one you ought to arrest for murder," Alida said. "She's the one who murdered that girl and left her body right there in the study for the rest of us to find it. She's going to murder the rest of us in our sleep before she's done. I want her out

504

of here. I want her out of here. Nobody wants her here and she ought to be gone."

"I want her here," Sheila Dunham said.

Everybody stopped making noise. Everybody. Coraline stopped crying, and Alida stopped making a fuss as the police officer tried to put handcuffs on her.

Olivia could barely believe the silence. She turned around and saw that Sheila had done her thing. She had managed to get herself off on her own, with nothing and nobody around her, and now, in spite of everything that was going on, she was the center of attention. There was no spotlight on her, but it felt as if there were. It felt as if there were a dozen spotlights on her.

Sheila advanced back toward the foot of the stairs, and the policemen, and Coraline and Alida.

"I want her here," she said again. "And I am the only person who gets to decide who does and does not stay in this house."

"She committed a murder," Alida said. "She did it right over there, in that room. They took something out of her bed. Something that she'd been hiding."

"I don't care if she shot the pope," Sheila said. "If I say she stays, she stays. If I say you go, you go. And you are going. This is your last night in this house. I want you out of here and on a plane first thing in the morning."

"She committed a murder! She committed a murder!"

"If she did, the police can deal with it. And as far as I'm concerned, the police can deal with you. I'll have your bags brought to the jail so you won't have to come back to get them."

"Bitch!" Alida said, and she was beyond shrieking now, she was beyond everything. Olivia didn't think she'd ever heard a sound like that before. It was as if she wanted to turn her voice into a weapon. Some people had voices that could shatter glass. Maybe Alida had a voice that could shatter eardrums.

"Bitch!" Alida shrieked. "Bitch! Bitch!"

Sheila Dunham stepped right up to her, and spat in her face.

SEVEN

1

They went out to Engine House in Len Borstoi's unmarked police car, with Gregor riding up front in the passenger seat and Borstoi's partner — who had never said a word, as far as Gregor could tell — riding in the back. The partner sent text messages, seemingly compulsively. Bennis sat in a chair at an empty cubicle in the police station while they all got ready to go, playing solitaire on her phone.

"I don't go out to Engine House," she told Gregor once again, when he asked her if she was sure she didn't want to come along for the ride. "And I'm really not going out to Engine House to talk about a murder. That other murder meant we almost didn't end up together, did you know that?"

"I did, to tell you the truth."

"I remember the day they executed her," Bennis said. "I was with Christopher, and we went to a bar, and sat on stools, and watched the television there. And that was the news. It was all the news. They went over and over it. Did I tell you I don't approve of the death penalty?"

"Yes," Gregor said. "Sometimes I approve of it, and sometimes I don't."

"Did you approve of it in her case?"

"I thought it was beside the point in her case," Gregor said. "The woman murdered for money, and she wasn't likely ever to get out of jail. But if she did, I think there was a good chance she'd murder again. I think you know she would have. In a way, she wasn't much different than the woman who is now calling herself Karen Mgrdchian. She killed to ensure that she had the money she wanted and thought she needed. There didn't seem to be anybody she wouldn't kill."

"The woman calling herself Karen Mgrdchian is a psychopath," Bennis said.

"So was she," Gregor said. "And it's like I said. I think you know that. I think you have known it at least since your father was murdered, and I think you could have known it earlier if you'd been paying any attention to the person who murdered him. But you never did pay her any attention."

"No," Bennis said. "Nobody ever did."

"That's part of the explanation, too," Gregor said.

He kissed the top of her head. "Don't go anywhere. We'll be back in a bit. Don't run your battery out. I may need to call you."

"I've got a charger in my bag," Bennis said.

And then, since that seemed to sum up Bennis absolutely precisely, Gregor let Len Borstoi lead him out to the car. It was nowhere near as nice a car as Bennis's, but it was bigger. Gregor didn't have to wonder if his legs would fit in it. He waited for the partner and was ushered into the front seat. He buckled his seat belt and thought about the first month or so after the seat-belt laws were passed, when he had deliberately refused to wear it because the government wasn't going to tell him what to do. It had made absolutely no sense. He always wore a seat belt even when it wasn't required. It was sensible to wear a seat belt. He believed in wearing seat belts. He thought human psychology was a very strange thing.

"Are you all right?" Borstoi asked him.

"I'm fine. I'm thinking about seat belts."

Borstoi let that pass. "What was all that you were talking about some woman calling herself something or the other."

"The woman calling herself Karen Mgrdchian," Gregor said. "Don't worry if you can't pronounce the name. You should see how it's spelled. It's something going on in Philadelphia. There's another woman, Sophie Mgrdchian, who's lived in her house since — well, I'd guess she's lived in one house or the other of a four-block area for all her life. And she's over eighty. Anyway, she was found a few days ago, lying comatose on the floor of the foyer of her house, with another woman with her. At the time we found them both, the other woman seemed to have dementia of some kind, and Sophie was an old lady, so she went off to the hospital and this other woman also went off to a hospital, for observation."

"All right," Borstoi said cautiously. "That sounds okay. Two old ladies in a house. One of them has dementia. The other of them has — what?"

"Good question. Nobody knew. The police looked through her house. I looked through her house. There was nothing to tell us who her doctor was. Or doctors. Somebody with the police checked with Medicare. She didn't seem to have been registered anywhere. But when she was found she had one of those plastic pill organizers in her pocket, and she had some fairly expensive prescription medication."

"Okay," Borstoi was growing ever more cautious. "That kind of things happen sometimes. It gets hard to find stuff out, even though it ought to be easy."

"Well, when the other woman got to the hospital," Gregor said, "it turned out they couldn't take her fingerprints, because the pads of her fingers were all scarred up, like they'd been injured or gone at."

"Now it's beginning to sound wrong," Borstoi said.

"It's definitely wrong," Gregor said. "It isn't hard, but it's wrong. It's just that we don't think of old people as people who would do — things. If that makes sense. First, it turned out that the pill organizer we found in Sophie Mgrdchian's pocket didn't belong to Sophie Mgrdchian, which was significant because one of the prescriptions in that organizer was for a drug to control high blood pressure, and Sophie didn't have high blood pressure. She sometimes suffered from low blood pressure."

"Ah," Borstoi said, "and the hospital, not having anything else to go on, was giving her that stuff because they figured that if she had it on her, then it must have been prescribed for her. And somebody else in the hospital wasn't doing the checkup and follow-up they should have, so they didn't notice —"

"That she was still comatose and they didn't have an explanation?" Gregor asked. "They did notice that. They've taken her off the medication now. With any luck, she'll come to, and she can just tell us what we need to know. But before we figured it all out about the medication, the other woman suddenly started behaving as if she was perfectly normal, and that's when she said her name was Karen Mgrdchian. If she was Karen Mgrdchian, that would make her Sophie's sister-in-law, the wife of Sophie's only surviving brother-in-law, Marco. And with Sophie unconscious, we had no way of knowing she wasn't."

"But she wasn't?"

"No," Gregor said. "Oh, I just dumped all this in the lap of the police over there, and they'll have to verify it, but I'm pretty sure that this is a con woman we have our hands on. I think she somehow made friends with or otherwise got herself into the life of the real Karen Mgrdchian, who lives in Cleveland, and that she probably took her for everything she was worth and then killed her. The Philadelphia police are going to ask the police in Cleveland, or wherever it is, to go look in the basement of Karen Mgrdchian's house. If there's a body, that's where it is. This is an old woman we're talking about. She isn't likely to have been strong enough to do anything complicated with a dead body, and why would she bother? The basement would be there, if the house has one, and the house probably does. Anyway, I think this woman took Karen Mgrdchian for whatever there was to be had, killed the woman, dumped her body in the basement, and then either ran out of whatever it was she'd stolen or got to the point where she couldn't continue without getting caught. If it's the first, then either she wasn't able to get hold of Karen Mgrdchian's bank card, or Karen Mgrdchian didn't have her social security checks direct deposited."

"And that would matter, why?"

"More difficult to get the checks cashed," Gregor said. "I don't know what the real Karen Mgrdchian looked like, but my guess is that she didn't look much like the one we've got."

"Then the other woman, the Sophie woman, must have known she wasn't really her sister-in-law," Borstoi said.

"Not necessarily," Gregor said. "According to the women on the block who did know Sophie, the last time Sophie saw Karen Mgrdchian was in the nineteen eighties, when Sophie's husband died, and his brothers and their wives came in for the funeral. That's a long time ago. Almost thirty years. People change a lot in thirty years."

"I guess," Borstoi said. "I still think I'd be able to recognize them, once I knew who they were supposed to be. But maybe Sophie didn't know this Karen very well."

"Hardly at all, I think," Gregor said. "But, to get back to it, I think this woman calling herself Karen Mgrdchian killed the *real* Karen Mgrdchian and shoved the body in the basement. My guess is that the police will find she hit her on the head or something. She wouldn't be likely to have as good a dodge as the one with the blood pressure medication. But whatever it was, she killed Karen Mgrdchian, and then when the money started to run out or she was about to be found out, she decided to take off. She probably heard about Sophie from Karen. Maybe she heard that Sophie had a big house on an expensive street. Whatever it was, she came out here and moved in with Sophie."

"And these women who knew Sophie from the neighborhood, they didn't think anything of it?"

"Oh, no," Gregor said. "You should see these women. We call them the Very Old

Ladies. They're that. They'd also make Miss Marple look like somebody who can mind her own business. The Very Old Ladies were up in arms in no time, and they were convinced that Sophie was being murdered in her bed. They kept trying to get in to see Sophie, but no one answered the door. Mind you, Sophie was not a social sort. She kept to herself most of the time. It wasn't necessarily all that odd that she wasn't talking to people, except that this woman was there. So they came and got me, and I went and rang the doorbell. And when the door opened, there was Sophie, lying comatose on the floor. And there was this other woman, acting as if she had dementia."

"Did she have dementia?"

"I don't know," Gregor said. "She might have had a mild stroke. It was her blood pressure medication she was feeding Sophie Mgrdchian. I think that if we hadn't gotten there when we did, she'd have shoved Sophie's body into the basement and gone on living in that house until she started to feel it wasn't safe anymore. But Sophie would have been dead. I'm going to have Bennis remind me not to turn into a recluse in my old age. It's a good way to get yourself victimized."

"And the fingerprints," Len Borstoi said,

"that's because her prints are on file some-where. She didn't want to get caught at this and have it come back that she had a sheet."

"Well, have you ever known a con artist who started as an old lady?" Gregor asked. "And have you ever known any con artist who worked for forty or fifty years, who never got caught even once? I'd be willing to bet just about anything that this woman not only got arrested a few times, but that she got convicted at least once. But we'll see how it works out. At the moment, we're in the position of not having a real reason to hold the woman. Sophie Mgrdchian hadn't woken up the last time I checked, so she can't tell us anything. And just yet, there's no sign there's ever been a crime. So —"

"It's like what happened with that Emily Watson," Len Borstoi said. "We got her in jail, then we checked out the gun and there was no ammunition in it. Did I tell you that before? It wasn't blanks. There was nothing in it. The gun was absolutely clean. It hadn't been fired. At all. Ever. So, when push came to shove, there wasn't a whole lot we could charge her with, and the judge wasn't going to let us hold her when the charges we did have didn't amount to much. So, the next thing we knew, she was out on the street."

"Yes, well. We don't want the fake Karen Mgrdchian out on the street. If she makes a habit of this, she's a serial killer as well as a con artist."

"And our guy here isn't?"

"No," Gregor said, "she's killed only this once. But it was cold as hell. And I wouldn't like to speculate about what she would and wouldn't do for the rest of her life."

"If you can really prove this, she'll spend the rest of her life in jail."

"You're the one who's going to prove it," Gregor said. "That's my usual deal with police departments. I come in. I consult. I go home. They get the credit."

"Well, I wouldn't have thought of looking for this stuff if you hadn't suggested it. I give credit where credit is due."

"There seems to be some kind of riot going on in Engine House."

2

Riot wasn't really the word. The front doors of the house were open. People were spilling out onto the front steps, all kinds of people. Uniformed police officers were backed up against their patrol cars. There were lights on everywhere.

"Damn," Len Borstoi said.

He pulled the car into the roundabout and

517

stopped it. Gregor looked out the windshield at the action in front of them. Then he opened his door and the noise hit him. Somebody was crying hysterically. Somebody was shrieking. Somebody was just plain yelling, and he knew that voice. That was Sheila Dunham in her best end-the-universe-now mode, reading the riot act to somebody she expected to just lie down and die. Apparently, this time, she was mistaken. Nobody was going to lie down and die.

Gregor got out of the car. So did Len Borstoi and the partner, who finally stopped texting and put his cell phone away. Nobody was paying any attention to them. Gregor looked through the crowd and counted quickly. All the girls seemed to be there. There were also a lot of people from the crew. It seemed odd to him that they would be there this late at night. He saw Olivia Dahl, holding a clipboard clutched to her chest and looking dazed. He saw a couple of people he thought must be the staff for the house. He didn't recognize them, and they didn't look like they belonged with a television crew.

"There is a car waiting for you," Sheila was bellowing. "It's sitting right there, and I want you out of here *now*."

Gregor looked around quickly. There was

518

indeed a car. It was an ordinary Lincoln Town Car, not a limousine, but it had a driver, and the driver had a uniform. He was leaning against the car's hood and watching as if this was all a show.

The girl Sheila was bellowing at was Asian, and she was not crying. She was furious. She was also not budging.

"I'm not going anywhere," she was saying. "I'm going to sue. I'm going to get on the phone and tell everybody on the planet what's been going on. You can't keep my mouth shut."

"Do it and *I'll* sue," Sheila said. "And I've got better lawyers."

"God, the way these people behave," Borstoi said.

"Just remember," Gregor said. "The most important point, here, is what ought to be obvious. Sheila Dunham is not dead."

"She goes on like that, she's going to be."

Gregor waded into the crowd. He asked girls politely if they would move out of the way. They seemed surprised to see him. They had all been concentrating so hard on the scene in front of them, most of them hadn't seemed to notice that a new car had driven up. Gregor saw one of the crew with a handheld camera and another with a camera mounted on a tripod. They were filming all this. It might even have been scripted. Gregor didn't think so.

He climbed up the steps to where Sheila Dunham was standing and tapped her on the shoulder. She jerked around as if a wasp had stung her, and then relaxed a little when she saw who it was.

"Alida here is just leaving," she said.

"Not right away," Gregor said. "Maybe we could get all this back in the house for a minute and talk? It's starting to rain again."

Sheila looked at the sky. It was starting to rain again. So far, there were only a few thick drops, but it could get worse very soon. Sheila looked around at the girls again. The girls had all gone quiet.

"All right," Sheila said. "Mr. Demarkian here wants us all to go back into the house." She turned back to him. "There's still crime-scene tape up all over everywhere. I don't know where you think we can go that's big enough to get us all into one room."

"Try the dining room," Gregor said. "I'm pretty sure that isn't a crime scene, and from what I remember, it's big enough for a small high school."

Sheila considered him for a moment. Then she went to talk to Olivia Dahl. Then things began to move. Gregor stood where he was and watched girls swirl around him. Alida Akido didn't swirl but stomped, still looking furious. Coraline Mays, who looked like she'd been crying uncontrollably, was being shepherded around by Janice Ledbedder. Janice had her arm around Coraline's shoulder and was whispering in her ear.

The crew went in last, except for the guy with the handheld camera, who had hurried up the steps to stand in the entrance to get pictures of the girls coming up. Gregor wondered if this was all going to show up on television as part of this season of *America's Next Superstar.* He had no idea if a murder would be a draw or a drag on ratings.

Probably a draw, he thought. People were like that.

He nodded to Len Borstoi. "The dining room is usually accessed through the living room, and my guess is that they're going to go tromping through there, tape or no tape, but don't worry about it. You're not going to need anything there."

"Is there another way to get to the dining room?" Len asked.

"You can go around the back hall the way the servants do," Gregor said. "I am constantly astonished that I remember so much about this house. I was only in it a few times, and it was years ago."

"You didn't come back here for your wedding?"

Gregor didn't begin to know where he would have to start to explain why that was never going to have happened, so he just went into the house, looked around the large front foyer, and followed the girls into the dining room. He had been right. They'd gone right through the yellow crime-scene tape as if it weren't there. They'd gone tromping across the living room the way they'd go tromping through a field on a hike. If there ever had been valuable evidence in that room, it was either gone or contaminated now.

There had never been valuable evidence in that room. This afternoon's shooting was not particularly important. It wasn't even particularly smart. The best Gregor could say about it was that it made sense.

When he got into the dining room, the girls had seated themselves around the table. There were fourteen of them, plus Sheila Dunham and Olivia Dahl, and a few anonymous young women with clipboards. The dining room table held twenty-four even when it hadn't been expanded. It could be expanded to hold fifty.

Sheila Dunham took the foot of the table,

sitting down and stretching out a little as if she were about to interview a not-very-promising aspirant for the next season. Gregor took the head of the table because it had been left free for him. Len Borstoi, his silent partner, and the two uniformed officers took up places against the walls, near the exits.

Gregor looked up and down the table. Alida Akido was right up next to him, looking triumphant. Grace Alsop was sitting on his other side. Ivy Demari, the one with the streak in her hair and the tattoo, was midway down the right side, on one side of Coraline. Janice Ledbedder was on the other side, still with her arm around Coraline's shoulder. Coraline had not stopped sobbing.

Alida had her arms folded across her chest. "I only said what everybody else was thinking," she said. "They found something in Coraline's room. In Coraline's bed. And Coraline was the only one of us who was here the day that girl was murdered. She was the only one of us who could have murdered her. And then they found something. So Coraline must have done it. And I don't want to go to sleep on the same floor as a murderer. You don't know what she's going to do next. You don't know why she killed that girl. She could kill me, too."

"You're an asshole, Alida," Ivy said. "Did you know that?"

"They found something in her room," Alida said again.

"Yes," Gregor said. "Well, let me clear that up. What they found in Coraline's room —" He looked around at the officers. "Was it in her things? Or just in the room?"

One of the uniformed officers stepped slightly forward. "It was in her bed. Sort of shoved up under a comforter thing that was on the bed instead of a bedspread."

"All right," Gregor said. He looked up and down at the girls again. "What they found in Coraline's bed was a beige net glove, made out of stretchy nylon mesh with things appliquéd to it. Butterflies, I think we were told. The glove was used to make sure there were no fingerprints on the gun used to shoot at Sheila Dunham today. Mesh like that has several advantages over a latex glove. For one thing, it's closer to the color of the human hand, so it's less noticeable than the white of a latex glove. For another thing, latex gloves sometimes retain fingerprints on the inside of the finger sheaths."

"Oh," Janice said. "I heard about that. That was on *Forensic Files.*"

"Yes," Gregor said. "That was on *Forensic Files.*"

"So," Alida said, "I was right. Coraline shot at Sheila Dunham and then she hid the glove in her bed. She wanted to kill Sheila Dunham. Of course she did. She was absolutely humiliated the day of the first challenge. Sheila grabbed Coraline's T-shirt and ripped it right off, in front of everybody."

"So that makes sense?" Ivy said. "First, this other girl shoots at Sheila Dunham, then the girl shows up at our house and Coraline kills her for no reason at all, then Coraline tries to kill Sheila Dunham. I mean, for God's sake. Try to indulge in a little linear thought."

"The girl calling herself Emily Watson did not shoot at Sheila Dunham," Gregor said. "The gun she was holding at the Milky Way Ballroom had no bullets in it. It didn't even have blanks in it. Emily Watson was not trying to kill Sheila Dunham. And her name was not Emily Watson."

"Somebody shot at Sheila Dunham at the ballroom," Grace Alsop said. "There were real shots. I heard them. And there were real bullets. The police found them, in the wall. I saw that on the news."

"Yes," Gregor said. "There were real shots

fired in the ballroom. They were fired from the same gun used to kill the girl calling herself Emily Watson, and the same gun that fired at Sheila Dunham today. Maybe I should say, sort of at Sheila Dunham. If they'd been fired directly at Sheila Dunham, she'd be dead."

"You mean whoever it was, wasn't actually trying to kill me?" Sheila said. "That's a relief. And a disappointment, if you catch my drift."

"Yes," Gregor said, "well. You can take that up with your psychiatrist."

"It's not her psychiatrist who's going to be interested," Olivia Dahl said. "It's the publicity people. You have no idea how excited they were about going to work on a story about somebody actually trying to kill her."

"I don't see why any of this matters," Alida said. "We're still back to where we started. Coraline was the only person in this house when that girl was killed. The only one. The rest of us were all out at the challenge. The glove was found in her bed. Obviously, she must have known this girl somewhere. There's got to be a reason. But she's still the only one who could have murdered her. And that's that."

"You're assuming the murder was done

while you were all away on the, ah, challenge," Gregor said. "In fact, it was done much earlier in the day, before you all left, while you were all getting ready. And it wasn't done in the study. It was done in the servants' access corridor that runs behind all the rooms in that wing and this one. It was done there. Then the body was dragged out into the study and placed in a way that made it echo another crime that had once taken place in this house. Then the study door was closed. It didn't take five minutes, if it took that. Of course, the position of the wall mirror was also altered, but I think that was probably done the night before, when the security camera in there was disabled. It was a silly thing to do. I think it was supposed to make the scene look like one that had happened here before, that I had been involved in, and to get me rattled, or to distract me. It didn't. It just made it all the more obvious what was happening here."

"Which was what?"

"Oh," Gregor said, "it was getting done what the murderer came here — to Philadelphia now, not to this house — to get done. It was so that Janice Ledbedder could kill a girl named Emma Ware, who was once her best friend in Marshall, South Dakota."

Everybody turned to look, but Janice was just sitting there, smiling.

EPILOGUE

Revenge is not a reason.
It's a way of life.
— Orania Papazoglou

1

On a bright day at the beginning of May, Sheila Dunham got arrested in Leonardo da Vinci Airport for hitting a skycap on the arm with her purse and then stepping on his foot with her very sharp stiletto high heel. She was in the airport with the last six girls in the competition, on the way to the European house that served as the setting for the last third of the show. She was hot, and tired, and frazzled, and feeling invincible. She thought it made sense to feel invincible. After all, she had stared down a murderer, given a hundred interviews to all those news shows who had been refusing to hire her for years, talked the network into a contract for four more seasons at twice the

529

money, and seen her own face on the cover of *Time* magazine. It couldn't have worked out better if she'd planned it, and she hadn't planned it. People called her crazy, but she wasn't half as crazy as the real crazy people were. You could tell this by the look on Janice Ledbedder's face in those perp walks they kept showing on the evening news.

Bennis Hannaford saw the story about Sheila Dunham's arrest sitting at the table in her own kitchen on Cavanaugh Street, drinking coffee she had made herself and pretending that she hadn't thrown out the coffee Gregor had made earlier. The picture on the front page of *The Philadelphia Inquirer* was fascinating. There was Sheila, whom Bennis had seen a dozen times in a dozen different situations, and there was a line of girls backed up against a wall, looking panicked beyond belief. The caption didn't give their names. The story did, but without faces to put to them, Bennis didn't know who was who.

Andra Gayle. Coraline Mays. Ivy Demari. Mary-Louise Verdt. Faith Stackdopole. Marcia Lee Baldwin.

Bennis looked back at the picture and tried to figure out who was who. It wasn't possible. There was Sheila Dunham, though, her foot half in the air, her heel headed

down to that poor young man's shoe —
somebody must have caught it on a camera
phone.

Gregor came into the kitchen looking as if
he'd been up and running the country for
at least the last several hours. Bennis liked
this better than the way he looked when he
was having trouble getting to sleep, but it
still disoriented her a little. Most people
had a morning look when they'd first gotten out of bed. Gregor just looked like
himself.

He stopped at the coffeepot to check it
out. Bennis could practically see him decid-
ing not to say anything. She didn't believe
he actually minded. Even Gregor knew what
Gregor's coffee tasted like. Gregor poured
himself some coffee and came to the table.
He looked at the newspaper spread out in
front of Bennis. She'd turned to the interior
page, and there were more pictures —
pictures of Sheila, pictures of the Italian
police, pictures of an old woman advancing
with her own pocketbook, looking like
something out of Greek myth.

Gregor sat down. "It's not going to tell
you who won," he said mildly. "I don't think
even they know who won. I don't think
they're done filming yet."

"I think it's annoying how long all this

takes," Bennis said. "And Bobby's no help. Not that he ever was any help to anybody, but you know what I mean. He doesn't know anything, and he wouldn't tell me anything if he did know. And then all he wants to do is wail about whether all this brought down the resale value of the house. I told him that if he wanted to sell the house, I'd buy it from him at any price he named, but he didn't go there. He doesn't really want to sell it."

"Do you really want to buy it?" Gregor asked. "Just a couple of weeks ago, you were refusing to set foot in the place."

"I don't want it to go out of the family," Bennis said vaguely. She wasn't making any sense, and she knew it. She was only making sense to herself. She looked over a few more of the pictures, the ones with the girls in them. "What's the name of the one you said she was convinced was a spy for Fox News?"

"Grace something," Gregor said. "Harrigan, I think, but that wasn't the name she was using. I mean Harrigan wasn't the name she was using. She was still calling herself Grace."

"There isn't any Grace here," Bennis said. "I know which one I'd pick if I was a judge. Just from these photographs. The rest of them just sort of fade into the background, but this one pops right out. Who's this?"

Gregor looked over. "Ivy Demaris. Demari. Something like that."

"I like the name Ivy. What was she like? Was she a bitch?"

"I really don't know," Gregor said. "How could I know? I didn't spend that much time there."

"You know their names."

"Yes, well. I would have to, wouldn't I?"

"You recognized the face," Bennis said. "Ivy's face. And it's Demari. They've got the names of the girls in the second section here. I wonder what she really did in that airport."

"Besides assault a skycap?"

"But there must have been a reason, don't you think? Even Sheila Dunham has to have reasons."

"In my experience, most of her reasons come down to figuring out what's going to get her the most publicity. You'd think she'd have had enough of publicity after the last couple of months."

"Oh, no," Bennis said. "There's no such thing as enough publicity."

Then she found it. She leaned much closer to the paper, and half lifted it up in one hand. She gave a passing thought to the possibility that she was going to end up needing glasses. The explanatory paragraph was right there at the end of the first section, so that, skimming, she had almost missed it.

"Listen," she said. " 'The altercation arose after Ms. Dunham became convinced that the baggage handlers had dropped her two leather suitcases deliberately.' What do you think that means? Do you think she saw them throw them on the ground?"

"No," Gregor said.

"No," Bennis said, "but I bet she thought she did. It's the kind of thing she would think. I wonder if they'll have video of this on one of the cable news stations. Fox will have it, I bet. Fox loves to trash her. Maybe it'll be on *O'Reilly*."

"Were you always this obsessed with cable news stations?"

"I'm not obsessed with them," Bennis said. "I just think it's too bad, the damned show is being filmed in my own childhood home, and I didn't get a chance to see any of it. And don't tell me it's because I wouldn't go there. I wouldn't have had to go there. They go places and film things. Restaurants. Parties. I should have thrown a party for them."

"I wouldn't have come."

"Yes, you would have. I would have made you. But you should have realized it all along. Nobody ever really murders people like Sheila Dunham. They're too easy."

Gregor looked like he wanted to break some furniture, but Bennis ignored it.

Then she got up, folded the paper, and said, "Time to check in on the situation with Sophie."

2

Sophie Mgrdchian recovered better than anybody had expected her to, but she did not come back to Cavanaugh Street.

"We talked it over," her niece Clarice said. "I've got no idea why she was fighting with my mother, and she either won't tell me, or she's forgotten. So we've decided she'll come live by me in Atlanta. If we can get a good deal on the house, I know a very nice retirement community with waterfalls and peach trees."

"Atlanta explains what I couldn't understand," Gregor told Bennis as they headed toward the Ararat at six o'clock. "I knew there was a daughter, and I thought the daughter would be watching out for the mother. But, as it turns out, the daughter had taken a job in Georgia a couple of years ago. Not that she wasn't starting to get suspicious. She even had the police run out there a couple of times, but they didn't find anything."

"And Karen — whatever her name was — was already gone?"

"Susan Lee Parker," Gregor said. "You should have seen the paper trail she had. A good fifteen arrests for fraud in ten states. Two incarcerations, one here in Pennsylvania for a scam she pulled in Altoona about twenty-five years ago. The other out in California. Where, by the way, they charged her with murder but couldn't make it stick. They never found a body."

Bennis made a face. "There are probably going to be bodies strewn across the landscape," she said. "You'll end up on *City Confidential* again, talking about serial killers."

"Not *City Confidential*. They've already done an episode on Philadelphia. I don't think they do more than one on a place. But they'll get her for murder this time. They've got the body. Or part of it. She did a fair job with the lye, but it was only a fair job. She's getting old, I expect. It's all gotten too much for her."

"Well," Bennis said drily, "thank God for that. Tibor said they were going to have a memorial service for her at Holy Trinity —

I don't remember when. I still say it was amazing that you knew there was going to be a body in the basement."

"It wasn't amazing at all," Gregor said. "Susan Lee Parker was a fairly run of the mill female serial killer. And con artist, of course. More of a con artist, a con artist first, maybe. I don't think she'd have killed anyone she didn't think she had to. But it's a well-established pattern. Male serial killers kill for sex. Female serial killers — with one or two exceptions — kill for money."

"I still don't believe she fooled Sophie Mgrdchian into thinking she was Karen," Bennis said. "I'm sorry, I find this a lot more confusing than you seem to."

"I don't know that she did fool Sophie Mgrdchian into thinking she was Karen," Gregor said. "The word from Sophie is that she was suspicious from the first, and that may be why she ended up on the foyer floor as soon as she did. That wasn't Susan Lee Parker's usual pattern. The idea was to worm her way into a house and then stay until she had all the money. She didn't have close to all the money when she knocked Sophie out."

"Mmmm," Bennis said.

"At any rate, she killed the real Karen Mgrdchian, but nobody else. I was wrong about Clarice being in the basement, too, because Clarice was off in Atlanta, and Marco Mgrdchian died a long time ago. No, that wasn't amazing. What you really ought to be asking is how I knew about Emma Ware."

"Mmm," Bennis said again.

They had been walking along at a steady but not very hurried pace. Gregor had not been paying attention. Now he looked up and realized that they had gone far past the Ararat. They were all the way at the other end of the neighborhood, in front of Sophie Mgrdchian's house.

"We missed our stop," he said.

"Not exactly," Bennis said. She reached into the pocket of her skirt and came up with a set of keys. "I've got the keys. I thought we'd go in and look around."

"What for? You're not going to find more evidence than the police have picked up already."

"I'm not looking for evidence," Bennis said. "I'm being practical for once. This house is for sale. Clarice Mgrdchian wants a load of money for it, but I've got a load of money. It's the last whole house in the neighborhood that doesn't belong to somebody we don't want to move. So . . ."

"You want to buy a house," Gregor said.

"We could throw dinner parties," Bennis said, "or, you know, not. Come on, Gregor. Let's go take a look. Maybe it was falling down on Sophie Mgrdchian's head, but maybe it wasn't, and maybe it would be easy enough to renovate. Then I can make a deal with Grace for my apartment, and she can have a place big enough to put a harpsichord in."

"I thought she had a harpsichord."

"She's got something call a virginal," Bennis said. "Come on. All you have to do is look around. It won't kill you."

3

Gregor didn't think it would kill him to look all the way through Sophie Mgrdchian's house, but he did think it might kill him to live with Bennis while she renovated it. In fact, he would not only have to live with Bennis. He would have to live with Bennis *and Donna,* because Donna would be part of fixing up any house Bennis decided to buy. Gregor had visions of upholstery fabric swatches and tile samples all over his kitchen, and then he followed Bennis through the foyer into Sophie Mgrdchian's oversized, high-ceilinged living room. There was too much furniture in it, and all of the furniture had little square lace things over the backs of it.

"So," Bennis said, staring at the walls. "I thought you were going to tell me about Emma Ware."

Gregor wanted to know why she was staring at the walls. Was she going to want to have them knocked down? Or painted pink? What?

"I didn't know her name was Emma Ware," Gregor said. "I was fairly sure her name wasn't Emily Watson, because that was the name she gave the police. And she didn't have a record of any kind. Her fingerprints weren't on file. She was just a very young girl who wasn't saying anything to anybody but her lawyer."

"Did she tell her lawyer who she was?"

"No," Gregor said. "She didn't. But here's the thing. I knew that whatever was going on had to be about the deliberate attempt to murder this girl. That had to be what was going on, because that was what happened. She wasn't a celebrity. She wasn't Sheila Dunham's daughter, Mallory. We did get in touch with Mallory eventually. She's older, she's married, and she won't talk to her mother if she can help it, but she isn't lying dead in a Pennsylvania morgue. So we had this young girl, and it didn't make sense that she was connected to one of the celebrities on the show, or even to one of the staff. She just wasn't — I don't know how to put it. She didn't look like she came from the city."

"You mean she looked like a hick," Bennis said.

"Something like that," Gregor said. "At any rate, I thought that what made sense was to look into the backgrounds of the girls in the competition and find one who might have a reason to murder somebody. As it was, I might as well have saved myself the trouble, because Janice Ledbedder kept telling me why she had a reason to murder somebody. She talked about it all the time. *All the time.* To anybody who would listen, and to a lot of people who didn't want to. Janice had a long-time boyfriend. His name was Brian Ellendorf, but she never actually used his name. She never used anybody's names. I should have picked up on that."

"Why would she use their names?" Bennis asked. She was drifting out of the living room into the dining room. "It's not like you would know who they were."

"No," Gregor said, "but it's her style of speaking. She usually does mention names. She just didn't when she was talking about this particular thing. Janice had a boyfriend, named Brian. They'd been going out to-

541

gether since junior high school, and then, right before the senior prom, Brian dumped Janice to take Emma. This was not a small thing to Janice. It humiliated the hell out of her. It especially humiliated the hell out of her because she'd always considered Emma sort of her protégé, the poor little plain girl that a girl like Janice takes on to make herself look good. I haven't had a chance to talk to Brian Ellendorf, but I'd be willing to bet anything that he had some sense that there was something wrong with Janice. Whatever the reason, he dumped the one girl and then took the other. And Janice started thinking of ways she could get rid of Emma and not get caught at it. And that's when she got the invitation to audition for *America's Next Superstar,* and that gave her her chance."

The dining room was a horror story. The furniture was so large and so heavy, Gregor thought it would sink the house. There were two display hutches, both with decorative plates behind their glass doors. There was a hanging light fixture that looked like it might come alive and bite somebody.

"That part still doesn't make sense to me," Bennis said. "I mean, I get that they both sent in audition tapes, and Janice's was chosen and Emma's was not, but I still don't see how Janice got Emma to come all the way down here to do — well, what, exactly?"

"Get famous," Gregor said. "By this time, Brian was no longer seeing Emma, and he wasn't back with Janice. So Janice was dumped and furious, and Emma was dumped and sad, and the letters came. And Janice convinced Emma to come down to the auditions with her and stage a stunt that would get them in the papers, and then they could use that to get themselves famous. The plot was ludicrous, but we're dealing with a couple of high school girls here. According to Janice's plan as she explained it to Emma, they'd both fire at Sheila Dunham, and then they'd get caught, and then they'd be in the papers. Janice had the whole thing worked out. They'd give false names. They'd pretend they didn't notice each other. It would look like the whole world was out to murder Sheila Dunham, and then they'd go on television and tell the world how they were really getting justice for all the rejected girls. It was all a lot of nonsense. A more sophisticated girl would have known it was nonsense. But it was a chance for Emma to get away from home, and she had a lot to get away from. I'd guess that she was also actually upset about not being asked in to audition. Janice had other things she could do with her life. Not many other things, and not anything spectacular, but she was on track to go to the local college and find another boyfriend and get a teaching certificate and find a guy and settle down. That's what people do in Marshall, South Dakota, at least if you listen to Janice tell it. Emma was on track for nowhere. She had a good chance of ending up like her mother if she didn't do something with herself."

"Where were Emma's parents in all this?"

"Emma's father is long gone," Gregor said. "Emma's mother is an alcoholic and a drug addict. She didn't even notice Emma was gone. Janice told everybody about that, too. She really couldn't keep her mouth shut."

"But I still don't understand what she thought she was going to accomplish," Bennis said. "They were going to shoot at Sheila Dunham, and then what?"

"Janice was never going to shoot at Sheila Dunham," Gregor said. "She was going to shoot at Emma Ware, and kill her. And before you get all indignant at how complicated it was, Janice didn't expect it to be complicated. She didn't think she was going to pass the eliminations and end up in the final thirty, never mind in the final fourteen. She thought they would be part of a big crowd, and Sheila Dunham would be up there talking, and Emma would point her gun and 'shoot' nothing, and Janice would keep hers low and shoot real bullets. Everybody would see Emma and her gun. Nobody would be looking at Janice. Janice would just drop the gun where she was and nobody would be able to trace it to her."

"But why not just shoot Emma on the street somewhere?"

"Because it's harder than you think," Gregor said. "You've got to get your victim to an isolated spot. That means either going out at night or going out into really bad neighborhoods. You know as well as I do there are more people around at those times and in those places than you'd think. And not all of them are junkies."

"Most of them aren't interested in calling the police."

"Some of them might be interested in mugging you. The thing about committing the murder in broad daylight in the middle of a crowd actually made a certain amount of sense."

"But she didn't kill Emma Ware at the auditions," Bennis said.

"She tried," Gregor said. "She missed. She

wasn't as close to Emma as she expected to be. In fact, nothing was working out the way she expected it to. There was no mass meeting of the whole lot of them, which was something she'd seen on previous seasons of the show. They didn't do it that way this time. She never expected to be in the final thirty. She really never expected to be in the final fourteen and living in the house."

"And then?"

Gregor shrugged. "And then Emma got stupid. When she was arrested, she clammed up. Completely. She wouldn't talk to anybody. She wouldn't even give her name. She was scared to death, so she just gave the name she and Janice had invented for their little project, and then she wouldn't say anything else. Then the forensics came in and it turned out that there weren't any bullets in that gun, blank or otherwise, her legal aid attorney got her out on bail. And now we come to an interesting point."

"This is a built-in bookshelf," Bennis said. "Who puts a built-in bookshelf in their dining room?"

"Maybe it wasn't always a dining room," Gregor said. "Don't you want to hear what the interesting point is?"

"Sure," Bennis said. "But I also want to see the kitchen."

There was a swinging door to the kitchen, and they went through it. To Gregor, the room was just huge and messy. To Bennis, it was obviously the greatest thing since — well, since whatever.

"If Emma Ware had just gone away," Gregor said, "she'd be alive and well right now, and probably have stayed that way. Janice did not get caught with the gun at the scene because nobody was looking for a gun at the scene. They had the gun Emma had and they thought they already had it. Emma got carted off to jail, and Janice ended up in the final fourteen with a bed in the house and a chance to be on the air. And it could have stopped there. Janice almost certainly would not have risked a chance to win the competition to pull another stunt. If Emma had just skipped bail and run on home, it would all have been over.

"Unfortunately, Emma didn't do that. As soon as she got out on bail, she went looking for Janice. For all the nonsense that these people talk about security, everybody on the planet knew where the house was. It didn't take Emma long to find out and it didn't take her long to get out there and contact Janice. She needed to know what was going to happen next. She needed to know what was going to happen to her. So she came out. And Janice still had the gun. And Janice agreed to talk to her. And Janice killed her."

"When?" Bennis asked. "I thought the house was full of people."

"You know Engine House better than I do," Gregor said. "There's the central core and two wings. The rest of the people living in the house were in the wings, in the bedrooms on the second floor. Janice met Emma on the first floor in the servant's area —"

"Why didn't the servants hear?"

"Because there were no servants to hear. They go home at night these days. Janice met Emma there, and killed her in the back corridor. She stuffed the body out of sight in a small closet. Then she came into the nearest room, which turned out to be the study. She came in behind the security camera, which was aimed at the main door out into the foyer. She unplugged it. She looked around. Then she got a really bright idea. She knew the room. She was always watching those television shows about true crime. And she told everybody about that, too."

"Lots of people watch those shows," Bennis said.

"Agreed," Gregor said. "Janice, however, made a point of telling me once that she had seen a couple of them on the murder of your father. She knew I'd be likely to be around, because she'd heard from Olivia Dahl that I'd been asked to come in and consult on the shooting in Merion. So she thought she'd do something to, well, steer the investigation into a direction that didn't have anything to do with her. She'd put Emma's body on the hearth. She'd make sure neither I nor anybody else could fail to make the connection. She played around with the mirror and managed to dislodge it just a little, so that it was hanging just slightly forward on these ribbons —"

"Safety tape," Bennis said. "I remember those. Just in case the mirrors somehow came away from the wall, there was safety tape to stop them from just crashing to the ground. The mirror in the morning room at Engine House has those, too."

"With the mirror just slightly forward like that, I was struck immediately with all the resemblances to the first scene. I looked in the door, and there was the reflection in the mirror. It hit me right in the face."

"But why didn't anybody else notice the body in the study?" Bennis said. "Weren't the girls wandering all the hell around when that was going on?"

"The body wasn't there when the girls were wandering around," Gregor said. "The body was still in the closet in the utility hall then. The girls and the crew and the staff went out to get into the limousines to go to the challenge. Janice insisted she had to go to the bathroom and ran back inside. Coraline was still in the house, but she'd run upstairs in tears. Janice ran around to the utility hall, got the body out of the closet, dragged it into the study by the utility door, left it in the house, and ran out. It took less than sixty seconds. Then she was off to the restaurant in Bryn Mawr, and it was just a matter of who was going to find it.

"I think, you know, she expected that Coraline would find it. Coraline was in the house. But Coraline never came downstairs again until everybody else got back. I don't suppose it matters. Having Coraline in the house was lucky for Janice either way."

"Why lucky?"

"Because it made Coraline a natural suspect. No matter what you read in murder mysteries or see on those true crime shows, in most crimes, the most obvious suspect is the guilty one, and the most obvious suspect is the one right there sticking out like a sore thumb. And that was Coraline. Emma Ware was dead on the study floor and Coraline was in the house, and she was the only one in the house. All Janice had to do to clinch the deal was to dump something on Coraline that could serve as a smoking gun."

"The glove," Bennis said.

"Exactly," Gregor said. "When she didn't have any more use for the glove, she just walked into the room Coraline shared with Deanna and shoved it into Coraline's things. That was the really easy part. The girls were almost never in their rooms except when they were getting up or going to bed."

"Wasn't Janice the first into the house when they came back, too?" Bennis said. "Didn't somebody say she had to go to the bathroom then?"

"Probably," Gregor said. "At least it wouldn't surprise me. What does impress me was that last bit, where she fired at Sheila Dunham in the living room. In a way, she had to do something, because it was important for the police and everybody else to think that the reason for all this gunfire was that somebody wanted Sheila Dunham dead. And maintaining that fiction was not going to be easy, since there was a dead body to contend with and it wasn't Sheila Dunham's. And Janice's safety, then as always depended on there being no connection between her and the girl who died. So she decided to stage another shooting, another case of somebody wanting Sheila dead. Except she didn't want Sheila dead. She didn't even shoot in the right direction. She just shot in the way least likely to get herself caught on camera or noticed by the other girls. She waited until everybody was screaming and jumping up and down and — can you tell me why it is people do that? The screaming and the jumping up and down, I mean. What the hell is that supposed to be in aid of?"

"It's supposed to show you're enthusiastic," Bennis said absently. Then she pulled a kitchen chair over to the cabinets and stood on it to get a look.

"It was an interesting case," Gregor said. "It's the first time in years it hasn't mattered if I knew anything about the people at all. Oh, I know now, but at the time, all I had was the certainty that somebody wanted that girl dead, and that that somebody had to be one of the people who were in a particular place in the room at the time Sheila Dunham was shot at for the second time. There were three girls who were more or less in the right place. I had the police check out all three of them, and there was only one with a little blond friend wandering around. Or not wandering around. Doesn't any of this interest you at all?"

"These cabinets are mahogany," Bennis said. "And yes, it interests me. Of course it does. But I want to buy a house."

"You want to fix a house," Gregor said. "That's the real problem."

4

Down at the Ararat, fifteen minutes later, Gregor told the story all over again to Tibor, and Bennis sat down with Lida Arkmanian to talk about commercial grade ovens. It really was a very nice day. There was no rain, and no extreme heat. There was good sunshine. People had come out to the Ararat who almost never made it for breakfast.

"It is a senseless thing, Krekor," Tibor said. "It is such a little thing. I do not understand the reasoning."

"I don't think it really was reasoning," Gregor said. 'What Lola wants, Lola gets,' as the saying goes. Janice Ledbedder is one of those people who is just . . . broken, I suppose. One of those people to whom murder does not feel impossible. I'm not making much sense here."

"No, no, Krekor, you're making sense. It is only — a date to a prom, a boyfriend. It's stuff for children."

"Children kill sometimes," Gregor said. "Think of Mary Bell, ten years old and she strangled two toddlers to death, and to this day, nobody knows why. Boyfriends and proms probably look less trivial if they're what matters in the place you live in."

"But she was getting out of that place," Tibor said. "She had this audition, and then she was chosen to be on the show."

"And, as I told Bennis, if Emma Ware had just gone off and left her alone, Janice would have let the whole thing pass. Exactly because she had something new in her life and somewhere else to go. It was only when Emma started to look like a threat to Janice's place in the competition, to look as if she'd let the whole silly plan out and get Janice booted off home, that Janice decided to go through with the original idea. In the end, it always was just a matter of Janice wanting what she wanted and being willing to punish anybody who got in her way. I don't know. Maybe the psychologists will say something different. I just know that I've seen them like Janice before, people who kill for reasons you and I would find incredible. There are too many of them out there."

"Yes, Krekor," Tibor said drily. "Now I will start to wonder about the man at the newsstand and the girl who bags my groceries. This is helpful."

Linda Melajian brought them cups of coffee, and Gregor leaned over the table and sighed. Bennis was still on the other side of the restaurant, deep in conference now with both Lida Arkmanian and Hannah Krekorian.

"She's talking about taking out walls," he said. "I knew when she said she wanted a house she was going to end up taking out walls."

A shadow came over the table, and Gregor looked up to find the three Very Old Ladies standing next to him, looking black and ominous as always. He could never understand why they always dressed like that, or how they could be so intimidating when not a single one of them could be more than five feet tall. Or maybe not. It was hard to tell how tall they were. They were like something out of Greek myth.

Viola Vardanian was in the middle, and she had her straight black walking stick that she used as a cane. Gregor thought they were all lucky that she didn't have a death's head on the top of it.

"So," she said. "Krekor. We have spoken to Sophie Mgrdchian now twice."

"It was very good of you to look into it

all," Marita Melvarian said. "It's like I told Viola when all this started, it didn't make any sense to do anything silly when we had our own policeman here in the neighborhood."

"He's not a policeman," Mrs. Vardanian said, "and I didn't need him to tell me something was wrong in that house."

"Well, of course you didn't need him to tell you that," Kara Edelakian said. "None of us needed him for that. But he did all the other things, you know, and —"

"And he got that woman arrested," Mrs. Melvarian said. "And we didn't get killed in the process, which I was sure was going to happen. I mean, that woman was a murderer, wasn't she, she did it all the time, and I don't see why not —"

"I want to know how you found out who she was," Mrs. Vardakian said. "She had done something to her fingerprints. She wasn't carrying her birth certificate."

"No," Gregor said. "She wasn't."

"So," Mrs. Vardakian said. "What did you do? How did you discover her?"

"This isn't," Gregor started. Then he stopped. "It wasn't as hard as you'd think," he said. "It wasn't a matter of intelligence, just of boredom. She made her fingerprints unreadable, but she still had her face."

"I don't understand," Mrs. Vardakian said.

"She hadn't had plastic surgery or any-thing like that," Gregor said, "not on her face, at any rate. And a woman like that gets arrested a lot. And Susan Lee Parker had been arrested a lot. And every time you get arrested, you get your picture taken. So, it was just a matter of circulating mug shots and waiting. Finally, one came in that had to be the right one. There was a little back and forth, some cops from Lincoln, Ne-braska, came in to see if they could make a positive identification, and once we had that it was just a matter of following the paper trail. When you get arrested a lot, you leave a big paper trail."

"Ah," Mrs. Vardanian said.

"I think it's brilliant," Mrs. Melvarian said.

"I think it is disappointing," Mrs. Varda-nian said. She turned her black eyes on Gregor, looked him up and down as if he were a prime piece of red meat, and shook her head. "This is not how a Great Detec-tive behaves, Krekor. This is not like Sher-lock Holmes. This is the kind of thing that could have been done by a secretary with a fax machine."

Then she turned her back to them and stalked off, headed for her usual table. The other two hurried after her, fluttering.

"Well," Gregor said.

"Don't worry, about it, Krekor," Tibor said. "They're not impressed with me, either."

ABOUT THE AUTHOR

Jane Haddam is the author of more than twenty novels and is a finalist for both the Edgar and the Anthony Award. She lives in Litchfield County, Connecticut. Visit her Web site at blog.janehaddam.com.

The employees of Thorndike Press hope
you have enjoyed this Large Print book. All
our Thorndike, Wheeler, and Kennebec
Large Print titles are designed for easy reading, and all our books are made to last.
Other Thorndike Press Large Print books
are available at your library, through se-
lected bookstores, or directly from us.

For information about titles, please call:
(800) 223-1244

or visit our Web site at:
http://gale.cengage.com/thorndike

To share your comments, please write:
Publisher
Thorndike Press
295 Kennedy Memorial Drive
Waterville, ME 04901